KISS YESTERDAY GOODBYE

By

Ralph Lafette

MAPLE
PUBLISHERS

KISS YESTERDAY GOODBYE

Author: Ralph Lafette

Copyright © 2025 Ralph Lafette

The right of Ralph Lafette to be identified as author of this work has been asserted by the author in accordance with section 77 and 78 of the Copyright, Designs and Patents Act 1988.

First Published in 2025

ISBN 978-1-83538-478-7 (Paperback)
    978-1-83538-479-4 (E-Book)

Book Cover Design and Layout by:
    White Magic Studios
    www.whitemagicstudios.co.uk

Published by:
    Maple Publishers
    Fairbourne Drive, Atterbury,
    Milton Keynes,
    MK10 9RG, UK
    www.maplepublishers.com

CONTENTS

Chapter One

What was I doing there in Canterbury police station, sitting in a freezing cold six foot by eight-foot cell? Even my forklift truck wouldn't fit in that cell. A quick look around the cell revealed it had a metal sink, metal toilet without any seat, no window wooden panel for the blue mattress to rest on and a very thin orange blanket, not a sheet or pillow. What was I doing there, being arrested for the murder of my baby brother?

How could they think that I had murdered my little brother when I loved him so much? I felt so cold as it was freezing in there. Normally I am always very hot. A police officer was sitting by the open cell door – God knows why. Maybe I could ask him for a blanket.

"Please can I have another blanket, Sir? I am freezing cold."

He stood up and walked into the cell and he put his awkward face right up to mine and said, "Freeze you murderer, I can't leave you alone 'cos I am on suicide watch."

I immediately became afraid but I did not say anything more. I just sat on the bed and curled up.

Then he went and sat down on the chair by the open cell door. I curled up with the one puny blanket that I had on the bed. My back was against the cold cell wall. I tried to pull the blanket over my back but it was only a single one. I twisted and turned as I pulled my knees to my chest and rubbed my toes to warm them up. Then a plain clothes officer, who was walking in from the passageway, looked in at me and asked the officer if I was aright.

"He wants another blanket as he is freezing".

"Freezing? He must be kidding; you go and get him one and I will stay here."

The officer left us. He came back with a blanket and gave it me and then the plain clothes officer left us.

"Have you decided which solicitors you are going to call?"

"No sir."

"I gave you the list of solicitors, look it's on the floor. Just pick it up and choose one."

"You pick one for me sir as they all look the same."

He did not take long to make a selection. He called out a name within a second of looking at the paper, then he walked over to me and pointed to the paper and said,

"Banks and Banks."

He told me I must call now as we would have an interview as soon as that solicitor got here. He showed me the telephone and said, "Call one."

For the first time in my life I felt embarrassed that I couldn't read and write.

"I can't read and write. Can you call for me and could you let my wife know what's happened?"

"What is your wife's phone number?"

"The phone is not working at the moment but the address is 51 Motive Drive CT1 1LT, and my wife's name is Linda Mundy."

"I will call the solicitors for you and I will ask the desk Sergeant to get in touch with your wife Linda."

He pressed the bell by the door and a few moments later another police officer came.

"Officer Phillips, how can I help?"

"Can you stay with Mundy? I have to make the call and speak to the desk sergeant. I will be back in a moment."

"Of course."

He came back and said, "Mundy, they will send someone as soon as possible to call in to your wife and let her know that you've been arrested. I also called Banks and Banks the solicitors."

I was still feeling cold and very nervous in the cell. I had been there since just before lunch time and I had not eaten since that morning. As a result, I was feeling very hungry.

Then a nurse came into my cell, a big-set woman in her mid-forties.

"Hello Danny how are you?" she asked, genuinely.

"I'm very cold and very stressed. I did not kill my brother."

"Do you want another blanket?"

"Yes Miss."

"Officer Phillips could you get Mr. Mundy another blanket, please?"

"Yes Mrs. Blake, I will be back in a jiffy."

"I've got asthma, high blood pressure and I take insulin."

She made some notes, then took my pulse and temperature and asked if I had eaten.

"No," I replied, desperately.

She packed her medical equipment and looked towards me again.

"When the officer comes back with the blanket, I'll tell the officer to get you something to eat."

The officer said, "I cannot leave him alone nurse. Could you please just wait a moment and I will get some food for him?"

Mrs. Blake waited and I wrapped myself around with the blankets.

"I am back thank you Mrs. Blake. Someone will bring him some hot food after they have heated it up for him."

I was feeling cold again, worrying about what my children and wife were going to say. When was I going to see them next and who could have killed Johnny and why? When he phoned me to meet him he did not sound that bad. Or was he that bad and didn't tell me he was in trouble with his gay friends? Maybe they killed him?

The cell door was opened a bit wider and a different officer came into the cell.

"Here you are son. It's very hot so be careful."

I took a sealed hot container of microwave food and a plastic spoon and fork off of him. He put the tray on the side of the cell ledge. The cell did not have any tables or chairs to rest anything on. This food was very hot and I could hardly hold it but I welcomed it and put it on the side ledge. It was still on the ledge when I peeled the plastic lid off. It was too hot for me to hold. It was mash, veg and a slice of beef.

When I opened it a little, plenty of steam was coming out. I then sat on the wooden ledge with a very thin mattress, wrapping the blanket around me. I put the container on the edge of the ledge and started to eat. It was good but I burned my tongue a bit. When I finished I asked for a bin and the officer said, "Leave the empty container on the ledge on the side and I will clear it away later".

I did just that and sat on the bed curled up within the blankets. The nurse came back and gave me some medication for all my ailments and an asthma pump, as well as a shot of insulin. Also some single packet ones for me to keep and use when I needed.

Overall, she was very kind and helpful, not like the other people that were at the station. Before she left she told me, "If you need anything, just let the officer know and he will get in touch with me."

"Thank you Mrs. Blake."

Another police officer came and said, "The solicitor has arrived from Banks and Banks at the main reception desk."

"Come on Mundy. We've got to go and conduct the interview. Room one is ready. Follow me."

"Yes Sir. Can I take the blankets with me as I am very cold?"

"Yes. Are you ready?"

"Yes."

"Follow me."

We walked past some other cells that were not open and prisoners were inside. I could hear them speaking, laughing and muttering.

"Here we are - room one. Go and sit down and the solicitor will be here shortly. He is speaking to the inspectors upstairs."

I sat down and the officer was still standing right outside the door.

Chapter Two

Upstairs in the front desk area, the solicitor was introducing himself. "I am Mr. R Patel from Banks and Banks solicitors, here to represent Mr. Mundy."

"Come in Mr. Patel. Step this way as the inspector is waiting for you."

"Hello Mr. Patel, my name is Joan Smith and this is Inspection Patrick Robinson."

"We met before Patrick."

"Yes we have Raj."

The two inspectors stood up and shook his hands. One of them said,

"We give your company a lot of clients. I think this the fifth one today."

"Thank you inspector Robinson, I am sure Banks and Banks will be very happy with you for choosing our company and your station will have a good Christmas box for your favourite charity as well."

"When can you tell me about my client and how long has he been here?"

"About six hours. He is thirty one years old, having being married for nearly ten years and he has been with his wife for eighteen years with two children. He works in a timber yard driving a forklift truck which he has done since before he left school. By the way he can't read and write, he is over 25 stones, medically obese and he has medical problems."

"Tell me when I can go and see him as I need to interview him. Once again thanks for all these clients."

"Follow us and we can take you to him in interview room number one, downstairs."

They walked through the long corridors and down some stairs and went past some locked cells and then reached an open room with a police man standing outside.

"Mr. Patel, this is the room we are going to use."

"Thank you."

Raj walked into the room where Danny was sitting. Danny immediately stood up.

"Hello Mr. Mundy, you called our company Banks and Banks to represent you. Is it alright if I call you Danny or is it William? Please be seated."

Danny had blankets wrapped around him because he was still feeling cold as he sat down.

"No sir. Just call me Danny. I am so glad you came. There is no way I would've killed Johnny. I love my little brother, Sir".

"Danny there is no need to call me sir as my name is Raj. Before we start, I need you to sign some papers so that I can represent you."

"What are these papers for? I did not kill my Johnny."

"No, no, this is your permission for me to represent you. I need to have it in writing."

"I cannot read or write so can you read it for me please? Do you want me to sign it? Show me where you want me to scribble my name."

"There are a lot of papers here. I'll just show you where to sign. Sorry Danny, I took it for granted that you wanted me to represent you?"

"Yes Sir. I do. I can tell that you are a good man."

"Sign here, here ...."

As Raj turned the papers, Danny could not keep track of where to sign so he interrupted.

"One page at time, Sir."

"OK, I will slow down Danny."

Raj took the pen and pointed to where he wanted Danny to sign. He could hardly hold the pen because he was shaking so much and when he put pen to paper he could barely press on it and very slowly draw an 'x.' He wondered when it would be over.

"Are we finished?"

It seemed like what he did was hard work and he felt relieved that he had finished.

"No, just a few more pages to sign Danny."

After they finished signing all of the paper work, then Raj explained everything to Danny.

Banks and Banks would represent him and he couldn't change solicitors in the middle of his case. As he had signed the papers for them alone, they would represent him through all of it. Judges did not change solicitors in mid-stream as they thought you were wasting tax payer's money.

"Are you ready to be interviewed by me now, Danny?"

"When you are ready to, tell me exactly what happened and how you happened to be on the scene of the murder of your brother."

"It was twenty minutes to twelve and my lunch was at midday. I was working on my forklift truck when Eden called me, saying that I had a telephone call. It was from my brother Johnny. I took the call and he said that he wanted to speak to me urgently at his home. I said I would come in my lunch break but he said he wanted me to come right away. I told him I had a job to finish off first. He said that would be alright and he would expect to see me afterwards. I wish I had gone when he asked as this might not have happened. I might have caught the killer, or if he had seen me he would not have killed him."

"Don't think about that now. Just tell me what happened."

"So I walked over to where my brother lived. It's only five minutes to get to his place. As I was walking I was also eating my lunch. I would like to say Johnny's house is on two floors. There is the basement, ground floor and first floor. I must have got there at about seven minutes past twelve when I realised his front door was open. I walked up five steps and his room was the first door on the right, about ten steps as I walked into the house. His door was open a little. I went in and he was lying on his bed with a knife in him, so I rushed and tried to pull it out."

"I shouted, 'Johnny Johnny, talk to me.' Just then the landlady walked in and screamed hysterically.

"Murder Murder!"

I said, "Call an ambulance and the police. The land lady was still screaming.

"Murder, murder, you murderer." Then she went outside in the street and was continuing to call me a murderer. A few other people started to come by the room. I told them to call the ambulance. I was holding my brother for what seemed like hours before the police and ambulance came. I just sat on the bed holding Johnny until the police finally arrived and arrested me."

As he was describing it, Danny did not seem sure what was happening to him. He was in a daze and he was very hesitant. He had a very babyish look about him and was ready to cry again. Not surprisingly, he had been crying a lot over the past few hours, thinking that he had lost his brother and he had also been accused of his murder.

"I did not kill my baby brother. I love him. I practically brought him up myself before my mother and dad died nearly five years ago".

Upstairs in the inspector's office, they were talking about the case.

"Who is on suicide watch Joan?"

"Officer Phillips, Inspector Robinson."

"Are we going to charge him with murder or not? It's been seven hours since he has been in custody." "I know, and we have made quite a bit of progress on the investigation so far regarding Mundy. We know he has been working at Mace timber as a forklift driver for over fifteen years. He has never had any convictions or any charges against him."

"But his father has."

"Let's stick with Mundy shall we? Seems he is a family man, married with two children aged ten and eight - Kim and Amanda."

"Why would he want to kill his younger brother? He practically raised him himself for the last fifteen years of his life?"

"Joan, people kill for reasons which are only known to themselves."

"Look at him. He is thirty one years old and must be over twenty five stones. He is medically obese and he is wheezing all the time, constantly out of breath. His hair is all covering his bald head like Bobby Charlton. He is so pathetic."

"Joan do you know who had his hair like that?"

"Yes he used to play football for the reds and he won the world cup for England."

"Which reds?"

"Liverpool of course. You see. I know my football."

"NO. No Joan he played for Man Utd. His name was Bobby Charlton."

"Patrick why are we waiting to question Mundy?"

"The captain wants to head up this one himself. He wants to get a promotion and we need an extension of hours to hold him in custody longer when we start to question him."

"Pat, I don't think this man is guilty because he's got no motive."

"Joan, like father like son his father hated gays. He has said many times in the pub that he would kill any one of his children if they were gay."

"We should arrest him then." "He is dead, that's why I think his eldest son is following in his footsteps."

"Is that all we have Pat?"

"Only the landlady found him with the knife in his hand."

The phone rang and Pat immediately answered it.

"Thank you Sir."

"We have got the extension."

"Pat, shall I bring him to the question room? By the way Mundy said that he is freezing cold, what does that mean?"

"In medical terms he is in a state of shock."

"Look Pat, the nurse Blake is coming over. She will tell you what she discovered when she examined him."

"We can now question him."

"Come in nurse and have a seat."

"Thank you Mr. Robinson."

"Have you examined Mr. Mundy ready for us to question him?"

"Yes and I think that he is fine to be questioned. You probably already know that he has a lot of medical problems, including high blood pressure, asthma, diabetes and obesity. I have given him all of the medication that he needs in order to get through the next six hours. I shall come back before I leave and check on him and leave the officer with one week's worth of medication for him. I have ordered him another blanket too."

"Why is he so cold?"

"Joan, he is in a state of shock. I think you should look after your prisoners a bit better."

"Mrs. Blake, we do the best we can. Thank you for updating us. That will be all, nurse."

After the nurse was out of ear shot they carried on talking.

"That was a bit hard, Pat." "She is always being cheeky, so I had to put her in her place. We've got a murderer on our hands."

"Sir, the solicitor is with Mundy and they are ready for you."

"Thank you, officer Phillips."

Chapter Three

The door knocked. Then it was opened as two plain clothes officers walked in. They introduced themselves as inspector Patrick Robinson and officer Joan Smith. Danny was about to stand up but Mr. Robinson put his hand on his shoulder indicating to stay on the chair. He and Joan sat down opposite him and Raj sat next to Danny, then she started to speak while getting the tape disc ready.

"Are you, Danny Mundy, ready to be questioned regarding the murder of Mr. John Mundy?"

The solicitor looked at Danny quizzically.

"Yes I am."

"Danny can you begin by describing to us exactly what happened today from the time you left work and went to your brother's place? Every word you say will be taped."

"Shall I start from the time Johnny rang me at work or when I went to his house?"

"Start from the time you went to his house."

"Alright. Johnny rang me at work and said he wanted to see me as he was in trouble. He wanted me to go to his house straight away but I told him I would come at lunchtime. I know now that I should have gone straight away to his house."

The officer looked him up and down.

"Danny, now tell us what happened at the house."

"Yes Miss, I will. I rushed to his house at lunch time and when I reached his house, I walked up the five steps to the open front door and went straight into the hallway. I went right up to Johnny's door which was the first door on the right. Weirdly that was open as well. As I got there I called Johnny and walked into his room where he was lying on the bed. He wasn't moving on the bed so I lifted him up and put him in my lap. Then I saw a knife in his side and yanked it out as fast as I could. I hadn't seen the knife at first as it was hidden from view. Just as I did that, the landlady walked in and began shouting 'murder'. I told her to call the ambulance and police and she said, 'don't worry I will call the police then the ambulance.' I stayed with him on the bed until the police came."

"Danny. Listen to the question," Inspector Robinson said in a stern voice.

"Did you love your father?"

"Yes I did."

"Did you share a lot of his views?"

"Yes I did."

"Did he like queers? "Patrick raised his voice more.

"Did your father hate queers?"

"What's that got do with my brother's death?"

"Danny just answer the question."

"My father has been dead for over five years."

Tears were about to come out of Danny's reddening eyes.

"I think my client would like a break from questioning, please."

"Ok Raj, I will stop the tape. The interview has ended for now and we can label and seal the tape, Joan."

"Would fifteen minutes be OK and would you like a drink?"

Raj looked at Danny and the response was a quick nod of the head.

"Yes, could you bring two cups of tea please?'

"Why are they asking about my father?" Danny asked as they walked away.

"They are trying to suggest that you and he are very much alike and that will be the motive for you killing your brother."

"Raj I loved my brother. You know he left home and was living with us in my house with my wife. In fact he was sleeping on the couch until he found his own place."

"It is not for me to say, but who do you think would have wanted to kill your brother?"

"I only know a few of his friends. Eden, the accountant at work, liked him and Big Ron's grandson- Terry- liked him. Oh and the landlady as well."

"What do you mean by like?"

"You know."

"Your brother had more than one lover?"

"You don't have to say it like that. He was a very good looking boy, so yeah, the landlady liked him. She definitely didn't like me or any of Johnny's friends."

"Did he have more than two like him?"

"I think so. As I said the landlady liked him a lot as he did not even have to pay his rent sometimes."

"Danny, don't you see that those men he had affairs with could have had motives to kill him as jealousy is a huge motive for murder."

"What can you do to find out who killed Johnny?"

"Legal aid does not allow a lot of money for private investigators but I will see what I can do. Just tell me all you can about the landlady first."

"She had the hots for him when we went out for a pint. She always wanted to know where he was going."

"What did Johnny say about her?"

"He would say just because she let him off the rent for a few weeks that she always wanted to know where he was and if there was another woman."

"Did he have sex with her?"

"I think so but he'd never admit it."

Raj made a sign to say someone was outside.

A quick knock on the door and it opened again.

"Here are two teas. The plastic cup is hot so be careful."

"Thank you Joan, could you give us a few more minutes?"

"Danny, is there anything you want to tell me before they come back in?"

"No."

Danny held the cup in both hands and started to sip it, little by little. A few moments later the detectives returned to the interview room.

"Is it alright if we all sit down and I will put the tape in so we can restart the interview? I will begin with the open question tape switched on and time noted."

"Danny tell me again what time did you leave your work place?"

"I must have left at about twelve noon."

"And what time did you get to your brother's?"

"As I said before, it takes about five minutes to get there, so probably about 12.07 pm."

"Did you rush to get there?"

"Yes I did."

"Can I say something inspector?" Raj interjected, "Danny told me he was eating his lunch on the way to Johnny's house."

"So Danny, if you were eating, wouldn't it take you longer to get there?"

"Yes, I forgot to tell you I was eating."

"So I suppose it could have taken about three minutes longer to get there after eating."

"I am not sure as I said I went there at about seven minutes past. Johnny could maybe do it in about two or three minutes."

"I walked from your work to Johnny's and it took me ninety seconds."

"What system does your work place have to keep a record of who is in there at any time?"

"I don't know what you mean."

"Do you have a clocking in and out machine and you all have your own clocking in cards by the side of the machine?"

"Yes."

"Do you have your own card?"

"Yes I do."

"What are the rules about clocking in and out? I know that if you can't remember it's written above the clock."

"I can't read but I was told we are not allowed to clock someone else's card or you will get a warning."

"Did you clock out today?"

"Oh I am sorry I forgot to tell you that Eden clocked me out."

"So you could finish any time you liked before lunch?"

"No we had a job to complete and it took all morning. We finished it at about five minutes to twelve. If you want to check, you can ask old Bill."

"I did and old Bill informed me that he was not sure what time you finished that day."

"Excuse me, can I ask a question Joan?"

"Of course you can Raj."

"Who is old Bill? How old is old Bill, Danny?"

"He is over eighty years old and he is a bit doddery. I bet he has been with our company since it started."

"Thank you Danny, you can continue Joan."

"Who told you that Johnny had called you and what time was it?"

Joan stifled a yawn behind the back of her hand as she waited for a response.

"I am not sure what time they rang me before lunch, but it was probably about twenty to twelve when Eden came and told me and I went straight to the office so Eden could hand over the phone."

Joan was making careful, yet unreadable notes.

"What's Eden job at your firm?"

"He works in the office and does all the books and wages."

"When employees clock out does someone else deal with that or discipline them?"

"Eden is supposed to but he does not so everyone gets on with their jobs and people clock out each other all the time. Nobody take the piss, it only takes minutes to wash their hands or use the phone so we don't clock out for this."

"Danny do you know what time your clock card reads for today?"

"When Eden clocks out it will be when everyone else clocks out so I'd I say about five minutes past twelve."

Joan rolled her eyes. She was starting to get irritated.

"No Danny, it was at twenty nine minutes to twelve. We have got your clocking card. I would like you to go and speak to your solicitors and see whether or not you wish to change your statement. The time is now 23.41pm and this interview is terminated."

After the police inspectors left there was an awkward silence in the room. Moments later, Danny started to plead to his solicitor.

"Raj I am telling you the truth. I did not kill my brother. Why did my clock card say twenty nine minutes to twelve? I don't understand."

"I believe your story, its coming on to midnight so I will come back tomorrow in the morning. I will try to get legal aid for a detective. You just wait here and I will get an officer to take you back to your cell. Bye, Danny."

"Bye Raj. I will see you tomorrow."

There was a new officer at the cell door. He must have been over sixty with grey hair and a very thin frame.

Danny was still feeling cold and in the office it was not too cold. An older officer took him back to the cell where he was really very cold. He still had the blankets wrapped around him as he sat on the bed. The officer sat on the chair quietly with the door opened.

"Sir. Can I have a hot drink please as I am feeling cold?"

"Ok son, I will go and get one for you but do not move out of your cell or I will get into trouble."

"Yes Sir.

A few minutes later he returned with refreshments.

"Here you are son."

"Thank you sir."

This officer was very friendly so Danny felt at ease for the first time in the station.

"What have you done to be in here son?"

"I have been accused of killing my brother and I did not kill him."

"If you didn't do it you will be fine. So don't worry about it. Just try and get some sleep and tell the truth when the inspector interviews you."

"I have and I will."

After a while they spoke again.

"Sir, why am I so cold when I am normally always a very hot person?"

"The reason you are cold son is because of what happened to you today. You are in a state of shock. Now try and sleep, there is going to be a lot more questioning tomorrow for you."

Danny finished his drink and curled up on the bed, trying his best to get to sleep. Danny twisted and turned all night and he couldn't sleep. Probably he missed his wife. She was his comforter. As he looked out of the cell he could see that the officer was reading so he wouldn't talk. Danny just twisted and turned, drifting in and out of consciousness now and again.

Chapter Four

"Good morning Danny. I have some medication for you. I need you to keep this asthma pump and I will give you the rest of your medication as well. Just hold still so I can give you your insulin injection. I have your tablets too. I will leave some water for you to take them with. The officer has gone to get you a sandwich and something to drink that will help wash it all down."

"Thank you nurse."

Danny looked down. He hadn't slept very well and knew he was in for a deeper inquisition.

"Here he is now. I will see you just before lunch but if you need me, let the officer know."

"Here you are Danny. Some crisps, a sandwich and a hot coffee."

"Thank you sir."

Danny was disappointed to see the short officer again as he was hoping to see the older officer who was always kind to him. Danny could not do anything but go through everything that had happened over and over again, playing it out in his head like a video on repeat. He sat on the bed and squirmed and when the officer saw that he was fidgeting he called out with a suggestion.

"Do you want something to read?"

"No thanks, Sir."

This was going to be one of the few times in Danny's life that he hid the fact that he could not read. For his entire life, he'd managed without reading and writing. But it had never been easy.

"Excuse me Sir. What time is the next interview?"

"I am not sure but its Saturday today and they normally come around about now."

"Will they tell Raj?"

"Of course they will."

"What time is it now, Sir?"

"Eight forty five."

"Sir, can I brush my teeth and have a shower, please?"

"I will check."

He stood up and waved to somebody in the passage. Immediately an officer walked up to him.

"Mundy wants to have a shower and brush his teeth?"

"That's fine. You take him to the shower then."

"Come with me, Danny."

Danny followed him through the corridor and across to the toilets and shower. When they got there the officer opened a cupboard and gave Danny a towel, a bar of soap and a tube of toothpaste. He had been in a night gown and the officer gave him a clean one ready for after he had showered. The officer then took him back to his cell and once again Danny curled up on the bed. At least he was not feeling as cold as before. The officer was now being a bit more relaxed about keeping an eye on Danny too.

"Danny, I am going to find out what time your solicitor is coming for your interview, will you be ok?"

"Yes Sir."

He wondered why Linda had not tried to contact him or leave him a message at the desk. Maybe his wife might know if anyone wanted to hurt Johnny and hadn't told him about it. When Raj came, he would ask him to go and see her and the children. He missed them so much, it hurt.

He hoped to ask Raj to ask her if she might know something about who killed Johnny. Maybe he could tell him how long the police planned to keep him there. To him it just felt so cold in there, surrounded by all those concrete walls. He would normally feel hot all the time so this was a feeling he wasn't used to and he didn't like it.

"Danny get ready. Your solicitor is in the interview room waiting to see you before your interview."

He was pleased to know that Raj had arrived and was sure he might have some news.

"Follow me. Mind you, you should know where the interview room is by now."

"Is it aright if I take the blankets again?"

"Yes - come along."

The officer knocked on the door before opening it with an audible groan.

"I will be outside, so just go in. I will close the door for you."

Danny went inside and looked around but he saw a different guy sitting there. He then went back outside.

"Is this the right room to see Raj in?"

"Yes that is what I have been told. It's Banks & Banks solicitors."

"But that's not Raj."

"Hello Danny Mundy. Come in. My name is Robert Taylor and I am from Banks & Banks."

"Danny go back into the interview room and talk to Mr. Taylor."

"Yes Sir."

"Come in and sit down Mr. Mundy."

Danny was in a state of shock and so confused. Inside he felt dread coming over him and started to feel cold again. In some ways he felt lifeless, lost in his mind. Raj was his only hope. Why wasn't he with him?

"Sorry about the confusion but Raj could not make it today."

"I am not happy. I thought Raj would come today. He was meant to do a few things for me."

"Well let me see if I can help you. What was it you wanted Raj to do?"

"He was meant to get a private investigator and I wanted him to go and see my wife and ask if she knows who killed my brother Johnny. I also needed him to ask her to visit me."

"Why are you here? Mr. Mundy I have not had a chance to read the notes."

"I told everything to Raj. I have been accused of murdering my brother Johnny."

"Danny, can you tell me again what happened again please."

"Mr. Taylor, I am not happy about this as I signed papers to have Raj represent me."

"But he does work for Banks and Banks and we all work for them. I will read his notes but you need to tell me again what happened when you left your workplace and when you met your brother."

Monday morning.

The short officer at the door was given a small paper by another officer, who was wearing a different uniform.

"Danny get yourself ready as you are going to be moved to Emely prison where you will be waiting for a trial."

"Sir! But my solicitors said that you were going to drop the charges."

"That could well be the truth but you are being moved so get yourself ready and this officer will take you in a van to Emely prison."

Danny started to think about how much he loved Linda. He knew that she had that affair and had eventually come back to him and he had been grateful because he could not cope with life without her.

The officer took him to the desk and asked him to sign some papers and then tried to ensure that he understood what they were for.

"Yes." Of course he understood.

"Come this way then."

He opened a door and could see sunlight for the first time that day. It blinded him for a moment. It was at the back of the station, in this large compound of parked vans and cars with two very large gates.

"Wait here a while."

Another officer came and handcuffed Danny and then another one from the van came and he handcuffed himself to him. They walked over to the van, yet Danny was still in a daze and caught up in worrying. He told him to hurry up as he had got other prisoners to load into the van. As he started to pull at Danny's arm, the cuffs hurt his hands.

"Follow me. We have to go up these little steps and into the van."

Danny followed him before being told to go into the first cubicle and to stay standing up. He put his hands out of the cubicle and then he unlocked the cuffs that had bound them both together. He did not uncuff his hands though, as they were still cuff together. After this he locked the door then told Danny to sit down. Danny was feeling claustrophobic, as if everything was closing in on him. He could hardly breathe and move in the cubicle. It was such a tight squeeze and it made him think he might be having an asthma attack, but he was too frightened to say anything.

He had forgotten his asthma pump and wondered if maybe he should ask for it, especially as he couldn't breathe as well as normal.

"Sir! Sir!" he shouted. He couldn't see anyone properly, just a haze of people moving around the bus.

"What do you want Mundy?"

"I need my asthma pump, Sir. I can't breathe."

Danny overheard another officer speaking about him.

"I've got all his stuff. I will look in the bag. Wait... here it is, let's give it to him before he dies on us."

"Thank you Sir."

"Here you are Mundy."

Carefully, Danny took the inhaler and did three very big sucks on it and started to feel a little better. Then he started to think about Linda and what had happened over the last few years.

Danny and his wife Linda had been lovers from their school days when they went to the same high school. Back then they would go to the park instead of going to school and, luckily, their parents did not care one way or another. By the time Linda was sixteen she had had one abortion and two miscarriages. She left school at fifteen and worked in the corner shop and Danny was working at the warehouse. In fact, he had been bunking off school to work at the warehouse since he was twelve.

By the time they both were sixteen they were already renting a single room and started living together. People said that they looked very grown up for their ages so they went into pubs without questions. Linda was growing into a very beautiful woman and she often sang at the karaoke. Everyone loved her at the local pub. She was a great singer and one day an agent came to listen to her sing. Her favourite song was 'Stand by your man' which she belted out with passion.

Danny and Linda were inseparable. Men would go to the corner shop and buy things just to see her and to speak to her. The manager did not mind as customers who never normally came to his shop would stop by and add their custom. At night she would tell Danny about these boys and men who came to the shop to ask her out but he did not take any notice of it. Selfishly he did not tell her he loved her or even console her. The truth is, he took her for granted.

Both of them would eat burgers every day. She would offer to cook something healthy but he always wanted beef burgers. Often he would eat two with egg and cheese in one bun.

By the time she was seventeen she was pregnant. Fortunately this time everything was going well and she still worked at the shop but once the men saw she was pregnant they stopped coming to the corner shop altogether. However, one man still did. He owned a large pub and night club in town and his name was Tony Romeo. This guy was about thirty five years old and he would speak and say nice things to her whereas other men now didn't bother so much, especially since she was expecting.

She had spoken to Tony many times about Danny. Bill had asked her on a few occasions to come and work for him. She must have told him about Danny putting on weight and eating six burgers in one sitting. He asked if after her baby was born she wanted to work for him in town and a cab could pick her up and drop her home at night. She was touched by his kindness.

Simon Stone, the owner of the shop, was now thinking the consumers were not coming like they used to and was beginning to be worried that he would have to pay her wages when she started maternity leave. So he told her that he was selling the shop and gave her two weeks' notice.

That night she told Danny what the owner of the shop had had say. He was very angry in response. It just happened to be a Friday night when the family would normally go to the pub and Linda would sing on the karaoke machine. He told his father - Danny senior - what happened and his father was very angry as well. He said he would go and sort him out. As always, that was what his father was like when he was drunk.

Linda worked for the next couple of weeks. She told Tony what Simon the shop keeper had done and he pretended that he was sad. Inside though, he was very happy. He did not say much but the second week he asked her to come to his pub to have a look around and reminded her that there could be an opening for her in a couple of months, before she even had the baby and that the pay would be a lot more than what she was getting then.

She agreed to go and see the place but when she told Danny he did not show much interest and got on with what he was doing. Tony said he would send a cab for the following Monday. On that Monday morning Danny had already gone to work. She was annoyed that he hadn't even wished her the best of luck. In fact, as usual, he did nothing.

She had a shower after she had tried lots of outfits on to hide her being pregnant. After several did not feel right, she finally found the correct one. On Monday at ten a Rolls Royce pulled up outside the house so she walked out and Tony was in the back seat waiting patiently. As she got closer, the chauffeur got out and opened the car door to let her in.

"Tony, what are you doing here? I thought you were going to send a cab for me?"

"I have but he has got another passenger as well, me. OK let's go driver. I must say you look beautiful this morning."

He tried to kiss her on her cheeks but she pulled away.

"If you are going to behave like this, let's not bother. DRIVER stop the car now."

The car stopped.

"I am so sorry. That will never happen again. I am so sorry Linda, please forgive me."

"You are like the rest of those men. I thought you were different but I am coming to see the job and if there is anything else attached then I am not interested. I've got a husband who loves me and I have a child coming and I could do with the extra money to pay for a pram, cots and all the things a baby needs. We also need to get a bigger room as well."

"I am very sorry. Honestly. Can we carry on now please?"

"Yes."

"Driver drive on."

She felt good about what he had said and especially telling the driver to drive on. It took a half an hour for the driver to take her and Tony to an assigned parking place. They had their dedicated parking space and as soon as they arrived, the driver opened the door for her. Straight away they went to the back entrance and into the place itself. The back door was opened and someone was having a fag outside. He stopped and said, "Good morning boss."

Then he opened the door wider and Tony led the way into the building.

"This is the ground floor. As you can see, it is wide open and it's got two bars and a large dining area. We employ about twenty staff in here."

"I thought it was just a bar but it's so massive. You've got a lot of staff working for you."

"Follow me up these stairs at the back. Are you alright with the stairs or would you like to use the lift?"

"I am fine with stairs, a bit slow but fine."

"This first floor of the night club is the same set up as down stairs but we have no dining. It holds over one thousand people. In fact it has a license for over two thousand people overall."

"My god this place is gigantic. So what job do you want me to do?"

"We have to go in the basement for that. Just follow me to the lift. By the way, above this is a self-contained one bed flat. To be honest I sleep here sometimes. We are going to the basement now."

Tony was smitten by her. He wanted to hold her and touch her but knew he couldn't. Right then he had never felt that way about anyone before. He did touch her shoulder when he led her to the basement office and he felt good. She did not mind or even notice as she was looking around all of the time.

He was quite tall so he had to bend his head a little in the passage way of the basement because of the heating pipes and sewer system. He led her to the door which opened to his office where there were four desks and a long one against and the wall with CCTV cameras showing up on screens.

"There are a lot of cameras."

"Yes there are thirty six CCTV ones on each floor and sixteen for all the doors leading into the building. We need these cameras as it is a requirement by the licensing board and, guess what, the police still want more cameras."

"You are joking, by the way you still have not told me my job role."

"I was hoping you can help me with the paper work."

"I must be honest with you I did not go to school much. I spent most of my school days with Danny going to the park and generally playing about, so I missed most of my education."

"It's not hard but we have a lot bills and deliveries every day. All you need to do is to get all of them together and put them in date order. You can read and write, can't you?"

"Of course I can but my husband can't. That's not going to take me long."

"Well can you look at the CCTV cameras and see what is going on and if anyone is stealing from the till or taking the drinks?"

"I wouldn't know what cameras are for where. They all look very confusing."

"Don't worry about it. Just take your time. Here is a box of delivery notes for the last two weeks. Hope you don't mind making a start at the work now. By the way I will pay you cash in hand. What time do you want to be back home?

"I would like to be home by four o'clock please."

"No problem."

"Please can you send me in a mini cab because I don't want the neighbors talking about me."

"That's fine. By the way, if you need me, just call me on this number. I will be out for a couple of hours but I will ask my staff to bring some coffee for you, or you can ring this number and someone will bring you what you need. If not I'll be back by lunchtime. You are welcome to go to the dining area and get your lunch free of charge. I am going now so if you need me call me any time. Alright, see you."

"Bye. You do realise it will take a bit of time to get used to everything."

"Just take your time today and have a look around."

Linda picked up the folder box with some of the invoices in and she looked through them, quickly starting to get into the swing of things and sort them out in date order. When she looked around the desk and drawers there were more and more invoices everywhere. They were all over the desk so she stopped and searched through all the papers on the long desk top table. She told herself that the staff must have just brought the invoices and put them anywhere on this long desk. Finally she managed to get all the bills together when the door opened.

"Hello my name is Kim and I'm Tony's sister."

"Hello I'm Linda and I only started today."

"That's good as he needed someone to work in here. He has told me all about you. Do you know what time it is? It's lunchtime. 1pm."

"You are joking. The time has gone so quickly and I haven't done anything yet."

"I can see you've done a lot, getting all the paperwork together. Come with me, let's go and have lunch."

Kim locked the door and gave Linda the key. They went to the dining area and Kim led the way into a corner table.

They met for lunch regularly as time passed.

"Over the last three months you've done a better job than I expected Linda. You've tidied the office and cleaned it all. The desk tops are empty and everything is filed and reorganised. All the documents are on the computer now and you've even done all the staff time sheets."

"Kim has helped a great deal by teaching me to use the computer and all the filing too. She is wonderful. In fact, sometimes I wish I had gone to school instead of bunking off with Danny but I have learned so much here."

"You have saved so much work for the accountant. He used to charge over fifteen thousand just for the bills and he has reduced that to ten thousand. As a reward, here is a bonus which you fully deserve."

"That is too much."

"Five hundred pounds is not enough. You take it for your baby and buy the things you need."

"I have a few loans to pay so that will come in very helpful, thank you Tony."

"If you keep progressing like this you will get a bonus with every quarterly pay packet."

"You know I've only got another six weeks before I stop work so you will need to get someone to replace me."

"I will keep your job until you come back if you want to."

"I do want to come back but I will have to see what Danny says."

"Always remember you have got a job here but that's a long way away. We will talk about that then."

In the three months that she had worked for Tony he had never tried anything with her apart from when he touched her many times. Often when he was showing things to her he would gently touch her arm or shoulder and that was enough to make him happy. Deep down he was falling for Linda more and more but he couldn't do anything about it. He thought all he had to do was wait and wait and show her kindness.

Tony payed Linda cash in hand. This was good because she and Danny had borrowed and owed a lot of money and the loan shark would come around every Friday night for payments. She started to pay him double every week and the debts were slowly getting smaller and smaller.

Danny and Linda's lifestyle involved playing pool on Wednesday nights. Both of them would go there on Friday nights and Linda would sing at the karaoke machine. Saturday was usually the same again and sometimes, if they had any extra money, they would go to the pub on a Sunday lunchtime as well. By Monday they were borrowing money to last the week till Friday.

Since she started to work at Tony's she looked at life differently, especially the money side of things. She had looked at the people coming into Tony's Pub and seen how she was just like them, living just for the day. The way Kim talked about them in the pub there was nothing wrong but no ambition. She and Danny were just like them and this made her desperate to save money to buy a house. She thought about how her mother and father lived and Danny's parents as well. Let's face it, there was nothing wrong with that.

She got Johnny and his friend Simon to wallpaper and paint the small bedroom. Then they bought new curtains, a cot, a cute pram and a new double bed with fresh sheets and quilts. Johnny was now working for the council so she asked him to help to get a new place with the council. He reassured her that once she had the baby it would happen quickly.

He told her off as she and Danny had not even filled in the application form he'd given them and there was a 20 year waiting list. He said that he had already spoken to his manager about them having a baby and wanting to start a big family, so hopefully she would stand a good chance to get a house eventually.

Chapter Five

The baby was finally born and it was a hard birth due to a bit of a complication. Linda had to stay in hospital for a couple of weeks. In the evenings Danny and the rest of her family would visit her and the baby, though Tony and Kim would visit her every day during work hours regularly too. Tony wanted to pay her full wages but he thought she would think he was trying to buy her so he payed her half wages.

When they visited her she was appreciative but told him he didn't have to pay her at all.

"Tony you don't have to pay my wages. After all I was only working for you for four and a half months."

Kim laughed.

"Don't worry about this, he should be paying full wages, the skinflint. The baby is beautiful. What are you going to name her?"

"Kim you have taught me and helped a great deal. I will name her after you and I want you to be a Godmother to her."

"Are you sure?"

"I am. I spoke to Danny and he is happy about you being her Godmother."

The next evening Danny and Johnny came to visit her.

"That is a lot of fruit and chocolates."

"Kim and her brother came yesterday and brought them. Help yourselves or take them home for Mum and Dad. I am definitely not going to eat them all."

Danny dived into the chocolates and Johnny took an apple and both started to eat. Danny didn't bother to look at the baby but Johnny did.

"I've got a surprise for you Linda. I managed to swing a new council house for you, not too far from your old place but it needs a bit of doing up."

"That is great news! You are the best brother-in-law anyone can have," she cheered.

"It needs redecoration. I will try and get the keys and do your bedroom before you come out but the rest will need to be done when you move in."

"I don't care. I always wanted my own house and I was fed up of that room. Danny we will have to stop going out every night and just do it once a week as we are going to need money to do up the house."

Danny was not the type to say anything when Linda spoke because she was the one in the household who did the shopping as well as organising everything in their life. The only contribution he made was his wages each Friday. He liked the easy life where he did not have to think very much. In fact, he was looking forward to the nights when he was able to go to the pub and play pool or darts.

"Johnny, when can we get the keys?"

"I will collect them tomorrow, but you've got to remember that this house is a bit of a wreck and needs doing up. The council will only pay for paint but you will have to do the rest."

"You mean me and Danny."

"Danny you have to do up the house and that will be a lot of work, like when you did that room up."

Danny wasn't paying attention.

"Listen Danny Mundy, the last two months were my happiest, living it that room with nicely painted walls and nice curtains. It wasn't a waste of time so make sure you help Johnny and his mate to do that place up. No more drinking or pool for you. I mean it."

"Ok Linda." Danny seemed humble.

"The doctors want to keep me in for another week, for observation. So you can get the work done and maybe get your dad and my dad to help. I will phone my dad later or if he comes to visit me before I will speak to him. Danny please help Johnny and redecorate the house. You always say you will do things and end up achieving nothing that you agreed to do."

"Don't worry Linda I will do it."

"Do you know something Danny? Once you use those words I start to worry."

"What words do you mean?"

"If you don't know by now, you will never know. Please, Danny, try to help to do the work and do not say a anything negative. Right... now visiting time is over so go home. See you later Johnny."

"What words was Linda talking about Danny?"

"Don't worry."

"How long have you two been together?"

"About twenty years?"

"Danny you are so stupid. What words that you use can make her so mad?"

"Oh 'don't worry' you mean Johnny."

"To her. That means you will not do what you said you will do."

On the day that Linda left the hospital with her baby, both her parents and Johnny came for her in a minicab. Danny had to go into work. Linda was disappointed that he wasn't there, but she knew they needed the money for the new house. Linda was happy going into her new home because now she had front and back gardens and she had never had that before. Even her parents didn't have them.

After about half an hour, the cab pulled up outside the house which had a concrete path leading to the front door. The garden was busy with overgrown bushes and weeds. They were just about to walk through the door and Linda held her breath. She didn't know exactly what to expect. Inside, the hallway was clean but there was no decoration. Linda gave Kim to her mother and went to have a look around properly.

"Johnny. Dad. Why has the work not been done?" she asked, feeling anxious.

"We did the best we could love. The place was full of rubbish so we had to take all the paper off the ceiling and walls. It was crumbling and bits of wallpaper were falling off. Don't forget we all had to do our full time jobs as well."

"Honestly Linda, there was a lot of work needed. I tried the council and spoke to the housing management team but they would not or could not help."

"Mum, I can't stay in the house in these conditions with our baby. Can Kim and I stay at yours for a little while?"

"Of course you can love. Johnny go upstairs and get all the baby's things and Dad, you and Johnny take the cot apart and bring it downstairs."

"Linda, take all the clothes you need. We have to get this house sorted out before you and Kim can come back here to live. If you stay here, she could get very sick in these conditions."

Linda and Kim were back at her mother's house, in her old childhood bedroom where she'd grown up. Danny finished work early knowing that his wife and baby would be at home already. He rushed back and opened the front door, then called out for Linda and ran upstairs. As soon as he noticed that no one was home he panicked, thinking something bad must have happened.

Quickly, he picked up the phone that Linda had bought him but he had never used as Linda did all the phoning.

He had no idea how to use it so he played around with it a bit before putting it down and sitting on the bed, agitated. Suddenly there was a knock at the door and he hurriedly opened the front door. It was the lady who lived next door.

"Hello, I've got a message from your wife to say that she has gone to her mother's and you can call her there."

Danny looked at the mobile phone.

"Do you know how to work this?'

"Let me have it. What is your wife's name?"

"Linda."

"Here, it's ringing."

"Hello Linda, why are you at your mum's?"

"For once in your life use your brain. How can I bring our baby to a place like that? She will get so ill. Just get it sorted out. I don't mind if we have to borrow money from Big Ron at the pub."

"We already owe him money."

"I have paid it all off."

"What do you mean you have paid him off?"

"When I was working for Kim's brother, I paid it off."

"I will go and see him tonight. Linda, his rates have gone up so if we borrow £100 we will have to pay £3 per week in interest. Then, when we pay it all off we will have given another £10 on top and we will need over £300 to do the job, I think."

"Danny I genuinely do not care. Just get the house sorted out. I am not coming back until it has been fixed up."

"Hello! Hello! The phone has gone dead."

"Give it here. Let me have a look," said the helpful neighbour. "Looks like she put the phone down on you mate. By the way, the people who had the house before you were very dirty and untidy. I feel sorry for you as you have got a big job on your hands. My husband is a painter and decorator. Shall I ask him to call around?"

Danny looked bewildered.

"Thanks miss for the help with the phone. That is really kind, thanks. I'd better start to do some work. See you later or when your husband comes around."

Danny was stressed and didn't know what to do first. One thing was for sure, he was hungry. So he went to the local fish and chip shop. Later, when he got home again with the fish and chips, the door knocked loudly.

"Hello Danny, my name is Paul. My wife asked me to come and see you about some decorating work."

"Come in and have a look around. I am starving so I'm just grabbing a bite to eat."

Danny started to eat his chips and did not wash his hands. Meanwhile Paul looked around the house. When he returned to the living room, Danny had finished eating his fish and chips.

"There is a lot of work needed here mate. I can see if a friend of mine might help me to do it quickly."

"How much would it cost?"

"You're looking at £1000, at least."

"You are joking. I can't afford that. What about if my brother Johnny and I helped?"

"I have seen your work in the bedroom. If that is the standard you want, I will charge £650 cash in hand. As long as you and your brother help to strip the paper, rub down, fill in and clean up all the rubbish."

Danny nodded.

"When can you start?"

"My wife told me your situation so I will help you and start tomorrow."

"OK. You have got a deal."

After Paul had left, Danny started to wonder where he was going to get the money from.

"What do want this early in the morning?"

"Not you."

Danny pushed his way past the landlady. He and the landlady did not get along and they had had run-ins many times before when he had been and knocked on his brother's door.

"Who is it?"

"Me."

"What do you want Danny?"

"Open the door." "Talk through the door. I am in bed."

"Could you come to the new house after work today to help me decorate? I've got a painter as well and he is charging £650. With our help that's cheap. Is that OK then?"

"I will see you tonight. Bye."

"Bye."

"He probably had someone in the room," snapped the nosy woman.

"What's that got to do with you? He pays his rent every week so just move out of the way and let me past."

Danny walked past the landlady and went to work. On his way there he was thinking about how he was going to raise the money. First he went his manager. Knowing that he'd been working there a long time and they have been good to him, he told his manager his situation and he agreed to lend him £300. All he had to do was pay back £5 per week out of his wages. There would be no interest.

That evening he went to the pub and bought himself a pint, then went to see Big Ron.

"That is a lot of money Danny. I am not sure you can pay it back."

"I have always paid you back in the past."

"You mean your wife did all the paying back and now she has a little baby she will not be able to work up west any more so it will just be your wages."

"I will pay you Ron. It might take me a little bit longer but you know my family and Linda's family are good people when it comes to paying our debts."

"I know that Danny."

Big Ron had to stand up to get the money out of one of his trouser pockets. It was rolled up so thick that he could not get it out of his pocket easily. Even when he stood up it took him a while to get it out. He peeled off seven fifty pound notes, gave them to Danny and whispered in his ear.

"I am giving you an extra £50. I am doing you a favour. You pay me ten pounds per week interest and when you pay me back it will be £400, is that alright?"

"Yes, yes Ron."

"What do want to drink Danny?"

"Pint of Fosters please."

"Same again and an extra pint of fosters for Danny please."

Danny ended up staying till late in the night drinking until Johnny came for him.

"You are a very silly man Danny. You know what Linda wanted and you have not done it and you asked me to help you and you are pissing money the money up the wall. She is going to leave you."

"She will never do that. We are soul mates."

"Come on, let's get you home."

For the first time in Danny's life he had done things without Linda. He felt better than he thought he would. Probably Linda was going to get upset with him. He did it all wrong. He thought he would not tell her but he somehow knew he would need to find the extra money needed to pay Ron. Big Ron charged more than usual but he must be able to get the money to do the work.

Kim had offered her cottage to Linda to use until her house was done up. It had been nearly two weeks since Linda and the baby came out of hospital and the house was not done up, so Linda was living in Bill Gates' cottage. Danny had sent Johnny to see her and asked when she was coming back. The answer was when the house was completed. Danny had no idea how to decorate and he had drunk most of the money rather than spend it on decorating. Sadly the work was not done.

Linda was usually the driving force behind Danny, so he was lost without her. In the meantime Bill had taken Linda and Kim out many times and spent a lot of money on her, whilst showing her a lot of kindness. By now, she was falling for him. Deep down she realised that she had get to get herself out of that situation before she fell for Bill entirely.

So she told him to take her back the next day to her new house as it was unfair to Danny. Bill was very understanding and did not put up any fuss, only asking what time she wanted to leave the next day."

Johnny got the message that Linda was coming home and he went over to the house. It was clear that the place was still a mess with bins overflowing, tins of paint, and brushes etc. all over the place. The place was a complete mess but he spent the whole night cleaning so there was no sign of Danny. He gave the bedroom a special clean then the rest of the house.

Danny came home with fish and chips and was going up to the bedroom.

"No no mate. You must eat that in the kitchen on the table."

"Hey Johnny what are you doing here? It's nice to see you."

"I have not been here for a few days and the place is a tip already."

"Why worry? Linda is not coming back as she is living with that Bill Gates."

"She is not living with anyone. She is coming home tomorrow."

Danny started to hug Johnny.

"She is coming home."

"Yes she is mate, so sleep downstairs. I have touched up with paint and cleaned the upstairs rooms. Try and keep the place clean for tomorrow."

"What time is Linda coming?"

"Not sure but you go to work all the same. Do you want me to stay the night?"

"No I will sleep well tonight, thanks little brother."

He went to bed that night but he could not sleep as he just wanted to phone Linda. But he did not know how to use the phone. Early in the morning, before he went to work, he popped to Johnny's house. Knocking on the front door again and again, it took a long time for it to be answered and it was the land lady.

"Johnny isn't here, he is out."

"I don't believe you."

Danny pushed past her and knocked on Johnny's door really hard but there was no answer.

"I told you!

Danny left in a huff.

Chapter Six

Since Danny had been a baby, his mum and dad had always taken him to the Red Lion Pub regularly. His parents had always played darts or pool for the pub and the kids would come along when they practised. This was the normal habit with most of the families that drank in the Red Lion and it was the same with Linda and her family.

The pub was a very large place and was split into different sections. There was a public saloon and an off license side of it. It was different to today's pubs which are often open plan pubs.

In the off license side Big Ron did his business. It had a small TV in there where they would watch the horse racing on a Saturday and Big Ron was the bookie so he would take any types of bets and he always paid out. If you were lucky, he might buy you a drink when you won, although that was not very often.

Ron Junior was into drugs. He did not bring drugs into the country but he was a very big dealer. With a group of runners working for him he would operate from the public bar where the darts, pool and all types of games were going on. He did nothing in the pub apart from talk to his runners. The stuff would be left in various places in the car park. There were no cameras in those days, which is different to how things are now. These days, pubs have CCTV cameras all over them.

The landlord was very happy with all the trade he got and enjoyed a good relationship with Ron. There were not many fights in the pub as punters knew they would have to answer to the two Ron's if they stoked up any violence.

Big Ron and his family had come to the area about six years earlier, when they found an empty site and moved there. Of course, they have been hounded by the local council for many years but nothing the council did intimidated them as they always had an answer. In fact, they spent a lot of money on lawyers and solicitors, which they could easily afford due to all of the business they did.

When they came, Big Ron had his family scout out all of the public houses within a five mile radius to see which one they could use for their benefit (in other words, for their business) and where the police would less likely bother them. The pub that came to the top of their list was The Red Lion because of the size and the nature of the car park. They found out all about its history with the police going there every weekend because of fights.

The landlord was warned that the pub might have to close if they didn't stop all the fighting. So, initially, the landlord -Jim- stopped all evening opening. He even closed at six PM at the weekends.

Big Ron was about fifty years old and he dressed responsibly in a suit and tie. His white shirt was turned up at the collars and you could see the dirt round his neck. He had a pot belly and braces and his button was about to pop out, struggling at holding in his bulging belly. He went in the saloon part of the pub and ordered a double house whisky and a pint of Fosters. Jim looked around to see if he had come with anyone else. As a rule, he did not allow any gypsies into his pub as he'd had many problems with them before.

Instantly, he knew Ron was a gypsy but Jim was losing money in the pub and someone ordering three drinks at the same time was good for business. Anyway Ron stayed until closing time which was six on that particular Friday. The bell rang at 5.45 PM.

"Governor, are you closing?

Ron already knew the answer.

"Yes mate at 6PM."

"Why?"

"It's a long story."

Ron had a good way with words and he knew how to talk to people after years of training, selling tarmac to people who didn't need it. Jim locked all the doors and Ron stayed in after all the other customers had left. There were not many anyway.

That night Ron was buying drinks for Jim. He did not let Jim buy a round although he tried to insist. Ron just kept paying for the drinks until he left and during this time Jim took a liking for Ron.

The next day Ron came to the pub where Jim was eager to serve him, especially as his takings that previous night were double what he normally took before the problems with the police.

"Hello Jim, this my son, Ron Junior. Can we have a double house whisky and two pints of Fosters?"

The drinks were put on the bar counter which they stood at. Then Junior started to walk around the pub with the whisky glass in his hand. After his look about, he came back and spoke to Jim.

"This is a big place but you haven't got a lot of people in here."

"I know I am just holding on as I have got some property developers looking to buy it but I don't think the council will give permission for houses or flats."

"Best of luck with keeping it going, Jim. Can me and my son sit in the off license part of the pub?"

"No problem. I normally keep that closed, though, so you will have to come to this bar when you want a drink. Tell you what, there is buzzer in there. Feel free to press it and I will bring your drinks to you."

"Thanks Jim."

The next day Big Ron and another boy came to the pub and walked up to the bar. Jim was doing the crossword as he was bored and there was only one customer in the whole place.

"Hello Jim, you are pretty quiet today."

"Yes mate."

"This my grandson, Ron. Can we get three pints of lager and two whiskies? That house whisky."

"Yes I know you prefer the house whisky."

Over the next four weeks Ron and his family were now drinking in the pub and all three bars were used. There was a lot more atmosphere in the pub and more and more locals came back to the pub. The thing they were not happy about was having to leave the pub at 6PM. Big Ron was now a regular in the off license side of the bar, yet his son was in the saloon and his grandson in the public side where the pool table was. Jim was very happy because he had to employ two new part time staff where it had only been him and his wife before. If Big Ron and his family came to the pub, Big Ron would just press the buzzer and the bar man came to take his orders.

"Same again, Ron?"

"Yes, get one for yourself and tell Jim I would like to speak to him."

"Yes Ron, I will tell him and then get your drinks."

Jim quickly popped in to chat to him.

"Hello Ron, what's up?"

Ron turned to his mates and said, "Could you leave me for a minute, please?"

Jim was a bit apprehensive regarding what Big Ron wanted. In the past few weeks Jim had found out all about him and his family and knew exactly what they did.

"Jim sit down, how is business?"

"Business is good."

"Would you like it to be even better?"

"Of course."

"Since I have been coming here you have had no trouble with your punters. Do you know why?"

"I have an idea."

"I am glad you do, so can I make a suggestion? Why not open Friday night till normal closing time again?"

"Listen Ron. I can't take a chance in case of trouble and the police shutting me down."

"I will ensure that you don't have any trouble. My boys will take care of that. Is that settled eh Jim?"

"OK Ron. I will think about it."

"Think about it? There is nothing to think about. I have assured you. You know me and my family will make sure there is no trouble."

"I will speak to my wife."

"Call her now. I will speak to her."

"Ok Ron. I will open late this Friday."

"Please tell my son to come here Jim."

"Sure Ron."

"Did he go for it?"

"Yes I want to put the word out that there must be no trouble or they will have to answer to me."

"The word is already out. All my lines know and their punters know not to come for gear Friday nights. They either get their gear in the daytime or meet somewhere else to get their gear. We are going to make a lot more money Pops. I heard there is an English family who run things in this area, though. We might have trouble with them."

"What is their name?" "Murphy. He has got three sons and lots of cousins."

"Have you ever seen them?"

"No."

"Ask Jim for photos of all the people on the pub list that were barred."

"I did not think of that Pops."

"When you get to my age you will. Just show the picture to our people so they can be ready to stop any fights. I will ask Jim to tell his customers that Friday night is just a trial and if there is any trouble he will open again on Friday nights regularly."

"But Pops, other pubs who don't want Jim to open might send people to cause trouble here."

"You know most of the locals so speak to them and get the heads up on who is from another pub that might cause trouble."

"Ok Pops and I will tell your grandson as well."

"That boy! All he does is play pool from the time he comes here till we go home. Is he bothering to learn the business at all?"

"You know he knows more about what we do than you do."

"I like to lend money. That's what I do. It is very rewarding and I make people happy."

"I do as well. We are doing really well here. Once Jim starts to open late we will make much more money and, touch wood, we won't get any problems with the council or police."

"Our solicitors are looking after us with the council and they love cash."

"I will see you later Pops."

Chapter Seven

Danny staggered home and when he got in, Linda was watching TV. Kim was sleeping.

"Don't go in the kitchen and make a mess. I will make the burgers. How many do you want?"

"I will have three if you don't mind love. I am sorry for being late."

"Sit in the kitchen and eat 'cos I am going to bed."

Over the next few months they just lived a mundane life. Danny was going to work every day and Linda stayed at home. The only enjoyment Linda got was going to the pub on Friday nights and singing at the karaoke machine but she didn't mind that as it was how their parents had lived.

Kim came around quite often and would take Linda shopping. She left an invitation card for a garden party.

"Danny, we have been invited to a garden party."

"What is that?"

"A party where people mix and talk and possibly play games."

"Who invited us? I bet it's from Kim and her brother."

"Yes it is. What's wrong with that?"

"Nothing. I just can't see me fitting in. How do I know what to talk about?"

"Your job and it will nice for our baby to mix with her Godmother and others."

"I suppose you're right, when is it?"

"This Saturday and Sunday. I've got a nice old dress that I haven't worn for a long time so I hope it fits."

"It will fit. You are back to your old self before Kim was born. This Saturday, did you say?"

"Yes this Saturday."

"Sorry Kim I promised old Clegg I will work overtime this weekend as we've got a big order to carry out."

"I am not going alone."

"Ask Johnny to go with you. He might meet some nice boys," he chuckled.

"Stop it. It's not funny."

"Sorry love."

"Tell him when you see him."

"I will, what time does it start?

"I think 2.30pm, so tell Johnny to come at 2pm and we will get a cab. Oh, no, Kim said if we were going they will send a taxi for us."

Johnny arrived on time and they got into a car.

"Kim is really growing a lot. She is a big girl now."

"15 months old Johnny. It is nice of her Godmother to send a taxi for us."

"This not a taxi, Linda. It's one of their cars that we are in. Are they wealthy?"

"I think so. I will pull the window down and ask the driver," she teased.

"Stop it, Linda."

When they got there, Kim greeted both of them with hugs and kisses. Kim grabbed Baby Kim while Johnny went to take the baby's things out of the boot.

"You and Kim will stay in the cottage and Johnny will stay in one of the guest rooms in the house. Driver, could you show Johnny the guest room that he will be staying in? I will take Linda to the cottage."

"Thanks Kim, but where is Tony?"

"He will be here later after sorting some business out. I must say that you look gorgeous in that dress. I am going to leave you now, so just come to the main house when you are ready."

"Thanks Kim. See you later."

Tony and Kim's place was surrounded by a six foot wall which enclosed three cottages on the left and a foot path leading to the main house. To the right of the path, a driveway led to the house which had thirty windows. The entrance had Roman columns by the front door and at the back of the house it had two tennis courts and an indoor heated swimming pool covered by a glass frame.

"Where have you been Johnny? I have been looking for you."

"Lots of nice and rich people here. I was getting to know them."

"Who?"

"Not sure yet. There are so many."

"Kim has hired a babysitter for me."

"That's good. You can go and enjoy yourself."

"Funny. But how can I enjoy myself without Danny?" "Come with me for a walk in the grounds or let's go and have something to eat."

"Yes."

The two of them walked to the cold buffet and took some prawns, then caught a whiff of the barbecue and went over there. The most of other guest's eyes were on both of the them, as they genuinely were very good looking people. Over the next few hours they ate and drank and mixed with the rest of the other guests.

Linda forget she had a baby and went with Tony to his room. He played Linda's favorite music and they danced in each other's arms. Gently, he began to kiss her on the arms, then cheeks, then on her lips. He rubbed his legs between hers then slowly took her clothes off. She had never made love like that. She melted when he went into her and was slowly thrusting. This went on for longer than she had ever known. She could not think of anything else but Tony. In fact, she hardly sleep that night. Linda went back to the cottage and her baby was still sleeping so she went into the shower. 'How could I have done that?' she wondered. What had come over her? It must never happen again. She decided to get Johnny and go home straight away. Johnny came to the cottage.

"What's that smile on your face?"

"Guess who I slept with last night?"

"I have no idea."

"I slept with Kim. What a girl! What did you do?"

"I've got a child to mind. Anyway I am going back home now."

"I thought we were all going into the pool and playing water polo or something."

"Johnny I am going home you can stay."

"I will stay here. Quite a few rich people here that old Johnny boy has still not met. Look, the driver is coming now."

"What are you up to?"

"Nothing, nothing my dear."

Several years passed and Linda had another baby, which she named Amanda. She and Danny were beginning to get used to having a family of their own.

After that night Linda did not see Tony anymore. The only one she met up with was Kim who would come around and see little Kim and Amanda and bring presents for all of them. Johnny was mixing with Kim and Tony's family and friends up to the time he was killed, though. Tony had sent lots of messages to Linda but she never responded to him. Kim must have told him that Amanda was his and it was easy to tell from her looks.

Nothing was said about Amanda. Johnny was still going out with Kim and spent a lot of time with Tony at the night club. Johnny saw all of what went on there and he wanted to be a part of it all, so he started working for Tony at the night club a few nights per week. His life was different now and although he still met up with Danny and Linda, it was not as often as before.

Chapter Eight

Back on route to the prison...
"We have all the prisoners locked up and we are ready to go." The officer signaled the van driver to leave.

"I have given the signal for the main gate guard to open the gates."

The van driver gave a thumbs up and did his final checks.

The engine started up and they started to move. Danny looked out of the window at Canterbury police station. They made their way past the council buildings and stopped at Canterbury court to pick up more prisoners just inside the court compound. The driver drove into the compound slowly. Johnny worked at Canterbury council so Danny found himself looking out of the window to see if he could see any of his friends from work as they passed.

Then he was thinking about Johnny and how he had worked for the council all of his working life. He'd helped him to get the new council house and that had changed their lives for the better. Johnny was such a good person, he thought. 'Why would anybody want to kill him?'

Even though friends knew he dabbled in drugs, he never spent much money on them. In reality, he always had money in his pocket. In fact, he lent Danny money lots of times over the years. When he tried to pay him back he never wanted it back. Danny still couldn't believe he was dead.

Danny heard someone say that it was a long drive to Emely prison but he was sweating and desperately wanted the journey to be over with so he could get out of that iron box. It was a long ride and he could see all of the road signs but he was in a daze. He didn't see them clearly and it didn't register that they'd finally reached the prison.

The driver said something but the officer hadn't heard him properly.

"What did you say?

"We have to wait outside."

"Why?"

"The prison said they have an incident so we have to wait until it is sorted, before they let us in."

"Did they say how long?"

"No idea mate."

Danny heard one of the prisoners in the van shouting, "Hurry up! I need a piss. I am dying for one." Danny also shouted the same thing.

"Wait a minute I will get you something."

He handed him a plastic bag and asked, "Anything else?"

Two prisoners were talking constantly. One of them was called Jake and the other was Gary. The officer knew them both from before. They were taking the piss out of everything that was going on and even the officer himself.

Someone else shouted, "I need the loo too, Sir."

Everyone else did as well.

"Hold on you lot! I've only got one pair of hands."

 Soon he started to hand out the plastic bags to everyone.

"What shall I do with my bag sir?"

"Leave it on the floor and I will pick it up later once you lot are out of the van. Be careful not to step on the bags when you go."

They waited for what seemed like hours and some of the prisoners were shouting, "Get us out of here. It's boiling hot and stuffy in here and we are so hungry."

"If anyone wants something to eat just let me know."

Everyone shouted that they were hungry.

"Give me a moment and I will get you all something."

The officer was run off his feet and the prisoners were loving it.

He gave Danny a packet of crisps and a bottle of water and they gave the same to all of the rest. One of the prisoners was loudly complaining about this as he wanted some decent food.

It seemed as though two of them had been in prison before. One of the names stood out as his name was Jake Wade. The officers knew him and he was the one that had started all of the shouting.

Moments later, Danny heard a weird splatter on the floor of the van and it turned out that someone had thrown their wee bag over the top.

"Wade that was you. I saw you. I am going to put you on report."

"I did nothing," he said but his smirk gave him away.

The rest of them started to shout as well and some of them also started chucking the plastic bags of wee over the top of the doors out into the passageway of the van. The van was now flooded with urine on the floor.

Danny wanted to shout at them to behave themselves but decided not to get involved as he wasn't prepared to get in trouble.

He could hear the officers talking about the ones who had been in before and how they knew each other and the ring leader was Jake Wade.

"All you lot who have thrown anything on the van floor will be put on report and get a nicking."

"Who gives a shit about nicking? I've only got three months in this shit hole."

"Mr. Wade, I would advise you not to start anymore trouble or you will be off straight to the segregation unit and you won't be going to reception."

"Listen mate, I don't give a shit what you do. Prison doesn't scare me. I have been in and out lots of times and after this stint I have no doubt I will come back in again. So keep your threats to yourself."

While this was going on, the driver got permission to drive into the prison yard.

"This is the driver. All be seated as we are now moving to the prison yard."

The officer in the van spoke to the driver, once he had parked up.

"We are going to need some extra staff in here when we transfer them to the reception as we are having trouble and we need the biohazard team to clean this van. I am not going to do it."

"Ok. I will let them know. What's that smell coming from the van?"

"They decided to throw their bags of wee on the passage floor of the van so we will need the biohazard team in here once we get them out. I will be checking who has still got their wee bags when they leave."

The van driver opened the side door and the officer met him by it.

"Fucking hell, it stinks in here."

Then he opened Danny's door and Danny picked up the bag of wee so that the officers could see that he hadn't thrown his. He was still in the van when they started to open the door next to his. The other guy was asked to move first.

"Hold on to your bags and go outside of the van and wait."

"I am coming out for some fresh air," said the driver as he walked outside and shut the door behind him. He heard some shouting.

Danny was standing outside with the two officers. Quickly, two more officers from the prison came up to them and asked, "How many have you got?"

"We've got eight."

"Mr. Mundy, please go back into the van and sit down."

"Sir what do you want me to do with the wee bag?

Nothing was said so he took it back with him.

Danny was very surprised that they didn't cuff him again. He opened the van door and Danny went and sat down again in the same box. He was trying very hard to look through the crack of the door but the frame was all he saw.

"Oi! Oi! Fat boy. Have you got your piss bag? I know you've got it. When you leave, they will pick it up. If you don't leave it I will kick your head in as soon as we get in the prison."

"Shut up Wade. I've put you under report already," snapped the guard.

Danny was shaking with fear, listening to what was being said. He was not normally afraid. In his mind, he remembered what Raj had said about not getting into trouble or fights. If he did start fighting, the judge would not believe he hadn't actually killed his brother.

Someone else shouted, "Fat boy - make sure you do what Jake said! Jake has a lot of friends in prison."

"My name is George Green and if any one of you misbehaving you will be charged for anti-social behavior. The biohazard team will come in the van to mop and clean up the passage way and any parts that they can reach to mop. Please be as helpful as you can by standing on your seats."

"Come in now boys. Clean it the best you can and try and make sure the passage is dry. Then we will let them out and clean it again."

The bio boys came and started to mop the floors. Danny sat on his seat and lifted up his feet so they could mop around his little cubical, under the door. The officer went outside of the van and spoke to another officer.

The van officer was talking about the men on the van. "One of them is giving us a lot mouth and has already given us trouble. It's Jake Wade. If we get him out first, the rest will crumble."

"Yes we will do that. I know that Wade very well because he has been here quite a few times before. Anyway, let's wait until the bio boys are finished."

Half an hour passed slowly. Eventually they were ready to let the men out of the van.

"Thanks men! Let's go and get Wade first then, follow me."

George went into the van and straight over to Wade.

"How do you want to do it? The hard way or the easy way?"

"You know me, governor, I never cause any trouble."

George opened the door slightly and said, "Stay there and put your hands through the gap between the door and frame."

He did that and Green handcuffed his hands together. Then George cuffed him to himself and led him like a baby to the reception. He did not say a word and was quickly placed in a holding cell for the time being.

"Danny!" said the officer, as he opened his door.

"Put your hands through the door and the frame."

"What do you want me to do with my wee bag sir?"

As he said that the officer handcuffed him and took no notice of what he had said. Then he led him away. As Danny was walking he was thinking about how lucky he was not having to meet up with that Wade guy again. To his surprise, the officer led him to the same holding cell as Wade. They could see each other through the glass panel and as the officer was unlocking the glass door, Wade was giving Danny the eye. Danny started to worry that something bad was going to happen. His asthma was playing up and he started to wheeze. Soon his breathing was getting harder. The officer told him to sit next to Wade.

Danny began to speak to the officer again.

"I've got to be very carefully not to fight anyone because the lawyer said if I do then the judge will get the report of me fighting. If he says anything to me I will ignore him."

Danny's eyes did not look at him.

Then the officers told Wade to go with them.

"Why are you taking me? I haven't done anything bad! It's always me."

"You know exactly what you've done. We are going to the segregation unit."

As he cuffed him, Wade looked at Danny. If looks could kill, Danny would have already been dead. In reality he was so happy that Wade had been moved.

"Come on. You will be in segregation for a few days until you become a good boy".

Officer Green was laughing to himself as he was happy as well. There was no way that he wanted any trouble.

One by one, the other prisoners were brought out of the van and into the room. Danny thought they would be in trouble but nothing happened.

Another prisoner was also brought there. There were quite a few prisoners in the large room about half an hour later.

Another prisoner came and sat opposite Danny on the left hand side and then they brought Wade's mates and they sat on the bench opposite the door, to Danny's right hand side. Then they brought a tall, mixed race prisoner and he sat on his left hand side facing the door. Danny could see that Wade's mates were agitated and were looking to do something. One of them was a skinhead and was covered in tattoos. He glared at Danny and asked, "What are you looking at?"

Danny didn't answer. He just turned and looked the other way.

"Oi! I am talking to you. Don't turn away when I am taking to you, you cheeky little cunt."

Danny turned and looked at him and still did not say anything.

"Come here."

Danny was not keen to move. The rest of the mates were joining in, saying, "Come over here now."

Again Danny did not move. He was trembling. Even if he wanted to move, he couldn't. The mixed race guy looked at him and saw that he was in a state and then he looked at them.

"Why don't you lot leave him alone?"

Looking at them with no fear in his eyes, it was obvious that things were getting heated up. Danny's body felt relieved and he didn't tremble as much. All of them stood up and immediately turned and looked at him. The skinhead turned to face him and the others did the same. He stood up with no fear in him whatsoever. He was ready and they must have seen that.

The skinhead said, "Look mate, it's none of your business. There are three of us so you will get hurt if you stick your nose in. So just keep out of this. That fat shit has nothing to do with you."

"I hate bullies. That's what it's got to do with me. So come on, let's have it. I will make sure one will never suck a dick for a burn again, because he will have a broken neck. SO COME ON LETS HAVE IT! Let's have it you bunch of pussies."

The skinhead took a step forward and the other two stayed where they were and said, "Look mate. We're just having a laugh with the old bloke."

"Just sit down the three of you and don't say another word you bunch of wankers."

As he stepped towards them they sat down on the bench. The skinhead said, "Ok mate we are done."

"I know you are done, so shut the fuck up."

As the three of them sat down, Officer Green opened the door and called one of the skinheads out. After he locked the door and the skinhead was outside, he shouted to the mixed race guy.

"I'll tell Wade about you. You will get a seeing to for not minding things that are not your business."

"Tell Wade my name is Delroy and I will be here for the next five years."

Green asked him what they were angry about when he locked the door behind him. Nobody answered him. The two skinheads who were left were not comfortable alone with Delroy and one of them said, "Sorry, mate we did not mean it."

The mixed race guy told them to apologise to Danny.

They both looked at him with contempt and said, "Sorry mate."

Danny started hoping that he would be next to be called or one of those two skinheads might be called next. He started to pray to God for the first time in years. He didn't want to defend himself then or it would go on his record when he got to the courts. He knew it meant getting a bigger sentence even though he wasn't guilty of murdering his brother.

Green came in and Danny looked at him and he then pointed to one of the other skinheads. Now that the other skinhead was all alone, Danny could see he was afraid, just as he had been. He looked straight at the door and did not move his eyes from that door. A few minutes later Green came and looked straight at the last skinhead and then called him over to the door where he was so relieved.

Danny looked at Delroy and said, "Thank you for helping me. This is my first time in prison."

"Yea mate, I can see that. I hate bullies but you are going to get a lot of them in here so just be careful. They would pick on you, even if you haven't done anything. You need to look after yourself and if a bully picks on you, stand up for yourself even if you get a kicking. When you stand up to fight, make sure you hurt one of them very badly, like biting their nose or an ear off. Make sure you leave a mark on them. When the rest of the bullies in prison hear about it, they will think twice before trying anything on you and the bullies who bully you won't like it, because they will see a mark on them. If there is no mark on them they will say they kicked the crap out of you and the rest of the bully boys will do the same. Look, this is how bullying works.

One to one they don't want to know but two against one they might take a chance. Three against one, they will come at you all the time. Listen to me mate. You are a very big fella so if you hit someone they will feel it. Go to the gym and start to go jogging and practice weights. When they see you they will know straight away that you are not someone they can pick on. Sit up straight. Stand up straight and put your chest out. All of these little things will stop them from picking on you."

"How come you were willing to fight three of them? Were you not afraid?"

"Afraid of them pussies? Listen, I was angry at getting caught. I wanted an excuse to smash someone's face in, so they were lucky they never started. Bullies pray on people like you. It is always three or four against one as they never take a chance. They will not take a chance one to one or two to one in case they get hurt. They always work in gangs. What are you in here for?"

"The murder of my brother."

"YOU MURDERER! You are having a giraffe aren't you? Hope you've got a good lawyer?"

"Oh yes, the police got one for me. They even chose them from Banks and Banks." "

"Banks and Banks are useless. You need to get yourself another law firm. I mean a decent one. Banks and Banks and the police work together so you are fucked mate."

"The solicitor told me they will drop the charges and I will out of here soon."

"Listen mate. I don't know you from Adam but I'm telling you, don't believe the police as they are crooks. They work together with the lawyers."

Delroy took a bit paper out of his pocket and gave it to Danny.

"Here mate. You do yourself a favour and give them a call. You could do a lot of time in here if you get the wrong lawyers to represent you."

He walked over to Danny and gave him the paper.

"This the name of my solicitor."

"Thank you Delroy."

Everything Delroy told Danny his father had already told him. He had had fights in the pub and he could handle himself but the idea of fighting in there frightened him. He was worried it would get him a bigger sentence if found guilty and the judge would use the fight against him.

"That Green will be coming for one of us soon so you'd better think about what I said to you. Don't forget, get yourself to the gym, and do a bit of boxing.

I will be in the gym so feel free to come and check me out and make sure you get yourself another law firm."

"Thanks mate."

Green came for Delroy next and Danny was alone. He found himself thinking about what he had said about the law firm. A little later an officer came and called him to follow him to his cell.

Chapter Nine

Induction Block.

Still at the prison reception, Jean Hughes had been posted to Emely prison after three months of training.

"Good morning. You must be Jean, our new staff member. My name is George Green."

He walked towards her and shook her hand.

"You don't know what you've let yourself in for."

"Don't you remember me then? I used to work here in the stores for nearly 10 years."

"Oh crumbs. It's you, Mrs Hughes from stores. Sorry I didn't recognise you in this uniform."

"Who is next Jean?"

"It's that Danny Mundy. He doesn't look like he can hurt a fly. I feel sorry for him as he had only been in the pen for a few minutes and he was being picked on already."

"He's just like the rest of them. They have to learn that crime does not pay. As far as I am concerned, they are all guilty and I cannot treat them any differently. I suggest you do the same."

"Thanks George. I will remember that."

"They all look like cons apart from the bald and obese one. I can't see him doing anything. He looks so harmless, like a lost sheep."

"That is Danny Mundy who murdered his brother."

"You should know never to go by looks Jean."

"You are right but he looks so different from the average prisoner."

"Mundy come here, what size are your shoes, trainers, shirt and bottoms?"

"Yes Sir. I am extra-large in everything and size eighteen for shoes and trainers."

"I don't think we have your size but I will give you the largest we've got. One minute. I will see what I've got."

"Here you are. Trainers, tracksuit tops and bottoms. I am sorry but that's all we've got. I will order some large ones of everything for you. I am not sure how long it will take though Mundy. Next one, please. You deal with Jean."

"This one's been in before, Jean. Just give him all large."

"But governor?"

"Move on. Next one."

Then Danny was made to queue up again. Someone gave him a big plastic bag. It contained a plastic knife, fork, plate, two plastic spoons, one big plastic cup, one blanket, a sheet, a sweatshirt, trainers, tracksuit tops and bottoms, soap, toothpaste and more. There was a small carton of milk, a made up bag of cereals, two tea bags, four sachets of powdered milk and some sugar.

"Mundy, come with me."

Danny followed them through the door into a passageway. It seemed like the journey went on for ages. He was sweating and blowing hard after carrying all the bags. Danny was taken to this very large hall which was a bit like a doctor's surgery, with cons sitting on chairs waiting to be seen. The cons would go up to a desk and speak to staff in order. There were about eight desks with chairs in front and behind. Prison staff were at each desk and he was told to sit down and wait. After waiting a while, he was then called to a desk where he sat down quietly.

"Have a seat and could you tell me your name?"

"Danny Mundy."

"My name is Father Phil and here is a form that you can fill in."

"Father, I cannot read or write."

"Danny, are you a Christian?"

"Yes I am."

"So I will see you in church?"

"Yes sir."

"Have you got a bible?"

"No sir."

"I am going to give you a bible and some leaflets. No doubt you will go to the ESOL class."

"Sir what does that mean?"

"It means English Speaking for Overseas Learners. It is like ABC."

"Thank you sir."

"Go and see Mr. White at the next desk when he is free".

Danny sat on the next chair and waited for Mr. White to be free.

"Next Please."

Mr. White's desk was empty so he beckoned Danny over and he sat on the chair by his desk.

"What is your name?"

"Danny Mundy, Sir."

"My name is Mr. White. Can you fill this form out please?"

"Sir, I cannot read and write."

"That's fine. You don't have any bad habits. You can enroll in my class and you will learn to read and write in less than a month."

"Are you sure, sir?"

"Perhaps a bit longer but providing you work at it and do all of your homework and don't miss any classes, you will progress really well."

"I don't know how the system works in here. Am I allowed to be in education full time?"

"Yes Danny, I expect to see soon. Next please."

"Thank you sir."

The next person he saw was a nurse called Avis. She was a big set woman and her uniform was very tight. She dyed her hair and you could see her grey roots. Her voice was softly spoken.

"Danny I see from our records that the police gave us that you suffer from various health problems. Asthma, high blood pressure and you are on insulin for diabetes. Is that right?"

"Yes Miss."

"I will give you your medication for your first two days and I will give you an appointment to see the doctor at health care."

"Thank you for the medication. Where is health care?"

"Go to see Brian next. He is a listener and will help with all you need to know in prison."

"Thanks once again."

At the next desk the officer did not wear a uniform. He was about five foot, five inches tall and thick set. He had glasses, a tie, a white shirt, black trousers and black shoes on.

"Hello, my name is Danny Mundy. I was told you will be able to help me by the nurse."

"First time in prison?"

"Yes."

"My name is Brian."

"Are you an officer?"

"No I am a listener. I am on the induction wing where you will be going, and as you can see there are a lot of cons here. I will find you on the block. It will be easier to explain everything to you there. See you later Danny. Just wait there and an officer will come for you and take you to the block."

Danny went and sat on the chair that Brian pointed to, then an officer pointed to him, ushering him to follow him.

Danny wanted to ask him why a prisoner was doing that job but he was in a hurry. Danny followed him down some stairs, then into a passageway, then to a main gate.

Opening it, he said, "This is your induction block."

They walked over to a square office with glass panels on the top half of it. Danny could see the block and all the stairs leading to lots of cells on the three different floors. There were a lot of prisoners moving up and down the stairs and filling the walkways.

"Put your bag down and wait here by the office. Someone will come and allocate you a cell."

"Yes sir."

Danny waited and waited for what seemed like forever, idly standing by the bag. The other prisoners were looking at him, probably sussing him out.

"More new meat," someone said. It made him feel awkward as he waited and waited. Nobody came.

Finally an officer arrived with two stripes on his shoulders and asked him what he was doing there. Danny told him that he was told to wait there by the officer who brought him from reception.

"Have you just arrived here?"

"Yes sir."

"Wait here. I will be back shortly." Then he left and Danny waited again. Finally he heard someone shouting his name.

"Mundy come here now."

Chapter Ten

Danny looked around and saw an office where he beckoned him in. "Go and get your bags, man".

Quickly nipping back to pick up his bag, he followed him quickly up two flight of stairs and onto the landing. He opened a cell door said, "This is the cell you will be staying in."

Then he said to the people inside the cell, "You've got a new cell mate, so make sure you look after him as it is his first time."

Immediately he went back down the landing and down the stairs. The cell smelled like someone had died in there. There were two prisoners already in it. They didn't introduce themselves immediately. So Danny looked around and there was a single bed on his left with a prisoner lying on it. He looked about twenty five years old with medium build. He was not more than twelve stone in weight. Straight ahead was a small cupboard with drawers and a TV on top of it and behind was a window with a black plastic bag covering the window as a curtain. It was very dirty and to the right was a bunk bed with another guy lying on the bottom bunk. This guy was about twenty and very skinny, not more than eight stone. Danny was looking at where the toilet was but he couldn't see it. He really wanted to go.

"Where is the toilet?"

"Are you blind? It's to your left by the door as you came in."

Danny didn't even see the door as it was so small. He just about fitted in as he went in. He had to have a wee and went to the toilet where it stank and was very dirty. The place had not been cleaned for months so he held his breath. He couldn't wee for a while. Then he finally managed to go and came out. The guy on the single bed said, "Don't block the door with your bags."

"Where shall I put them?"

"Put them on your bed which is the top bunk."

Danny wondered where he was going to sleep with those bags all over the bed.

"Can't I put them under the bed?"

The other guy on the bottom bunk bed said, "My things are under the bed. Listen mate, you've just got here so don't start making trouble and when you get to your bunk don't put your feet on my sheet that's on my bed."

"Where is the ladder?"

The one on the single bed said, "This is prison mate. There is no ladder, you've just got to get on with it."

The one on the double bunk pulled out a white chair from between his bed and the chest of drawers.

"You get to your bunk using that."

"Thanks."

The one on the single bed sounded as though he had an American accent.

"I am giving you a warning now. Do not take any burn from anyone, because if you take a burn from anyone, or from the shop and you don't pay for it, the cell has to pay for it. I don't want to pay anyone's bills."

"I do not smoke."

"What are you doing in this cell? This is a smoker's cell. So you shouldn't be in here."

"I was told to come here. I had no choice."

"Listen mate, you best go and see one of the officers and tell them you don't smoke and take your bags with you when you go."

At that moment the bell went off.

"Dinner time."

The two of them quickly got their plates and left. Danny dug into his plastic bag and took out the plastic plate and spoon and followed them. By the time he got outside they were gone. As he made his way down the stairs, one of them came back and spoke to him. It was the skinny guy.

"You stay here. We can't leave the cell unattended or someone might nick something out of it. Wait until me or Joe come back, then you can get your dinner."

"Ok. Danny then turned and walked back up the stairs. He waited in the cell and had a good look around. They had pictures on the wall where the single bed was. It was dirty in there and after a while Joe came into the cell and said, "You best hurry up before there is no food left."

Quickly he went downstairs and there was still a queue at the server. He managed to get quarter of a pizza, some potatoes and carrots. Then he went back up to the cell but there was nowhere for him to sit and eat and he didn't take a chance to sit on their beds to eat. Danny ate standing up as he was so hungry. They finished eating at about the same time.

"Where I can wash the plate?"

"There is a sink on the end of the landing or in the toilet."

He went to the landing sink and washed the plate. There were a lot of dirty plates left in and around the sink. There was water but no washing up liquid. He came back and they had washed their dishes in the toilet sink. It was obvious that they did not want him there as he was not their type. Let's face it, he had nothing in common with them. Joe was lying on the single bed.

"Go and see an officer about you being a nonsmoker and ask them to move you to a nonsmoker cell. You best hurry up before its bang up time."

"What's bang up?"

Both of them burst out laughing as he was about to leave. Danny went downstairs and onto the ground floor. He called out to one of the officers on the other side of the bar.

"SIR! SIR!"

One of the officers came over and asked, "What do you want? It's bang up time."

"Sir! I don't smoke and I was put in a three man cell with smokers and I have asthma. Anyway, could I be moved please?"

"Look! What's your name?"

"It's, Danny Mundy sir and I am new here."

"Mundy, it's coming up to bang up time and roll check so come and see me tomorrow and I will try and put you in a different cell. That is all I can do now OK."

"Yes sir."

On the ground floor there were tables and chairs outside of each cell. He looked around and some of the prisoners were playing table tennis, while others were waiting with bats in hand and playing pool. The prisoners were playing chess, backgammon and other board games on the tables too.

Remembering how good Johnny had been at all these games, it brought back good memories. He tried to teach him but Danny was useless at them. His brother had always beat him. He stayed there a little while longer and had a look at the pool game. He would make sure he didn't look at anyone in the eye just like at the holding cell.

A few moments later the bell went, causing all the prisoners to start moving around (like ants building a nest). It looked like they were going back to their cells. Danny was dreading going back to the cell, but was thinking of what Delroy had said to him about being brave, even if he might get a kicking. But what was the judge going to say? He walked up slowly as people were pushing past him, going into each other's cells. It kind of looked like they were getting things. Finally he got to the cell and an officer told Danny to get in his cell.

It was the same officer that he had spoken to earlier. As he got inside, he shut the door behind him and locked it. The two of them were playing chess and he noticed they wore the same clothes all day and they were sweating. He took the top and bottoms from in the bag and went into the toilet so he could wash his face and body as he had been sweating too. Danny changed his clothes, then put the dirty clothes back in the bag. He somehow managed to get on the bed without touching Joe's sheets but it was difficult It made him realise he needed to lose some weight, especially now that his top didn't even go over his stomach and the bottoms couldn't go any higher than his legs.

Danny got onto the bed to find that his feet touched the end of the bed and his head nearly touched the head rails. He lay on the bed thinking about Johnny but could not feel sleepy. He hadn't really slept since that day when he found Johnny. Instead, he started to watch them play chess. He wanted to talk to them but decided not to, preferring to just watch them playing chess.

"STOP SNORING!"

All of a sudden he woke up. He must have dozed off.

"Listen mate you are going to wake us up in the night with your snoring and we have to go to work in the morning," moaned Joe.

"Sorry mate! I can't help it."

The other said, "You best keep that snoring down."

He wasn't sure what to do. They were still playing chess. He wanted to get down and have a little walk to wake himself up but it would take a lot of effort to get back up on the bed. Deciding to sit up instead with his back against the wall, he was thinking that may stop him snoring if he did fall asleep. Linda always complained about his snoring but he kept telling her to wake him when he snored. It felt like he was waiting hours before they went to bed. The two of them were playing chess for hours and the cell was full of smoke. It caused him to start coughing.

Joe was now talking to the other one while they were playing chess.

"Now the fucker is coughing. Listen mate, make sure you fuck off tomorrow because I can't put up with this shit."

Danny remembered what Delroy said regarding not being a pussy. He would say 'speak up for yourself even if you get a kicking.' He also didn't want the judge to think he was a fighter and trouble maker because the lawyer told him all the things that happened in prison would be put on a report that the judge could read.

"Listen it's not my fault they put me here. I can't help snoring. I don't smoke and I suffer with asthma."

He said that loudly and firmly and they seemed a little set back. After this, Danny noticed a difference in their demeanor but how long would that last? He didn't know what time it was but was feeling very sleepy. He couldn't tell whether it was day or night outside. Hopefully they would stop playing chess soon and go to bed, so he could at least try and get some to sleep. He wouldn't brush his teeth until he was bursting to go the toilet and do that at the same time.

Later they stopped playing chess and the skinny one did not say anything. He just made tea for Joe and didn't look at Danny who felt like a cup himself. As they were getting ready to go to bed he struggled to get off his bed and went to the toilet. He did not brush his teeth. The skinny one was already in the bottom bunk but Danny managed to get on his bed. He was sitting up and waited until they fell asleep. Then he plucked up the courage to lay down. Ironically, he could hear them snoring a bit. His wife Linda always complained that he snored too much. He used to go into the kids' room to sleep in the night.

"Stop snoring mate. You are waking us up."

Danny woke up and said, "Sorry, I can't help it."

"We've got to go to work in the morning."

Danny decided to sit up and think about his situation. He was just like his dad with no ambition. In fact he had worked all his life and had nothing to show for it. Having lived in a council house all his life he had been content. Not like Johnny who wanted more out of life.

Johnny went to school and night school. Following that he went to college because he always wanted to better himself. Later on, he'd had a good job at the council. Recently he had just applied for a manager job and he was in the middle of buying his own house. He'd asked Danny to lend him some money which they did. He had borrowed £300 of their savings. Whoever killed Johnny could have owed him money or someone owed him money. Danny's head was hurting due to thinking about Johnny.

He started to look at himself again. He was reflecting on his weight, his life in general, his dad and mum and even his children. He was hoping that would keep him awake. Danny knew he had a good job and had been there for nearly twenty years. The wages could be better though. The boss said because he couldn't read he couldn't pay him more but he argued he was doing the same job as the other fork lift drivers. It didn't make sense that they were getting more money than him. In fact they asked him how to do certain jobs all the time.

"STOP FUCKING SNORING mate! You are driving me crazy. If you wake me up again I am coming over there and kicking your head in." Joe was getting angrier.

Danny didn't know what had happened but he was on the floor when he woke up. He knew that he must have jumped off the bunk bed. Somehow he hadn't hurt himself but it was dark and he could not see anything. The two of them did nothing. All they said was, "What the fuck?"

He got up as he walked and felt for the chair, then the bunk, and climbed onto the bed. He wondered what happened. Danny guessed he must have jumped while asleep and that must have scared them or they would have done something to him. He remembered what Delroy had said to him. He sat up again on the bed and looked into the darkness with his back against the wall. Knowing Linda all his life, he had never felt lonely before. She had come to his dad's house when he was fourteen years old. This was the first time in his life he was alone and he hated being in there. In fact, he wanted to kill himself. That's probably why subconsciously he jumped off the bed. He had gone to church a few times and had got married in church and his kids were christened. 'God please help me get out of this place. God please help me.' He fell asleep and later heard the cell door open.

"Wake up and get to work now," a different officer said. Instantly, the two of them got up. Joe went to the toilet but the skinny one got there before him with the kettle to fill it up. Joe waited for him and then he went into the toilet. The skinny one put his clothes on while waiting to make the tea, then Joe came out of the toilet and the skinny one went into the toilet. Danny didn't know what to do as he hadn't been given a job.

Perhaps he should stay in bed until they went. Then he could go and see that officer about a non-smoking cell. They had their tea and were about to leave then Joe turned to him and said, "Seriously mate. I couldn't sleep last night. I did not even wake up to get myself ready. I am the number one at art class and now am going to get a blocking for being late."

The other said, "Me as well. Go and see an officer to tell them you are a non-smoker. You need to move out before we come back or there are going to be problems."

Then they left together, meaning Danny could finally go to the toilet, wash up and change, put the kettle on and make some tea. But when he looked into the plastic bag, all his tea things were gone. There was nothing to eat or drink. He made up his bed for the first time in ages as his missus normal did it? He really missed her and just wanted to know who killed Johnny. Danny was so confused about what he was going to do. He fantasized about the solicitor saying the police were going to drop the charges. It didn't make sense they had charged him with murder so how could they drop the charges? He would go and look for the officer that he met yesterday. As he walked out of the cell, he realised they said not to leave the cell unattended. Why should he listen to them? They wanted him out, after all.

Chapter Eleven

Danny looked over the landing towards the ground floor but he couldn't see an officer anywhere. He walked down and took a chance. No one would go into their cell, he thought. He walked back and looked into the cell where there was not much to steal apart from the chess bits. Deciding to go down and look for the officer, he found there were not a lot of people on the block. Some of them were sweeping and mopping the floors, stairs, landings and shower areas. Danny walked to the main gate where there was an officer by the gate. Perhaps he was making sure they did their work. He approached him straight away.

"Sir! The officer who was on duty last night told me he would arrange for me to move to another cell if I came to see him this morning."

"He is off for the next four days. You are new here, aren't you?"

"Yes sir. I do not smoke and I was put in a smoker's cell, even though I suffer with asthma. Please can I be moved?"

"Come and see me later as I am the cleaning officer today. I will try and sort something out for you."

"Yes sir. What is your name?"

"My name is Officer Mr. Taylor."

"What sir?"

"Officer Mr. Taylor."

"Thank you sir."

As he walked away, Danny felt relieved. Walking up the stairs and onto the landing, he remembered closing the cell door without locking it. It was opened and someone was in it.

"What do you want mate?"

"Nothing. I was looking for Joe."

Then he left and Danny thought to himself that he must know that the lads had gone to work and probably came to nick something. Danny went and lay on the bed and fell asleep.

A while later, the door opened as Joe had come back.

"Don't tell you've been in bed all morning. Did you go and see an officer about moving?"

"Yes," Danny said proudly.

"His name is Officer Mr. Taylor and he said he will see later on when he's finished with the cleaners."

"He has finished ages ago so you had better go and see him now."

He got off the bed and left the cell to look for Mr. Taylor. He reached the ground floor where everyone was queuing at the server. It must have been lunchtime and he could not see Mr. Taylor. Danny went back up the stairs and into the cell and was about to get his plate but Joe and skinny were getting their plates too.

"Did you see him? "Asked Joe.

"No. Everyone is getting lunch."

As he said that, the two of them just left the cell so he decided to get his food too. Should he have told them that someone was in the cell? He knew that if he did they would have a go at him. After they came back, he went downstairs and when he was on the ground floor he saw Mr. Taylor at the server, shouting. He was about to go up to him but changed his mind. Maybe it was better to wait until he got closer to him in the queue and then speak to him.

"Next five. You! (Pointing to someone who had slippers on) No slippers at the server. Go and put on shoes or trainers and make sure the rest don't have slippers or shorts on."

The person who left the queue was pissed off because he had already been waiting in the queue for ages. He was also hungry and he swore to himself as he left the queue. Danny was now in the next five in the queue.

"Next five."

Four passed him to get their food and Danny stopped, about to ask a question.

"Mundy! I will have single cell ready after tea time. Come and see me then."

"Thank you Sir."

He was so happy that he turned back to go and tell them upstairs.

"Don't you want lunch Mundy?"

He quickly turned back around and went and got his lunch of tinned tomatoes, boiled potatoes and fish fingers.

He was the second to last one in the queue.

The guy serving the food asked him, "Are there any more for lunch in the queue?"

The guy in the queue with him said, "No, just the two of us left."

"Do you want some more food?"

"Yes please. How come you're offering us more?"

"We will only throw it away as not many people eat this shit."

He filled his plate up and left the serving hatch happy, as he could fix his hunger. He suddenly felt so happy. Looking around there was an empty space on a table. He went and sat down next to this guy and he looked at him. He nodded. Then he said, "You are sitting in someone's seat mate."

Awkwardly Danny nodded and went upstairs to eat on one of the landing tables.

Two Muslim prisoners were at the landing, looking down.

"Are you OK mate?"

"Yes."

"If you need anything just ask us. My name is Khan and this is Jamal."

"My name is Danny Mundy. Thank you very much."

"Any time. Just come and ask."

Khan was tall and had a slim build and he was clean shaven. Jamal was very much the same but he had a beard and darker skin tone.

Danny was very surprised by this kindness. They were good people like Delroy and he couldn't wait to move from those two that he'd been sharing the cell with. In fact, he dreaded going back in there. He went and washed his plate in the landing sink by the showers then went into the cell.

Joe immediately said, "You don't want to be talking to those Muslim scum bags. They are trying to recruit white people to go to their church. Keep away from them. Did you speak to the officer about moving cell?"

"Yes, he said after tea time he will sort out a single cell for me."

"Hope he is not a lying shit like the rest of them," growled Skinny.

"You said it was Mr. Taylor who will sort out the move?"

"Yes Joe."

"Well he is one of the best screws on the house block so he will definitely sort it."

Danny had to wait till tea time with these two. Just then an officer came and shut and locked the door.

"That's us banged up for another two hours. I am going to have a kip as I did not sleep last night," whined Joe.

"Me as well Joe! I told you, didn't I? After my last sentence they tried to recruit me."

"What those two?"

"No, no, another lot. I was down on my luck with no money. I was on the gear a lot then. I'll be honest with you, I would have joined them if they gave me anything I wanted. A white brethren helped me as he was doing alright. He had just come in and he brought a lot of gear in and I helped him sell it so he looked after me. I was lucky 'cos I might have been a suicide bomber now."

"His name wasn't Jake who helped you, Skinny, was it?"

"Yea, do you know him? I hear he's back. He came back yesterday and he must have brought a lot of gear to sell."

"Excuse me but how can he bring gear in here when they strip search everyone that comes into this place?"

"Where do you think he put it? Think about it."

"Jake must have come in with you yesterday. Did you see someone of that name coming in with you?"

By this time Danny was on his bed and they were on their beds also.

"I don't know."

If they knew Danny had been threatened by him, they would do him in. These people must come in and out of the prison all the time. It was obvious they didn't care about being in there. He hated this place and the people that came in, apart from Delroy. They fell asleep he decided he would not sleep. Instead he sat on the bed with his back on the wall, looking through the corner of the window where the black plastic bag did not cover. He couldn't stop thinking about how those Muslims were more kind to him that his own countrymen. These cell mates were not his countrymen. They were the scum of the earth. He bet they had not worked a day in their life. Danny couldn't wait to get out of that cell and out of prison.

The door opened and the officer said, "Work, men."

They woke up but did not wash their faces. They just went out like that. Danny was glad they had gone as he had the cell to himself now. What was he going to do? He would go onto the ground floor and see what was going on. Just like the other morning people were cleaning. Some of them were reading, exercising and doing push-ups. Two of them were taking it in turns to do pull ups under the metal stairs, holding on to the steps. Danny knew he had got to try and get fit and learn to read and write as well.

He had a good look around and then went back into the cell but had nothing to do. He was bored and went and lay on the bed, falling asleep.......

The door opened. Joe had come in to get a towel and go for a shower. It must have been tea time so he went downstairs with his plate. On the ground floor, nobody was there. The server people were cleaning and then looked at Danny.

"Is it tea time?"

"No mate. You're three hours too early."

He laughed and walked away. Why did Joe come back so early? He waited on the ground floor for a while and then saw Joe and a few other prisoners dressing up and walking to the gate.

"Where are they going?"

"They've got visitors, mate. They are going to the visiting hall".

"Thanks mate".

Still unsure if the police had told his wife, he hadn't heard anything from anyone. He wondered when the lawyers were coming to see him. He had no belongings. The police had kept all his belongings. He had to speak to someone to tell him how everything runs in the prison. Nobody was telling him anything. He was sure the officers were meant to tell him.

If he went back to the cell there would be nothing for him to do. All he was going to do was fall asleep again. Instead, he walked around the house block, up and down the three floors and did a little exercise up the stairs to the end of the landing and back down the stairs to the servery. Round and round until he was tired. Mr. Taylor came onto the house block and, when he caught sight of Danny, he called out to him.

"Mundy! After teatime cell number twenty, on the second landing, is free. You can have that, so move your things after tea."

"Thanks sir."

Today was a good day for him. God must have been listening to him. 'Thank you Lord.' He went back in the cell and lay on the bed. He couldn't wait to leave that cell.

The bell went, just as Joe came back and Danny quickly got his plate before he said anything to him. He left the cell before Joe did. Soon he arrived on the ground floor where there was a queue waiting at the servery. Danny joined the queue and when he got his food he ate it standing up. When he finished he went and washed his plate up then went into the cell. He told them that he'd got a cell on the second floor before putting the plate in his plastic bag. Danny told them he was going and had got a single cell on the second floor. As he left they said nothing to him. He went down the stairs and walked across to number twenty. The door was open and he was about to walk in.

This guy in his early thirties said, "What do you want?"

"This my cell. Officer Mr. Taylor said I can move in after tea time."

"I was given this cell by an officer and I am having it so you can piss off and get your own cell."

Danny did not know what to do, so stood outside the cell with his bags. The guy came out of the cell and spoke.

"Listen mate, do you want to come in the cell and we can have it, or clear off?"

Danny knew plenty about prison and that you don't grass. So that meant he couldn't go and tell anyone. The only thing he could do was go back to his old cell with those two. Going up the stairs the bag all of a sudden felt heavy. Finally he got to his old cell. Joe and Skinny stood in the door way.

"What happened?"

"I went to the cell and there was a prisoner in it. He said it was his cell, so I have come back here."

"You can't come back here. I want to sleep tonight."

"Where am I going to sleep?"

"That's your business."

Then they slammed the door shut. A few other prisoners were watching and laughing at him.

"Don't let them do that to you mate. Sort them out."

Chapter Twelve

Because of what they said it gave him the courage to start banging on the door. They took no notice but then the two Muslims came out of their cell next door.

"What is all the noise about Danny?"

He told them what had happened.

"No problem. Come into our cell mate and you can see the officer tomorrow and tell him what happened."

"Thanks, are you sure?"

Khan picked up his bag and took it to their cell. They took their shoes off as soon as they got inside the cell. Danny did the same. As he got in, he was amazed to look at the cell. They had proper curtains and they had quilts on their beds. They had mats by each bed and carpets in the middle of the cell. Even a clock sat proudly beside the TV.

He moved the quilt from the single bed and Khan said, "You are our guest so this bed is yours."

"Thank you."

"You are our guest. It is a Muslim custom to please."

As he pointed to the single bed, he picked up Danny's bags and looked for the blanket but he had forgotten it next door. He looked at them and they could see he didn't want to go next door and ask. Instead, Khan went under the single bed and took out sheets, a pillow and blankets and gave them to him. They did not wear slippers in their cell and the floor was spotless. In fact, the whole cell did not have a speck of dust or dirt anywhere. The kindness these Muslim showed him reminded him that his own people did not show him any kindness at all. He was amazed how this cell and other cells could be in the same building.

Khan put the kettle on. The bell went and a few minutes later an officer came and locked the door. He did not even notice him there.

Khan asked him, "Would you like some tea?"

"Yes please."

Danny finished making the bed they had given him. It was the bottom bunk bed and he sat on it and got out his plastic cup from his bag and gave it to Khan. He waved his hand and gave him a proper ceramic cup instead. Jamal offered some biscuits from a tin and he showed him a little bedside cabinet that he could use.

Khan spoke the Queen's English perfectly and he was the teacher's assistant in the English class while Jamal was working in the workshop. Jamal could see that Danny did not have proper fitting clothes and he said he would try and get some clothes for him but couldn't promise because of Danny's size. For the very first time in days he felt safe and was not in fear of anything. They asked why he was in prison and he told them his story. They found it hard to believe that he could kill anyone and certainly not his brother.

Khan asked Danny who his solicitor was.

"Banks and Banks."

Jamal shook his head, "They are rubbish because they work for the police."

Khan agreed.

"They are no good. Where are your papers? Let me have a look for you."

"The papers are at reception. I will ask for them tomorrow."

The door unlocked and an officer appeared.

"How many are in here?"

"Three sir."

"Oi Mundy, you are meant to be next door. No wonder the count was wrong."

He locked the door and went.

"Do you think he will move me back Khan?"

"No. He is in a rush to get the count right so he can go home."

"The officers know what goes on in here, even if you don't see them. They have their little stooges that tell them, so they know what happened to you today."

"So why don't they go and say something to the two of them or give them both a nicking for locking me out of the cell that I'm meant to be in?"

"They probably have nicked them and didn't bother to tell them. That's how they work in here. Prisoners get nickings all the time and they are never told until they get loss of their privileges. That's when they find out most of the time. See… he did not come back to move you," said Jamal.

All three of them started to drink the tea and it tasted very good. Danny looked around the cell and noticed they had some charts on the walls with times on them.

"What are those charts on the wall?"

"Those are the times we pray, so we will be praying in a few minutes."

A short time later they got their prayer mat out and started to pray towards Mecca. Danny wanted to be respectful so he decided not to look at them while they did it. He turned his head, facing the wall. This went on for about fifteen minutes. He had never seen anything like this before. They really prayed aloud. He felt good being with them as there was no pressure. In his original cell it had been like waiting for something bad to happen every second.

After they finished praying they folded their mats and put them away. Jamal took his Qu'ran and started to read and Khan started to do some writing. Danny thought to himself that he must learn to read and write. Johnny tried to teach him a few times but mostly they ended up in the pub playing pool. It was nine o'clock so he went and brushed his teeth and lay on the bed in shorts. They did the same.

"Danny what are you going to do tomorrow. Have you had induction yet?"

"Not sure what that is Khan."

"They are meant to tell you about the prison and you are meant to be assessed for education and various things that you can do in the jail. I can see you can't read or write so you need to enroll in our ESOL class."

"What does that mean? I will do that but can you tell me things about the prison please Khan?"

"It means English Speaking for Overseas Language. What do you want to know?"

"Everything."

"We are on the third floor. Outside here it's called the threes, the second floor is the twos and what's on the ground floor is called the ones. 'Burn' or 'snout' is roll up or tobacco. 'Bang up' means locked up in the cell. 'Seg' is the segregations unit where all the bad boys go and spend some time."

"What is that?"

"That's where prisoners are put as punishment for fighting, stealing, being late or too much nicking."

"What's nicking?"

"An officer or teacher gives that for having things in your cell that you are not meant to have, basically if you're doing anything wrong. Roll check is when they count how many prisoners are in the prison. They count how many are in each cell and the total in each block and then they add all the blocks and other places prisoners are currently hanging out, such as medical wing."

Jamal said, "The count is always wrong. Sometimes they will open the cell six to seven times in the evening after bang up to count us again."

"Roll check is 7am in the morning, then the officers open the cell doors and count how many are in every cell. Then they open cell doors at 8.45am for education, work etc. After that, there is no movement between house blocks. Then at midday they allow movement again and we all go back to our house block for lunch. Then at 1.40 they do another roll call while we are all banged up. Then it's open at 1.50 for work or education again. We stay there and no movement till 4.30. We are all back and evening bang up is 6.50pm. So when we come back we have free time and you can play games or go outside in the yard until roll check at 7pm. Those are the important things you need to know. You've got to be behind your doors at those times. If you are in work or education you have be there by 9am and there is no movement after everyone is locked up where they are."

"I must warn you and Jamal, I snore very loud."

Both of them took out ear plugs and smiled.

Danny knew he wouldn't have to worry about them complaining, so he could finally have a good night's sleep. He woke in the night and went to the toilet but both of them were sleeping. He felt so good not having to climb down the bunk bed. At six in the morning they started to pray aloud, though he did not mind and quickly went back to sleep. He woke up again but did not see them. On top of his side cabinet there was a note. Obviously he couldn't read it. Danny was very angry with himself as a youngster for not bothering to learn to read and write.

He washed up and closed the cell door as much as possible without locking it. Going down to the ones, he wanted to see if he could find an officer but he did not see any so he went back to the cell and lay on the bed with not much to do. A few minutes later he got up again and started to walk like he did the previous day, up and down the landing.

"Mundy what are doing out of your cell?"

"Nothing Sir."

The officer came up the stairs.

"Get in your cell."

Danny went into the cell and slammed the cell door behind him. Laying on the bed with nothing to do, he started to think about why Linda hadn't got in touch and questioning who could have killed Johnny. He really needed to speak to someone. Hopefully the lawyers would get in contact.

The cell door opened.

"Sir. Sir, what time is it?"

"11.30. Oh here you are."

"Thank you Sir. There was a clock right in front of me."

The officer gave him a slip before he could ask him to read it, then disappeared and left the cell door open.

Danny walked up and down the stairs until it was lunch time when everyone came back from work and education. He got out his plate as Khan came into the cell nodding. He did the same and on his way down the stairs he bumped into Joe, who spoke to him.

"You'd better watch out as someone is going to get you for staying with those Muslim cunts."

"You locked me out, what do you expect me to do?"

Danny looked him straight in the eye for the first time.

He just walked past him on the stairs. If he had Skinny with him he might have tried to attack him. Danny remembered what Delroy had said as he walked past him. He went to queue for dinner but it was a long queue and he waited for his turn.

Mr. Taylor came up to him. "You will have a single cell tomorrow and I have got a listener coming to see you. His name is Brian and he will explain about phone calls, education, church, application forms and anything else you want to know. This should have been done on the first day you came here."

"Thank you Sir."

It gave him some hope that he could phone his wife soon and he wanted to persuade her to come and visit him because he missed her very much. He had known her all his life and didn't know how to manage without her. Danny had not thought about her and the kids so much in all his life.

After getting his tea, he went back to the cell.

"What have you got to eat, Danny?"

"Oh. It's pork, mash and peas, Khan."

"I'm very sorry Danny but me and Jamal don't eat pork. Please could you eat it outside and when you've finished wash your plate on the landing sink."

"Very sorry. I won't take it again at the server."

Danny left the cell and ate his food near the landing sink. This was the best food he had had since being there. He felt so stupid that he should have known they don't eat pig. He decided to get another plate and throw his one away. There were dirty plates, cups, spoons and forks which prisoners left in the sink all the time. So he knew he must wash his plate on the second floor and hope that wasn't as bad. He would wait a little while before going back to the cell. Danny would tell them he would not eat pork again despite it tasting so good. After a while he went back into the cell.

"Thank you for respecting our wishes Danny."

"I am sorry Jamal, I should have known. I was stupid. I will not eat pork again."

"Don't worry about it. Let's go down on the ones and play some pool."

"If you don't mind I will stay in the cell till I move tomorrow. Mr. Taylor told me today."

"No problem but we are going to cook in the kettle tonight, so you can taste some of our food as we cook."

"That will be good."

"Come on down, it will be fun."

They were talking as they made their way down to the ones. The other prisoners were looking at him, but they did not say anything. Khan and Jamal said hello to a few prisoners, some Muslim and some non-Muslim. He could see that they were friendly with everyone and when they got to where the pool table was, Khan spoke to someone waiting in the queue.

"How many are waiting to play pool?"

"There are six waiting mate."

So Jamal said he would begin to cook.

Danny went with him and Khan stayed. Jamal and Danny took their shoes off and he went and got another kettle. He then got some onions, garlic and ginger and started to cut them up before he put butter in the kettle, then waited for it to melt. After that he put garlic and ginger in the kettle and gave Danny a spoon and told him to keep stirring the kettle and make sure any ginger and garlic didn't stick. While he was doing that, he opened three tins of Tuna and drained all the oil into the kettle. Danny was still stirring the kettle then he put the onions in, then he put a tea spoon and a half of curry powder and a bit of all purposes seasoning in. Danny looked at him and he made an action with his hand for him to keep stirring. Even though his hands were getting tired, the aroma smelled really good and he couldn't wait to taste it. A few minutes later he took the spoon from him before adding in the tuna and giving back the empty tin to put in the bins outside.

As Danny went outside someone said, "That smells great."

He went back in the cell where the smell was even better. Jamal was still stirring the kettle. He took over then he got some bread, pickle, pepper and salt out and he took three plates out as well. Khan came back and he had a tub of boiled rice from the server. They went and washed their hands and Danny did the same. Then they sat on the mats and put newspaper in the middle of the floor. They put the bread, kettle and the rest of things on the paper. For Danny it was a struggle to sit down crossing his legs.

"Can I stretch my legs because I can't cross them?" "Sure you can."

Danny waited for them to start. Immediately Khan said a prayer thanking Allah for the food. Danny was very surprised at just how good the food tasted as it was better than his home food. He took his time to eat as he was watching how slowly they ate and savoured the dish. If he had been at home he would have finished the whole lot ages ago. When they'd finished, he struggled to get up and turned on his knee and then on his arms and got up holding the bed post.

Khan said, "Leave the cleaning to me."

In his head they probably thought he wouldn't clean it properly. He went and washed his hands, then lay on the bed.

"How come the officers have not come to bang us up Jamal?"

"Today is Wednesday so bang up is at seven pm".

The clock said it was only six thirty.

"I think I will do some exercises and do some walks up and down the stairs."

Then he left the cell and was feeling a bit better. However he couldn't wait to hear what the solicitors said. Shit, he was meant to get the solicitors papers from reception for Khan to look at. He walked till 'bang up' time and had never walked so much in his life. Normally all he did was walk to and from work to home, eat, watch TV then go to bed for five days a week. After work on Friday he'd go to the pub then grab a take away. Sunday was pub in the morning then home for lunch and lazing around before bed. That was his life whereas Johnny was always doing something active.

Danny lived his life day to day, not thinking about the future. He was happy and contented with his life. Now looking back on his life he could see why Johnny wanted to better himself. But could that have caused his death or was it because people knew he was gay and certain people hated him for that? Even their father hated gay men and woman so he had probably turned in his grave. He started thinking about what he was going to do with his life. If what everyone was saying became true then he would get charged for murder. He wanted to change and exercise a lot more. The doctor at work said he had to lose weight. He wished he never had this asthma condition that left him out of breath all the time. Annoyingly, he had to remember to keep using his asthma pump. There went the bang up bell so he made his way back into the cell where the boys had already tidied up and had started to pray. Danny took his trainers off and walked quietly to his bed to lie down. They took no notice of him and carried on praying. He wanted to go to the toilet but he kindly waited until they finished praying. After that he washed up ready for bed.

"Did you bring the solicitors paper work?" asked Khan.

"No I forgot, sorry Khan."

"In prison you must try and get things done yourself. Jamal and I feel sorry for you and we will try and help you, but you must help yourself as well. People in prison don't ask more than once. Look at your friends next door. You know they will be in and out of prison all their lives because that's the only life they know."

"Why? You might ask. They are thieves and that's all they know. It's the environment they have come from. Their dads will have done the same. They will rob kids coming from school, taking their phones or anything they may have. Even old age pensioners. They run in a shop and steal things and run out again. Coming to prison is nothing as they get fed, a roof over their heads in the winter. In their home they spend the heating money on drink so they can't pay their bills. That's one type of cons you've got in here but the other are small time drugs dealers who have two or three lines".

"What are lines?"

"Very small drug dealers have one or two lines. This is when one drug dealer gets five to ten people selling drugs for them. They have a bit of money because the bigger drug dealers give them drugs on tick or they have money to buy bits of a kilo, then they mix it and give to their lines to sell. They sell as little as twenty five to fifty pounds worth and the smaller drug dealers sell ten and twenty pounds worth. Those next door will not be trusted to work in a line because they will use it. Then you've got the guys who sell to the guys who have lines. Big fish are the ones who walk around in Gucci, Prada, Hugo,

Boss, etc. gear and they tend to show off. The very big boys you don't really see about as they stay quiet in their cells. Prisoners go to them and they don't cause any problems. In reality they are doing ten to thirty years plus in jail and still run their operation and the money goes to wives or partners."

"How do you know all this?"

"I deal with these people in here all the time and they tell me their stories to big up themselves."

"So some of it is not true."

"When you've got Bank, Post Office, Armed van robbers again they tend to do a little business in here like a little drugs protection or bullying for money. They are on nothing, meaning they have no other business outside, so they have to make money for their families in here. They are very dangerous men because they can pick on anyone if they think you could have money. Then you've got people like me who did insurance fraud and Jamal, who got done for money laundry. Generally they won't pick on me or any Muslim as there are too many of us or gypsies in here. Same as the prison officers, they are racist against blacks, Albanians, Russians, as a matter of fact all foreigners, because there are not a lot of them in prison in England. If they did they could have riots in all the prisons in the country."

"Another thing is that most of these officers grew up with prisoners."

"What do you mean Jamal?"

"They went to school with some of them or are cousins so their families know each other. Some of them even live in the same streets as them."

"What about pedophiles?"

"They're put on a separate house block and they are kept away from the rest of the prison populations. Some have been killed in here."

"Someone gave two prisoners some spice to go kill one pedophile. They killed the guy and put him under his bed and he was not found for a few days. That goes on a lot and later we were told he was not a pedophile but the cons that killed him thought he was a pedo. It just shows that anything can happen in prison. They burn prisoners or set alight their cells, or they will pay someone to stab someone. If you look at some of the very big guys in here you see they will always have someone behind them to cover their back or, if they don't, they will have a couple of towels or sweatshirts covering their back and neck in case someone tries to stab them in the back from behind."

"You were saying that bank robbers make prisoners pay money in here for protection. How?"

"Their family have to pay on the outside."

Jamal was listening as well. Danny thought he was not in there long, maybe just seven weeks. He was very interested and he wanted to know what everything is.

"Are you listening Jamal?"

"Yes my master," said Jamal jokingly.

"Prisoners borrow things or buy drugs and they can't pay their depts. They will tell the people who they borrow from that their family has got plenty of money to pay off the debt. They then phone the family and ask to put money in an account of the person they owe. Most of the time they give large to say their family has money. When they don't, then the family will be told if they don't pay then their husband or son etc. will get beaten up or lose an eye. So they put their family in problems. This is where it gets interesting. Some of the families do have money so even if they don't owe money they will ring and threaten them the same way."

"How would they if they have money?"

"Good question Jamal and when they don't have money they make excuses or make them wait till next week or month or say they don't have it. If they have any sense they pay up straight away because they are in trouble."

"Danny you've been promised a cell tomorrow right? Do you know whose cell it will be?"

"No. Mr. Taylor didn't tell me."

"I can tell you. That coloured person who took that single cell from you yesterday on the twos. That's whose cell you will be having."

"No way! How do you know?"

"Jamal it doesn't matter how I know. He just hasn't got many coloured guys in here to kick up a fuss. He will be going to the segregation unit for bullying you."

"What about those two next door who locked out Danny? Why aren't they going to the segregation?"

"What colour are they Jamal?"

"But that's wrong, so wrong."

"Jamal this is a local prison so most of these local prisoners know the officers' families."

"So they will threaten them."

"NO, no they went to the same school together with some of their fathers or elder brothers or they all know each other so why rock the boat?"

"When I came here for my first day why did the officer not put me in this cell?"

"I told them we don't want anybody who isn't a Muslim in here. If Jamal didn't come in this cell they would have mixed me up but because there's two of us they will listen to us plus next door was empty. They're very understanding when it comes to religion. What religion are you Danny?"

"I am Church of England. All my kids are christened and I got married in the church. I don't go to church lots but I have been asking God to help me."

"It looks like Muhammad did listen to you and put you with us."

The door clicked as the officer checked and then locked the door.

"How can I get some new clothes, like underwear, T-shirts etc. Jamal?"

"Khan knows."

"Clothes from outside or prison ones Danny?"

"Any, it doesn't matter. I have eaten nothing compared to what I normally eat outside so I will have lost some weight. The clothes I have outside will be too big for me, so prison clothes Khan."

"I will get some for you tomorrow."

"Thank you Khan. I will remember to get my papers from reception too."

The both of them got books to read and Danny turned to face the wall. He thought these two Muslims were really good guys and knew they had helped him so much and he felt guilty that he had done nothing for them. Was it Allah or Jesus?

The next morning they had left and he got his things together and made his way to the gate.

"Ah Mundy you can go to the cell on the twos you were given last time and Brian, a Diversity Rep will come and see you."

"Thank you Mr. Taylor."

Danny made his way to the cell with his bags and, as he opened the door, he noticed it was filthy. The guy before had not cleaned it. He put his things on the bed and then went to get a broom and swept it out but the toilet and the sink were very dirty so he needed special cleaning stuff for that. The door knocked and he opened it.

"Hello Danny, remember me. My name is Brian. I am here to help you in any way I can as I am the Diversity Rep and a Listener."

"What is a Listener?"

"I listen to all your problems and see If can help you."

"Thank you Brian. I need to get my papers from reception because I need to get hold of my wife. Since I was arrested I have not heard from or seen my wife. Can you help me? I also need some cleaning stuff for the toilet. Generally I need a lot of help as I cannot read and write."

"Don't worry, I will help you, no need for you to ask anyone else. I will be back in a few minutes."

Danny continued to clean the best he could. If only his wife were there. She would have done it in no time. Oh, how he missed her. He felt that his life was nothing without her. He sat on the bed but the mattress was so thin he could feel the metal slats under it.

Suddenly the door knocked.

"That was quick Brian."

"I have brought some goodies for you. Two bags of things you will need."

Danny quickly open it and looked at it. There were lots of cleaning things and he put it under his bed.

"Mr. Taylor will bring you a pin card and the papers from reception. I have enrolled you in E.S.O.L classes as well here so you just have to fill this out. Oh sorry! I will fill it out for you as I have got all your details. I am going now. If there is anything you need, come to me or any other listener. You don't need to go to anyone else."

After Brian left, Danny got the bags from under the bed where he found loads of cleaning materials, extra blankets and sheets, a pillow, a dustpan and a small brush. He was so happy. The bell went for lunchtime so he got his plate and went down to the ones and saw Khan and Jamal. He went behind both of them in the queue and they acknowledged each other. Then he saw Brian who gave Khan and Jamal a bad look. Luckily, they took no notice of him. The only people that helped Danny didn't like each other. What was he going to do?

Khan said, "I'll bring your clothes for you later."

"Thanks."

Danny felt the tension! He was four behind him in the queue and Brian had just got his meal and left. Danny got his meal and went to his cell and sat on the bed. He wasn't feeling hungry, which was unusual for him. He was thinking about Khan and Brian. Starting to try to clean his cell, he tried fixing the TV but there was no Ariel. He did have a kettle but he needed so many things. The door knocked and he opened it to find Khan there. He called him in and he had a bag with him. Instead of walking in, he chose to stay in the passage by the door.

"Here are the clothes I promised you but they need washing."

They were still in the passage way when a prisoner said, "I will wash your clothes for you."

Khan said, "No thanks mate."

Danny looked at Khan and wondered why he said no.

"I needed the clothes washed. Why did you say no?"

"Have you got money to pay?"

"Oh I see. Can you please get me a kettle and an Ariel for the TV? You have done so much for me and I feel bad asking all the time. I don't want you to think I am taking the piss." "No, no, not at tall. I like to help new people that come to prison. I was lucky to find a lot of Muslims here when I first came here and they helped me a lot so I am doing the same in return. I'll see what I can do for you. See you later."

He looked into the bag of clothes. It included some good stuff. One of the tops was Ralph Lauren so Danny was very pleased as he'd never worn designer clothes before. He continued to clean whilst thinking of his wife. She usually did all the work in the house. He hadn't even emptied the bins before and realised he must have been a very lazy person at home. Having to clean this little cell was so hard for him but he knew she would never moan or complain. Let's face it, he was a very lucky man. The cell door knocked and he opened the door. The same person who asked him about the washing stood there. He was around thirty five, medium clean built and with a sharp cockney accent.

"Do you want that washing done mate? I will only charge a tin of Tuna. My name is Archie."

"I don't have any money to buy Tuna."

"Look, you have been here at least three or four days by now. The prison pay you fifty pence a day on your canteen sheet. A tin of Tuna is only seventy pence so you can buy that and have your washing done for you. You don't want dirty clothes like those other muppets and when you start work or education you will get more wages."

"Explain to me how the wages work then."

"Look mate, I not here to teach you how the prison works. If you want your washing done it will cost a tin of Tuna and you pay when you get your canteen. No rush, just pay me when you have it."

"Ok." Danny was about give him the clothes then he looked inside the bag which had three tops and one bottom in it. The guy was about to take the bag.

"Hold on."

Danny fetched the rest of the dirty clothes and put them in the same bag.

"You are taking the piss. That will be double."

"Give it back then."

"No I was only kidding. I will be on the ones, number three, just by the laundry room so come for it this afternoon. My name is Archie.

He took the bag and left. He was about to finish making the bed and have a lie down when Brian came back with his solicitors papers and a pin number for the phone.

"How does that work Brian?"

He tore the paper, revealing a four digit number.

"You have to remember, every time you ring anyone on the outside, you have to put the pin number in which is 7, 3, 8 and 9 then you ring your number on the out. You do that and you need to write all the numbers in your book or diary."

"When can I ring my people?"

"You can in a couple of weeks. It will be clear for you to use."

"But Brian, you know I can't read and write. I have to ask my wife to send me all the numbers and addresses. Then I would need your help to fill this form with all the numbers in it. It's going to take a long time before I can speak to my wife."

"I will speak to a senior officer and try and get permission for you to speak to your wife."

"Brian it would be good if I can get a visitor pass for my wife and she can bring all the numbers on the visit as well."

"Ok Danny I will see what I can do. But all of this takes time and all the officers are stretched and under staffed. You should start education tomorrow at nine am. Don't be late."

"Where do I go?"

"I will come for you in the morning and take you there, don't worry."

The bell went for bang up so he lay on his bed, looking at the cell and thinking about outside, his brother, the solicitors, his wife, the children and how long he was going to be there. In prison there was plenty of time for thinking. All the time outside you just did what you had to do but there you were always waiting for someone or something and always thinking. An officer locked his door. He looked around his cell and needed plastic bags for curtains. He also wanted a cupboard with drawers, a table, a chair and so many things.

He couldn't keep asking so was just going to do without until he got to see his wife. Hopefully she could send some money but she wouldn't have any spare money as they always lived week to week with his wages. His head was bursting with what was happening to him. Who could have killed Johnny? Why? Why? He felt his face and his beard had grown and but his stomach felt smaller.

Danny knew he needed to do something about his lack of reading and writing skills. This was his chance to do something about improving generally. Danny got off the bed and lay with his back on the floor, hooking his toes under the radiator pipes and started to do sit ups. He did one and two but the third was a struggle. Eventually he managed to do five without pushing himself too much. Then he turned onto his stomach and tried doing press ups but could only do three before once again struggling. After this he stood up and jogged on the spot for a few seconds and was out of breath which made him stop quickly.

Danny went back and lay on the bed. Perhaps he needed to push himself on. He must not lie on the bed anymore apart from when it was time to sleep. So he stood up and walked up and down the eight feet cell. At least he could tell himself that he was doing something. He did nothing besides jogging on the spot, press ups, sit ups and walking all through until lunchtime when the door opened. He was about to lie down on the bed but changed his mind and sat on it instead. A few minutes later he walked on to the passage way when he saw Brain coming. He beckoned him and he walked up towards the officer's office. Danny managed to catch up with him by the door and he opened it and followed him.

"Ah Mundy. Brian spoke to me about you, so follow me."

"You can phone your wife now Mundy."

"Thank you sir."

Danny picked up the phone and tried to dial but could not remember the number. The officer was sitting on the chair looking at some paper work when he noticed him shaking his head.

"Do not tell me you cannot remember the number."

"Sorry Sir."

He picked up the phone and asked someone to get the home number. He waited a few minutes and then he wrote it down and gave it to Danny, telling him not to lose it in a stern voice.

He took it and dialed the number. It rang and rang and then it was finally answered.

"Hello Linda. This is me, Danny."

"What is going on? How could the police arrest you for the murder of Johnny when you loved him more than your own children?"

"I don't know love. They just did. I need you to send some money and book a visit to come and see me. I am using the officer's phone so I can't stay long. Oh and all the addresses and phone numbers please."

"I will try and send some money but your firm will not pay me your wages as they want you to sign for it. I have being trying to visit but could not get through. I will keep trying."

The officer was looking at his watch.

"I've got to go now. Bye love. See you soon. I miss you so much."

He put the phone down and tears were about to come from his eyes, when the officer said, "Go back to your cell."

"Thank you sir."

As he walked back to the cell, tears were filling his eyes, thinking what his wife had said. He loved Johnny more than their kids. That wasn't true but that's what she thought so he must have shown it. He had learned so much about himself since being in there. He had to make a change in himself and his attitude. By the time he got back to the landing everyone was doing what they normally did, cleaning, running up and down the landing, doing press ups, playing chess etc. He went to his cell, closed his door and started to try to do press ups but struggled to five then stopped. He did a few sit ups and stopped again, then jogged on the spot and again he was tired and out of breath. He was walking up and down the cell and knew if those prisoners saw him they would laugh at him. After a while he heard shouting outside. Danny opened his door and went into the passageway that looked down on the ones.

"Look who's back, Wade."

"Wade!"

Danny was not impressed. He must have just come back from the segregation. Danny quickly went back into his cell and was about to sit on the bed when he realised he needed to do exercises. He thought he saw Brian talking to Wade. Going back outside, he had a good look around but he did not see them together. He came back into his cell and locked the door, then he started to exercise again. He had not had a shower since he was at the police station and he was all sweaty. He went back out on the landing and locked his door. He went to the showers the other day but there were a lot people in there so he did not bother. The next time he went, Joe and Skinny were in there again so again he did not bother to shower. He must not be afraid of getting into trouble if it wasn't his fault. The judge would know that. If he was going to get a beating he would just have to be brave. Unable to open the door, he realised he must've locked it by mistake. He knew he had to go to the office and ask an officer or hope he might see one on the way. No officers were about so he had to go to the office. Danny knocked on the office door so they could see him through the glass windows.

"What do you want?"

"Sorry sir. I locked myself out of my cell."

"Mundy why have you locked the door?"

"Sorry sir."

They walked up to his cell but Danny was walking slowly. The officer could overtake him and open his door.

"Do that again and you will get a nicking."

"Sorry Sir."

Danny got his stuff and went to the showers. He was ready if anyone troubled him. He went into the showers to find that two prisoners were in there already. Danny went and showered. It felt good not to be afraid for the first time since he had been arrested. When he finished he went to his cell. After he dried himself he could do with some clean clothes. He hadn't thought about that at the time. He changed back into the dirty clothes he was wearing earlier. A few minutes later, Archie came to the cell with the clean clothes.

"Don't forget a tin of Tuna on Saturday when you get your canteen."

"But!"

He was gone before he was able to say he was not getting canteen on Saturday. However, he was glad to have clean clothes and could change back again. With the new clothes, he felt good, but he had no idea what time it was. He'd have to ask his wife to send his watch. There were so many things he had to remember. Thinking about it, perhaps it was at the police station. He was about to walk around the house block when Jamal came.

"Danny I have some things for you from Khan: a kettle and an Ariel for your T.V. I've also got you a curtain."

"Thank you Jamal, are you busy?"

"No, what do you want?"

"Could you explain what money I would get for education or work or just explain everything about wages please."

"If you do work or go to education, you get fifty pence per session. When you work in the Gym or as a cleaner or server you get one pound five pence a session so if you go to work or education you will get about ten pounds per week. There are other ways that pay more but I don't know exactly."

"How does the canteen work?"

"You should get your canteen sheet which has got a list of all items for sale on Wednesday and you fill out what you want. Make sure you have money to buy it otherwise you will not get it. Also make sure you hand it in, then on Saturday we queue up and get what we order so you should have had your canteen sheet yesterday but because you are new you will not get one till next Wednesday. I will show you a little trick to put these curtains up. I've got a tub of glue and some match sticks. What we do is glue two matches together so we have four like that. Then we glue two together, not the full length but glue them together, overlapping half the length of the match stick. You probably noticed these match sticks do not have sulfur as prisoners use it for building things such as ships, houses or photo frames. When they are dry we stick them to the wall where we want the curtain. You can see the gap between the match stick and the wall and that's where we will hook the curtain but wait till it dries. We will do that tomorrow. Do you want to come to church tomorrow (Moshe)?"

"On a Friday?"

"Yes that's the day we go to the Moshe in prison. Do you need anything else Danny? If not I will see you tomorrow."

"Thanks for everything and bye."

What had he done? The English boys were going to have a go at him going to Muslim church. Brian would get upset with him. In fact, he had put himself in a right pickle. He couldn't break his word due to getting a kicking soon. He'd had some lucky scrapes so far. Now that Wade was going to be dragging him into more trouble. The next morning he woke up and didn't have a watch or clock so had no idea what time it was. He was used to waking up in the morning then having a wash and starting to do some exercise. He was feeling better.

Where was he going to get match sticks? He made a cup of tea and watched the breakfast TV, laying on the bed but remembered he must sit up. Danny decided to just walk up and down the cell, then tried to do press ups and sit ups, finding his breathing was getting better, partly because he remembered to use his asthma pump. The door opened at a few minutes past eight and he looked around his cell to check he hadn't forgotten anything.

"Good morning Danny, are you ready?"

"Bit nervous but I am ready Brian."

"Follow me then."

<u>First day in Class</u>

He was thinking of telling Brian about going to the Moshe that afternoon.

"Here we are. E.S.O.L class 10. Mr. White this is Danny Mundy."

"Hello Danny, take a seat and I will be with you shortly. Thank you for bringing him Brian."

"Sir, Can I quickly speak to Brian before he goes?"

"Yes go ahead but don't take too long."

"Brian you might not like this but Jamal asked me to go to Muslim church. I am sorry but they looked after me, when Joe and Skinny chucked me out of the cell."

"Don't worry about it Danny. You are your own man but be careful as this prison is going to kick off soon, so make sure you are on the right side. It is my job as diversity and listener rep to look after new prisoners. I get paid to do this. The most important thing is I like you. I don't think you killed your brother and I consider you a friend. I will always try and help you."

"Thank you so much Brian. I really appreciate your help and friendship."

"Mundy, class is ready."

"Yes Sir."

Mr. White had white hair and was about fifty five and he spoke very softly and slowly. There were ten in the class: three English, four African and two Indians and a prisoner classroom assistant who was putting out the books and pens on the tables. He sat in front and was nervous when he picked up the pen. He could see his hands were shaking.

"We've got Mr. Mundy who will join us today. I know some are new here but this class started on Monday. Some have already missed a few lessons but by the end of next week we should be aright. Everyone should be on par with each other."

Mr. White turned to the chalkboard and someone made a farting noise. He quickly turned around and said, "One more silly noise and I will make sure none of you will get paid for your sessions in education and I know who did that, stupid nose Williams."

"It was not me Sir."

"I don't want to hear any more noises."

"How many of you can read and write?"

"Not many put their hands up so this is what we will do today."

Mr. White went to the chalk board and wrote A, B, C, a, b, c.

"Answer me. Who knows what these letters are?"

"Not many put their hands up again I see."

He got out a ruler and pointed to A.

"That A is a capital a."

The rest of the lesson went nicely, with no more noise. The bell went for the lesson to finish. As Danny was about to leave, the teacher spoke to him.

"Mundy I think you did well today. There's no class Friday afternoon but here is a book I want you to learn over this weekend. It's just your simple ABC book. Hopefully it will come back to you from when you first went to school but don't worry if you don't finish it. I am glad at your age you wanted to learn to read and write in this class. See you on Monday Mundy."

"Thank you Sir."

He made his way back to the block and was just going to his cell when Brian called him to his cell. Had he changed his mind about him going to the Moshe?

"Come in Danny and have a seat."

As he walked into his cell he was dressed in a Hugo Boss top and bottoms and Gucci trainers. He had brand new tables and chairs and he had his own shower in his double cell. He had a carpet on the floor and his cell was like a proper room. He had pictures of his family and friends on the wall. In fact he had everything you needed. His cell was spotless.

Someone came to his cell and asked, "Can I have quarter?"

"You still owe me an eighth so that will be three-quarters you will owe. You know what will happen if you don't pay."

"I have put down on my canteen sheet for this week already Brian."

"Come back in five."

"Can I have it now before bang up at lunchtime?"

"I said come back later."

"Oh ok, sorry Brian."

A few minutes later someone else came to his cell for burn and he told them to come back later.

"Danny you best get back and get your lunch. Don't forget any time you need anything just ask me. Are you actually going to the Muslim church?"

"Thanks for everything Brian."

As he left he didn't answer him as he couldn't tell him who to be friends with. They were nice people the same as him. If they asked him not to be friends with him then he would just ignore them. His cell was nice with his own shower. Brian's cell was double the size of his so he wondered how he got so many things. He supposed he had been there a long time. He'd got to learn how things work in prison and had to be a changed man and stop feeling sorry for himself. He knew there were a lot of people who were innocent of crimes they had been convicted for.

After lunch, Khan and Jamal came to his cell, dressed in their sherwani (long frock) and wore their caps on their heads. They went to the Moshe and Danny was surprised that it was not a church but they used the same room that Christians used. He followed them into the Moshe and Khan left him and Jamal and went to the front. Everyone was in lines facing the front where the Imam was. There was a gap so people could sit and cross their legs, which some of them were doing.

Jamal and he were in the second line. Danny sat down next to Jamal but could not cross his legs. He took up three spaces. To his surprise there were quite a few white faces and they had on their frocks and caps and a few of them had beards like Khan. Danny looked to the front where Khan and the Imam were taking like they knew each other for a long time. The service had not started as people were still coming in.

"Danny what did you think of it?"

"Don't know really but definitely different from the church services I normally go to. That's all I can say. I'm glad I went."

"Will you come again?"

"Not sure really. We will see if I understand it a bit more. If I do then I will come again."

"We do have Muslim class so you can join and you could learn a bit more about our culture, how we pray and our Qu'ran."

"That's an idea. I think I will do that. I can still go to my church?"

"Oh yes, no problem."

"It will be tea time soon so get your tea and you can come to my cell and I will speak to you about Mohammad."

"Mohammad?"

"He is like your Jesus. It's all very similar to your Bible."

"I am expecting a letter from my solicitor. I will check and then I will come up."

"On second thoughts we are not going to have enough time after we get tea because they are going to bang us up straight after tea. This weekend its bang up all weekend. You can only go out if you go to church on Sunday morning. Otherwise they will not let you out, so put your name on the list for Sunday Church. This weekend we are locked down and they are only letting us out to get lunch and tea, or they might feed at the door."

"Feed at the door?"

"They will wheel a trolley with baguettes for dinner etc. look! Over there they have started to queue up for evening tea mate. So you'd best get your plate."

"Ok I will see you later Jamal."

"Jamal. Where is Danny?"

"He expecting a letter from his solicitors so he went to his cell, Khan."

"What did he think of the services?"

"He liked it but he did not understand so I told him about Qu'ran classes. I think he was interested in joining but he wanted to go to the English church as well."

"Jamal, I think Brian wants to recruit him and use him to work for him because he is big guy. You know these white guys who love the gym in prison because they can't afford it on the out. Once he starts to lose weight and train he will be useful to Brian. Danny is a big unit."

"Why would he want someone new that doesn't know anything about how the prison works and his business? He can't even read and write!"

"Jamal what do most white people do when they come into prison?"

"You are right. They go to the gym as often as they can."

"He is a big guy and if he was going to the gym and knew a little more about what a good recruit he would be for Brian and the same for us, well he would have a good hand of cards. The main thing for Brian is that he does not get used or anything."

"What do you mean anything?"

"He does not use drugs as far as I knows. I want you to work on him. Go and see what he needs and get it for him and make sure he goes to Qu'ran lessons."

"I will my brother."

Later on.

"Mundy are you in there?", "Yes sir, in the toilet."

He heard the door locked after he'd finished in the toilet. He lay on the bed and dozed off. He woke and tried to go back to sleep but couldn't, so put the T.V on and watched a little before switching it off. Bored, Danny looked at the ABC book but his mind was not on it. Once again he started to think about his brother and wife. He started to feel depressed but instead of laying on the bed got up to try to do some exercises. After a bit he stopped and turned the T.V back on. His head was in a twirl and he wanted to get out of there. He had done nothing wrong so why was he there? He wished he was home. He needed to sleep. Then he remembered Brian said if he was feeling depressed and wanted to talk, all he needed to do was press the bell. So that is what he did. Then he waited and waited for over an hour until the door opened.

"What do you want Mundy?"

"Can I speak to a listener please sir?"

"I will get in touch with Oscar One and let them know what you need. I don't know how long they will take but I will let them know."

"Thank you sir."

After he shut the door, Danny went and put the kettle on and did not lie down. Instead he just walked up and down the cell and waited for them to come. He must have waited for over an hour then the door opened. To his surprise, three officers were at the door.

"You wanted a Listener?"

"Yes sir."

"Tonight is a very busy night as prisoners are calling for listeners all night. It's never usually this busy. Here is Brian. He is by himself and normally there are two but because we are so busy Brian doesn't mind seeing you by himself. He says he knows you. Press the button when you are finished."

They left Brian and locked the door behind them.

As he sat on the toilet Brian asked, "What's wrong Danny?"

"I am feeling very depressed as my mind is all over the place. I can't sleep because I keep wondering who killed my brother. I am going to get charged for his murder and I didn't do it. My wife is all alone and I haven't heard from my solicitors. I am just out of my mind with worry. I can't even study this ABC book because I feel suicidal."

Brian stood up and put his hand on Danny's shoulder.

"Don't say that or they will put you on suicide watch and someone will open your flap every twenty minutes for months and you will never get any sleep. I am supposed to report that but I won't. Listen Danny. Just talk to me as I am here to listen. Talk about anything to get it off your chest. A lot of people that come into prison for the first time are like you and they do the same thing. You're looking at twenty five plus years in prison, if they find you guilty of murder so I can fully understand what you are going through."

What Brian just said hit him like a ton of bricks. He just lay back on his bed and started to cry like a baby. Brian held him as he slouched on the bed.

"You've got to be strong for your wife and kids and your mind has to be cleared for when you go to court. That's going to be well hard because you will have to wake at five thirty every morning and go to court, being double cuffed from here into the wagon and in the court cells for hours, often waiting hours upon hours every day. Two and a half hours going there in the wagon in that tight space, having to hold your piss or piss in a bag and possibly wetting yourself while you piss and the same coming back. Then after waiting in the cells you are taken into the courts where your wife will be watching. Then you will listen to all the lies from the police and the so called witness about how you could have killed your brother. When you come back from the courts you will find cold food waiting for you. You will not have time to shower apart from on weekends. It's going to be hard mate so you've got be strong for the road ahead."

After Brian had said what was going to happen, Danny's face changed. His tears stopped then he stood up.

"I always thought British justice is the best in the world but thinking about how many people are wrongfully convicted on the news is making me realise that it will probably happen to me. I think the solicitors were lying to me that the police will drop the charges."

"Danny if they were to drop the charges they would have given you bail. I am sorry but that's the truth. Have you thought about who could have killed your brother?"

"My brother was gay and I did not know his friends because I worked five and half days a week. We went to the pub at least once a week to play pool and we were in the pub's pool team. Everyone in the pub knew us because our dad used to drink in the same pub all his life before he died. My brother and I were totally different. He was a very ambitious person who was buying a house and he was a bit like you, always doing some deal or another. I thought about who could have killed him but I have no idea."

"I will be honest with you. Best try and figure out who would kill him. As you said, the landlady saw you with the knife in your hand that all the jury want to know is what an eye witness has to say. So you are bang in trouble mate."

"Thanks for coming Brian. I know what I have to do now. I have got to be strong for my family."

"Shall I press the bell Danny to let Oscar one know we are finished?"

"Yes Brian, you have been very helpful mate."

"You are a big lump Danny. If you tone up you could earn yourself some money for your family in the future and I like you. I could do some enquiries where you live to see if anybody knows anything about Johnny."

"I am no good to anyone."

"Not like how you are now, but in a few months when you go to the gym."

"What would I have to do?"

"Don't worry about that now, we will talk another time. I will get a table and chair for you and if you need anything else, let me know. I can hear Oscar One coming."

The door opened.

"Are you all done?"

"Yes sir."

After they left, Danny sat on the edge of the bed thinking. He then stood up and did some jogging on the spot, saying to himself he had to get fit and earn some money. He was not going to feel sorry for himself any more.

In the morning the cell door opened. The officer said, "Go and get your canteen and come straight to your cell. I will be watching you."

Then he opened the next door and said the same thing before Danny could say he had no canteen. He then stood by his cell door in the passage way.

"What are you doing there Mundy? Get your canteen."

"I have got no canteen sir."

"Get back in your cell."

Danny went back into his cell and took the ABC book out, starting to study it. He did that for an hour, then did press ups, sit ups and jogging on the spot. Smiling as he finished, he was certain he was getting better. Trying to alternate all the time, he hoped he might not get tired doing the same thing.

The flap opened on the other side of the door and when he looked it was Archie looking through the flap.

"Have you got my tin of Tuna?"

"No."

"That's double next week."

Then he closed the flap and went.

About midway an officer's door opened suddenly.

"Go and get your lunch and come straight back."

Danny got his plastic plate and went and queued with the rest of the prisoners to get lunch. He saw Archie pointing at him with Wade. Danny turned his back so he was facing the server. Quickly he got his lunch and went back to his cell. It was his favorite: eggs, boiled sausages, bacon, beans and half a slice of fried bread and he could help himself to as much bread as he wanted. He got into his cell and ate lunch before going through his training routine and learning from his ABC book.f

Chapter Thirteen

On Sunday morning the door opened.

"Are you going to church?"

"Yes Sir."

The officer left the door open and went to the next person who was going to church. Danny made his way to the gate where he could exit out of the block. There were at least seven prisoners waiting to be let out for church. Then an officer came and opened the main gate and the prisoners followed him to church. When they got there two officers were by the entrance. One was standing and one sitting by a table with a sheet of all the prisoners who were on the list to enter into church. If your name was not on the list you were not allowed in. There were two officers searching the prisoners as they were going in.

As he got into the church the front seats were empty, only the back seats were being filled. He walked over to the back seats as well, picked up a hymn book that was on the chair and took a seat. The minister was standing at the front facing the prisoners. There were two officers at the back and two each at the sides and then two by the door. Danny was sitting in the middle of the back row with hymn book in hand. When mostly all the seats were taken, the Father spoke.

Quietly, he started to pray but while he was praying the prisoners were talking to each other. Danny stopped and looked up. For a moment they stopped talking and then when he started to pray again they started talking again.

Danny continued and finished the prayers and then the Father said to them, "You come into the Lord's house to worship. No more talking. The next person who talks will be asked to leave and banned for one month from this church. Time for hymn number thirty one - Amazing Grace."

They all started to sing but again most of the back was talking. Then other prisoners were taking things from their trousers and passing to each other burn, money and other contraband drugs in plain sight. When the hymn was finished they stopped passing things but continued to talk. These prisoners did not come here to worship God but to meet other cons from other house blocks so they could do various deals.

The officers did not say anything. The Father was in charge of the church and guards only got involved if a fight broke out. They were able to see what went on and made mental notes on who did what. There was a group that kept talking all the time again and eventually the Father pointed to them.

"Stop talking or you will be asked to leave. That hymn Amazing Grace… does anyone know who wrote it?"

All the cons were looking at each other, then a black man from the choir put his hand up and stood up.

"Go on tell us?"

"He was a slaver who sold slaves."

"Well done Isaac."

"His name was Robert Newton and he is known for going to Africa and kidnapping Africans to sell to the Americans. Was that a Christian thing to do?"

The father looked around.

"Was that a wicked thing to do?"

Again he looked around and cons were saying, "No. No. No."

"You are right. He stopped doing wicked things and he became a Christian and he wrote that amazing song. The moral of this little story is that you all can change."

The Father continued to read from his bible but every time he looked down to read the bible, some of the prisoners started talking again. He stopped reading, looked up and pointed.

"You three please leave now. Officers escort them out please".

The officers walked towards them and one of them said, "We've done nothing."

"Come this way now."

As the three were escorted out they were protesting their innocence.

"Thank you officers, I will take no more talking in church."

They were marched out and there were similar disturbances throughout the service but at least it was a lot quieter than before.

When the service was finished the officers instructed the front row to move first and so and they were escorted back to the house block. When they reached the house block, the officer opened the main gate to let them in.

"Go straight back to your cell but do not stop and talk."

Danny got in his cell and put the kettle and TV on. He was about to lie on the bed then sat up on it instead, made a cup of tea then started his excises. After that he studied the ABC book. The whole day they were all locked up and dinner and evening tea was all served at the door. The server staff, escorted by two officers, served from food trollies. All through that day Danny studied the ABC book though sometimes he did not understand it. It made sense to break it up into sections between exercises and reading.

That night all he was thinking about were his wife and kids, wondering when they were going to come to see him. Who killed Johnny? He thought about his friends. Eden, Kim and her brother Billy, Big Ron's grandson and the landlady. He didn't know Johnny's gay friends at work or at the other pubs he went to. He had no idea why Eden did not clock him out when he said he would. Danny had asked him in the past and he had forgotten a few times. Because he is the wages clerk he would laugh and say, 'Who is doing the wages?' Thinking about work, Danny remembered that he would go in from eight in the morning and stay on the fork lift truck and not move till lunchtime and then the same from lunch time till five o'clock. He hardly moved all day until he went home to eat and watch T.V. till bedtime.

Monday morning came and he knew he had been in prison for over a week now but had still not heard from his solicitors. He put his TV and kettle on at about six thirty then did his exercises and study routine. He knew the ABC book better now, as it came back to him the more he studied. Generally Danny was feeling better and noticed that when he did his routine he didn't worry about anything except for when he sat down on the bed.

The door opened at ten past eight.

"Education Mundy."

Danny wanted to have a quick shower but there was not enough time so he just tidied his cell a little and went to his English class where he turned out to be the first one there.

"Good morning Mr. White."

"Ah good to see you are early. On a Monday not many come in."

"I have finished with the book."

"What? You've finished reading it and memorised it and you know everything in it? So if I ask you any question on it you will be able to answer?"

"Yes the more I studied it, a lot of it came back to me from when I was a youngster."

"Well done Danny! You have answered all the questions correctly. Here is a spelling book which I want you to learn from and I want you to copy the letters on your ABC book as well. Take them with you when you go to lunch."

Some of the class were coming in so Danny went and sat at his desk. After the morning class he went and got his tea then walked straight back to his cell to eat and did his routine. The cell door knocked and he went and opened up. He saw a boy who couldn't be more than twenty years old and under five foot tall, with a baby face.

"Hello mate, can I borrow some sugar?"

He was about to come in.

"One second mate. Wait there, I will get some for you."

He grabbed three sachets of sugar and gave him them, knowing that his supply would be replenished later in the day.

"Have you got two more please mate?"

Danny went and got two more. While giving it to him, it gave him a thought. Now he'd got to stop taking sugar in his tea. That might help him to be fitter and so he gave the lad all he had.

"Thanks mate I will give the same amount back to you. My name is Kevin and I am two doors down."

Danny closed the door and carried on what he was doing. An officer looked in and locked the door at lunch time. Hour an half later the door opened again.

"Mundy, education."

He went as quickly as he could so he could speak to Mr. White alone. Weirdly, when he reached the door it was locked. Then another teacher came and said Mr. White could not be there this afternoon. As Danny was going back to the house block, the classroom assistant met him and said. "We've got a different English teacher today, so you'd best come back with me."

"I will be taking the class today. My name is Mrs. Mills and what is your name?"

"Danny Mundy, Miss."

"Sit down until the rest of the class come, Mundy. Is that the book you are studying? Well done! I am glad you decided to make use of your time while you are here as a lot of prisoners don't make use of the education facility in prison."

Mrs. Mills was in her fifties, slim with no wedding ring on her finger. She was a little posh. The other prisoners were coming in dribs and drabs, though in total, only four more prisoners came for class.

"We will start then."

She turned to face the chalk board and heard a wolf whistle.

"I will not stand for this kind of behaviour in class so please stop."

This went on for a least half an hour and Mrs. Mills called an officer and said, "I will not be teaching these prisoners because of the way some of them are behaving like animals."

"Can you tell me what is the problem or who is the problem Mrs. Mills?"

She pointed to the only English prisoner in the class apart from Danny and the officer pointed his finger and called him.

"I have done nothing."

"Come on. Before you get into more trouble."

"I would like to apologies to you for calling you animals, let's carry on with the lesson because we have lost enough of it already."

The rest of the lesson went well as Danny and the other prisoners wanted to learn. He later discovered that to get a better paid job in prison you needed to pass level one in English. That was about five levels above his class.

"Thank you for the lesson today Mrs. Mills."

"See you later Danny."

The assistant joined him while walking back to the house block and said, "She fancies you."

"Get lost. I've got a wife and kids. Why did you say that?"

"That's the first time she has ever called anyone by their first name."

"But she is married. She is over fifty years old."

"No she is not. Play your cards right and you've got a chance mate."

Danny made his way back to the house block and Brian called him into his cell on the ground floor as they walked by. He went into his cell and left the door half open.

"Hi Brain, can I come in?"

"Yes and have a seat. Would you like a cup of coffee?"

"Yes please."

He sat down on one of three chairs next to where he put some biscuits on the table. For the first time he noticed Brian talking very slowly, pronouncing his words slowly and longer than usual.

"Help yourself to coffee. You know how strong you want it. Just use a proper mug and have some biscuits."

He got a bar of chocolate out of his cupboard and gave it to Danny.

"Have it later, eat the biscuits."

"Thanks Brian, are you sure?"

"YES."

As he was making the coffee, Danny took the chocolate and put it in his pocket. Then he took a biscuit off the table and shoved it in his mouth. Someone came to his door.

"Brian can I have a quarter?"

Brian closed the door, leaving the person outside, then went into his cupboard and got a brand new Amber leaf ounce tobacco. He took a plastic knife, cut it in half and then cut the half into two quarters. He suspiciously looked at the two quarters. He then took his finger and thumb and pulled a chunk out of the quarter and put it in a tin. It was wrapped in toilet paper and he opened the door and gave it to the prisoner who looked at it. He was going to say something but didn't bother and left. Meanwhile Danny drank the coffee from the mug and it felt so good to be drinking out of a proper cup. He took another biscuit and took his time to eat it.

Brian said, "I've got to watch that one. Did you notice I gave him the smaller one? Look what I am going to do now."

He took the bigger quarter which was left and took the razor and carefully cut an eighth of the quarter and then he got a small plastic bag and wrapped it in toilet paper and put it in the bag. The rest was wrapped and he put them in plastic bags.

"Did you notice what I did?"

"No, not really. You got an extra eighth out of an ounce of tobacco."

"Well done Danny! You are learning and I think you have lost a lot of weight in the week you've been here. Keep it up."

He took another biscuit and finished the coffee off.

"A little treat for you. Take that mug when you go. You can have it. Put some biscuits in your pocket as well. I want you to take five packs of burn to my dad. His number is thirty-two."

Brian lifted his mattress up and took a five pack and gave it to Danny, instructing him to put it between his legs. Danny took it without thinking and did what he said.

"Thanks for everything."

Danny hurried up the stairs, hoping no officers would stop and search him. Quietly, he knocked on Brian dad's door.

"Brian sent me."

"Come in son and have a seat. Do you want a drink?"

"No thanks. I just had one with Brian and he gave me this to give you."

"It is supposed to be six packs. You haven't nicked one have you?"

He started to doubt himself.

"No that's all Brian gave me sir."

"Well what have you done with the other one?

"Honestly I did not take it as I don't even smoke."

"Stop worrying kid. I am only kidding son. Here, have a can of drink."

Danny took it and left straight away without saying a word. Soon the bell went for tea so he went and got his plate and queued up. He met Kevin on the way to the queue.

"Hello Danny. The food is crap on Mondays. As a matter of fact it is crap every day."

"OK Kevin."

He really didn't want to talk to anyone but just wanted to grab his food and go to his cell. Thinking about what Brian's dad did today was not nice. He couldn't trust anyone, He could have said six packs and what could he have done? The dad would have made him pay for it. Anyway he got his food and went into the cell, ready to eat. Kevin followed him in and sat on the toilet seat with his dinner in his hand, about to eat.

"Aright mate?"

"No, I need to go to the toilet mate. Can we chat later?"

"Oh sorry mate. I will come back later as you are the only friend I've had since I got in prison."

After Kevin said those words, he left. Danny was surprised as he'd only given him some sugar but he definitely wanted to be alone. The door opened to check if he was in his cell and then locked by an officer.

He found himself thinking about what Brian had said to him regarding making some money and about him losing some weight. He looked at himself and he'd lost some but not much. He heard movement next door but took no notice. He looked at his food which was fish fingers, peas and mash. He picked up his spelling book C.... A.....T. Then he did his training routine. By his door there was a letter and he picked it up and looked at it. With typed letters it must have been from the solicitors. He opened it and on top of the letter he saw a capital B for Banks. He looked at the rest but could not make out what it had said. He wondered if the police had dropped the charges and decided to ask Brian.

Danny pressed the bell and waited, though he kept looking at the letter. He opened it and could make something out but had no idea what it said. The door opened.

"What do you want?"

"I got a letter from my solicitors and I need Brian the listener to read it to me."

"THE BELL IS ONLY TO BE PRESSED FOR EMERGENCIES. IF YOU PRESS THAT BELL AGAIN YOU WILL GET A NICKING!"

It was Officer McCarthy. Someone told Danny about him that he was not very nice.

The door slammed and locked. He was a bit taken aback and started to feel sorry for himself and lie on the bed, getting very depressed. Reminding himself to be strong and not give up, he knew that officer was a bully who wasn't worth worrying over. He would see Brian in the morning so he started his routine until he was tired and went to bed. After his routine he always felt good.

The next morning Danny woke up at six thirty and did his routine. He couldn't wait for the door to open so that he could go and see Brian to read his letter. That morning he kept looking at the TV for the time but it was going so slow that he decided not to keep looking. The door opened and he was ready. As soon as it undid he ran to Brian's cell and knocked on the door but there was no answer. He knocked again but still no answer. The cell door next to his opened.

"He was called out lots of times last night for his job as a listener. He will sleep all day now mate."

"Thanks."

He ran upstairs to Khan's cell and knocked on their door instead.

"Come in Danny. What's the matter? You are breathing heavy."

Catching his breath, he thought that he must remember to use his asthma pump more.

"Morning Khan, can you please read this letter for me? I think it's from my solicitors."

Within a few seconds he read it.

"It's not much Danny. All it says is your solicitors are coming to see you on Thursday at 10am."

"Is that all? Nothing about the police dropping the charges?"

"I told you that when I read your papers, they have charged you. Now you've got to defend yourself against charges or go guilty and I know you are not guilty. Sorry about that. Where are you going now?"

"Thanks, I am going to education."

Khan went back in his cell.

"Who was that?"

"Danny. He wanted me to read his letter from the solicitors who are coming Thursday. Did you manage to get the table and chair for him?"

"I am working on it. Brian has reserved some at the stores."

"It must be for Danny. Tell you what Jamal. Let's go and get them before he does and give them to Danny. That would put us in a good light with him."

"I'm pretty sure he already likes us."

"He can like us a little more then."

"You said that Skinny next door was asking about the Muslim class."

"I bet he wanted sugar or something?"

"Yes you are right again. Just give it to him but be very careful as he and Joe are working for Brian and his dad hates Muslims. Also Wade is back as well."

As he opened the class door, Danny realised he was late. Most of the class were there and everyone was sitting down.

"Sorry I am late Mr. White. I had a letter from my solicitors and had to ask someone to read if for me."

"Any time you want help with any forms or letters you are welcome to ask me. Have a seat."

Mr. White faced the class.

"I had reports that this class was badly behaved during the lesson with Mrs. Mills. I am not happy about that as when I am not here you represent me. Do you understand? Do you all understand?"

"Yes Sir."

"I understand the main culprit is not here today anyway. Let's get on with today's class."

When the class was over Danny stayed back as Mr. White wanted to have a word.

"You've done so well with the spelling book and now need to start copying from this new book. I think you are improving so we've got to keep it going. By next month you will be able to write your letters. It will be nice to write to your wife and kids. Maybe in a few months' time you will be able to read your own letters too."

"Thank you Sir."

He made his way back to the block. When he got back to the block Kevin was there. He wanted to go and see Brian but he stopped him.

"Where are going mate? I was looking for you."

"I am going to see Brian."

"Oh that's why I came looking for you. Brian was looking for you this morning."

"Thanks. I'll see you later."

Danny went to Brian's cell but he was not there. His dad and Wade were in there and the door was wide open as he looked in.

"Come in son. Brian will be back in a minute."

Wade looked at Danny strangely.

"Don't I know you?"

Brian's dad said, "No, he is new. You don't know him."

"I've got to get something. Tell Brian I will see him later."

He left as quickly as he could and raced straight to his cell. There was Kevin waiting for him. Danny went into his cell and he followed him in.

"Danny, I want to give you a heads up to keep away from Brian and his dad as they run this induction block."

"What do mean induction block?"

"After three or four weeks we will be moved to another block, probably house block two. Brian and his dad run this block so make sure you don't borrow anything from them and if you do make sure you pay them back. I think they've got people in other blocks working for them as well and the whole of the prison. They've got people on the outside collecting money for them as well."

"How do you know all this?"

"From the other jail I was at, they warned me to keep away from them."

"They only give me things. They've never charged me for anything."

"Then they must be recruiting you to work for them in the other blocks. Once you go to the gym and lose that Bobby Charlton hair do you will be all right to work for them."

"How do you know all this?"

"I've being in jail since I was fifteen and I have learnt a lot. If I was as big as you I could make a lot of money. I don't talk to a lot of prisoners but notice all what's going on. I see how cons move and where they go, who they go with and who they speak to. I notice who is hiding from who. Who lock themselves away and don't come out of their cells because they owe. In the other jail I came from, because of my knowledge, a drugs dealer used to ask me who to trust and who is a grass. Who can pay back any information needed about anyone? They will ask me and pay me for that information. They don't want to chase cons to get their money or burn back as they like a clean deal with no problems because that can come on top chasing of cons for what they owe."

"So what did you do to be in prison for so long?"

"After my father died it was just my mum and I living together for years, then she met this fella. At first he was good but then he started to beat me and tell me to get out of the house all the time."

"Didn't you tell your mum?"

"He bullied my mum and she kept telling him to leave."

"He took no notice and threatened mum that if she went to the police he would kill her. She was scared out of her wits."

"So what happened?"

"I went to the petrol station and bought petrol then waited until mum was out and he was upstairs sleeping. I poured petrol all over the stairs and all of the downstairs then put a match in the letter box and ran across the road. By the time I got across the road the house was on fire. I saw a raging fire through the windows."

Chapter Fourteen

Danny was shocked and spent the rest of the night reflecting. The next morning he was called in to meet the Solicitor.

"If you can think of anything else, no matter how small, let me know. I am afraid I've got some bad news for you though. I am leaving Banks and Banks. This will be the last time I will see you."

"That's all I need - someone new. Can't I stay with you, or can you give Raj the details? You know my case. I don't want someone new."

"You will have to write to Banks and Banks and ask to change solicitors but, as I told you right in the beginning, the judges don't like to change. But try. There is not much more we can say at this moment in time. I have to say goodbye and all the best for the future. Here is my card for my new firm."

They both stood up and shook hands then he left and Danny sat down and waited for the officer to say when he could go back.

Danny went back to the Wing like he was walking in a dream, thinking he was going to spend the rest of his life in prison. He needed to provide for his family. Brian said he could make money in here working for him, and help his family who had nothing. They lived in a council house. Danny would try and work for Brian and buy a house for his family. He reached his cell and there was no Kevin so he started to do his exercises. Lately he found he was getting fitter. As a result he didn't need insulin and his breathing was a lot better. He had got stronger and he was doing all the right things so he would start going to gym next week. He'd already been to the gym induction. The door knocked and he opened it.

"What happened with the solicitors, Danny?"

"Bad news, Kevin. They need to find out the time my brother was killed but that could vary. It's very bad news and he reckons there is no chance. I will spend the rest of my life in jail unless I can find out who killed my brother and no chance of that with me being in here."

"I don't know what to say mate."

"I think I will work for Brian and start gym next week to get fitter and stronger."

"I will come with you and train you."

"What do you know about training in the gym?"

Kevin took off his shirt.

"Wow, you are a pocket battle ship. You are all muscles."

"I took all my badges for gym instructor. In fact I have over thirty certificates for different subjects."

"How come you say people bully you?"

"The cons that are twice my size. Why do you think I have been in prison so long? I burned three people's cells that had bullied me. So, because of what I have done, they have kept me longer. Nobody bullies me anymore but this is a new jail and people don't know me, so I will probably get bullied again."

"I'm not looking forward to tomorrow, having to tell my wife what the solicitors said. I am not going to see her if I have to spend the rest of my life in prison. How much do you think I will get if I go guilty?"

"You don't want to go guilty mate. That's twenty five years plus and then you have to wait for parole. You've got to fight it. If you lose that thirty years there is a chance you might be lucky. Dinner time mate. Just get your plate and we will go down together."

"I don't feel hungry but you go and get yours."

Kevin left Danny and shut the door, putting his TV on and lay on the bed. He felt like crying then he thought he had got to be strong for his family. He would go and see Brian later. The door knocked and he opened it.

"I've got you some grub as you need to eat something mate. You don't want your wife and kids seeing you like this tomorrow. Many times when my mum came, I felt like crying because I am here. I need to look after her. That's why at this jail, I will keep out of people's way and try not to get bullied."

"Thanks for the food Kevin. You are right."

They sat down and started to eat. Kevin was on the toilet eating then a pink sheet of paper was put under the door and he picked it up.

"What's that Kevin?"

"This is your canteen sheet and the white sheet underneath is your wage slip. You've got nearly nine pounds on your sheet Danny."

"How come?"

"Your pay for education and Muslim time and church."

"They payed me for church?"

"Yes so you'd better fill in the canteen sheet and hand it in in the morning as if you put it in late you will get no canteen."

"Can you put two tins of tuna for me?"

"Nothing else?"

"No I don't need anything else as I have to pay Archie."

"All done. I am going to do mine now."

After Kevin left, Danny looked at the sheet and the wages sheet and saw what he could figure out.

The door locked and he looked at the food. He picked at it then left it on the table, thinking about life, work, wife, kids and Johnny having been with him in the pub. He just watched TV now but did not know what he was watching. Danny didn't feel like moving from this cell or going to education.

The cell door opened and he jumped up.

"Mundy... education."

The door knocked and opened at the same time.

"How are you feeling?"

"Shit Kevin, I don't want to go to education this afternoon."

"Go mate. It will take your mind off things. If you don't go you will lose money plus the time will go quickly for you rather than being banged up the rest of the day. Otherwise the time will go slowly."

"You are right mate. I will go, it will take my mind off things."

Danny went to the class where Mr. White gave them so much interesting work with lots of questions and answers. The time went so quickly after the class was over.

Danny had not seen Brian for a few days. He decided he would go and see him. He went to his cell but it was locked so he went up the stairs. There was no Kevin. What was going on? He went into the cell and sat down. The door was open very wide without been knocked. It was Wade. He was as tall as Danny but very slim. He just had a T-shirt on. All Danny could remember was what Delroy told him. On their own the bully doesn't want to know. Danny shouted at him loudly.

"What the fuck do you want in my cell? Get out!"

"Move me out."

He slowly came towards Danny. Danny rushed him and he put his two hands on his throat and tried to push him out of his cell. He got him onto the landing and then pushed him towards the safety rails. Danny saw Brian on his left.

Wade said, "OK mate. I was only having a joke pal. Ask Brian."

"I am not your pal so just keep away from me."

"OK, OK."

"Hello Danny?" said Brian.

Danny did not answer him. Instead he kept looking at Wade.

"Go away Gary. I want to talk to Danny alone."

Danny let Wade go.

"What is going on Danny? This is not like you."

Danny went into his cell and Brian followed him in.

"Have a seat. I saw my solicitors today."

Danny sat on the toilet seat and gave Brian the chair.

"I am sorry mate, you just have to got to face up to it. You must make a bit of money on the side as you are getting fitter and you were already strong. If I hadn't stopped you, you would have put Wade over the rails. You've got to be very careful with your temper in here because you will get shipped out in a flash. You have to let the punter know what you can do then they will be scared of you. If you want to get someone, you get them in the showers or in their cell, not in view of the cameras or the screws. Wade told me you owe Archie four tins of Tuna. I will cover that and I will see Archie and tell him."

"I owe him one for my washing that he did. I don't owe four. He said that because I didn't pay him last week I've got to give him two this week. Work it out. I've only been here just over a week."

"Are you sure?"

"Yes. Listen I will speak to him myself. I have put down two tins for him."

"Who filled in your canteen sheet?"

"Kevin. He is being very helpful to me. So what do you want me to do to earn money for my family?"

"Do you feel up to it? You are a big man and you were going to damage Wade. You can't let something like that happen in plain view of everyone like you did just now. It is good in a way because Wade has a bit of a reputation so the word will get around and you will earn respect off other prisoners. You will probably go to Wing four when your induction is over. I've got Burns working there for me but he is starting to take the mickey. His money is supposed to go in my account by Monday and Thursday and he has not been paying money in my account."

"I can't go there and take over just like that."

"No, I will tell them you are coming to help him and to learn the trade."

"There is not much to learn is there?"

"There is a lot to learn such as how to cut the burn, spice, heroin, crystals, weed, paper and banking money on the out. All these things you have to learn. I am selling in here and mobile phones, trainers and clothes. You need to learn the prices of everything."

"How do you get all these things in here?"

"Easy, you need not worry about. You have not asked what you are going to earn a week."

"Ok, can I earn £10 per week?"

"You are having a giraffe. A lot more than that. At least ten times more."

"What, a hundred? Starting from when?"

"Today, but you have got to drop the Muslims completely."

"You stop talking to them completely."

"I am a man of honour and they helped me when no else did. I can't forget that. I need the money but I can't do that. For the first time since I have been in prison I feel good, like the man I did on the outside."

"Sorry to hear that Danny. I thought you would have taken this very generous offer I made you. If us English and the Muslims were to have a head to head which side would you take if you were working for me?"

"I would take your side. I will be loyal to the man I work for."

"Let me rethink my offer to you. I will speak to my dad and come back to you. I will speak to you later."

He shut the door, leaving Danny thinking about £100 per week. He was an idiot to refuse that but fair is fair. The Muslims had been kind to him and when it kicked off he was going to be in the middle. The door knocked.

Kevin knocked on his cell door and walked in.

"I heard everything. That's a good offer mate. The Muslim means nothing to you, they are not your family. That £100 could look after your family."

"Let's get our food and we'll talk when we come back."

They walked down the stairs.

"Why are the cons looking at us?"

"They are looking at you. They either saw or heard what happened with you and Wade."

"Some of them must be Wade's mates."

"Yes, you've got to be more careful now."

They got their food and came back into Danny's cell where Kevin sat on the toilet seat and Danny on the chair.

"Kevin do you know what honour is?"

"Yes you look after me and I will look after you."

"Suppose Brian offered you £100 to burn my cell and nobody would know and you are going home the next day. Would you do it?

"Your cell?"

"Yes my cell. You see... you had to think about it so I know the answer."

"NO, no I would never do anything to you, you are my mate."

"Well that's honour. If you do not burn my cell."

The door opened. The officer came in looking for Kevin.

"Don't you have your own cell?

"Sorry sir."

The door locked. £100 per week. That was a lot of money tax free. It was half what he got from the warehouse after tax. Danny would see his wife tomorrow and speak to her about the offer. That meant he would have to tell her what the solicitors said. Maybe he shouldn't tell her yet as it might upset her.

Danny supposed if he asked Brian to help him find who killed his brother he might help. His head had been so confused since his brother's death. He was a bit surprised about what he'd done to Wade. Would Danny have done that if he hadn't heard the news from the solicitors? Deep in his thoughts was the worry of fighting with anyone in prison as he knew that would go against him in court. He had fights in the pub when his dad kicked off a few times but that was years ago. The men in there were fit and some of them were super fit. Being fit earned money in there. They had got to be to get their money if prisoners that owed them didn't want to pay.

The radiator pipe knocked but he took no notice. It knocked harder and there was shouting out of the window.

"Danny it's me."

He put his head close to the window.

"Is that you Kevin?"

"Yes, I am next door in number eleven."

"How come?"

"That guy moved out yesterday and I asked if I can have his cell. I forgot to tell you and something else. Put your ears by the radiator pipe, I want tell you something that I don't want anyone else to hear."

"I was cleaning the showers when Joe, Skinny and Wade came in so I hid in the last cubical and they were talking about getting someone."

"Who? Who?"

"Wait wait, when I knock the pipe twice or you knock you can talk."

Knock and knock again.

"Who did you hear they are going to get?"

Knock and knock.

"The only person I can think of is you. I will keep an ear out tomorrow. I have your back Danny, don't worry."

Knock and knock.

"Thanks. I will see you tomorrow."

They wanted Danny so if he was going be in there for the rest of his life he was going to hurt a few of them. The officers knew Danny doesn't cause any trouble. They knew Wade and his mates were trouble makers. Probably that would come up in court as they were known as trouble makers. He would defend himself like when he was with his dad. Danny would start to practise his routines for the rest of the night. Danny's dad taught him never to be afraid of anyone.

Chapter Fifteen

The next morning he woke up at six thirty to make a cup of tea and start his exercise routines. When he was tired he stopped and read his book and did copy writing. He looked at the time which showed seven forty-five. He must have been training for over an hour which meant he was lasting much longer now. He had some cornflakes. Waiting eagerly for the cell door to open, he was keen to have a shower and wear those jogging bottoms and top to go and see his wife. The door opened.

"Visits, Mundy."

He had his towel ready and he ran to the showers. When he went in and started to shower someone was coming in and he'd forgotten what Kevin had said the night before. All he was thinking about was the wife. However he got ready for a fight. Someone came in the showers just after him. Danny was about to punch.

"Don't do that Danny, it's only me."

"I could have hurt you."

"I told you I will watch your back."

"Piss off. Let me have my shower in peace. It's too early in the morning for them cunts, they are all asleep."

"I will see you later at your cell."

About ten minutes' later he got out of the shower and as he walked out of the shower unit there was Kevin waiting with the mop in his hands.

"I told you to go."

"I am here to do my job, my job is to clean the showers."

"OK, OK you made your point. I can't be too careful."

On his way to the cell he looked around to see if Kevin followed him but he didn't. He dried and changed. He looked at himself in the plastic window and noticed that his beard was long because of two weeks growth. Also his hair was long so he thought he ought to cut it off. People looked at him and laughed at his Bobby Charlton hair. Danny wanted to cut it off and shave his head so he'd got no hair instead of trying to cover the bald patch in the middle. Kevin came into his cell again.

"You look smart mate. Your missus will love you. Why don't you get rid your of your hair? Especially that bit you've got covering that bald patch in the middle?"

"You are right. When I come back from the visit, let's borrow a pair of clippers and cut if off and my beard."

"I've got a pair of clippers. I will cut it for you now."

"How comes? I haven't seen you cutting anyone's hair on the wing."

"Not bothering yet here. People don't want to pay a tin of Tuna and then I've got problems getting my Tuna."

"Well when I come back from visits you can cut mine and I am telling you now I am not giving you a tin of Tuna."

"See you later Danny. Have a good visit."

THE VISIT

Danny was very nervous going to the visiting hall. This was the first time he had been apart from her in nearly twenty years. He walked slowly to the exit of the block. They all waited for the officer to let them out. When he was let out, all the other prisoners ran to the visiting hall. He walked, even though everyone else was running when he got there. The officers were searching everyone and they collected the I.D. cards. Then the prisoners were given a coloured sash and searched, then told a table number to sit at. Danny was given his number and he looked for it but there she was at the seat. The kids saw him and ran to him. Amanda was ten and Kim was twelve. They both ran towards him. Danny picked both of them up with each hand and took them to the seats where his wife had tears starting to fall from her eyes. Danny sat down and he somehow managed to hug all three of them.

"What has happened to you Danny? You have lost so much weight. I would not have recognised you if it wasn't for your hair. Where did you get those clothes?"

"Some of the Muslims gave me them. They have looked after me. How have you been managing? Did my firm give you my wages?"

"Yes but I had to fill out a lot of paper work for it. I had to go to the job centre to get a full time job. I have asked where I did my part time job for full time work and they said they will sort something full time for me. But why have you lost so much weight? You look better for it. What did the solicitors say?"

"He said he needs to know exactly the time of Johnny's death. He said that could be either way. You told him I love Johnny more than the kids. That's not true."

"I know. I only said that. I know you love them. So we've now got to wait for them. Oh Danny I don't know what to do without you. I miss you so much and the kids."

"You can get something for them at the tuck shop and get me a burger please."

"Can we come to the tuck shop mummy?"

"Don't you want to stay with daddy?"

"I will stay with dad."

"Good girl Amanda, come and sit on my lap. What have you been doing while I have been away?"

"Mum has been sorting paperwork out. She's been crying a lot about not having money. Then she got your money from your work place so we are good now and she is going to get a full time job. She is spending more time with us on our homework now."

"That is very good. I am learning to read and write now too."

"You are not?"

"I am. The teacher said I am a natural. I will be better than you soon."

"Ok spell my name."

"That's easy. I gave you that name, A.m.a.n.d.a."

"Ok I will give you a hard one. Spell apple."

"A...P...L...E."

"Nearly right but you missed another P. You are getting good dad. Here comes mum with our stuff."

They all were so happy when they ate. They were laughing and joking but he could sense the sadness in everyone. Linda was crying most of the time while the kids were testing him on spelling. He didn't know if he was right or wrong but they were laughing so much. In the old days if anything was wrong he would go on and on about it. Linda would get fed up with him. Danny did not talk about being inside or what she going to do. She took the lead and he followed. They smiled a lot at each other. The bell went.

"Visiting time is up."

"They have rang the bell. That means you've got to go love."

He kissed and hugged the girls and then his wife.

"I nearly forgot I've written you a letter and I put twenty pounds in it. They've got it at the desk."

"Thanks love. When I get it I will write you back."

"What Danny?"

"Dad can read and write now mum, only a little."

"That's very good Danny, looking forward to receiving a letter from you. Bye love."

"Bye dad. Bye Dad."

Danny stood up and watched them leave. He did not want them to see him crying. What were his wife and kids going through? He must do what he could for them. They needed money. His girls were growing and it'd only been two weeks. Soon they were going to have boyfriends. Danny was going to see Brian and ask for the job even if he would have to take sides. Danny would go and speak to Khan and tell him. No hard feelings but that was the least he could

do, to pre-warn them about what he was going to do for his family. Surely they had to understand.

END OF VISIT

As he walked back to the wing, three officers were running towards his block, just as he got to the entrance gate.

"Mundy go straight to your cell and lock you door."

"Yes sir."

Danny walked slowly back to the cell, looking all around to see what was going on but everyone was banged up. When he got to his cell he sat on the chair then got up and filled the kettle with water, put it on the pipe, knocked and sat down. The pipe knocked again, he put his ears to the radiator's pipe and knocked.

"Did you hear what happened to Jamal?"

Knock, knock.

"No I have just come back from visits but I saw some officers running here. What happened to Jamal?"

Knock, knock.

"I am not sure but the word is Jamal came back early from work to prepare the Moshe for the afternoon when three people attacked him in his cell."

Knock, knock.

"Is he badly beaten? Did an ambulance come for him or is he at health care?"

Knock, knock.

"I don't know where he is. It was not you they wanted when I heard them plotting in the showers".

Knock, knock.

"You think it was Wade, Joe and Skinny?"

Knock, knock.

"It must be them and Brian and his dad must have set it up. Don't forget I heard them in the showers."

Knock, knock.

"The Muslims won't like that. They have Jamar this afternoon, and do you think they will stop it?"

Knock, knock.

"The prison will not stop it, but it will be lock down for the next few days. We will feed at the landing, one at a time. The only people that they will let out are kitchen and server workers."

Knock, knock.

"Kevin, I've got somethings to do, I will speak to you later."

Danny wanted to go and see Jamal or Khan and let them know how sorry he was. He wasn't sure he still wanted to work for Brian and his dad. He needed to look after his family now. His wife had to do full time work now. She had never complained in all the years they were together and he hadn't helped her at all. She had done everything herself in that council house. All he did was work and give her the money and take it back to buy drink.

The door opened.

"Lunch. Do you want a baguette or a baguette?"

"Are you trying to be funny mate?"

"Sorry mate, cheese or ham," the server worker replied.

"We haven't got time to mess about. Give him a ham one as he is not a Muslim and hurry up about it," said Officer McCarthy.

"Thanks."

The door locked but he did not fancy anything to eat. He had a burger normally. In the past he would eat until he couldn't eat anymore on the out. Danny now didn't do that. He preferred exercising and he was studying so he could write to his wife a letter. Later the door opened.

"Get packed. Here are two plastic bags. You are going to another Wing."

The officer left the door open and then opened Kevin's door and told him the same thing.

Danny started to put everything he had (which was not much) into the bags and the officer came back.

"Meet me by the gate and I will take you there."

"Danny I am glad we are moving, aren't you?"

"I am but I wanted to see Jamal or Khan before I went to thank them for what they've done me. I will go and see them in the Moshe next week if I don't see them before. Come on, let's go to the gate."

"Meet me by the gate."

"Where are you going?"

Danny went to the gate and waited until the officer came.

"Where is your mate?"

"I think he is still in the toilet sir. Look, he is coming."

The officer opened the gate and went ahead of them.

"Where did you go Kevin?"

"I went to listen outside of Joe and his mate's cell."

"And?"

"They were still in there."

"How come they are not in segregation unit?"

"They probably didn't beat up Jamal."

"Come on you two, hurry up. I've got to get back here."

As they reached the wing Kevin spoke.

"Sir I forgot my I.D. card and paperwork. Can I go back and get it?"

"Yes hurry and get it. Meet me at A wing."

They walked along a long causeway until they reached a door which he opened that led into A wing. They strolled into A wing.

"Wait by the office Mundy."

"Yes Sir."

A few minutes' later.

"You, Mundy, follow me. Go on the threes. Number thirty-three will be your new cell."

Danny picked up his bags and walked up to the threes. When he found the cell he knocked on the door and went in. There were two prisoners laying on their beds and there was a cloud of smoke in the cell.

"What do you want mate?"

"Nothing."

Danny went back outside and shut the door. He thought to himself that he was not going through all he went through again. He went back downstairs and to the office and knocked on the door. The same officer opened the door.

"Sir I suffer with asthma and I don't smoke. That was a smoker's cell you sent me to."

"Wait there. I will be out in minute."

Danny was looking for Kevin but he had still not come. He looked around the block where it wasn't as clean as the induction block. A few of the prisoners looked at him and shook and nodded their heads when they saw him looking back at them.

"Mundy go on the twos and to cell number eighteen."

"Yes Sir."

Danny picked his bags up and went up the stairs to the cell. There wasn't far to go. Danny opened the door. There were two single beds, not three. It had two cupboards, a table and a chair. It was looking good, just needing a little cleaning and would be good to go. He looked at the two mattresses on the bed, pressed them, turned them over and picked the best one. He looked under both of the beds but spoke too soon as they were full of rubbish. He left his bags outside and went and got a mop, a broom, a dustpan and cleaning stuff. He put disinfectant on the toilet and sink, then he pulled all the things from underneath the beds and put them in a plastic bag. He looked up and there was Kevin.

"We are going to be banged up together. You can't mate because you smoke. I don't want a smoker in my cell."

"I told the officer I didn't smoke so he will not put me with you."

"I told him I don't smoke. I won't smoke in our cell mate so don't worry."

"If you do, we will fall out mate. Please start cleaning the toilet and sink. Just leave the bags outside as I am going to mop up the cell. Come on. Don't just stand there and look at me."

"Yes Sir."

Danny cleaned the cell. The walls were very dirty and the window sills were dirty. He wiped down his mattress and Kevin's. He thought he would need to do it all again later. Danny checked the toilet. Kevin did a good job, to his surprise. Danny brought the bags in and noticed the other prisoners on the block were looking at new meat.

"It looks like grub time Kevin. Get your plate mate."

They both got their plates and queued up. Lots of the prisoners had their food already so they didn't wait long to get theirs. They went and sat in their cell and just when they got in the cell it was bang up time so the door locked.

"The afternoon went quick. Do you know anybody on this block Kevin?"

"No mate."

"How are we going to get news on what happened at the induction block?"

"We will Danny. Jail is where the news travels the fastest. What are you going to do about working for Brian and his dad?"

"I don't know mate. I really don't know."

"How about us setting up on our own without Brian. Just me and you together?"

"Kevin he has someone over here working for him and his dad. Burns. That means if we set up, we are going to clash with Burns and his crew. Plus we have to find out who else is selling on this block."

"How are we going to get drugs and phones etc.?"

"We have to start just with burn and go from there. I could speak to Burns and tell him what Brian said but I think we will hear something soon before Monday. Have you got any burn coming tomorrow?"

"One pack."

"That's a start. You don't need it. You are not going to smoke anymore."

"But."

"No buts, we've got to start somewhere mate. Let's look at the cell and what we need to do. Your bed on the left, mine on the right, plenty of space between the toilet at the end of your bed. We need two small cupboards underneath the window and two big cupboards at the end of my bed."

"I plan to give the sink and toilet another going over. We need to paint the cell and do the floor. The painters normally charge a pack of burn and the same for the floor. We can strip and polish and get proper curtains."

"My wife sent me twenty pounds in a letter. I am waiting for that then perhaps we can do the cell."

"I will start cutting hair again."

"When they want a haircut, say they have to pay you."

"The first thing I am going to do is get rid of Bobby Charlton so come and sit on the chair while I get the shavers. When I've finished with you, nobody will want to mess with you or us."

"Look in the mirror Danny. What do you think you look like man?"

"I don't look the same. I look mean, my wife will not like it."

"I am glad you like it."

"Thanks. I am going to do my exercises and study."

"How many press ups can you do Danny?"

"Not many. When I first started I could just do two or three. Now perhaps fifteen. Now I am getting stronger."

"Look at me and start counting."

"1, 2, 3, 4, 5, 6, 7….55, 56…150.

"How many can you manage in one go?"

"About five hundred in one go."

"Stop it. That's enough. I see why you've got no weight to lift. I've got to lift twenty five stones."

"You've just got to keep doing it every day. I did it now for nearly eight years. One thing we need to do is shadow box because when we start our business we are going to get trouble and we have put our marker down on someone. By the way you are about twenty stone now mate and you must have lost a lot of weight since you have been here."

That evening they talked. Kevin was a wealth of knowledge about prison and how it works and about the types of prisoners. The murderers, fraudsters, the pedophiles, street crime and rapists. His best knowledge was about who were good payers and could possibly have money and scams outside. They were doing their exercises when the door opened. All through that night they talked and it was good to have someone in the cell with him. In the morning he woke up and did his exercises. Then he took his book out. Kevin was up as well.

"Morning associations."

"I thought we would be banged up all weekend. We are lucky Danny."

"Kevin try and learn who is doing what and if you find Burns let me know. I am going to stay in here and I want to do some copy writing. I have to write my wife and kids a letter."

"I will see you later."

"What have you come back for Kevin?"

"We can go to the yard outside."

"That's good news. I need some fresh air. I am coming."

They went outside where the yard had green grass in the middle of a square of concrete. Where the prisoners walked around some were jogging at a slow pace. Some were laying on the grass. Some were playing chess and draughts and some were doing pressed ups.

"There are not many outside prisoners here Kevin."

"It's too early for most of them because they are probably sleeping. Come, let's jog around Danny."

"Don't go too fast. I've got asthma so let's just go at a walking pace please or I will not keep up with you."

They were jogging for about two minutes then a walking pace. Danny started to get out of breath and started to walk but Kevin was still jogging. Danny continued to walk around when someone called him.

"You Mundy?"

"Yes I am. Who is asking?"

He was dressed in a sleeveless Hugo Boss shirt and wasn't particularly muscly but the sleeveless top showed what little he had. He wore Hugo Boss shorts and Gucci trainers.

"I am Burns. Brian sent a message that you were coming to see me to learn the business. But there is no business to teach mate. Brian and his dad are going to be finished after what happened to Jamal the Muslim. I am working for myself, so when you see him tell him what I said."

Three prisoners joined him to reinforce what he had said. They were shabby, dressed in old clothes. At that moment Kevin stopped jogging and walked towards them and stopped.

"Who is this your minder?" Burns said, looking at Kevin.

Kevin looked back at all of them and said.

"Are these your three stooges?"

The four of them walked closer to them in a menacing way, got to arm's length away and stopped.

"You two want your heads kicked in?"

"No need for that is there. I am only little. Come on Danny. We should carry on jogging."

"Listen Burns you've got to tell Brian that he is out of your business yourself. I am not your lackey."

"Mundy don't think about starting your own business here. This Wing is mine."

"I will see you later, come on Kev."

"Kevin did you see how he was dressed and did you see his boys were dressed like tramps? He does not look after them."

"Danny I don't think he is all that. He is just a showoff. Let's go and get our canteen."

They got their canteen and took it to their cell.

"I've got two tins of Tuna for that Archie for doing my laundry."

"That debt is squashed as you are not on his wing anymore. So you don't have to pay him because he's got to catch you first."

"Kevin what about putting out the burn?"

"I will be honest with you. I could do with a fag, I am dying."

"It's yours. Do what you like but you did say you were not going to smoke and we're going to do some business with the burn you are getting this week. Remember when I spoke to you about honour I asked you a question. Keeping your word is honour. It's your choice mate. I am not telling you nothing."

"I really need it Danny. I will take a quarter and give out the rest. I will cut this into four eighths and keep the quarter whole and only cut when needed or it will get too dry. I will show you what to do."

Kev put the pack of tobacco on the table. Then he took a plastic razor and broke off the head where the blade was. Then he pushed an old blade that he had in between the blade and plastic and cut out the tiny plastic rivets. He pulled off the plastic covering and then got a brand new blade.

"Danny do you see how I get the blade?"

"Yes."

"I will show you something else. Get me a prison toothbrush."

"Here it is."

"Thanks. Look what I am doing. I will get the blade. Slit the handle side of the brush. It's hard work. Now you see the blade can fit into the toothbrush. I will tape it up to half of the blade and now you've got a blade with a handle. The cowards make it longer by taping another brush to it, taking off the brush side of it."

Danny cut the ounce first in half, then cut that in half again and the same again so he'd got four eighths, then he wrapped it in toilet paper. Then he packed them tightly in plastic bags and took a bit off each eighth before bagging them up. The other half ounce he cut in two and wrapped before taking a bit off each then wrapping them tightly. The quarter he had left made four roll ups for himself and he put the rest in his pocket.

"I think I will sell one roll up for a milk."

Then he took the tobacco he had put in his pocket and made four more roll ups but they were a lot thinner than the ones he made before."

"Why did you make those last four so thin?"

"Those are the ones we are going to swap for milk."

"There is hardly any tobacco in them roll ups, what are we going to do with the milk?"

"We then sell the milk for Tuna or anything we want on the canteen. You will need stamps soon so we can swap for that or money, maybe fifty for a tenner".

"What prisoners would be so low to do that?"

"There are the spice heads that soon as they get their canteen go and buy drugs or pay their debts, then borrow straight away again. That is how the circle is."

"Can't stop. I've got to go and look for some business before lunch and bang up for the weekend."

"I am going to church Sunday morning and shall put the word around that we do burn or snout which is what old time cons say."

"See if you can find out about Jamal?"

"See you later."

At lunchtime Danny couldn't see Kevin. The yard was shut so he must have been in the block. Danny went and got lunch. He went and queued up. Danny still couldn't see him but hoped he was not in trouble. Danny got his lunch and went to the cell.

"Where you been? I have been looking for you. Go quickly and get your lunch before it's all gone."

"I will thanks."

Kevin went and got his lunch. Danny had got to keep an eye on Kevin or the business wouldn't get off the ground. He knew he couldn't do things that were going to draw attention to either of them. Danny carried on eating his food and when Kevin walked back to him he seemed excited.

"Go on tell me then. Tell me what are you so happy about?"

"I got rid of all the burn."

"The four eighths?"

"Yes plus I have buyers for the other quarter."

Danny took everything in and thought about it.

"These prisoners you gave the burn to, do you know them?"

"No not really. They live on this spur."

"Do you know where they live? Like the number of their cell?"

"No."

"Everyone got their canteen today and they are skint already and are borrowing. How do you know when next week comes they might not bother to pay us and go and buy from someone else?"

"That's where you come in. I told them I am working for you and they wanted to know who you were. I told them you were the guy who was going to throw Wade over the railings in plain day light. The guy with that shaven head looked like a scared man. One eighth I swapped for some spice that's worth as much as a half an ounce of tobacco. We've started Danny so get ready to make money."

"Or get ready for trouble. I do wonder what I am getting myself into."

"I forgot to tell you Brian said to call for a listener tonight."

Danny did all his exercises and reading and writing. Kevin was not his normal self. Something was wrong but Danny didn't know what. Had it been a good idea to share cells with him? Laying on the bed and thinking, Danny pressed the bell.

Later that night, the door opened.

"Who called for a listener?"

"I did sir."

"Come this way," the officer said.

He took him to a small waiting room and told him to wait. He locked the door and later on the door unlocked then Brian walked in.

"How are you Danny?"

"Not bad, Kevin and I are banged up together. I spoke to Burns and he said you and your dad are finished and that he is working for himself. Those were his exact words. I don't know what to say."

"I heard he'd been shouting his mouth off about being his own boss. When he can't get any gear to sell, let's see what is he is going to do. He had better not leave the Wing or he is a dead man."

"Why did you sort out Jamal?"

"I will be honest with you, my dad is old school and he hates all foreigners, pedophiles and gays. I could not stop him. I am his son. I've got to do what he tells me. I am his son and it had to be done. What are you going to do about it?"

"I don't know, I will be honest with you. I am grateful for all the help you gave me. I didn't like what happened to Jamal. When I came back from visiting my wife I was going to join you. I heard what happened to Jamal and I changed my mind. I have been banged up with Kev and we are going to start on our own business, in fact we have started."

"I am glad you told me, I know already. A little warning that Kevin is a spice head. You picked a good partner to start your business. Little advice - you could do well in that Wing as it makes a lot of money. I could supply you, but you will have to clash with Burns. To be honest that will suit me fine. You take him on and put him out of business. Going back to you and Kevin being successful you've got to be in charge of everything going out and coming in, keep an account of everything and that will hold him off for a little while using drugs. Eventually you will have to break your partnership with him because he is a user. Why do you think he is in prison for so long? He should have been out at least five years ago. With users the more they get, the more they want and it will come to that stage. Whatever they get will never be enough. I like you Danny and that is why I am telling you about Kevin. Ask him when you go back. You need someone to teach you the ropes. Kevin can do that."

"I had a little feeling he was like that, but I did not think it was that bad. I can add and multiply. I know my maths. I think that is all I need. Oh and the names. That should be easy as I am in Mr. White's class. What's going to happen about the Muslims? Are they going to retaliate?"

"Danny, I'm not sure as their Imam and Father Tim are sorting things out. I hope things will be alright but things might still kick off in a big way. One way or another, sooner or later."

"You and your dad have been in a long time?"

"I've been in longer than him, he's only been in five years. I have been in nearly seven. I've got two girls. Another three years then I am out."

"What area are you from out there?"

"Canterbury and around Kent. Originally my dad was born there."

"You are in for breaking the law. I am in here for nothing."

"That's how it goes mate. Sorry but you've got to try and look after your family. That's what I did. I got two houses and I rent them out. I make £1,000 a month off each of them and my missus lives in our council house. You are going to be here for a long time. Don't let that Kevin mug you off. He is going to use you for his drug use. We've been here a long time now. Any time you want a chat, let me know. All the best."

He rang the bell then a few minutes later an officer came and took Danny back to the cell. On the way back he was thinking about whether to confront Kevin or not. Could Brian be lying to him? He would sleep on it and keep an eye on him so he could see how he behaved. Just like Brian said, Danny needed to learn the business. That was strange that his dad was from Kent and so was Danny's. He wondered if they knew each other. Both of them didn't like the same kind of people and they were about the same age. They followed the officers and one of them opened Brian's cell door and walked Brian to his cell and then Danny to his.

As he went in Kevin said, "You've been gone a long time. What did Brian say?"

"Nothing much. Only he wants to supply us once we get rid of Burns. I am going to have a dry wash and go to bed as I am knackered."

"I'll join you. It's been a long day."

Chapter Sixteen

For the next few weeks they were doing well in the business. Danny still had not received a letter from his wife and kids. He was getting better at reading and writing with Kevin's help. Also he didn't need to use insulin anymore. His health was getting better all around. He had lost a lot of weight and his mind seemed to be on business every minute of the day. He was always giving out burn or receiving payment. His time was very busy with the selling of burn.

He was not thinking like before about the outside. Danny kept a count of everything and knew he'd got over one hundred cartons of milk and loads of tuna and canteen and it all seemed to be right with no trouble between Brian and the Muslims either. Danny spoke to an officer about the letter but was told that was not their department. He was thinking Brian was pulling his leg about Kevin. Then the door knocked. Danny opened the door. One of the customers called Mick stood there.

"Is Kevin around?"

"No, can I give him a message?"

"I've got this pack of burn for Kevin. I should have given him it yesterday but can't find him."

"Thanks mate. How long has he been supplying you?"

"Since he came on the Wing."

"Thanks mate. If you want anything, come and see me. Kevin and I are partners. Where do you live?"

"Yes I know mate. Kev told me. I live on the twos - number two. I will you see you later thanks."

After Mick left, Danny looked to find his name in the book but it was not in there. Even though he knew him he couldn't remember his name in the book. What was he going to do now? It wasn't a lot of damage. He did not show signs of taking anything, spice or drugs .They only showed signs when they didn't get anything to take. What should Danny do? Could he run the business without Kevin? Did he need someone to watch his back? Yes that Mick seemed ok and now Danny might have to look at recruiting someone else as well.

"Where've you been?"

"Getting more business for us."

"Kevin where is the book?"

"We don't need it now."

"Just get it Kevin. Let's make up the book to see what we've done so it's all written down."

"We can do it later."

"No Kevin. Let's sort it now. You always say later and end up doing it wrong because you can't remember who you gave stuff to."

"Here it is. I am putting it on the table. I'm just going to the toilet. I am dying for a piss, I will just be one second Danny."

Danny sat on the chair and got the book out on the table. He started to count all of their stock and what was out, matching all the names in the book. Kevin was ages in the toilet.

"What the fuck are you doing? That was a long piss."

"I am coming out."

"Did you wash your hands?"

He went back in the toilet and a few seconds later came back out. Kevin knew something was up.

"Have a seat mate in front of me or come next to that. It will be better if I'm not sure what you've written. Maybe you can explain to me. You are sweating, are you alright?"

"Yes I am fine."

Kevin moved the chair next to his and was rubbing his eyes because they were red. He thought he knew what he had been doing.

"I am your friend and business partner. ARE YOU ALRIGHT?

Danny stood up and put his arms around him and said, "I am your mate. Just speak to me."

"I have been using heavy drugs again. Sorry Danny. It all started when I began working at the server. I hid stuff there and used it there. I wanted to tell you so many times."

"Which ones you being using?

"Spice, that's all."

"That is the worst in here, it slowly sends you crazy."

"I could not get anything else, without you finding out."

"What can we do? Tell the screws to put you in the drug free block? Go to health care in the segregation or you can do it with me here. It will only work if you do not come in here and help yourself to our stock when I am not in here. We cannot do any more business. I will get a new partner to work with me. I will still split with you, but I will keep everything with my new partner. If I can get one. I can get your mother's address and I will get your share to her somehow and we will share with a new person, what do you say?"

"I don't know what to say?"

"Today is Friday so if we will bang up all weekend it gives you a chance to clean up and not take drugs. I will tell the screws you are not well so you don't have to leave the cell. I will not go to church. I will ask someone to look after all our stuff. Give me all you've got. Your choice, what do want to do? You are no good to no one or yourself. That's why you've been in prison for such a long time."

"Danny what would I do on the out? What type of life would I have with my mother? She is old now and can you imagine the type of man she will have now? Do you really think I want that life again? In prison I have shelter, food and a bit of pocket money and people I can talk to. It is frightening me to think about life on the out. I am not going to the screws so I have to do what you said and stay in here for me to get cleaned up."

"It is not going to be easy Kevin."

"I will try my best Danny."

Somewhere on the same wing as Danny and Kevin.

"That dope screw Taylor is on duty. He is always doing Sudoku. He carries it everywhere he goes. He is in the office now doing it, Burns."

"Sam, I want you to go to the gate by the office and if he comes out you stall him, make sure he does not come out. Stall him. Go now and wait by the gate. Actually, go by the phone as you can see better from there and they'll think you are on the phone instead of thinking you are watching the office."

"Get the tins of tuna and put them in your socks lads."

"I've got no tuna, Burns."

"Ken get any tin you've got and put it in your socks, stupid."

"I have not got any tins but I have got my tooth brush knife I made."

"Do you think you are going to get up so close to them to use your knife, Ken?"

"No."

"Ken, go to my cell and get any tin, stupid, go quickly."

Danny and Kevin were looking through the book of customers.

"Have you put down everything you have taken from our business?"

The cell door flew open.

"Who do they think they are coming to our house and nicking our customers? Let them have it boys."

Before Danny and Kevin could do anything, a tin of Tuna was hitting them from all different angles. Danny picked up the table that he could use to protect himself and Kevin picked up his pillow and stayed behind Danny. He managed to hold the legs of the table and push the table onto the attackers. No one could pass as the single beds were on either side of the cell. Burns' men tried to get onto the bed but Kevin pulled their legs from them and one fell to the ground, hitting the table with the tuna.

They were banging at the table with their tins in their socks and not hitting anyone. They were banging arms. The one that was on the floor tried pulling Kevin's legs but he just stamped on his hand and he screamed. Danny started to push harder with the table towards the door. Another fell to the floor. Danny was just pushing blindly due to the fact he could not see anyone behind the door. He dared not show his face or try to look at his assailant, knowing they would hit him. Another one of them fell by the door outside. They all managed to get up, they got their socks with tuna tins and were swinging from all different directions and at different angles, all at Danny and Kevin.

Danny and Kevin started to protect themselves better and were pushing them back. Kevin got hold of one of their socks and started pulling it. The others were still swinging their socks with tins in. They were hitting the table and some were missing and were hitting themselves. Danny was still holding the legs of the table firmly. Burns' lot were coming back strong and one of them managed to get on the single bed and got Kevin until he pulled him down to the floor. The rest were swinging around the table and trying to pull the table away from Danny but he was too strong as he held the legs of the table firmly.

Kevin got hit on the head then he fell to the floor with a big thud. Someone said, "You killed him. He is not moving."

Another one of burns crew said, "He is dead."

Burns said, "Let's finished them off."

The lookout shouted, "SCREWS!"

"Let this be a lesson to you. Do not trade in this Wing anymore or I will do the same again but worse."

Burns and his boys left the cell in a hurry and ran up the back stairs. Sam joined them and spoke. "Sorry Burns, false alarm."

"Never mind you idiot. Let's get back to our own cells just in case."

"They have gone, Kevin are you all right?"

"Course I am. It's a trick I learned a long time ago. When my mum's boyfriend used to beat me I used to fall to the floor then he would stop hitting me. My mum would say exactly what they said, 'you killed him,' but my arms are sore and my head must be swollen."

After they had gone, they started to tidy up the cell and put things back in order. Kevin had sat down and Danny was doing most of the work.

"Look at the table. The Formica is all dented up and that's oil on the table so one of the tins must have broken."

"Kevin take your shirt off. Let me look at you. Fucking hell you are full of bruises all over your body. I did not get as badly hit as you. I had the table to protect me, but my arms are bad. Fucking hell, both of them have swelled up. I will get some water in a bowl for you."

"You use the bowl. I will use the sink. Your arms will not fit in the sink, Danny."

"You run the cold water on your arms in the sink. I will use the kettle water and pour on my arms. I will use a damp cloth and dab my arms. Kevin, your face has swollen up a little."

"I can feel it but it's OK. I had worse than this before."

"I'm going to get lunch. You stay here as I will get yours."

"I am ok. Danny I will open some tuna."

"I am going to the server. So they can see I am not scared of them. They will think you are badly hurt when they don't see you Kevin. They would not know if you are OK or not."

"OK. I feel like shit."

"Yea you look like shit. I'm going to get my tea. I will tell the officer at the server you are not well and I can then get your food. Is it OK if I leave you love?"

"Piss off."

"That was quick Danny."

"Everything is running late and the food has not come from the kitchens yet. I did not see Burns or his boys but a few of the prisoners were looking at me to see if I was marked up. My arms are killing me."

The door knocked and he walked to the door. Danny was ready for trouble this time.

"Be careful Danny!"

He opened the door slowly and was ready.

"Hello my name is Karim. I am a friend of Khan and Jamal. I just heard what Burns did. Can I be of any help? Let me know, is Kevin OK?"

"We are fine. Thanks for your concern Mr. Karim. I will see you later."

"OK."

"My arms are not too bad but my head is hurting."

"Kevin are you sure that is not the lack of drugs talking?"

"You could be right Danny, what are you doing?"

"I am putting everything in bags and I am taping it up so you cannot get it and swap for drugs. Have you finished with the sink?"

"Yes it does make a little difference running it under the tap but your hands are too fat to fit in the sink."

"Ha. Ha. I will use a cup to pour the cold water over my hands. I don't think I am going to go and get tea. I can't be bothered. I will join you with tuna and biscuits then you can help me finish off this letter to my wife and kids after we've finished eating."

"You've being writing this letter for the last few weeks."

"I am getting better but I want it to be perfect. I can't understand why I have had no visit from her and the kids or solicitors."

"What about all the cons who are going to come for roll up and burn?"

"I think we shut up shop and let Burns think he has won."

"Good idea Danny. I'll the shut the door as I want to get some sleep."

"I am going to run cold water on my arms to get the swelling down. Do you want a basin?

"No Danny. I just want to rest and sleep."

A few minutes later the flap opened.

"Kevin can I have a quarter till next week?"

"We are shutting down for this week."

"I heard what happened. Seems it's all over the block. I will come still to get my stuff from you. I don't like getting stuff off Burns and his boys. I will see you later mate."

The flap opened several more times with cons asking for stuff that day until bang up.

"Danny, I need some pain killers as the pain is too much."

"Kevin we've just got wait for the morning for them. I don't want to alert the screws. I am in pain as well."

"The word will get to Burns that we have shut up shop. I am glad it's bang up. I thought the flap will come off its hinges. Are you going to help me to finish this letter off to the wife and kids?"

About two hours later.

"Are you happy with the letter now Danny?"

"Yes."

"Danny what are you doing now?"

"I am pressing the bell. I am going to ask for a listener."

"Why do you want a listener? I need a listener."

"I want to speak to Brian."

"You don't need to speak to him Danny."

"We need some experience for the right bit of advice about what to do. He has being doing this for years and he hates Burns. It will be worth listening to what he has to say. I have not seen him for weeks. I bet he will be surprised as he must have heard what happened."

The door opened.

"What do you want?"

"I need a listener Sir."

He shut the door again and came back half an hour later.

"Mundy follow me."

"He took him to the same room he went in last time. The door locked and he waited for Brian. As he sat down he felt the pain all over his arms and body. His arm was throbbing, the door opened.

"Hello Brian."

The door locked and there was just Danny and Brian in the room.

"That's not you Danny Mundy. You look mean without the hair and where's that stomach? Even your arms look bigger".

"Nice to see you too Brian."

"Danny I hear you've got double trouble."

"Double?"

"Your partner is drugged up and Burns and you are at war."

"Yea I suppose you are right, I called for some advice."

"No I don't think you need that, you want some help?"

"No I don't. Well... you could say that. Have you got something in mind?"

"Well I have. I will pay you two hundred and fifty pounds to take out Burns and I will supply everything you need for that wing. By the way, the rumour is that you got your head kicked in today."

"Do you see any marks on me? Brian it was four against two."

"More like four against one. I knew from day one you could handle yourself. Even my Dad said so and he did not even know you. So have we got a deal?

Give me your wife's address and I will have someone drop it off to her and the kids."

"I am not giving you my wife's address. Brian, you should have seen the fight. Burns and his boys came in swinging their cans of tuna in their socks and were hitting each other when the missed us. My table has so many marks on it. It was not funny at the time but now I know they did more damage to themselves than us."

"That's not what I heard. I heard they gave you and Kevin a good hiding and you were too frightened to come out of your cell for tea this afternoon and you were turning customers away from your cell, saying you are not trading anymore."

"All of that is true apart from one thing."

"Yes I know - the good hiding. So what is your plan Danny because you have got one I hope?"

"I have to think about it first if I am going to accept your offer or not. How can I deal with Kevin's problem without the screws knowing about it? By the way do you know Karim?"

"What another Muslim?

"Yes, after the fight he came to my cell to ask me if I needed anything."

"I told him I was OK and he left."

"That's a very hard one because I think the screws know already. I would tell health care and let them take care of him at the hospital or you've got to watch him twenty four hours a day, seven days a week for two weeks at least."

"I have to do that Brian. I have to dry him out but I don't think he is so far gone. He helped today. In fact he did a lot. If he was not there I would have been in trouble. I need someone to watch my back."

"There is someone in there you might like to use. He is into weights and all he does is smoke. He seems honest but he is always skint because he spends all his money on protein for his body building."

"I think I know him. Mick."

"How do you know him?"

"You are not the only clever one around here mate. Anyway thanks for all your help. I will take your offer. I could ask for more but I won't. I know you will pay more but I am happy to do it for the £250."

"I will meet you in the church on Sunday and give it to you."

"No, no not in the church. I will call you as a listener."

"You know Mick works in the gym and he will be very useful to you as he can move stuff in the gym as well for you. One of my guys works in there so he could give you the stuff as well. I will ring the bell for the officer."

Danny was taken back to his cell where Kevin was lying down. Danny's new next door neighbour, Cyril, was there.

Cyril was about sixty five years old, very thin with long white hair and a beard. He looked after things for Danny.

"Is Cyril helping you?"

"Yes he is alright as he does little things for me."

"I always give him burn. They say he is a pedophile. He plays with little girls."

"No he is not, he is in here for fraud. He is married and he's got kids."

"Loads of those pedophiles had kids, are married and still play with other people's kids."

"Kevin he is as good as gold so you best put the word out that he is straight and not a pedophile. I will be asking him to help me to keep an eye on you and get what you might need when I go to education."

"You still have not told me what Brian said."

"He wants me to take out Burns and he is going to pay £250 so we get £125 each. You can send your share to your mum and he says he will supply us after. We need to get someone else on the firm so he suggested Mick. Do you know him?"

"Yes, I was meaning to tell you about him. Thanks for the money. You don't have to share it with me."

"Don't bother saying any more. I know about you and Mick."

"You are not mad with me?"

"No mate, we are partners. You made a mistake but you are only allowed one and after that if you do that again we are finished. At this moment in time you have got to get well and prepare for the worst. Is there anything else I need to know?"

"I will not be the same person so just ignore me, whatever I say."

"I will do my exercises and you do yours as well."

"I don't feel like it mate."

"Up to you mate, though if you want to get better you have to work at it."

Chapter Seventeen

The next morning Danny went to church and when he came back he opened the bags of stock. He checked it all to make sure none was taken.

"Don't worry I did not take anything. It's all there. I am starting to feel bad. My stomach is cramping up on me. I had some tea and biscuits and I could not keep it down."

"Look, you need something heavy to eat so you can keep it down. It will be lunchtime soon. Are you alright to get your own dinner?"

"No mate you get it, the officers knows I am not well."

Danny went and got his and Kevin's lunch with no sign of Burns and his crew.

"Here you are mate. Just get this down you."

"I don't fancy it mate. I'm just going bring to it all up again. My stomach is getting worse. I need something. Maybe even a smoke."

"Come on Kev, I have not stopped you from smoking, I will get a packet for you. No, no I won't. I will just give you some. Here you are, one eighth."

"Don't you trust me? You think I will swap burn for drugs?"

"Yes I do. Try and eat something with your roll up."

All through the weekend and Sunday night Kevin was moaning about pain in his stomach as well as his head going around in circles. He was walking up and down the cell nonstop. It was soon Monday morning.

"Kevin I am going to ask Cyril to look after you as I have to do education."

"I don't need any old Pedophile to look after me."

"What are you going to do today? Will you just lie on the bed?"

"My stomach is cramping up badly."

"Here is some burn, so have a smoke. Are you sure you don't want Cyril to keep an eye on you or even talk to you?"

"No go. I will see you at lunch time."

"Remember what I said. One chance only. I am taking the bag of stuff to Mick to look after and don't go and ask him for it. I am going to education."

After dropping the bag off he hurried to the classroom to speak to Mr. White about the work he had done over the weekend. When he arrived, the classroom door was open so he walked in and Mrs. Mills was in there.

"Good morning, Danny how are you?"

"I am good, are you taking the class today?"

"Yes I am. I see you've got some work there. Can I have a look?"

"Here you are. It's some copy writing and I've done the whole book on spelling."

After a few minutes the other prisoners started to come into the classroom.

"This is good work Danny. Please stay after class and I will give you some more work to take to your cell. Now go and take your seat."

The class was good that day. Nobody messed about. It was over in a flash then he stayed back and Mrs. Mills gave him some work to read and copy. She said his handwriting was very good. That was the same thing Kevin had said. Danny hurried back to the block to see Kevin, hoping he was OK. He went into the cell where Kev was on his bed curled up in a ball holding his knees to his chest. He went and sat on his bed and spoke to him calmly.

"Keep it up mate. You are doing well. Is there anything I can do?"

"If you make this pain go away that will be great. It's all over my body. My stomach is full of cramps and no matter what I do it does not go away."

"Have you tried to eat?"

"No mate it will just come up and this is not the worst. The worst is yet to come. I don't reckon I can cope with what's going to come. Just get me some spice or anything and it will go away, please mate."

"Kevin you don't want to go back to that. You want to be clean for when you go and meet your mum. So think of your mum and what she is going through. She will want to see you well. No mate I will not get you anything. Just three more days and you will get over it."

"My days are like months. It's taking forever. I don't know if I can do it anymore."

"I will stay with you today and I will not go to education this afternoon."

"Listen mate. You go. They did not open my door after you left this morning so they will do the same this afternoon. The pain is unbearable. I have tried so many times in the past to give up the drugs and I have always failed. I have got a friend that's helping me. I never had a friend before so I must do it. This pain just won't go away, no matter how I twist and turn my body or move! I've got to go to the toilet and be sick although nothing comes out."

Five minutes later Kevin came out of the toilet holding his stomach.

"This pain again. I wasn't sick, just my stomach erupting and my head is starting to spin. I can't do this. It's too much pain in my head."

All of a sudden Kevin started to hit his head against the metal frame of the bed. Danny quickly went and grabbed hold of him to stop him from doing it again."

"What are you doing Kevin?"

"I just want the pain to stop, but no matter what I do the pain will not stop. If I eat anything it comes up and when I go to the toilet nothing comes out."

Danny started to get very worried. He called Cyril to come to the cell and he took a long look at Kevin.

"What do you think I should do about Kevin?"

"Fuck me he is in a bad way. You should let health care take care of him as he is going crazy with the pain. I heard him bang the cell just before you came back."

"Cyril I have never seen anyone like this before. He's totally gone. He is not the same person I know."

"He is in a bad way and he will not recover from this. Only health care can help now he has gone this far."

"You can go now Cyril, thank you."

"Kevin I will go and get our lunch now."

"Ok mate."

Danny went downstairs to get lunch, luckily finding there was no queue at the server. He spoke to the guy behind the counter.

"What happened?"

"Lunch is all gone mate. You should have come earlier, sorry."

"We missed lunch?"

"They have finished Danny - sorry mate."

As Danny went into the cell Kev was curled up in the bed rocking from side to side.

"Sorry mate, no lunch, all gone."

"I could not eat anything anyway."

Danny lay on his bed looking at Kevin, feeling helpless.

The cell door opened and Danny stood up and went towards it to open it wider. It was an officer who walked into the cell.

"What is the matter with your cell mate Mundy? I could hear him shouting this morning."

"He's got a bad headache sir."

"Listen Danny I know what you are trying to do. It's all over the block but just let healthcare take care of him."

"I am fine, governor. There's nothing wrong, just my head where I fell over is painful. I will be OK in a few days' time."

"If you say so Kevin. I will take your word for it."

He left and locked the door.

Danny felt so helpless where Kevin was concerned. He knew that he couldn't actually do anything for him.

Then he opened the door again and said, "Kevin I will let it go this time but if I hear any more screaming I will come back and take you to healthcare myself."

The officer pulled the door shut and double locked it.

"Danny, I can't help the screaming and shouting. These pains are always there and they just don't ease up. The only thing that will make it stop is if I had some drugs."

"That's not going to happen. There's only a few more days to go mate."

Over an hour and a half passed but there was no improvement with Kevin.

The door unlocked. McCarthy came in.

"Is he OK Mundy? Does he need special treatment from healthcare? If I or any other officer hear him screaming he is going straight to healthcare."

"Yes sir."

"Education now."

"I will see you later mate. Just hold on a few more days."

Danny hurried on his way to class where he met Brian.

"Hello Danny. What's going on? When are you going to do that thing for me?"

"Sorry Brian. I am going through it at the moment. My wife has not written to me. I still haven't received the letter she sent or the money and with Kevin he has taken my mind off the job but I will do it."

"If you are short I can help."

"No mate. It's not that. It's her letter. I want to read it with all what's going on. I have not had time to post the letter I have for her. I have got to go. I will see you later mate."

When he got to the class Mrs. Mills was there and most of the class.

"I am going to show you a movie."

All of the class were cheering for joy as she was setting everything up.

"Danny be ready at the light."

"Yes miss, am ready."

"Switch the light off please".

When it started to show there were lots of boos and shouts of 'what a load of rubbish'. It was a documentary of Alan Sugar, not a film.

"Lights on please Danny."

"Light on miss."

"This is going to part of your exam question. I do not want to hear any more noises or you will lose your wages for today and you will not be asked back to education. That means some of you will not be able to get a job as you need level one to get a job, or will not be able to do your sentence plan. This man Alan Sugar started with nothing so you will see for yourself what he achieved. No more noises please. Let's watch the film and you will learn something."

After the film was over it was time to go back to the wing. Danny was on his way out and Mrs. Mills stopped him and said, "Put the blinds up for me and did you learn anything from that film?"

"I was very surprised how he did it. That was all very hard work and a will to win and not give up. In my life I always found the easy way out, no problems in my life. Nothing to worry about. I was different from my brother who was filled with ambition. I just lived from day to day."

"I have seen how you have wanted better for yourself. You have changed your mind, lost so much weight and you are now helping your friend to give up drugs. I think you are a changed man since you have come to jail, your mindset is different now."

"Yes I have. My eyes were blinkered to life when I was living on the out. I was like my father and his father."

As Danny was putting the blinds down, Mrs. Mills put her hands on his and said, "Keep the good work up and you will achieve a lot. I just hope your lawyers will prove your innocence of the murder of your brother."

"I want the same but everything takes so long and I can't do anything about it."

He looked at her and she looked at him with her hand still on his and it was nice to have the feel of a woman.

"I got to get back to the wing miss, before they lock the gates."

He moved his hand and she looked deep into his eyes. He turned, walked outside and ran back to the wing. He went towards his cell expecting noise from the cell but there was none. As he walked to his cell Cyril was by the landing outside.

"How is he feeling?"

"Still the same Danny. One of the officers kept walking by. That's why I came in here to keep him quiet. He didn't want anything to eat because it goes through him like water. He says his bum is like a tap but the officer wants him to go to the healthcare."

"What they will do at health care is put him back on some drug medication and he will be back to where he started. Get your plate, let's get our tea."

"Ok Danny I'll meet in you in a second."

Both of them walked to join the queue for tea then waited in the queue. Wade and Burns happened to be together in front of them in the queue. Burns said,

"Here he comes with his crew - a drudge and a pedophile, what do you think of him now Wade, fancy taking him on again?"

"I'd love to. He has not got anyone to help him now."

Danny was looking at them and thinking he needed to check himself and not get involved in trouble. He could control himself and took no chance with his court case coming up. They were looking at Danny and teasing him loudly so that other prisoners were looking at them in the queue.

"Take no notice of them Danny. Let's get our tea and go back to our cells."

They got their tea then Cyril went back to his cell and Danny went to his cell. Kevin had been sick in the sink but nothing was coming out so it seemed that his guts were bursting but he brought up nothing. Danny sat on the chair, put the spoon on his plate and looked at Kevin. Leaving the spoon on the plastic plate, he then went over to Kevin and held him. There was nothing he could do but to look at him. It made him feel totally helpless. He put him on his bed and sat at the edge and all he could think of was to get on his knees.

"Dear God, please, please help Kevin get over this terrible time in his life. Help him to stop feeling this pain and help him to recover from the drug illness."

"What are you doing Danny?"

"I am praying, I have to ask God to help you. I can't see you in so much agony mate."

"I don't know how much more of this I can take Danny."

He left the bed and went back to the sink, trying to bring up his guts but nothing came up. Danny looked at his food and turned away, looking back at Kevin at the sink yet now he had gone to the toilet. This went on for the next few hours until bang up. Danny was getting a bit worried he was not getting over his drug problem. In fact he was getting worse. He thought it would get better for him, though this was not the case. He went by his bed and sat at the edge. He held Kevin and listened.

"Danny I will do anything for some spice. I will give you a blow job. Please put a line out the window. I will give you a blow job as long as you want."

He tried to pull his shorts down but Danny slapped him at the back of his head. He fell back on his bed and said, "I will do anything 'cos I need some spice please mate."

"Keep away from me and don't ever do that again Kevin or... nothing."

Danny just hoped he slept that night and he would be better in the morning. This went all through the night, him going to the sink then the toilet, curling up in the bed. Danny was up all night and doing his routine exercises and thinking about what he had said to him. How could he say that to him? The door opened.

"How is he this morning Danny?"

"He is getting better sir."

"He needs to go to Health Care."

"Sir if he goes to H/C they will put him back on drugs and he will be back to square one again."

"As I told you yesterday, if he makes any noise I will order him to H/C or take him myself. On your way to education Mundy."

"I will see you later Kev."

As he left, he knocked on Cyril's door which was open. Danny pointed to his cell and Cyril nodded as Danny walked to education. His mind was still on what Kevin said to him. How could he want to give his best friend a blow job for spice? He understood now what Brian had said to him about how cons suffer with drugs. It gets a hold them and their lives are finished once they start using it. Danny normally hurried to education but today his mind was very much on Kevin. He took a slow walk to the classroom and it reminded him what it felt like when he first came to prison. His mind was not on education. The next few hours felt like a week and somehow the teacher knew and left him alone when education was over. He rushed back to his wing and everyone was looking at him as he walked to his cell. Cyril came out of his. Danny took no notice of him and went into his cell. There was no sign of Kevin and just then Cyril walked in.

"The officer told him to go to healthcare and they came for him as he was screaming all morning with the pain. I tried to stop him but he took no notice of me. The officer said he is going to health care, sorry Danny."

"Not your fault Cyril. Go back to your cell. I want to be alone, oh and bring the bags. I told Kevin I gave the bags to Mick. If he knew you had the bags, he would be on you for it. Go and bring the bags, I will look out for you Cyril."

"Come on its clear - bring the bag."

"Here are the bags, are you going for dinner?"

"Thanks, no I won't bother as I don't feel like eating. You know healthcare are going to give him some sort of drugs, probably give him methadone, and give him a high dosage as well. He will never get over his drug addiction in healthcare."

"I know mate, I have seen it time and time again. They come to prison without any drug problems and when they leave they become drug addicts."

"If they ever get released, that is."

After Cyril left all Danny could think about was how Kevin got that desperate he offered to give a blow job. His life was all fucked, with no letter from the wife or the solicitors. The only thing that would take his mind off things was to do his exercise routine and think about the business and not feel sorry for himself. Danny was going to exercise till he dropped, then the door knocked. He went to the door and opened it.

"Come in Mick, what can I do for you?"

"Have you got any burn? I did not come just for that, mate. I wanted to see how you were. I see they took Kevin to healthcare. He will be in jail all his life now. I knew him from his last jail where he did the same but not once, loads of times. He will be on permanent medication."

"Thanks mate, fancy doing a bit of work for me?"

"Doing what?"

"Do some selling and put out some burn and a bit of drugs."

"No thanks mate. My people give me money every week on my visits. I don't need the hassle. I'm not afraid of doing it. I just want enough money for some smoke, eggs and a portion for the gym and my family send all I need to buy those things. Thanks Danny but no thanks".

Danny needed someone to look after his back. Mick did not want to know and Cyril was too old to help in case of trouble. So he thought he would take up Jamal's offer to help. Plus he told Brian he would sort out Burns. Danny decided to go and see Jamal.

He walked up to Jamal's cell door and knocked. Jamal soon opened the door.

"Hello Danny, come in."

"Hello, it's so nice to see my two Muslim friends, when did you come on the wing?"

"We came just after dinner. If I had seen you on the causeway I would not have recognised you Danny. You've cut your hair and you have lost a lot of weight, you look great."

"Thanks Khan, I am sorry to hear what happened to you and Kevin. Jamal I thought there was going to be murders here. I am glad that it's over and you are back to normal health now?"

"I don't think it's over and done with. They are the type that need things to be sorted out sooner not later."

"Now is not the time to talk about that Jamal. We've only come to see how Danny is and he is looking good. Don't forget Danny, if you need anything just ask, we are going now."

"Thanks for coming and take care. Oh you know that Wade and his boys are on this wing."

"Yes!"

Chapter Eighteen

The next morning Danny quickly went to education. In reality, he was enjoying education and he was learning all the time. When he was doing English and exercises, his mind was away from all his troubles and his case. If he let that take over his mind he would just be in bed all day and night. He felt like that every day so it was not easy for him to be motived every single minute of the day. Linda used to wake him up in the mornings to go to work with a cup of tea. As he reached the class, Mr. White was there in the classroom and he started thinking about Mrs. Mills.

"Good morning sir, here is my homework."

"Good morning, Danny have a seat. I have decided to give a mock level one test."

"Sir I don't think I am ready. Can I wait a few more days as lots of things are on my mind at the moment?"

"Ok I understand Danny but you've got to do it soon. I will give you a few mock test papers to go and study tonight. If you don't understand anything, let me know during the next class."

"Thank you sir."

The rest of the class made their way in one at a time. When Mr. White shut the door there were only five in the class which went on for a while. Then an officer opened the door.

"Is Mundy in this class?"

"Yes sir."

"You've got a visitor. Please come with me. You are meant to look at the notice board to see if you've got visits. You are lucky I know or you would have missed your visit. Come on, move yourself. Half your visit is nearly over."

"Thank you sir."

He was questioning who it might be. It must be his wife and kids. It would be good to see them as he hadn't seen them for a long time. He was given a red sash to put on, then he was searched and told that he must go to seat number six. He remembered the low numbers were at the other end of the visit hall. He looked for his wife as he walked past other prisoners and their visitors but he couldn't see her. However he did see two men at number six.

He nodded to Mick as he passed him and went to the table where the two men stood up and shook his hands. He went into the visit hall and he could see two of his mates from work.

"Hello Fred and Eden. Nice to see you both. I did not know I had a visit, thanks for coming."

"I cannot believe it's you, what have you done? You look so different now. I must say prison has changed you. By the way your missus gave us the details."

Fred was the manager of the loading bay department and seemed happy to see Danny. Eden was the accounts clerk and also started talking.

"As you can see we were waiting a long time so we bought some food and drink for you. Help yourself. How are you finding this in here?"

"Thanks Fred.

"How are you getting on?"

"Not very good Eden. I am in here for the murder of my brother but you all know I love him and I would never do anything to him."

"But have you not been charged yet Danny?"

"Eden, my solicitors said I've got no defense because I was found with the knife in my hand and the landlady saw me. The jury will believe that I killed him."

"Eat something Danny."

"I will Fred."

He took a burger and started to eat it.

"Fred, my wife said she had problems getting my wages for the last week I worked. Is it OK now?"

"She has all your up-to-date wages now. The firm don't owe you anything now. She has asked for a part time job and I think she will get the job Danny."

"Eden, I know you and Johnny were friends. Is there anything you can think of that can help. Is there anyone he owes money to or they owe him and are not paying anything Eden? Anything will help. Or you Fred."

"Danny you know if there was we would tell the police."

"Danny I will make sure your wife gets the job. I will keep an eye on your family and if you need anything let me know."

"Thank you both. Fred that will be good if you can help my wife with the job and keep an eye on her and the kids. I will be very grateful. I don't know what is going to happen but it does not look good for me and the family."

"Have you got any ideas at all Danny who could have killed Johnny?"

"Eden you know him and his friends better than me. We went out once or twice a week but I never met any of his friends. You and he went out a lot more than me and you know his friends, don't you? I don't know them."

"Danny sorry, as I said I can't think of anything."

The bell for the end of visiting time sounded.

"The visit is over so we've got to get going Danny. Nice to see you. We will come again soon."

"Nice to see you as well."

Danny shook hands with both of them then they left. Sadly, he sat on his seat and waved bye to them. Then he remembered that Fred the manager had made a pass at his wife at the Christmas party and he had spent a lot of time with her buying her drinks. When he spoke to her about it she just laughed and said he had imagined it. If he was going to be found guilty he won't have wanted her to wait for him. Fred could give her a lot more that he could. After all the visitors had left, an officer shouted.

"Rows one to ten can make their way back to your wing."

The officer shouted out again. Danny quickly made his way back to the wing and Mick joined him on the way.

"Had a good visit Danny?"

"Not bad. I think I have lost my appetite. Normally I would eat at least two burgers and have two or three cokes. I can only manage one of each."

"You know why. Your stomach has shrunk since you've been in prison. You don't eat a lot in prison. I do because I train and I burn a lot of energy. By the way are they partners?"

"No why do you ask?"

"The younger one is a definite queer boy, but the older now thinking back I think not. But that younger one is gay as fuck. Was he one of your brother's boyfriends?"

"I don't know Mick? Any second thoughts about joining me? My business is really going good."

"No not really Danny. Just want to do my time and go to the gym as much as I can. Anyway what about Burns and his crew? I thought that fight was to stop you and Kevin from selling."

"I am thinking about it and want to start up again."

They both got back to the wing where he walked slowly up the stairs and he looked around before entering his cell. He always did that now, anywhere he went. As he got in there was a letter on the floor. He sat down and opened it. Now he could read and write, he could get by. He read it again though he was not sure how to take it. He went and got Cyril.

"Read this letter for me. It's from my wife."

"Are you sure?"

"JUST READ IT."

"Dear Danny. I and the kids miss you a lot. As you know, it's very hard for us as we've got no money.

The water tank burst and flooded the whole house and damaged all our belongings. I've got nobody to help........"

"Go on. Why have you stopped?"

"I just looked at the date on this letter. It was posted two and a half months ago."

"You are joking. Never mind. Just keep reading it to the end."

"Do you remember that Kim, our Kim's God mother? I rang her to help and she came and got me a little cottage on her land and got decorators to do up the house. She asked Tony to give me my old job back and I will pay him back for the decoration of the house weekly out of my wages. Remember she used to send a cab for me. The same cab will take the kids to school and they will not miss their education. I will try and come and see you but it's very far for me to see you in prison. It's very painful to see you like that. The children are doing well at school and there is a big improvement in them. They love the cottage and getting a lift to school. Nothing more for me to say. I will try and see you. Your last letter was good so keep it going. You will soon be better than me. Lots of love, Linda and the kids."

"That's it. Done, Danny."

"Thanks. I will see you later mate."

"OK."

What could he do to help her? Kim and maybe her brother as well were helping her. He had never thought about that before. He must have fancied her. Why would a man help if he didn't? They always wanted something. How come the letter took so long to get there and had no money in it? She'd got none herself.

Brian promised him £250 to do Burns so he would have to do him now for the money. He wanted to give Brian the address of his house, so his people on the out could mail it there. He couldn't do anything to her and the kids, if he had problems with him in the future, because he would not know where they lived.

Was this a Dear John letter? Why had she not come to see him and why was there no money? Perhaps she was busy with the house, kids and work…… Or with Tony. That was all he needed. Kevin was in hospital and now he wished the letter never came. Danny just felt like getting in bed and stay there forever. He put the T.V on and started flicking through the channels but there was nothing on so he put it on the music channel…. Dolly Parton. 'Stand by your man'…. That's all he needed so he switched off the T.V. again. Danny opened two tins of tuna and put them on the plate, switched his kettle on, found six slices of bread and stacked them with butter and ketchup. Looking at the mirror, he felt his stomach and looked at his arms. Then he lay down on the bed and started feeling sorry for himself.

Knock, knock, the door was open.

"Come in."

"Are you going for tea?"

"I was about to have something but yea I will come with you. Why do you think the letter took so long to get to me?"

"I don't know mate. Why not ask one of the officers on duty."

"They will give some stupid excuse. I am not in the mood to listen them. Just let's get our food and go back to our cell."

When they got their tea he ate a little and gave one tin of tuna to Cyril and chucked away the bread, trying to take his mind off the letter. Thinking what Mick said about Eden and not wanting to join him, he would have never considered Eden and Johnny being lovers. His mind was racing so he must try and see Kevin at the hospital. He would ask the officer on duty. Danny went outside of his cell and looked to see which officer was on duty. He wouldn't bother as it happened to be bloody McCarthy on duty. There was no sense in asking as he would say no anyway, so he went back in his cell and closed his door. The door knocked again.

"Who is it?"

"Me. Cyril."

"Come in me old mate, what's up?"

"You know the Muslims on the twos?"

"Yes what about them?"

"One of them got attacked today by Burns and three of his mates. They took all their gear. It was very quiet today, not many officers about 'cos of some union meeting today."

"How do you know all this? You are normally banged up!"

"McCarthy came and asked me to clean the threes landing as it had a load of rubbish from last night. While I was cleaning I saw Burns and his mates by the shower on the twos. I hid so they could not see me, then the four of them went into the Muslim cell and must have beaten him up and came out with a pillow case full of stuff. I made sure they did not see me and nobody was about."

"Where were the other two Muslims?"

"They were not there, but I saw them come back, just before you did. There is going to be a lot of trouble when the Muslim kicks off."

"I have got to try and stop that or we will be locked down for days and people will be shipped out to other prisons."

"What can you do? You are only one man Danny."

"I am sure I can handle Burns by myself."

"But he has at least two of his boys with him all the time, why get your self-involved?

"They helped me when I first came here and one thing I gained since I have been in prison is honour and self-belief."

"That's not going to help you, four against one."

"You are right Cyril, that's why you are coming with me."

"Me? You are joking."

Cyril was scared out of his wits and started to tremble with fear.

"No I am not. For the next few days I want you to spy on Burns and all his crew. None of them are over five feet five and they can't fight to save their lives. Look how thin they are. They live on what drugs they can get. Go on the threes with your newspaper then sit on a chair and read. I want you to tell me what and where Burns and his crew are all day."

A sense of relief came across Cyril.

"Yes I'll do that, no problem."

"The key to this is you get to tell me the times when Burns is alone."

"I can do that Danny."

"Start now but don't forget your papers. I am going to see the Muslim boys now."

He walked to the Muslim cell and knocked. The door opened and Khan had a large tin of salmon in his hand in case of trouble.

"Oh it's you Danny. Come in."

"I so sorry about what happened to Jamal. I wish I could help Khan."

"Don't worry about it, by next week things will be sorted out. I am just waiting for the word from the Iman."

"Thank you for coming, I respect you for coming to see us."

"I see you are about to cook so I will see you later."

"You can join us if you like mate. There is plenty."

"I have got something that needs sorting out."

"OK."

As Danny walked back to his cell he felt that they did not want to talk to him about what happened. For the next few days Cyril became busy reporting to Danny. Burns' movement with his boys had been spiced up with their haul from the Muslims so Burns had been alone a lot more. He was training extra hard since Jamal got beaten up. Danny was about to wash up when the door knocked.

"It's me - Cyril."

"Come in."

"Burns just went into the showers by himself and one of his boys is outside the shower. Here - take this."

"Bloody hell where did you get this baseball bat?"

"Quickly put it inside your jogger's leg and go before he's finished showering."

He took it and put it in his trouser leg. He quickly hopped along to the shower on the threes. Just before he got near them, he hid in a doorway and then he took the bat out. Without hesitation he walked up to Burns' man by the showers. He pushed the bat with all his might into Burns' guard's stomach which made him fall to the floor and he started to cough.

"Stay where you are and be quiet, or the next one will be on your head."

He did not say a word and Danny dragged him by the collar more into the showers. He was moaning but not loud enough for Burns to hear. Danny heard the water splashing from the showers where Burns was. He quickly walked into the showers and punched him in his jaw. He fell against the wall, hit his head and fell onto the basin. There was water everywhere. Then he punched his ear drums while he was on the shower floor. He was about to say something.

"You aahh."

He bent down and punched him in the face again and blood was pouring like in the film 'Psycho'. He was about to hit him again but he was out cold with water showering his face and water and blood pouring down the drain.

He went outside to see Burns' man still on the floor. Danny dragged him into the showers with Burns. Then he went by the entrance of the shower. Cyril was waiting to receive the baseball bat. Then he walked to Burns' cell and went in. Only two of them were in there and they were out of it on spice, one lying on the single bed and one on the bottom bunk.

"What the fuck do you want?"

"Nothing."

He slapped the one that spoke first on the side of his ear so he fell on the bed. The other one put both hands up in the air.

"I don't want any trouble."

His hands remained up in the air.

"Take what you want 'cos it's all in the cupboard. I want no trouble."

He turned the cupboard around so he could see the back of it. Then he kicked the back in. In the cupboard was a pillow case packed full of stuff. He took it out.

"Where is Burns' gear?"

"Here it is under his single bed. I will get it for you."

"Stay there. I will get it out."

Danny got on his knee and took out a shoe box that was under that bed. He was dripping with water, being careful not to slip as he got up. The other one said, "That's Burns' stock."

"I am taking it all. Tell him that Danny Mundy has taken it. I am going to my cell now."

"Burns is going to get you Mundy."

Danny turned back and slapped him on the side of his face again. He screamed with pain, then Danny left the cell. Danny walked slowly to his own cell with the bag in one hand. Cyril was waiting outside.

"Any screws about?"

"No mate."

"Go and give this bag to Khan for me please. I must get out of these wet clothes. Check for screws and before you go, let me take this box out, thanks mate."

"I will."

A few minutes later, after Danny changed back into his clothes he reappeared.

"That was quick Cyril."

"The Muslim boys were coming to say thanks, but I said to them not today. Wait till things die down. What do you think Burns is going to do?"

"You know what. I am not going to wait for him. I am going back to his cell now."

Danny waked to Burns' cell and waited and listened outside for a while then pushed the door wide open. Burns was on his bed alone, one of them on the top bunk and two were on the other lower bunk bed. Before they could react, Danny said, "Do we finish this now or is it ended?"

They were shocked so they could not move. They never expected to see Danny come back to their cell."

Burns said, "You broke my ear drums and my face is bleeding. One of them said you hit me with a baseball bat."

Danny went over to him on the lower bunk and punched him in the face so his head hit the wall.

"I don't need a baseball bat to sort you out, you must be dreaming. Burns you are not answering me - is it over or not?"

Burns said, "Let's get him lads. There are four of us and we can easily smash him."

As he said that Danny kicked him in the face but his boys did not react. In fact they stayed where they were.

"Come on boys. Just get him."

They could see Danny was ready for anything they had.

Burns tried to get his crew to fight but it was a waste of time. The one on the lower bunk bed spoke.

"Look what we got working for you. Nothing. We get a bit of spice and a few bits of burn."

The two on the top bunk said, "Yea look at your clothes. You get the best and we get the rags."

The one at the bottom joined in.

"I am not working for you anymore. You two on the top bunk, what do you say?"

"That's it! We are finished with you Burns, I am not going to get a hiding for you and get nothing."

"Well Burns - it's time for you to leave this wing and if your boys want to work for me, they can?"

"Yea, Yea, Yea, we will work for you."

"You bunch of wankers go and work for him and you are dead meat."

"Burns if you are still in this wing in 24 hours I will get you again. You are finished."

"I have still got a few friends."

"Remember my words Burns, if these three want to work for me come tomorrow, I am sure you three can handle Burns if he gives you any trouble. I'll see you later but remember what I said Burns. Get out of this jail."

Cyril was outside waiting and acting like a lookout.

"Everything OK?

"Yes."

As Danny went towards his cell he was surprised that Burns had never said about the box he took.

"Cyril I am going to see the Muslim boys now. I'll catch you later."

"No screws about Danny".

He walked to their door to find that it was open slightly and so he knocked on their door.

"Come in Danny. We were just having tea, would you like some?"

"Yes. Thanks Khan."

"Sit down and have some biscuits as these are special ones the Iman gave us."

"These are nice, thanks."

"Here take this packet and thanks for getting our things back. You gave us a lot more than was taken. I have put back some in a bag for you. Did you hurt them badly?"

"No need for that Khan, I did what I had to do. Hopefully they will not attack you again. I told Burns he has to leave the wing or else. Please forgive me, I've asked his crew to come and work for me."

"Why? They will attack us again. What about Wade and his mates?"

"Jamal - the reason is that they will not trouble you again. I will be their boss. I don't know about Wade or what he is going to do."

"I heard the only reason you got Burns is that Brain paid you."

"Jamal do not say that," said Khan.

"I will be truthful and honorable with you that is not the reason. I will never forget the kindness you and Jamal showed me when I first came to jail and Brian helped me as well."

"I believe you Danny, me as well," said Karim supportively.

"Jamal have you anything to say?"

"Khan, I got beaten up very badly and I am not thinking straight, sorry."

"Danny I am sure it was Brian's dad that told Burns to attack us and steal all our belongings."

"Khan I will find out and let you know. Look, I am going now but thanks for the biscuits and the parcel. I will open it when I go back to my cell."

"Cyril is everything OK?"

"You've been a long time with them."

"Anything happening? Burns left his cell just after you. He is watching table tennis on the ground floor, probably waiting for someone?"

"Any of his boys with him?"

"No."

"Look - the server is ready so let's go and get our tea. Burns is coming up the landing."

Danny got his plate and Cyril followed him and by the time they got to the ground floor Burns was gone.

"Where did he go? I did not see him Danny."

"I did. He went into someone's cell on the ones. Just forget about him and let's get our lunch."

That night Danny didn't feel like doing anything and just he lay on the bed with the TV on, watching it but not really taking it in. His mind was thinking about Linda, but not about the kids. It was like their early days meeting after and before school when he was just constantly thinking about her. Danny was thinking he must speak to Brian. He pressed the bell and waited for over an hour before the flap opened.

"What do you want Mundy?"

"Can I speak to a listener please Sir?"

The flap closed again and he was once again waiting... Later the door opened and it was Oscar one.

Oscar one are the night staff that patrol and in are in command of a prison at night.

"Come this way Danny."

He opened the listener door and Brian was already sitting on a chair waiting there. Danny sat down and the door locked.

"How are you Danny?"

"Not too bad."

"What's up?"

"You are joking with me. Don't you know what went down today? What's wrong with your network of spies?"

He told Brian what took place that day and asked if his dad had set up Burns and his crew to beat up the Muslims.

"Well mate I am glad Burns got a good hiding. I knew you had it in you. My dad didn't know anything about it or set it up. So you will be working for me now."

"As told you, I need as much money as I can get for my wife and kids. I gave you the address where your people can send the money."

"You will need me to supply you with phones and high end drugs."

"Yes only that. I don't need anything else."

"I will give you a good deal Danny. Some of Burns' crew will be working for you?"

"I don't see why not. Burns never looked after them. I will look after them, I can read and write a lot better now and Maths was my strong point so they can't rob from me."

"I will get that money to your house within a week OK?"

"Thanks Brian."

"We are done then?"

"Yes I will press the buzzer for the officer to take us back to the block."

Danny was taken back to his cell, thinking that Brian had lied to him about his dad. Danny was sure he knew what really went on that day and his dad set up Burns to do the Muslims.

Chapter Nineteen

Over the next few days Ted, Bill and Liam joined Danny. Bill would only be in a few months before his sentence would be finished. So he needed someone on the outside to work for him and Bill was the answer. He would give Bill lots of work and high end drugs and phones to sell for him. Danny would make him his right hand man while he was still there.

During all of the sales he had done, he never tried to steal from Danny. He was always on point. Danny looked after him and they trained together. As a matter of fact, they all got on well. The crew were happy working for Danny because he looked after them. They did a lot of business in the church, gym, health care, library, and workshop and anywhere they could.

They started to have lots of paper money which he gave to Cyril to look after for them. He had a great hiding place. Brian said his people put money through letter boxes in envelopes.

Burns had been shipped out. Wade was now working for Brian on the same wing as them and they had their own customers. Burns had cheated prisoners when they first come in. When they realised that, they started to come to Danny's crew to get gear. Danny's crew did not cheat people and his crew got a lot more business that way. Danny soon had ninety percent of the business on the wing. Wade liked Danny's work in the other wing as well.

Kevin was still in hospital but he was now working as a cleaner in the hospital and still doing drugs. Danny soon realised he could not help him in prison. Kevin said he got food every day, somewhere to sleep at night when it was raining or snowing and a bit of pocket money for cutting hair again. He had ruined himself and knew he would never come out of prison. Over time Danny had seen quite of few similar to Kevin, stuck in prison on a cycle.

The door knocked and he went to open it.

"Come in Billy. What's up?"

"I just want to tell you that Burns has lost an eye. His dad is in and out of prison as well so you'd better watch out in future."

"Don't worry about me. I always look out for myself. Thanks anyway Bill, I am going to see Cyril now."

"Hi Cyril - any news this morning?"

"Quite a few being released. I think ten or more."

"You are serious?"

"Yes I bet a lot of them owe you money Danny."

"You are dead right. It's never more than one or two being released at the same time. I hope we don't get any nutters to replace them. I don't want to be fighting again. Is Bill around?"

"I will and go and get him."

"Do you want me?"

"When are you getting released?"

"Only got five days left."

"Bill how have I treated you since you started working for me?"

"Listen Danny you have been great to me. You gave me better clothes, more money, far better than Burns."

"Any hard feelings about me hitting you with the baseball bat?"

"No mate, what baseball bat?"

"That's good, in that case we have to go over our plan. As you know, my wife is not living in my house so you can go there and live. Here is a letter for my wife and the address where she is. She will give you the key for the house but you will have to pay the rent. You open two bank accounts, one for yourself and one for the gardening business. Then open a building society joint with my eldest daughter Kim and here is another letter for you to give to Kim. A bank account for yourself and one that I will get the punters to put money in for the things we sell in here. Use the same account for the business for the time being.

Later, when the gardening business gets bigger we will get another account opened just for the business. If we have problems in here with cons not paying us you will go and see their family. The money I am giving you should set up a gardening company and buy all the tools you need and you've got money for yourself. By the way, do you know anything about gardening?"

"No but what is there to know? I will get by."

"You've got five days left to get some books and read up and learn about it."

"Hope I get some jobs, I will advertise in the Yellow pages and some shop windows and get some cards and leaflets printed as well."

"You are really getting into this. I hope we make it as a business."

"Danny do you know how much money you are going to give me?"

"I don't know at the moment. I will have a count up later on tonight."

"Do you want me to get a job on the out? I am sure probation will want me to get a job. The other thing is that they might put me in a hostel."

"If they do, take it and don't say you've got your own place. How old are now Bill? I will be twenty three at the end of the year."

"You've got to promise you keep your word and look after the business on the out. In years to come you will be a very rich man so keep away from the drugs."

"I've done that since I joined you. I can see that drugs don't pay. I am sad that you are going to get done for murder and get over twenty years plus. By the way, when are you going to court?"

"Next week mate. You can come to the court."

"Which court?"

"I think that Old Bailey court."

"I will try and come."

"We got to make a code when you write inside."

""No need you got a phone in the jewelry box. After your sentence they will move you to another prison."

"Suppose they find it when the search?"

"I forget about that. OK we will do a code when you call me."

"I will have to start the business all over again, that won't be a problem."

Danny was going to have a meeting with Ted and Liam. They had being working for him since Burns left. Liam didn't have much common sense. He made mistakes when giving out burn (snout) but he was strong and always paid up. He will have a go and get back what they were owed. Ted was very clever and his memory was better than Danny's. Bill and Liam would chase their punters, but Ted would wait until Danny got involves and ask him why so and so had not paid up. He also ran the shop. That stocked sweets, drinks, and tins, like a normal shop on the outside. The only thing was if they took a tin of tuna they had to give back the following week one tin and a half. That's why people took two tins as it was easier to count the following week. Three tins if they didn't pay then four and a half tins. The same thing applied to everything in the shop. Bill used to check everything in their once a week meeting.

There were a lot of new faces over the last few days. Danny wanted to tell the crew not to give out a lot of stuff to these new prisoners.

"Now that Bill has gone, Ted and Liam have got to do more work and, of course, more money for both of you. Do you think we should recruit someone else Liam?"

"Some of these new cons are not like what we normally get. They look mean."

"What do you mean?"

"Danny - you know there have been quite a few fights already."

"Have they been to the shop and taken things without paying?"

"They have and they have paid back Ted but they take it again."

"Yes they have, but some then are asking for the large pack of coffee and three or four cans at one time."

"Did you give it to them?"

"No I told you they can only have one can and a couple of tins and a half pack of burn. One of them was arguing and saying he'd got the money on his canteen sheet. I told him to bring the sheet then he started calling me names. Then Liam came and asked if everything was OK."

"Look mate, Ted and I work for Danny and it's his shop so if you have problems go and see him, he is on the twos."

"Just give me a couple of tins of Tuna."

Ted said, "What's your name and cell number?"

"Why do you want that for?"

"It's for my records. I can't remember everyone's who takes thing from me and I have to keep a record for my boss."

"Fucking hell my name is Phillips and I am on the threes - cell thirty one."

"Here you are mate. That's three tins on canteen day back."

"I know prison rules, my mate wants an eighth of tobacco too. He lives in the same cell as me, his name is Mark."

"Here you are."

"Thanks."

"Thank fuck they've gone. I thought it would have kicked off if you had not come Liam."

"From what you are saying we need to get someone else. Any ideas boys?"

"I see we are going to get trouble with these new cons."

"Well Ted who do you suggest? It seems you are giving it some thought?"

After bang up Danny thought about these new boys. They had not clashed with him as yet but they must know of him and probably had seen Danny around. Danny would just wait and see what happened at court on Monday. That afternoon the solicitors had nothing new to report other than to keep telling him to go guilty and get a lesser sentence. Danny had not bothered to write to his wife and children since he'd got the Dear John letter. The lawyer today said he would write a letter to Kim and the children. As a matter of fact he was going to write to her during lunch time at bang up. She had not written to him since her last letter, not even with the address that she was living at now. Danny will write to her at their address, his home.

'Dear Lindy and kids

I miss you all so much,

I don't know what to say

The door opened.

"A letter for you Mundy."

The door was locked.

Danny quickly opened it. It was from his two daughters, but Kim had been doing all the writing, nothing from Linda. 'Dad we miss you very much and Mum, she told us to write you. Since we have moved to this cottage it is very nice. It's got a big, big front garden and swings at the back. We've got bikes now and we ride around the ground. We go swimming once a week. (The writing changed) Dad we've got piano lessons as well. Mum said we are going to get a piano as well and we get a lift to school. All the other kids are jealous of us. (The writing changed) Dad we want to come and visit you but mum says not yet. We are going to learn to play tennis. Even Mum is learning now. Dad we do really miss you, bye for now.....'

"Legal visit Mundy."

"Yes Sir.

It was the same procedure. He would queue up with the rest of the prisoners. One by one they were searched then told where to sit, waiting for the lawyer to come. He was probably going to be late again. Danny had spoken to a lot of prisoners at the police station. They have a list of solicitors and they always call them for you, unless they know someone themselves. They all do the same thing, make their clients wait. They are never on time, but they still book the time to get paid. He was still waiting and so were the other prisoner. They wouldn't come for a while.

A young man was walking towards him. He must have been in his mid-twenties with a very thin frame and ginger hair, wearing a black striped suit and a pink tie.

"Hello Mr. Mundy I am from Banks and Banks. My name is Toby Wells. I will be representing you at the trial next week."

"What another solicitor? I am fed up with Banks. All they do is keep sending different lawyers to me. I am fed up and I go to court next week."

"I am sorry Danny, can I call you Danny?"

"Yes you can. Let's go over my defense please."

"I read your case last night. I managed to secure a barrister for next week. Your wife rang the Banks and Banks and told us she wants the best barrister and her boss will pay for it instead of legal aid."

"What is the difference between the legal and paid for?"

"Many of the top barristers do not work for legal aid but their private clients pay a lot more."

"How much is he costing?"

"I am not sure. £1500 to £2500 per day."

"Where is my wife getting the money?"

"I am not sure. I think it's from her employer. The barrister will be here shortly. His name is Phillip St. John. Oh look here he is now."

He was about forty and was big set with jet black hair, a pin striped suit and a red tie. He came to their table so they both stood up and shook his hand and introduced themselves.

"Mr. Mundy, Toby and I went over your case last night. I am afraid we do not have much time before the case on Monday. Is there anything you specific you want to point out to me now that I have read all your statements?"

"Sir I was not looking like how you see me now when I was arrested. I was obese and over 25 stone and I had a lot medical problems."

"What are you getting at Mr. Mundy?"

"Now I could walk to my brother's room from work in about ninety seconds. I could not do it then and when the jury see me now they will think I got to my brother's room and kill him in the time frame."

"I read…"

"One moment Toby."

"Sorry."

"Danny we've got that on record, but even if you went there at 12.10 that is still in the time frame of your brother's death. We don't have a lot to go on I am afraid. The jury will hear what the landlady says and there is no defense for that. The time you clock out at work does not help as well."

"What about the detectives Banks hired, did they come up with anything?"

"I am sorry to we not did hire any."

"Looks like I will be in prison for the rest of my life. Banks and Banks have been no help to me at all. They are taking the legal aid money and sending six different people to represent me. Having so many different lawyers does not help me John."

"You are right Mr. Mundy, can I suggest if I was prosecution I would win the case hands down. No problems because you've got no defense. We could tell the jury how you've been raised and look after him for years and you love him as if he was your best friend. The fact remains that the landlady saw you with the knife in your hand and there was no one else remotely around at the murder scene apart from you."

"Did Banks speak to my wife and kids about my relationship with my brother? One of her favorite sayings is that I loved my brother more than her and the kids."

"Yes they did. I got statements from her and the children. I am afraid they won't be coming to court as the children have got school and it will be too much for her and the children."

"Yes I think she is right. I don't like the kids seeing me in hand cuffs."

"Danny, Phillip St John and I spoke at length last night and as he told you he would rather prosecute this case. He said he will win hands down. Have you thought about going guilty and throwing yourself at the judges mercy?

You will get a lighter sentence."

"I understand what you are saying but I did not kill my brother and I cannot do that. I don't think there is any more to say about that."

"Well Danny I will do my best for you in court and I will see you on Monday morning before we go to trial."

"Thanks to the both of you."

They shook hands and they left. Danny sat on the chair thinking of how other people might look at his case. They would be right. Looking at his case from the outside he would think the same. His kids were happy and Linda looked like she was happy. If Danny stayed in prison for a few years he could earn money for them to go to university like Johnny wanted to do. Danny did not kill Johnny and he would not go guilty. He would stay in prison and earn money and send the kids to university. The visit hall was empty of lawyers and they got to wait before they went back, waiting in line. Then they were taken up to the small room, searched then walked back to wing to wait for the iron gate to be opened, then walked up to his cell. Cyril was there.

"How did it go?"

"They are telling me to go guilty and I will get a lesser sentence. I will not say I killed my brother, even if they say I will get five or ten years."

"It's up to you my friend. Come get your plate as its tea time."

"I am not hungry mate, you go. I will see you in the morning."

"Danny if you are going to court tomorrow, you'd better eat something. They will come for you at 5am to go to court, it's going to be a very long day."

"I have my plate. Let's go."

After he had his tea he took out the letter that Linda had written and he read it again, thinking about how happy the kids were, doing things that he could not afford to give them. Linda seemed happy too. Was she having an affair with that guy? He was paying the barrister, giving her somewhere rent-free. Also he must have been paying for the lessons that the kids were having. He must have been stupid not to think that.

He never took the kids out as a dad. He only went on holiday once every three years or so. Danny's life was pub and work and sleep. He could not even help his kids with their homework. He was a useless father. If this guy was a good father figure, good luck to him. Danny was not going to deprive his kids of what they were having now. Danny would not rock the boat. He would say nothing but he would write them a nice letter when he came back from court the next day.

All through the day and night he was thinking about how happy the kids were without him. What if he was found not guilty? He would go back to them and what kind of life would his kids have? His mind was all mixed up. Maybe he could get more money from the company but would they take him back and pay him more? Danny must try and get some sleep as Cyril said it would be a long day. Danny wondered who would be there. The kids did not write if he gave them money. He must try and sleep........

The door opened.

"Mundy – court now. So get ready. I have to take you to reception by 5.15 am."

"Sir can I have a quick shower?"

"We've got no time for that, sorry. I've got to get a prisoner, I will be back in a second."

The officer came back with another prisoner and said, "Go downstairs by the gate and wait."

When he got by the gate Danny knew he had met this con before. He was one of the new ones and he nodded to him. Danny did the same but he was still half asleep when they waited and waited. At 5.45 an officer opened the gate from outside.

"Come this way lad."

They made their way to reception and were placed in the very big room. When he first came to this jail that seemed like a lifetime away. He was called and he went to a little room to be strip searched. Then he was put back in that large room. He could see officers coming on duty still in their own clothes. Danny could see the con who worked at reception cleaning. Then they took the other con to be searched and when he came back it was 6.15. Both of them were waiting again. Another officer came and asked their names in order to double check all names were correct. Then he left. At 7am he was still waiting and falling asleep.

"Are you ready lads?"

The other con said, "We've been ready for ages."

"Mundy come here. I am going to handcuff your hands together and then handcuff one hand to the wagon."

Another officer opened the gate and Danny walked with him to the front desk where he was met by a sergeant.

"What's your name?"

"Mundy, sir."

"That's ok, take him in the wagon."

They walked together and another officer opened the exit door and they walked for about ten more steps. Then an officer was waiting and opened the door to the van. They quickly went up the small step and he put Danny in a cubical and told him to push his hand in the small space between the frame and the door, then he unlocked his cuffs from Danny's. Soon the officer brought the other con in the van and then he told the driver, "We are ready to go."

Danny heard a loud engine noise as the van moved towards the exit out of the yard and towards the main gate. He stopped and switched off the engine and he could see him going to the main reception for vehicles. Within a few minutes he came back and opened the van door.

"They've got a delivery coming in, we've got to wait."

"Why don't they just let us out? We are going to be late for court."

"They don't care about that, it's just their jobs. I am going to wait in the reception office and grab a quick cuppa."

Danny was not thinking whether or not they were going to be late. His mind was thinking how happy his kids were playing tennis, swimming and having horse riding lessons. They must've been having the time of their lives. He wondered if his mate Bill would be there and if Brian's mate put the money through the letter box. He hoped the crew handled themselves while he was at court. He brought the book to read. He was reading it but it was not registering in his mind. When they got on the motorway, he did not even realise that they'd left the prison. At 8.30, he wondered what was going to happen at the court. Danny was feeling hungry.

"Governor I am feeling hungry, any grub?"

"Sorry nothing in the van. When you get to the courts you will be given something to eat and a drink."

The other con asked, "Governor, what time are we going to get there?"

"Should be by 9.30 am."

Cyril said it would be a long journey so gave him a book called 'The Lincoln Lawyer' to read. He couldn't get his head into it. He'd tried to read it but couldn't get past the first page. He put it down and looked at the roads and watched the people on the road going about their business. He was nodding off.....

The van stopped and parked in a compound when they arrived at the court. The officer took the other con first and about ten minutes later he came back for Danny. He opened the door slightly.

"Put your two hands through the door."

He did that and handcuffed one of his hands to him then opened the door fully. They walked together down some steps and in an area where other prisoners were waiting and some were in cubicles. He took his handcuffs and told him to sit next to the cons he came with. He spoke for the very first time to him.

"You are Danny Mundy, you run things in our block?"

"Yes I am Danny. What is your name?"

"Jake."

He was small but he was built like Kevin, in the mid-twenties, clean cut but no fashion statement. Just plain. You could see he was not like other cons trying to be something he is not.

"What are you here for?"

"Fight in the pub. G. B. H."

"You should not get much for that?"

"That's what my lawyer said - two to four years. I might get a suspended sentence because I work for a living and have never been in trouble before."

"I hope you get out buddy, who is your lawyer?"

"Raj Patel."

"You are joking me, he used to represent me. Then he left the company and set up himself. Have you got his number?"

"Here is his card, who is representing you?"

"Banks and Banks."

"My mother said they were useless."

"How would your mum know?"

"She is a social worker."

"Your mum's right, they are useless."

A door opened.

"Danny Mundy, your barrister is here so follow me."

They walked for a few steps and he opened the door where there was Toby and Phillip.

"Good morning Danny, have a seat."

"I have been travelling since 5am, can I have something to eat or drink please?"

"I will see what I can do Danny. Phillip will go over the case with you."

"Thanks Toby."

They went over the case.

"You must show a photo of when I first came to prison. I told him he must ask Eden if everyone asked others to clock them off and he also does it for staff. He must show the statements what my wife said about. I loved Danny more that I loved her and the kids. Make clear that I have no motive to kill my brother."

He nodded and made notes.

"I must tell you the landlady always hated me. We somehow never got on since Johnny moved into her room, I don't know why."

"Here you are Danny. A ham sandwich and a hot drink."

"Thanks Toby."

"Toby any more you want to add to what Danny has told me here? Have a quick read."

"I am afraid I did not manage to get a photo of Danny all those months ago."

"What about the rest?"

"Yes I have."

"Danny - the landlady is the key. Why do you think she hated you?"

"I went to pick up Johnny to go to the pub and he was in the communal kitchen and those two were having a good laugh. I said in jest 'what are you chatting to this old bag for?' She said, "Who you calling an old bag? Get out of my house and don't come back.' I took no notice of her and waited for Johnny. As we left Johnny said 'she lets me off the rent so I have to humor her.' We have been at war ever since."

"I think our main defense is no motive and you were not a healthy man then, but you were still a very big man. I think that's it so let's get up there and wait to be called by an officer when it is time."

Chapter Twenty

The court case. DAY ONE

On their way back to the prison.

"How did it go Jake?"

"I got two years and two suspended. I've done one year and just got a year left. My boss was there and he said I can have my old job back. I think that swung it with the judge. By the way, Raj said to give him a call then he will come see you. How did you get on?"

"Police and forensic did most of the talking. I will be honest with you. I did not listen too much as my mind was in a daze."

"Did you see Bill your mate?"

"No I did not but he is a good fella. I am so tired. I just want to go to bed when I get back because this is so draining."

On the way back there was a lot of traffic and traffic jams. They got back to the prison at about 7.45. Security check took place under the van and looked over the van. Then Danny was cuffed and taken to reception, strip searched and put in a holding cell. Then he waited for an officer to take Jake and him to the Wing. At around 8pm an officer came.

"Ok lads follow me. I will get you something to eat and milk and cereal for the morning. Long day eh?"

"Yes Sir, a very long day. I've got weeks of this. Hoping I don't go crazy."

"Here you are, curry and rice. Just get a plate and take as much as you like. It still should be hot. Take some milk and cereal each."

They put the cereal and milk in their pockets and took as much as the plate could hold.

"Come let me take you back to the house block."

The officer was walking fast and some food was falling off the plate. He must have been rushing to watch Coronation Street on T.V. or something. He quickly opened the wing and opened Jake's cell and ran up the stairs and opened Danny's door on the way down.

"Close your door. It will lock itself."

"Yes sir."

He locked the main gate before Danny got into his cell. Danny lay on the bed and fell asleep. He heard the central heating pipe knocking which woke him up. He got out of bed and put his ear to the pipe.

"How did it go today?"

"Nothing much - just the police giving their findings and forensics report. You're right, it's a very long day. I fell asleep as soon as I got in. You woke me up."

"Sorry mate. I think your boys had problems today, but it was sorted. People must know you are in court today."

"Thanks for telling me. Just keep an eye on things for me and tell the boys to give you any messages for me."

The next night he came back from the court after a long tiring day again. He went into his cell and sat on the chair. The food from the day before was still on the table and he got up and put it in the bin. He started to eat then the pipe knocked.

"Hi Cyril I am eating. Just knock back in half hour please."

Danny put the T.V. on and finished eating and tidied up. His head was still in a daze. He was thinking he didn't really care if he was found guilty or not. He never helped his kids when he was out, so staying inside would help no end. It would not be nice for them when people were saying their dad was a murderer. They might get teased at school.

DAY TWO

The next day the same thing happened, they were up and 5am, waiting at the gate and at reception, then off in the van to go out waiting in the traffic. After that was waiting time at the court to see the lawyers. Then waiting to go into the court room. After court waiting in the courts to go back then waiting to get out of the compound, then waiting in traffic, then waiting to get back in the prison, then waiting at reception. Then waiting to be strip searched. Then waiting at reception for an officer to take him back to block.

He got back to the wing when it was nine o'clock. The traffic had been bad. Danny put the food on the table and went and sat down on the toilet. He had a lot of wind in his system and wasn't used to waking up and eating early. The pipe knocked but he did nothing. After a few minutes he went and knocked on the pipe.

"How did it go today?"

"Nothing much. Just the prosecution talking about how I am guilty and saying I had ample time to kill my brother. The jury were looking at me like I was guilty already."

"Don't let it get to."

"I never thought I would have to go through all this every day. I am out of it."

"Quick question. Did that Bill come to court?"

"Yes, shit he is going to ring later. I will speak to you later. Let me get ready for the call."

Danny got the music box out and pushed it the right way to open the box. He'd got into bed where there was a phone under his pillow and put the box back correctly on the table. Pulling the cover over him in a seated position, he then took the phone out and noticed it was still on silent. There was no missed calls. He knew he would phone any minute now. With an eye on the phone, Danny kept one ear listening for the door and turned the light off. The phone call came.

"Hello Bill, nice to see you today. Can you give a full report about the house, daughter, account and job? Did you find the key in the shed OK?"

"Yes it was where you said it will be. I opened two accounts. It was hard as some banks will not open an account for ex-cons. £700 in a joint account with your daughter providing I take her to the bank and we do it together. It's in my name at the moment and I opened the other in my name."

"Text that account to me. I will get our customers to start paying into that account when they buy things from us. Did you manage to get a job?"

"You are not going to believe this but your old firm took me on. I start next Monday."

"Bill do not trust them and do not tell them what we are doing. I don't have to tell you the reasons why."

"Have you started to advertise for garden jobs as yet?"

"No. I will work for a while and then start to advertise for work. I prefer to be my own boss."

"No problem."

"Just to say the house has had a leak in the bath but its ok now. I can't see any bill though, your missus must have paid but there is an envelope. I think its money."

"Open it."

"Yes it is money. £250. What do you want me to do with it?"

"Put it in your account. You need to set the gardening business up as well, in case the old Bill want to know where you get the money."

"How am I going to meet with your daughter?"

"I will write to her and tell her. Ring me tomorrow Bill. I want to speak to Cyril and don't forget to text me those account details. See you."

"Phone you tomorrow."

Danny got of out bed and returned the phone under the pillow. He switched the light on and got a pen and paper. He took the phone with him to the toilet and checked for account details. It was there and he copied it for his diary. He took the music box into the toilet, opened it and switched off the phone, putting it in the box and closing it. You could open the window just enough for your hands to go outside of the window. Danny sat on the table and wrote the account details and instructions for what the crew had to do. He mentioned the account details and told them to inform punters they can pay for gear on the outside. They must put the money in the account once they'd checked money into the account and got the stuff they wanted. The money would be in the account straight away. He knocked the pipe twice, hard.

"Cyril I've sent a laundry bag with a tin in it. I wrote a letter that I want you to give to Ted. By the way any problems or any news?"

"I will swing the bag first when you get it. I will tell you the news, are you getting ready?"

A knock on the pipe.

"My hand is ready so swing it."

"I am swinging it now. Stretch your hand all the way out of the window."

Knock on the pipe

"Hold on, I forgot to put a tin in the bag. Get ready I am swinging again."

Speaking by the open window now, he said, "I bloody am. I got it. Hold onto your string at your end. I am pulling the bag in. Wait. Let me put the letter in. Pull it."

"I am pulling. I got it."

Speaking by the window.

"Go to the pipe and tell me the latest news."

"The crew miss you. They told me to tell you the business is good. They gave £115 to me. I have hidden it with the other stuff. I should give them a phone call tomorrow."

"Someone wants to pay 50 packs for a phone."

"Are they new cons on the block?"

"No, they have done business with us before."

"That's OK. Look, I am knackered."

"What happened in court today?"

"Just police and prosecution. Good night Cyril."

Danny sat on the table but the food was stone cold. He picked at it and had a little of the chicken and bit of the rest. Then he put the kettle on and T.V. He made a cup of tea and lay on the bed. Danny felt so lonely without Linda but if she was happy, he was happy for her. He thought the house would be done up. He didn't want to rock the boat with her and the kids. He would leave it as it was. Hopefully he could write the kids a letter tomorrow. He changed his mind and wrote it right then.

'Dear Amanda and Kim.

That was a nice letter you sent. I am so happy you are doing all these lessons so keep it up.

You will be too posh for your old dad. Who is best at sports?

The trial is this week. There are long days up at 4.45am and back at the prison at 8.30pm.

It's a shame mum and you can't come in person as it will help my case, the lawyer said. It will be better to say I loved Uncle Johnny more than her and the kids in court rather than a letter. But never mind. Make sure you do your studies. I am very proud of the two of you. I love you very much.

Tell mum I love her.

Bye for now - love you lots.

DAY THREE - WEDNESDAY

He got to the court at about 9am. It seemed the officer knew the routine. He went and got drinks for everyone then the lawyers came and had a chat with him. They went at about 9.55 and he got taken into the court.

The clerk called the first witness.

"Mr. Gordon Cleege."

Old Gordon in the witness box was swearing on the bible to tell the whole truth and nothing but the truth.

"Mr. Cleege how old are you?"

"82 sir."

"How long have you worked at Webb and Sons?"

"Since the war was over, about 60 years."

"What is the rule about clocking out?"

"Everyone must clock their own card or they will receive a warning."

"What happens when they do it all the time? Will they get another warning and get the sack?"

"What time on the 23rd of July 2005 did Mr. Danny Mundy leave Webb and sons to go for lunch?"

"I think midday, same as everyone else?"

"Did he leave any earlier?"

"I am not sure?"

"You covered for him and he left early. Didn't he?"

"You are making me confused."

"Mr. Miller you don't need to shout at Mr. Cleege."

"Sorry your honor."

"Mr. Cleege tell us in your own words what happened that day. Did you serve in the army?"

"Yes your honour, I signed up in 1940. I lied about my age."

"How old were you?"

"16 years old."

"Where did you serve?"

"I was in the African campaign before Monty came."

"I was there in 1946. I missed all the action. Thank God, so tell us what happened that day."

"Danny got a phone call from his brother at about 11.30 and told me he wanted to shoot out as soon as it was 12 and Eden the accountant would clock him out and he could leave dead on 12. Your honour, can I speak about the landlady?"

"Yes you can Mr. Cleege."

"I object your honour as this is highly irregular."

"Objection overruled. When you serve your country like Mr. Cleege I would listen to your objection. Carry on Mr. Cleege."

"One day Danny had to work overtime to get a special order out. It was Friday and he asked me to give Johnny his wage to give his wife Linda. I went to Johnny's house and knocked on the door. The landlady opened the door with a rude manner."

"What do you want?"

"I want to see Johnny."

"He is not here."

"I could see Johnny's lights were on and I could knock on his window if I stepped on the steps so I knocked the window and the curtain opened. Johnny saw and beckoned me in."

"Look he is in why are you lying?"

"Why do people are always disturb him?"

"Are you going to let me in?"

"She slammed the door in my face, then Johnny came out."

"Are you ok?"

"Yes I am fine. She hates people coming to see you. Danny is working overtime and he wants you to give this to Linda."

"Thank you Gordon. Are there more questions?"

The prosecution was vexed. He said, "Yes. Mr. Gordon Cleege do you suffer with any health problems?"

"Yes I do."

"What are they?"

"I have slow signs of Parkinsons and also signs of Alzheimer's disease."

"That will be all, thank you Gordon."

"But judge, I would like to ask a few questions, your honour."

"Gordon how long has Danny Mundy worked at the firm in your own words please?"

"Danny worked while he was at school. In fact, he came after school and Saturday and Sunday. If we had extra work then he used to bunk off school and come to work. Then he left school at 15 years old and worked full time. He was a bit like me."

"Tell us about his character. Do you consider him honest?"

"Danny is a very trustworthy man. I trust him with my life as many times he was left with cash in the office yet nothing ever went missing. All the boys working for us are trustworthy."

"Have you clocked anyone out at lunchtime or in the evening?"

"Yes many times, if the boys want to go to the shops, banks, anything I would clock them out. Sometimes I would clock out 6 or more at a time. I don't go out for lunch, my wife makes sandwiches for me."

"Did you think Mr. Mundy could murder his brother?"

"No he loved his brother. He looked after him for years. No way would Danny do that."

"Gordon do you at present suffer from Parkinsons and Alzheimer's and might that affect you at present?"

"Thanks to God they do not affect me at the moment."

"That will be all."

"Next witness - Mr. Eden Walker."

Eden sat in the box and swore on the bible.

"Mr. Miller how long have you worked at the company?"

"About seven years."

"Do you remember the 23rd Of July 2005?"

"Yes I do."

"What time did Danny get the call?"

"I think about 11.30."

"Are you sure about the time?"

"Not really as it could be earlier."

"What happened after that?"

"Danny asked me to clock him out at 12 midday, normally he asked Gordon."

"You mean Mr. Cleege."

"Why do think he asked you this time?"

"I suppose I was in the office - that's why."

"Could it be he wanted to leave the factory early so no one would see him? You know the office is just by the exit of the factory?"

"No I don't think so. They had a special order to fulfill."

"But is it possible he could have left early?"

"Yes it is possible."

"That will be all."

"I have a few questions for Mr. Walker."

"Were you friends with the late Johnny Mundy?"

"Yes we were, we were very good friends."

"What time did you clock out Mr. Mundy on the 23rd of July 2005?"

"I think just after he left the office at about 11.40 am."

"Why did you clock him out at this time?"

"I was going to lunch this time as well as I am doing the wages. It did not matter what time I clocked him out because I knew he was at work."

"What is the penalty for clocking someone out?"

"A warning. If they do it again they will get the sack."

"Do you think Mr. Mundy killed his brother?"

"No way, he was the apple of Danny's eyes."

"That will be all thank you."

"Call Mr. Webb."

"Mr. Webb how long have you had this company?"

"Gordon and I started it after the war around 1947 and we built it up from nothing."

"Do you know Danny Mundy?"

"Of course I do. I know all my staff?"

"Your clocking in and out system leaves a lot to be desired. It seems anyone can clock out any time and no warning will be given?"

"Is that so?"

"You have got one of your staff clocking out six people at a time and there is no warning or the sack."

"Ha, haaa."

"What do you find so funny, Mr. Webb?"

"Sorry your honour. He is talking about Gordon. How can I sack him when he owns 25% of the company? I trust all my staff and if any of them wants anything the company will help them. Danny can have his job back as soon as you find him not guilty."

"Thank you Mr. Webb - that will be all."

"I have one question for you Mr. Webb."

"Do you think Mr. Mundy killed his brother?"

"No he did not, his brother was his life."

"That will be all thank you."

"We will break for lunch, back at 2.30."

"Court adjourned till 2.30."

Danny was taken back to the cells where he was put in a single cell and brought lunch. It was beef slice with Yorkshire pudding, green peas and boiled potatoes; a microwave lunch. After's was custard and cake. It was the best lunch that he had had in ages.

At 2pm the lawyers came to see him. They both told him it went better than expected that morning. In the afternoon they wanted to produce his wife and children's statements.

The barrister said, "It would have been better if your wife had come in person."

The lawyer said, "I asked her again to come but she said no, I could not force her."

"When is the landlady going on the witness stand?"

"Danny that's the key. The prosecution will call the landlady. We've got no defense for what she was going to say and she will say it with venom. The only defense we have for that is you have no motive for killing Johnny."

That afternoon they read the statements from Linda and the kids. It was clear that it did not help the case.

"The prosecution made it out that Linda did not believe me. That's why she did not come to the trial. That's the reason she made a statement. I don't think it went well, nor did the lawyers. After the letters were read the judge adjourned the case."

It had been a long day but he would get used to this. He was fully drained. This time it was 9.15 pm and it seemed to be getting later and later. He put food on his table and went to the toilet where he was full of wind. His eating and going to the toilet system was out of sync. Somehow today he felt hungry. He started to eat, the pipe knocked.

"I am eating, I will call you later."

Bill was going to ring and if Danny didn't answer he would ring back later. Each time Bill would only ring once and put the phone down. Danny was hungry for his favourite pizza and got a whole one due to the officers telling him to take want he wanted. Perhaps he should have grabbed another one for the morning. Never mind. That was good and a nice cup of tea washed it down. He texted Bill to ring him tomorrow. He supposed he'd have to tell Cyril what happened today. Gently he knocked the pipe.

"How did it go today?"

"Nothing much, tomorrow is the day mate."

"Why is that?"

"The landlady will go on the stand. How did the sale of the phone go?"

"A bit of a problem there, they wanted to give only 25 packs this week and 25 the following week."

"So what happened was the crew gave them the phone and kept the charger."

"That was good thinking. Was the phone fully charged?"

"No only 75% worth so they have to come back with the rest of 25 packets."

"Did they give it out to our keepers?" (Keepers are prisoners who look after things for the dealers so that the screws do not think they are up to no good)

"Yes I still have a lot of gear."

"Tell the crew they've done well. I am tired so I am going to bed."

"Good night Danny best of luck tomorrow."

DAY FOUR

There was not much traffic on the road so they reached court at about 8.45am. Danny had some coffee and two sandwiches and noticed there were not a lot of cons today or perhaps he was early. Why did he get extra sandwiches and crisp? It was like he was back to his old ways of eating. It's the coming and going to court that made his body out of whack with his head. He ate everything and drank the coffee, while looking at the graffiti. Kilroy spoke to him.

"Banks were the worst lawyers. If you got them you are dead meat."

Danny stopped reading and was the only one there. It was coming close to 9.30 and he hoped the lawyers might be there soon.

The door opened.

"Mr. Mundy follow me. Your solicitors are here."

"Good morning Danny take a seat."

"Thank you Mr. Johns."

"Where is Toby?"

"He is running late."

"Typical Banks."

"Not to worry. I've got the brief for today."

"You are been called Sir."

"We are coming, thank you."

They were soon in the court room.

"Call Hilda Hunt."

"Call Mrs. Hilda Hunt."

She got into the witness box and she was looking all around, wearing her thick rimmed glasses.

"Hold the bible please Mrs. Hunt. Do you swear by almighty God that you will tell the truth and nothing but the truth?"

"Yes I do."

"Where do you live?"

"I live at number six, Bishop Road Canterbury."

"How long have you lived there?"

"Over twenty years."

"Do you work?"

"Yes I do. I have lodgers. Some pay for room and board and only Johnny rented just the room."

"Is it a good living?"

"Yes my husband before he died bought the freehold. I make a living."

"Cast your mind back to the 23rd of July 2005, can you tell me what happened that day?"

"I was cleaning the kitchen."

"Sorry to stop you. Where is the kitchen in relation to Johnny's room?"

"As you walk into the ground floor the basement is below. You open the front door and the wall to the left leads to Johnny's room, the first room on the right and if you carry on along the passage you come to the kitchen."

"I will put up this drawing. Take a good look at it. Does that look right to you?"

"Yes it does."

"What made you go into Johnny's room?"

"I could hear the traffic from outside."

"Soon as you heard it did you walk to Johnny's room?"

"I am not too sure. I had my hoover on doing the corners which get really filthy, then I did the dishes."

"Tell us what you did when you heard the traffic?"

"I walked to the front door which was wide open. I wanted to shut it. Johnny's room was open so I looked inside. In there was Mundy with a knife in his hand. He said something. I can't remember what. I shouted 'murder murder', then I went outside and called for help."

"Mrs. Hunt is there any reason you think Danny killed his brother?"

"Objection."

"Withdraw the question."

"Mrs. Hunt, did Johnny and Danny Mundy have any arguments or did Mr. Mundy threaten Johnny?"

"They always argued. Mr. Mundy always wanted money off Johnny."

"That's a lie."

"There will be no outbursts in the court room Mr. Mundy."

"She is lying, your honor."

"Be quiet or I will have you removed from the courts. Carry on Mr. Miller."

"Thank you my lord but that will be all Mrs. Hunt."

She was about to leave the box.

"Please remain seated Mrs. Hunt as the defense will cross examine."

"Mrs. Hunt how many lodgers do you have?"

"I have five, four now."

"How many pay full board?"

"Four."

"Did Johnny paid full board?"

"No he didn't."

"He said he ate at his sister-in-laws."

"Since you have been renting, how many people have not paid for full board?"

"Only Johnny."

"Why is that?"

"I felt sorry for him, his father and mother had passed away and he was saving to buy his own house."

"Is there any other reason Mrs. Hunt?"

"No."

"I put it to you that you were in love with Johnny Mundy and you were jealous of the men that came to his room. That was why you always say he is not at home when he is."

"Yes we did like each other. He told me if anyone knocks to tell them he was not in."

"Did you make Johnny's breakfast and evening lunch even when he did not eat it?"

"I always cook extra anyway. I did not want the food to go to waste."

"Mrs. Hunt could you explain how you get to the basement and first floor from the ground floor flat please?"

"To get to the basement use the front door or the stairs in the hallway next to the kitchen that take you to the basement or the stairs in the passageway that take you up to the toilet which has a window leading to an outside flat roof. That leads to the outside garden and back yard and then to the room on top."

"Can anyone get to the back and outside of the house?"

"Yes there is a door to the back yard in the basement, though nobody ever uses it and from the toilets you can get through the window and you are outside."

"Is it possible that someone could use the stairs to the basement and go to the backyard?"

"No I would hear because I was in the kitchen."

"Let me read your statement. You said you could not hear anything because the hoover was on."

"Yes that was true."

"So it is possible that someone else could have been in the flat without you hearing?"

"I am waiting for an answer?"

"Yes it is possible."

"No more questions."

"The court will be adjourn till tomorrow."

On the way back in the van he was thinking the case went well, as the landlady showed her real character. If released back to the same job, disturbing the kid's life would be no good for them. He was a different man now. Danny wasn't sure what he wanted anymore. In just under two years in prison he had achieved a lot. What more could he achieve if he was in prison longer. That was his trouble. He thought too much.

At 8.30 he got back to his cell, not feeling hungry but he put the kettle on and the pipe knocked.

"How did it go today Danny?"

"It went well. I am going to eat now. You have anything important to tell me?"

"Couple of Muslims beat up one of Wade's men in the causeway. The officers didn't find them as they wore their dress and they all looked the same. It's been lockdown today so we were all fed at the door. Only workers were allowed out."

"How is my crew doing?"

"Everything is good. I've got some cash for you."

"Hide it with the rest, I am going to bed early so see you tomorrow."

"Good night Danny."

Danny hoped there would be no lockdown at the weekend as he needed to give this cell a good clean, mop and sort his clothes. He would give some to Cyril in the morning if lockdown was coming as he wouldn't be able to do it. Tomorrow he was taking his turn going on the stand. He wished Linda would come, though she'd got her own life, therefore he shouldn't think about her."

He did not sleep well last night. Bill was apparently doing OK and he'd started decorating the place. That Monday Bill would be starting at Danny's old place.

The door opened.

"Mundy, court."

"Sir. Can I give my washing to Cyril?"

"Yes."

He opened Cyril's door and put his washing in and closed the door.

DAY FIVE

The van got there at 10.15 because there was an accident on the road and they were seeing long delays. He was sweating in the van like he used to when he first came to prison. Just as he arrived there they were called and there was no time for a drink and a sandwich. Danny's clothes were wet. He was taken into the court and was called to the witness box where he must swear on the bible to tell the truth. He gave his name and address.

"Mr. Mundy can you tell us what happened on the 23rd of July 2005?"

"Eden came and told me I had a call from my brother."

"I think about 11.30 but I am not sure."

"We have the telephone records and it was at 11.20."

"Our clocks must be wrong at the factory then."

"We checked that the clocks there were saying the correct times. What did you do after the call, and what did Johnny want?"

"He wanted me to go to his room straight away. I should have, but we had an urgent job to finish off so I told him I would come at lunchtime. He insisted that I came straight away. I did not listen to him. After putting the phone down I asked Eden the accountant to clock me out as I had to go and see Johnny at lunchtime. He said he would do it. I told old Cleege I might be late back from lunch and he said ok. Then at 12 o'clock I rushed out, grabbing my ham sandwich and eating it on the way.

When I got there the front door was open. I thought Johnny left it open for me not to disturb the landlady. I walked up the six steps and Johnny's room was open. I walked in and Johnny was sitting with his back against the bed and legs on the floor. He was not moving. I lifted him up and put him on the bed and I did not notice the knife in him until he was on the bed. As soon as I saw that, I pulled the knife out but he was dead. I was in a state of shock. I could not speak. Then the landlady came to the door and shouted, 'murder murder, you killed Johnny.' I said call the police and the ambulance. I think she ran out in the street and shouted 'murder, murder.'

It took ages before the police came then the ambulance came and took over. I sat on the bed in shock, looking at Johnny. That is all I know."

"What time did you leave the factory?"

"According to the clocks at work 12 midday."

"What time does your clocking card say?"

"I have no idea?"

"The time we got is 11.35 on the clocking machine."

"Did the landlady see you with the knife in your hand?"

"But I took the knife out of Johnny."

"Answer the question - did the landlady see you with the knife in your hand?"

"Yes she did."

"Mr. Mundy when did you find out that Johnny was gay?"

"I knew a very long time ago."

"How long ago? Give a date please."

"Since he was ten years old he told me he did not like girls and I said make sure dad don't find out."

"Why did you tell him that?"

"Our father hated gays."

"How do you feel about gays?"

"I am not one and don't mix with them apart from when I am with Johnny."

"So you have the same feelings about them as your father?"

"I do not hate anyone."

"I put it to you that you did hate gays and you had an argument with your brother to stop being gay. The business that he needed your help on the phone was a lie. I put it to you Mr. Mundy that you had an argument with your brother and you killed him, then you were found with the knife in your hands. You cannot deny that."

"I loved my brother and I could never kill him."

"I put it to you that you hated gays like your father and you killed your brother, no more questions."

"Danny did you kill your brother?"

"No sir. I did not. I loved my brother."

"Tell me, did you have cross words then?

"No sir, we did not. While we were growing up we never had a cross word. My wife teases me, always saying that I loved my brother Johnny more than her and the children."

"I will read out the statements Linda made and the children."

"My husband is a very good man. He did not kill his brother as he loved him more than me and my children. That's his little brother."

"Our father loved our uncle and he would never kill him because we all loved him very much."

"No more questions."

"The court will be adjourned till 2pm today."

That night they got back at 8.30 pm and the wing was very quiet which made Danny figure something was up.

He asked the officer.

"The block is very quiet tonight - why?"

He kept walking up to his cell but did not answer.

"Sir was there a problem today?"

"Nothing for you to worry about. There, your cell door is open, get in."

He knew that Cyril always listened for him. He would tell him what went on. As he got in the pipe knocked.

"Hi Danny, how did the courts go today?"

"Nothing to report. What went down today?"

"Today is when the Muslims have their church and about 20 cons somehow got into the Moshe with pool balls in their socks. Some had chair legs and various other weapons and attacked the Muslims in the Moshe. There were only two officers on duty and they got a very bad beating. Not as bad as the Muslims as they were on their knees praying on the floor."

"Anyone got killed?"

"Let me put it like this - they had to call outside help with ambulances and helicopters. I don't know if anyone was injured or killed."

"Who were the ring leaders?"

"I am not quite sure but I think Wade and Brian's dad."

"Do you think it will be lockdown tomorrow?"

"It definitely is. I am sure cons are getting shipped out tomorrow."

"I am going to have an early night. See you later."

"Good night Danny."

Danny got his musical box and went into the toilet where he took the phone out and texted Liam to ring him at 9.30 pm. Then he put the phone in the box and on the table, so he would be ready. After that he started to eat. Then he had thought to call a listener and ask Brian to tell him what happened today. He pressed the buzzer and carried on eating. Looking at the time it was 9.15. If Liam rang it was on the lowest sound. No one would hear it. If he didn't answer at one ring, he wouldn't ring any longer. He tidied up and wondered how that cell could be so untidy when he was not there during the day. The door opened and an officer spoke.

"What do you want?"

"A listener."

"The listeners are very busy tonight. It is going to be a long night."

"Sir I will wait."

The door locked on time. Danny got the box and went under the blanket. He took the phone out of the secret compartment, went and switched off the lights and went back to bed when the phone rang.

"How are you Liam and Ted?"

"We are good. Ted will do the talking Danny."

"The guy who bought the phone comes with the phone with no charge every day for us to charge it for him and we've got to keep a watch on it in the cell."

"He can't talk to his family alone for the phone to be flat."

"You are right. Liam said one of his friends said he has a business outside selling sports cars and he is in for some sort of fraud."

"He said he will pay the rest tomorrow, so if he doesn't, make sure you tell him he will have to pay interest on the twenty five pack. That will be 37.5 packs the next Saturday and if he does pay he will be charged two packs per a charge on his phone and ask Liam to find out where his garage is or show room. How is business? Did any of our punters go with Wade?"

"I am not sure who went with Wade. He paid them two packs of burn each to go with him and I don't know a lot more."

"Hopefully I will see you boys tomorrow."

"See you later boss."

Packing the box away on the table, he began thinking about the day. St John said that the prosecution can't prove a motive, only the flimsy notion that because of his father he hated gays. The knife in his hand was their case. It was up to the jury. He had fallen asleep when the door opened. He looked at the time and it was 11.30.

"Do you still want a listener?"

"Yes."

"Follow me."

Danny was half asleep, following the four officers down on the ground floor and to the listener's room. He opened the door and went in. The door was locked behind him.

"Where is Brian? I wanted to see him."

"Sorry mate, you've got us."

"Why are you taking that attitude with me?"

"Sorry Danny. I did not mean it to come out like that."

"That's better, one – tell me where Brian is and two - tell me what happened today."

"What little we heard is there are going to be mass shipping outs and new listeners will be trained up. Brian and his dad are shipped out to different prisons."

"What evidence do they have on Brian?"

"As you know they don't need evidence, they can do anything they want."

"Are you going to see Brian?"

"We are on the same wing so I suppose so."

"Give Brian my number and ask him to call me."

"I do not think Brian has got a phone. His cell and his father's cell were searched and stripped with all new beds and tables."

"Tell Brian I asked for him to give you the number. You know how to do that without getting caught and ask him if I can do anything for him. I am pressing the bell and I hope they don't keep us here too long."

That night he lay on the bed and fell asleep. He didn't change his clothes or anything, wondering what was going to happen the next day.

Banging and shouting woke Danny up so he looked up to see it was Cyril.

"How did you get in?"

"We've been open since 7.40am yet you were sleeping when the officer opened the door. Come and look out on the landing."

"I am half asleep, leave me be."

"Come outside now."

Danny went to the landing and by the rails there were at least 12 officers on the ground floor.

"Look Danny they are now opening Ware's cell."

"He is in a three man cell."

"Yes Wade will be led out in handcuffs and his crew are handcuffed as well. They are being taken to the ground floor."

"Look Cyril they are opening more cells and cuffing more. They must be all the ones who attacked the mosque. Cyril they have not opened the Muslim boys' cell as yet."

"Danny there must be 16 they have arrested and they will be shipped out to all different prisons."

Half an hour later they were all gone. Danny went to the Muslim cell, which was now open wide and all three of them were in bed.

"I'm so sorry what has happened to you boys. If I can do anything let me know."

"Don't you think you white boys have done enough?"

"Shut up Karim, Danny is a valued friend of ours - apologies."

"I am sorry Khan. I spoke out of turn, please accept my apology Mr. Mundy."

"That's OK Karim. I understand how you feel, I could see you boys are tired. I will take my leave."

Danny left the Muslim boys and went to see Ted and Liam. He went into their cell again and both of them were still in bed.

"Everywhere I go this morning everyone is sleeping. Good morning."

"Morning boss."

"I won't disturb you but come and give a report of everything this week but before you see me go to all our keepers and take a stock of all the things they've got for us and both of you do the same with your stock. If you've got any cash, bring that to me as well."

"Hold on Danny. I will give you the cash now. We are expecting a lot more today."

"Today is canteen day."

"Yes we know, we were up late last night doing the figures."

"We'll have you sent money to your family this week Ted?"

"No. I wanted to tell you how much first."

"That goes for you as well Liam?"

"Yes."

"OK I will see you later."

He went back to his cell where there was Cyril waiting for him. Danny didn't know what he would do without him as he had taken over from his old mate Kevin.

"Here is your washing. I see you've done your rounds."

"Thanks buddy for the washing. It's got to be done. Got to keep on top of it. Those boys will do that as well and you. By the way have the officers searched Wade's cell?"

"No but his cell has got a large padlock on it."

"What about the rest of the people that were shipped out?"

"No they only shipped out Wade."

"Go and count all of the cash and stock you have."

Danny was still on the landing when Cyril came back.

"Here it is Danny. I always have it updated."

Cyril gave a paper with everything he had and Danny looked at it then tore it up and flushed it down the toilet. There was another knock on the cell door.

"It's Ted, Danny."

"Come in."

"It's me, Ted."

"Here is the cash we have. First of all £90."

"Give it to Cyril, let's go outside because they have opened the yard. We could walk and you can tell us everything outside."

They went out in the yard while Cyril stayed and hid the money. The boys gave all the updates on stock, including two things that could be problems. A couple of the new cons in the house owned twenty five packs.

"Ted are they a problem? You want me to visit Phillips and Webb?"

"They have not caused any problems as yet but I think it could be bad for you to visit them. It could flare up when you go to court."

"You are right Ted. I will leave it to you two. I still think we need another member as we will have lots of business now Wade and Brian are not going to be here."

"I don't trust anyone as yet Danny."

"Have you been looking Ted?"

"No Danny, but there is enough for one more I think."

"Cyril does a lot for me. He does not get paid though he is under my protection so no one will trouble him and he is happy about that. Look here he is coming now. What's up Cyril?"

"There is a lockdown this afternoon so canteen will be at the doors."

"Shit that's all we need. Just make sure you see the main guys who owe the most first."

"Ok boss, by the way, you have not said anything about your trial, how is it going?"

"Sorry with all that went down yesterday it took my mind off it. I think it's about fifty/fifty but I have no idea what the jury will do. I will just carry on assuming I will be in prison for the next twenty five years."

"Boss why don't you try to go the mosque today? You have been before."

"If I go, the Muslims will think I am taking the piss."

"But they know you."

"Not all of them know me."

He went back to his cell and lay on the bed thinking how Ted and Liam got everything sorted out with no problems. Everything was good in prison. What would they do when he was found not guilty? Would Linda come back or would she let the kids come back? He couldn't do that to the kids when they had brilliant lives now. He couldn't take that away from them. Danny couldn't go back to his old life on the out anymore. Now he wanted a lot more out of life and would not be contented with his old life. He would leave it in the hands of God. Nearly two years in prison and he was a different man. Falling asleep, he was roused up as the door opened.

"Go and get your tea and come straight back to your cell."

"Yes sir."

He got his plate. Cyril was outside so they went down together to find there was not a queue. He got his meal and Cyril got his and they walked back to the cell.

"We've got new cons on the wing already."

"How do you know?"

"The pipes can talk haha."

That night he did a bit of reading and the first exercise for the week. He ached when he started doing them but he'd got to keep fit so did his whole routine.

Sunday morning he went to church, came back and went to the gym, then had a long shower. No one was in there so that was good. He got back from showering and it was dinner time. There was a letter on the floor of his cell which was put on the table and Cyril was outside. Together they got their lunch.

"You were lucky the officers let you shower as the Wing is in lockdown."

"I think he said to get back to the cell but I didn't hear him. That's probably why no one was in the showers."

"Anyway we are locked this afternoon."

"I will see you later Cyril."

After eating, he opened the letter and it was from Mrs. Clare Miller. Danny didn't know who she was. After reading the letter he never thought about another woman in his life apart from Linda. What was he thinking about? She was only wishing him all the luck with his case and she didn't believe he killed his brother. He looked out of the plastic frame and then out of the window. It was the first time he'd done that. What was he looking for? He'd best do his workout routine and when finished that do some reading. Who could have sent him that letter?

That morning he woke up at 4am and did a workout and a bit of reading as last week he did nothing. Were there going to be any more witnesses, he wondered?

DAY SIX

They reached the Old Bailey at 8.25am and he was very glad to have time to eat something and have a chat with the lawyers to see what they thought of the trial so far. He spoke to them and they were saying that the trial was going well as the Prosecution couldn't find a motive for him to kill his brother. The only problem was the landlady. All they could do now was hope.

They walked into the court room around 10.15 then the judge came in and they all stood up. Danny was told to be seated.

The prosecution made summing up statements and then St John went over and over the fact that there was no motive. He sounded very good so Danny believed that there was no way the jury could find him guilty. After that, the judge sent the jury to deliberate whether he was guilty or not. Danny was taken to the holding cell. One of the guards came up to him and spoke.

"I don't think you are guilty son and your barrister did a very good summing up. I think you will be going home today."

He locked the cell and said, "I will bring you some grub."

After this he left Danny thinking about home and what he was going to do about Linda and the kids. Perhaps she wanted to stay at the cottage but he hoped he could at least see the kids. He didn't think he would go back to his old job. He would set up his own business. He'd got the feeling and smell of it and he loved it. The food came and Danny ate it, while making plans for his release. Realising he wasn't sure of the outcome, he mustn't make any plans or he might not get free. He fell asleep and was awoken by the guard who said, "The jury are still out and it is 3.30pm now. I don't think they will finish today son but that's good news for you."

"Why do you say that sir?"

"I have seen many cases and if they don't come back in an hour or so they will not be coming back today. I could be wrong."

"Thank you sir, can I have a cold drink?"

"All I've got is water."

"That will do, thanks."

He brought the water and he had a big gulp and sat down, looking at the clock. Time was going very slowly so he stopped looking at the clock. There were magazines and newspapers there. Danny picked one up and could now read it in his head which was full of expectation and disappointment at the same time. He finally found the wanted ads and started reading them.

"Come on son. It's time for you to go back to the prison."

"How can the jury find me guilty when there was no motive?"

"They have not come out yet as they are still discussing your case. It is time for you to go back to the prison."

"Thank you. I was confused."

"Once they are out you've got a chance son. Come on, let's get you back in the van."

He was so pleased to get back in the van and wondered if he could still run the business in prison on the out. There was no way so sooner or later it would come to the end. Danny was in limbo now as he didn't know what was going to happen. He forgot Bill had started working at his old firm that day. That is why he did not see him. He got back to his cell at about 9pm, put the food on the table and washed up and then the pipe knocked.

"Hi Danny how's it go today?"

"Nothing to report that's new. Has anything happened today?"

"Do you remember those new prisoners that live on the threes? They gave Ted a lot of problems today and they took stock from Ted and said they will pay back on canteen day."

"Where was Liam?"

"He was at the gym. When he came back, Ted told him and both of them went on the threes and had words with them. They assured Liam that they will pay back on canteen day."

"They are taking the piss so Liam and Ted came back with their tail between their legs."

"It was at least five of the new boys with Phillips and Mark. I don't think Ted and Liam could do anything."

"Thanks Cyril."

The food was getting cold.

Knocking on the pipes.

"Cyril pass all the cash you have."

"Give me a few minutes'."

Knock on the pipes.

"I am going to swing the bag over so get your hand out of the window ready."

"I am ready, swing."

"It's not swinging Danny."

"Did you put a tin with the money in the bag?"

"Sorry Danny I forgot. I will now."

"Swing hard....... I got it."

He pulled the laundry bag in and took the money out.

"You can pull it back now Cyril."

Danny wanted to take the money with him the next day, by squeezing the money in very tight rolls so it could fit in his back passage. If he was searched they would not find it. He would do that in the morning as he didn't fancy doing it but knew he needed to. If he was released tomorrow he would at least have some money to start with. He was not going to think about Linda and the kids as he wanted to get some sleep.

DAY SEVEN

Danny could not sleep due to twisting and turning all night. He was ready when the officer came to open the door. They reached the Old Bailey at about 8.55am and saw the same guard as last time. This was a kind man who brought a sandwich and a cup of coffee and crisps for him.

"I wish you the best of luck today. I don't think you killed your brother and neither do many of the guards that work here. They've got the wrong man. I think that landlady knows a lot more than she is saying. I am locking the door now."

"Thank you sir."

Danny got The Lincoln Lawyer book out, sort of reading it but it took him ages. He did not understand it fully but wanted to keep trying to. If nothing else. It would take his mind off things. He started to read it again and now it was slowly becoming a lot clearer.

"The Jury has finished making a decision and they are calling you. I will open the door. I am sorry I have to handcuff you and take you upstairs."

Danny was seated in the court room.

"How are you feeling Danny?"

"Very nervous Mr. St John."

"Sit down, not long to wait now."

"All rise for the judge."

The jury came in and he was sweating like he'd just had a shower. His whole body was soaking wet when he stood waiting for the jury to read the verdict. One of the lawyers put his hand on Danny's shoulder for him to be seated. He sat for a while then the jury passed a note to the judge.

"Mister Danny Mundy will you please rise."

The judge spoke loudly.

"The jury has come to deadlock. They cannot come to a majority decision. I am afraid there will have to be a retrial. I will note this case for attention in future."

"All rise."

The judge left quietly.

"Toby and I will come and see you before we leave."

"OK"

"This way Danny."

As the old guard handcuffed him again and took him downstairs in the cell and locked the door, he said, "I am sorry mate. I will bring you a cup of coffee."

A few moments later he returned.

"Here is the coffee. I've got to take you to the interview room."

He opened the door but there was no one there and they locked him in. Danny quickly took the money out and put it in his pocket, before sitting sipping the coffee. He had to go through all this all over again. It would take so much out of him. The old guard said about the landlady. Maybe he had a weird feeling for him to say that. He must have seen thousands of cases. The door opened only for St John to walk in.

"I am very sorry Danny, I couldn't do any more."

"But Banks and Banks could have."

"I can't answer that. We have to prepare for a new trial."

"I do not want Banks and Banks, I want Raj Patel."

"I know Raj. He is very good. He was with Banks but the judge might not agree as more of the tax payer's money will be spent. Still, I will see Raj and put in a request to the judge for a change of solicitors."

"I want you to give this money to Linda."

"Where did you get that money?"

"I found it in the van."

"I can't do that."

"Why are you giving it to her? Bill should have it as he is spending a lot of money on her and your family."

"What has that got to do with you?"

"He is a very close friend of mine. That's why I took your case for him. Your wife is using him. Your children have swimming, tennis, horse riding, private lessons and he is paying for all that and your wife still lives at the cottage he provides for her and the children."

"Look just give the money to who you think is the right person please."

"I will do that but if you ever bring money to me again I will call the guard."

"Thank you. Talking of the guard, he said that the landlady knows more that she is saying. What do you think about that?"

"If the judge agrees I will ask Raj but if he does not it will have to be Banks. I am going now so is there anything else?"

"No. Thanks for all your help. Good bye."

Danny got back to the prison quite early, just after lunch and he managed to get some lunch before it was bang up time. The pipe knocked.

"How come you are back so early Danny?"

"Long story. I will tell you later when we are open."

"OK."

He didn't mind coming back to prison as he had lived a more wholesome life there. He was glad that Linda and the family were happy where they were and he didn't want to disturb them. Soon he was falling asleep.

The door opened and he had forgotten what day it was.

"What day is today?"

"What's wrong with you today?" asked Cyril. "It's Monday."

"What classes do I have?"

"Level two English."

"Sorry Cyril - I am half asleep still."

He told Cyril what had happened and went to class. On his way to class people were saying hello to him but he didn't acknowledge them. He got to the English class and Mrs. Mills was there. Only two had showed up for the class so far. She looked at the time which said 2.02 pm.

"I think we will start now." As she started writing on the chalk board one con walked in and then another. She was vexed and sat down.

"I shall wait until everyone is here. The registered time is 2.09."

No more cons came and there were six students. She stood by the chalk board and said, "I will be taking level 2 English in future."

Someone shouted, "What happened to Mr. White? Did he get caught?"

"Be quiet. In future if anyone is not on time for these classes, they'll be sent back to their block. The class must start at exactly 2pm. We have wasted nearly half an hour today."

Everyone behaved themselves for the rest of class until it was time to leave. When Danny was leaving she stopped him and asked, "What happened with your case?"

"It was a hung jury and I have to go through it all over again. It is so soul wrenching and tiring."

"Sorry to hear that but the good thing is that they never found you guilty."

"Is it? I am sorry I have to go."

Danny went back to the block. When he got there Cyril came running to meet him on the ground floor. He had a black eye, there was a few officers around by the main office, and they could hear what was being said.

"What happened to you?

"Nothing. I slipped and fell."

"You old dip stick, you should not run."

They walked to Danny's cell.

"Now tell me what really happened."

"A couple of the new guys came in my cell with balaclavas on and punched me and told me to lay down on my face and they searched the cell but they got nothing. I was lucky they did not beat me up to tell them where your things were but they searched everywhere and then left."

"Do you know what they wore or smelt like?"

"They did not smell clean but one of them had on an old pair of blue trainers and he had Christmas socks on."

"How do you know?"

"That's all I could see facing down on the bed."

"When I am not here, I want you to stay on the ground floor and read your paper, if the officers let you out of your cell."

"They are supposed to let me out all the time because I am retired but they don't. Their excuse is that they are short staffed. That's why they keep me locked up."

"When I am not here go by the Muslims or by Liam and Ted's instead of staying in your cell alone. Go and tell the crew who to look for, but keep it quiet. Don't worry about them bunch of cowards. We will find them. I know exactly who to ask. Are you sure you are telling me the truth? I looked in your cell and it was not disturbed."

"I tidied it up."

"I am going for a walk and I will see you later."

How would the new cons on the block know he was looking after things for Danny? Ted and Liam would not say anything and the other keepers didn't know, but they could have guessed. Everyone knew he liked to tell everyone Danny was his best mate so cons wouldn't bully or take the piss out of him.

Danny went to Ted's cell to find the two of them were playing chess.

"Can you give me a half pack of burn Ted?"

"I heard what happened to Cyril. What are you going to do about it?"

"I got that in hand, what about those three upstairs? Are they paying on time?"

"Yes and no."

"What do you mean yes and no Ted?"

"They are paying and taking it all back again."

"That OK, once they pay back the interest, what about the packs for the phone?"

"They want to pay the rest in cash."

"That's OK. Just tell them if they want to pay cash its double on top on the outside. Make sure you get their home address and bank details and I will give it to Billy to collect it."

"Here is the half pack. Do you want any more?"

"I think this is all I need mate. I'll see you later."

Danny went to the laundry room which had one very big washing machine and two dryers. There were lots of bags of washing between the bars. One side of the bars was dirty washing and the other side was clean. All the bags had cell numbers written on them. All the bags of clothes are thrown in the large washing machine and washed together and the same with the dryer. If you want a private wash you have to pay a tin of tuna or what the laundry man wants to the same value. Danny normally got a private wash from Sam who was in charge of the laundry.

"Sam how are you?"

"I am really busy with all the lockdowns. I am just catching up now but I can fit you in Danny. Where is your washing?"

"Do you know who is still wearing Christmas socks at this time of year?"

"Danny I would not know because all the clothes are in the bags. I can't see it all."

"Here is half a pack. I want you to look for the person that has those socks. When they have come tell me but do not tell anyone that I am looking for them OK?"

"I don't need that Danny."

"I am paying you to do the job. Keep it, I will see you later."

He quickly went to Cyril's cell and sat on the bed.

"How is your eye?"

"It's OK - not painful."

"You are the man that knows what's happening in this prison, as a man that hardly leaves the block. What do you know about the English teacher, Mr. White?

"I am not sure but someone from Wing four set him up with a newbie but he did nothing, yet they say that he tried to have sex with him and he is suspended. There is an investigation, I don't think he is coming back here."

"Go and have a look outside to see if there are any screws about. Then show me how to open this panel by the window."

"No one about, this is how you do it. Push that panel in, then pull this panel. Can you see?"

"Yes OK. You can put everything back now."

"It's been a few weeks and we still can't find who beat me up, Danny."

"Yes I know mate, I am still looking. I am taking my clothes to get washed and you want me to take yours?"

"Here they are, thanks."

"I will tell Sam to do a private wash with mine. I will see you in a few minutes."

"Sam me old mate, here's some washing."

"Danny, the cons you are looking for are those there newbies. Look, they are on the twos landing, sitting down playing cards."

"Are you a hundred percent those were the guys who had those socks?"

"Yes boss. One had those socks but the three of them always come here together."

He went back to his cell and stood outside by the rails on the walkway. He saw the three of them going to the queue to get lunch.

"Cyril go and get your lunch now quickly."

Cyril went downstairs very quickly and he was just behind the three that attacked him. They looked and talked to him in a bad way and Danny was clear it was them. Cyril came out of the queue and other cons went in front of him. Danny got his plate and went and sat next to Cyril. He told him they were calling him names. They decided to eat in the cell and when Ted and Liam came in, Cyril went to his cell.

"How is business?"

"You know, Danny, we spoke today already."

"Just testing Ted."

"Boss, Liam and I think we should get a bit more."

"Why is that Ted? Are you the spokesman for the two of you?"

"No he is not speaking for me Danny. I could do with a bit as my mum lost her job on the out and she has to wait a long time for the benefits to come through."

"And you Ted? What's your reason?"

"We do all the work and you get most of the profit."

"Do you boys remember when you were working for Wade and you had nothing? Look at what you're wearing now, Ralph Lauren and Gucci trainers."

"Ted you are sacked. Liam give me your Mum's details and I will send her £250. Liam you have to run the business until I get a replacement.

"But boss I am sorry."

"Once you think like that I have no need for you. Liam get a new cell mate. Ted you have to move out of the cell then out of this block then out of the prison. I give you seven days to do that. I will see you later Liam to go over things."

Later on in Liam and Ted's cell.

"You idiot Ted. You are lucky he didn't give you a good hiding and take away all the designer gear from you. You know what he did for us. Wade gave us crumbs."

"I know I fucked up. Can you talk to him?"

"It's not going to do any good, you know why he sacked you. Your mindset. You'd best get out of this cell and find some excuse."

"Can I have some gear?"

"Why did you punch me?"

"That's your answer."

"But Liam."

"You still don't know do you, get out."

Danny had to sort those three out plus get someone to replace Ted who was an ungrateful son of a bitch.

On his way to class, Danny went past their cell and there was not a lot of movement. That meant they must have been still sleeping. He went back upstairs and told Cyril to keep an eye on that cell and tell him about their movements for the next day or so. Cyril did that for the next few days.

The next morning he went to see the men that attacked Cyril's cell. They were still in their beds. On the left single bed Danny grabbed him, pulled him up and punched him. The other two on bunk beds were still in their bed turning. He pulled the one on the top bunk down and lifted and pushed him on top of the one that was sleeping below him. He didn't hurt them now they were fully awake. The one on his left rushed him and he punched him in face. Immediately he went flying back on his bed. Danny held the top bunk and started to ram his right foot onto their faces, necks and legs until they stopped trying to get up. The one on the single bed said, "No more mate."

"I am not your mate."

"Remember me. My name is Danny Mundy."

"We know who you are. Sorry mate, I have had enough, we've all had enough."

"That's good, I will see you later."

The one on the left said, "You bet you will."

He went back towards him and punched him in the face with his right hand and followed it up with a left hook.

"What did you say?"

"Nothing mate."

"I am not your mate."

He punched him again. That was a nice wake up call for them. He was sure it was the English teacher that sent him that letter. He was not going to say anything. He'd got no time for women. He needed his education and to get a new trial but he had not heard from anyone. He hoped the judge allowed Raj to represent him. He wondered if St John would represent him again as he was quite good.

"Good Morning Miss."

"Good morning Danny, how are you doing?"

"I am fine."

He was glad when that was over and wondered if they would say anything to Cyril. Not long after he got into his cell, Cyril came in.

"Hi Danny."

"What did they do today?"

"They have not come out."

Danny went and listened outside their cell door. There was a lot of talking and movement. He opened their door which went to the left. The one on the left had a broken cue stick in his hand and the other one had a sock with something in it. They were ready to have a go, not like before. Where was the other one?

"We're ready for you Mundy. Let him have it."

He knew the one on the left would attack first and he was ready for him. As he lifted the cue to hit Danny he stopped him in midair, taking it away and pushing him onto the single bed. The other swung the socks and hit him on the side of his chest but hit himself on the way back. Danny punched him then he fell back and Danny went for the other one. He was coming for him again and punched hard on the side of his body. Then he punched him. As he hit him he came forward again then with all his might he punched him in the face. Then he felt cold down his back. The missing one cut him down the back with a blade and he was not ready for him. He turned and hit him as hard as he could and he fell to the floor out cold.

"OK, OK I had enough."

"What about you?"

"No more."

"I will see you guys later."

Danny quickly ran to his cell holding his back and stopping the blood from dripping. Cyril was there.

"Get me a clean towel or sheet."

He took his top and vest off and both were soaking wet. He got his towel and ran hot water over to soak it. Cyril came back and he lay on his belly first.

"Take that hot towel and wipe my back Cyril."

"It's bleeding."

"I know - just wipe it and then put your clean towel on top. I hope it will dry before I go back to class, as the bell has gone. Go to your cell and tear strips of your clean blanket and when they open this afternoon come and wrap me up."

Danny should have known there was someone in that cell because Cyril told him there would be. He was too confident. Luckily, the blood had dried up well and it wasn't as bad as he first thought. He would stay still until the bell went and Cyril came in. He felt stupid but was going back to see them after lunch.

The bell rang and he was soon back at his cell door which was open but there was no sign of Cyril. He decided to wear two T shirts and a top. He wanted to walk to their cell. When he got there the cell was locked. Scratching his head, he rushed back to class.

"Hello Miss, not many in class this afternoon."

"Have a seat Danny. We will carry on as just the two of us."

"Miss I've got a visit. I only came to tell you bye."

"Just the two of us Danny."

"Miss have you got the first aid kit?"

"Yes."

Danny lifted his top at the back and showed her the injured back.

"Oh my God! What happened to you?"

"Long story."

"Do you want to go to health care?"

"No."

She went to get the first aid box and he closed the blind on the door. He put the kettle on.

"I've got the first aid box. I've also got these large plasters."

"That's good, two of them can fit nicely on the cut."

"I've got to clean it first."

"The kettle is on."

"Take all of your tops off completely."

As he did that he saw her eyes looking at his body. Her eyes looked pleasing when she saw him looking back at her.

"Turn around. Let me wipe all of it with disinfective. You need to stop moving."

"It stings."

"You are a big boy. I'll just put the plasters on now."

"That felt good. You've got tender hands."

He held her hand and kissed her but she did not move.

"Stop. Someone might come in."

"Ok miss."

"You are the only one in class and I am not supposed to be alone with a student. I will ask the officer to take you back."

Danny looked into her eyes and she into his. She was right that the last thing they both needed was to be caught. He had put all his clothes on and sat in a chair as she went for an officer.

"Danny the officer wants you to join the Maths class as we are in lockdown. That's the room next to mine."

"Thanks miss."

As he walked out of the classroom he quickly kissed her cheeks and she smiled. He knew it was her that wrote the letter but she was being quiet about it. Nothing happened in the Maths room.

He went back to the block after it and everyone was unlocked.

Danny went outside the three boys' cell. He walked in and the three of them were waiting, ready for him but he was not confident now. Despite that, he was more determined. He reminded himself they were only young and much smaller than him.

"So you boys are ready for me? I think someone will get badly hurt today. You on the left, what is your name?"

"Larry, my mates are Simon and Peter. Listen Danny. We don't want to fight you but that Cyril is a pedophile and he messed up Peter's thirteen year old little sister and she has gone insane because of him."

"Look he is not. I have seen his charge sheet. Stay here and I will go and get it."

Danny called out to Cyril as he approached his cell.

"Go and get your charge sheet."

A few moments later Cyril gave it to him.

Their door was still open.

"Here is his charge sheet, read it."

Larry took it and read it aloud.

"Tell you what boys we can carry on and have it or you guys can work for me."

"What is the pay?"

"To start Larry, you can have a pack a week and you two half per week. Larry will be working a lot more than you two as he will move in with Liam."

"I don't want to leave my boys as they are not good with reading and writing."

"Peter and Simon are you going to English Class?"

"Shut up. I could not read and write when I came in prison. I will get you a full packet each if you two go to English class. Working for me you need Maths and English. Have a think about it."

After that he went to his cell and Cyril was there.

"Here is your paper."

"Liam is in your cell."

"Hi Danny. Ted's gone. How did it go with those three?"

"All good. In fact, one of them might start working for us. He will have to move in with you."

"Here is my mum's details."

"I will ring Billy and give him your mum's details."

"Cyril can you excuse yourself please?"

"OK."

"That was a bit hard Liam."

"Sorry boss I didn't mean it like that. Ted told me some stuff before he went - not like I wanted to listen."

"Go on."

"Did you know that Cyril worked in the print shop before he came to this jail?"

"So if he is a pedophile why have they put him in this block?

"I think he got done for pedophile stuff and he made his own sentence sheet himself boss but I am not sure."

"It's a touchy subject. I don't understand it, change the subject. If the officers put some new con in your cell, send him to those three's cell and hopefully Larry will come to yours."

"On slight problems, those on the three that are messing about did not pay all last week."

"But they borrowed again yes?"

"Yes but there's going to be a time when they can't pay at all. I can see it coming."

"We are still making money from them yes?"

"Let's run with them until they can't pay but just give them less each week."

"That's what's been happening."

"You want to stop giving gear or food?"

"I would like to stop the gear now."

"You know them better than me. Do what you think, those boys with the car dealership have paid Bill. Hope they come again as that was a good bit of money without any hassle."

That night he gave Liam's mum's details to Billy.

"Billy, Liam tells me you and him wear the same size shoe. I want you to buy two pairs of trainers the same size you wear."

"Why?"

"Wait. I will explain everything to you when you get the trainers and take them to a cobbler."

"What's a cobbler?"

"I did not think you are so young. A cobbler is a shoe mender and maker of shoes. Take the two pairs of trainers to them and ask them to do a lift in the inside of the trainers and take bottoms and leave voids so you can put drugs in the trainers and in the lift area. Let them take it apart and pay the guy when you go next time with the drugs to put them in the shoes and for him to seal them so it's done professionally."

"Suppose he doesn't want to do it. Go and shop around until you find someone. After he has done it, post one pair to Liam and when you visit Liam wear those trainers. When you come to visit Liam don't walk in alone, walk behind a crowd of people coming to the visit at the same time. Remember the crowds are at the start of the visit, so make sure you are early. Then when you and Liam think it's safe, exchange trainers. Do you understand?"

"What happens if I am caught?"

"What do you think? Back in prison. Are you making good money?"

"Yes."

"If this thing comes off the way we planned, we will be making a lot more money in here, OK buddy see you later."

Over the next few weeks everything went fine. Larry moved in with Liam and Peter and Simon started doing English class. The English teacher and Danny were getting very close. Still he had not heard anything from the lawyers.

He had to go and visit the boys on the threes. They understood that their debt was getting too big so they had to cut down. The good news was that one of their family was going to give Bill £200 and that would clear what they owed, while putting them in credit by £100. When it was quiet like this something always happened but fingers crossed.

He came back from gym but, to his surprise, there was no Cyril to greet him, just a note on his door saying he was not well. Cyril had not been well for the last few days but he always met him. He missed him being there. Danny wondered if he was coming for lunch, knowing he would have eaten in bed. When he opened his flap he was sleeping like a baby. Deciding to get his lunch, Danny didn't bother him.

The next morning there was no Cyril again. The officers must have been short staffed as he wasn't opened on time. Going to his lessons he missed the old guy.

Lunch time came and again there was no Cyril. He'd not opened his cell and Danny looked at the flap where he was still sleeping in the same position. He thought he would go and see the officers at the Wing office and knock on the door. They saw him and carried on doing what they were doing. Then a few minutes later an officer came to him.

"What do you want Mundy?"

"Sir I think something is wrong with Cyril."

"For your information he left a note on his door. He does not want to be opened."

"But sir I think something is wrong with him."

"Leave it with me. I will check on him later."

The bell went for lunch time bang up and he was only now coming to check on Cyril. Danny waited by Cyril's door. The officer opened the door and Danny tried to get in.

"Stay there Mundy."

He stayed by the door and the officer pushed Cyril's door but nothing happened. Then he pushed again and a manekin head fell on the floor.

The officers said, "He has escaped."

Then he blew his whistle and the rest of the officers started running from the other doors and the office. Before he knew it there were over ten officers by Cyril's cell.

"Mundy get in your cell now."

"Yes Sir."

Chapter Twenty One

He could still hear things. They'd locked up the rest of the Wing now and they called the prison governor.

Danny looked out of the peep hole in the door. They had passed his door before getting to Cyril so he could see what was happening. More officers were coming from different Wings. They had not had an escape for as long as he could remember. He just stood at the peep hole looking. Presumably the prison Governor was there and his deputy also. It must have been an hour now but still officers charged about. He was getting ready to go to English class when a paper was pushed under his door.

It was a letter from the prison Governor. There would be a lockdown for the rest of the day and evening meal would be at the door. He went to see what was happening but couldn't see anything as they'd blocked his peep hole. They don't normally do that. Why would they do that? Who left the notes then? Danny's head was a mist so he made a cup of coffee and rested his brain. All he could say was best of luck to Cyril.

"Joe you are manager of the Wing, have you checked the CCTV?"

"Governor Hurst the video is showing lines and jumping up and down. I have put in a request for the engineers to fix it. When they last came it was working properly and they said they will come back and check it but they have not."

"Can we see anything positive on the CCTV?"

"No sir."

"What about the causeways?"

"Sir our CCTV also covers the causeway."

"Get the engineers on the phone now. Deputy Perkins I want only the officers to feed the prisoners tonight. No server workers. Start from Wing one."

"Yes Mr. Hurst."

"The engineer is on the phone Sir."

"It that Mike? I want you come to Wing two and fix the CCTV system now. Here is the phone back Joe. This is the first time anything happened on my watch. All you officers must come out of your offices more and see what is going on in your wings. I hope you can learn from this."

The door opened.

"Here is your lunch Mundy."

Before Danny could say anything the officers locked his cell and were at the next door. He got a bag of goodies containing a chocolate bar, bag of crisps, orange drink and an extra milk. Later that night he phoned Liam to see if he knew what happened. He didn't know anything and none of his people were aware either. They would find out in a few days. They always found out what's gone on in a few days. He forgot to ask Liam if he got the trainers from Bill. He rang Liam again.

"Has Billy sent you the trainers?"

"Yes."

"Have you checked them?"

"Yes I can't tell any difference. I've pulled and took out the lining yet I can't see nothing."

"Liam, Liam, you are meant to open the lift innersole part of the trainers. The drugs are in there. Pull off the soles of the trainers and the drugs are in there. Then I want you to fold that cash as tight as you can and put it into the trainers. Then glue it all back together."

"Boss, you did not tell me sorry."

"Ok I told you now so sort it out and then give it to all the keepers tomorrow. Make sure you split in eight parts for the keepers."

"Yes boss - are you sure it's going to work?"

"Liam - we are not sure of anything, but the trainers went through reception. They checked the trainers. Everything we do in prison we might get caught for one day but we've got to take a chance. If we did not your mum wouldn't have £250 and more money to follow."

"I understand boss."

"When is he visiting you?"

"Next week Monday."

The next morning the cell was still not open but there was lots movement in Cyril's cell. Another letter came saying to bang up all day. No social activities and food at the door.

They couldn't do that, he thought. He supposed they could if they thought more prisoners were going to escape. Spending time in his cell all day meant he did his exercises and reading. He wrote a letter to Mrs. Clare Miller and Banks and Banks.

The next day he was expecting bang up, but the doors opened for everyone so he was able to go to his class. He knew he would have to find a different class. He would join business studies because that would help him for the future. He went into the classroom.

"Sir I would like to do business studies as I am getting nowhere in this English level two. I will come back to it at a later date?"

"That's fine Danny. I could see you were struggling and you were trying hard. I will ask an officer to take you to the business class. Here is a note for the teacher."

"Thank you sir."

"I am Officer Jean. Follow me Danny."

"You were at reception when I first came to prison?"

"Yes I was. You have a great memory Danny."

She took him to the class and he handed the note to the teacher. He was short and about sixty five, wearing a pin stripe suit with a tie and black shoes and he had a head full of white hair. He read the note.

"Mr. Mundy as you can see this is a small class of only eight students and we work from these books. There are five in this series, book one to five. Everyone is on a different section and different books and you will be starting from book one. Also you have to do a business plan so if you want to start a business when you are released you will have an idea how to start a business of your choice."

"Will I be able to take book one with me at the end of lesson?"

"Sometimes when I give you homework you can take the book away for research."

Over the next few days Liam had switched the trainers in the visits no problems and distributed the content to the keepers. Quickly he began enjoying business studies and his head became a bit clearer than the last week.

His cell door knocked so he went to the door.

"Liam come in, what have you got there?"

"The local papers."

"What about it?"

"Let me read the first bit to you."

"Look just tell me, have they caught Cyril?"

"He was murdered in his cell and his body was stored under his bed."

"Oh no."

"The papers say he was caught with children and for fraud on his sentence but they only put fraud on his sentence sheet. He was a pedo after all. I will leave the papers with you and you can read the full story."

"Why did he not tell me the truth? I would have still looked after him."

"I think he was afraid."

"Do they know who done it?"

"The CCTV was not working, but they are all working now.

"Has Larry said anything to you about it?"

"He never mentioned a word about Cyril though he is enjoying working with us."

"That's good. Could you leave me alone now please?"

"Boss - Cyril has gone, so don't do anything. The governors and officers are keeping a very close eye on things now. Daily they are patrolling more and we've got a lot to lose if anything goes wrong."

"You are right Liam. If he had told me the truth and that happened I would have done something to the cons that did it but he did not. There's something else Liam. Everyone on the wing knew he was under my protection and they still killed him."

"I see what you mean boss."

"Put the word out that anyone who knows anything needs to come to talk to me. I give will them 48 hours to come forward from today."

"Ok boss."

"I can't be fairer than that."

Danny knew that the police had been in to investigate Cyril's room. They looked around and didn't seem overly interested. He guessed it would be the coroner that determined if it was a murder or not. There was a cloud of mystery hanging over the whole prison.

It had been a hell of a day since he put it out about who killed Cyril. Liam came to Danny's cell.

"Boss you remember Simon, Peter and Tom. He was the guy I sent to their cell and Larry came to mine."

"Of course I know those two and I've seen Tom around."

"My name is Tom. I instigated the killing of Cyril."

Danny held onto himself as he was angry and wanted to smash his head against the wall but Liam stepped closer to him.

"Go on, tell me why."

"Mr. Mundy he damaged my little sister. She was only ten years old. Right now that girl is still in hospital because of him. Peter's sister is only seven years old. Cyril sex assaulted her and she will never be the same again and there are quite a lot of other children he did damage."

"Have you got proof of all that?"

"Yes, I think he only had ten months of his sentence left and he would go and do the same to other mother's children if we did not stop him."

"Did you know he was under my protection?"

"Yes."

"Peter and Simon you work for me. I am surprised at you. What punishment do you recommend then Liam?"

"I am not sure boss."

"What do you think Tom?"

"Not sure Mr. Mundy."

"Where do you work Tom?"

"I work in the Library?"

"That's one of the better paid jobs?"

"Yes Mr. Mundy it pays £14.90 per week if I do all the shifts."

"Do you want to work for me like Peter and Simon?"

"I am helping them already."

"Ok I will start on half a pack of burn a week and the punishment is £5 a week each from all three of you. Any questions?"

There were smiles on everyone's face.

"No boss."

"That's all. I will see you later."

"Thanks boss."

"Liam, Cyril told me he got another six years leave. What a lying cunt, if I was to see him now I would definitely knock him out. That nasty man."

"Boss he has gone so that's the end of it. I see his cell has not been occupied yet boss. I got a lot of work to do. I will see you later…"

A few months later he got a date for his new trial and Clare had been writing to him, sometimes sending three letters a week. He would meet her in the education block and sometimes she taught him in the Business studies course. They kissed a lot but nothing serious had yet happened.

There was a knock on the cell door. He opened it.

"Come in Liam."

"Boss we are getting very low on stock."

"Burn?"

"No we've got plenty of that but we need more drugs."

"We will organise with ten of our crew to get visits from their family all on the same dates. Then tell Billy who their families are and give him their addresses. He will then get the drugs to them. Don't forget they've all got to be women so when they kiss they can pass the drugs through their mouths."

"Do you want me to do the trainers scam again?"

"We have done that a few times already. I don't think I will press our luck as things are really going well for us. We are selling to at least three wings now."

"How soon do you want this done?"

"If we are getting out of stock, now it would take at least a month for the visits to be organised so do it now."

"Ok boss. I will get onto it now and do the phone calls tonight. See you later."

Cyril's cell had been locked for a week. Danny went outside of his cell onto the landing. There was an officer coming with a newbie.

"Mundy I've got a new neighbour for you. Wait here while I unlock these locks on the cell door."

"Yes Sir."

The newbie looked at him and nodded his head. Danny nodded back and went back in his cell. He looked like Kevin. He wanted to go and speak to him later and get the gear out of Cyril's cell. What was that noise outside?

"Listen newbie. Cyril said I could have the little cupboard and the chair."

"The officer gave me this cell and everything in it and you can't have anything."

Danny went outside and looked into the newbie's cell.

"What's going on?"

"Nothing Mr. Mundy just getting the stuff Cyril said I can have."

"You got it wrong mate. Cyril said I can have all his stuff."

"Sorry Mr. Mundy, can I go now?"

"Yes and don't bother this kid anymore."

"I am not a kid, my name is Vincent."

"Ok Vincent, how old are you?"

"Nineteen."

"Yea that's old. Where is all your stuff you got from reception?"

"I left it by the office."

"Go and get it before someone steals it."

Looking down from the landing, Danny watched him go to get his bag. Soon he was coming back up the stairs.

"You got everything?"

"I think so."

"I will let you mop and tidy your cell, I will see you later."

Another one Danny would have to look after, making him feel like a regular Robin Hood. He seemed strong but they all did at that age and they thought they could beat the world.

The next day in the evening, Danny went to Vincent's cell.

"Can I come in?"

"Yes come in mate."

"My name is Danny Mundy but you can call me Danny."

"I know who you are. I spoke to someone I knew from the out."

"Don't believe all you hear. What are you in for? I know we don't normally ask cons what they are in for. The unwritten rule is wait until you have been told."

"I don't mind telling you."

"I want to know all about my next door cell mate and everything about him, do you understand?"

"What I did was not nice but that was how I survived. I and two guys followed an old couple from the City Centre until they got into their house and rushed them as they opened the front door. They never stood a chance so the other two guys roughed them up too much while I went and got their jewelry upstairs. When it was time to go the two wanted to stay and have the drinks in the fridge and the cabinet. I left them and went to the park and met a guy who deals with stuff. He gave me a hundred pounds and some drugs for it, though it was worth a lot more. I didn't care as I wanted the drugs. I normally sleep in the park and do my drugs there. I got arrested in the park then went to court and got five years but the other two guys gotten years' sentence each."

"That was a bit rough."

"We had lots suspended sentences. I think that the judge gave us so much."

"Did you have a home?"

"Yes the park."

"No I mean a proper home."

"Yes I did until I was seventeen. My mum is a druggy. When I was very young my mum had lots of men come to the council flat. It was a one bedroom flat so when her men friends came I had to go outside and play in the park with my friends until very late. From the age of eight years old I went to the park."

"What about school?"

"I used to go and get registered then bunk off. They would make appointments for mum to go to the school but she never went. Then I was put into a home though I did not stay there long. In the meantime my mum was about to lose the council place. When I was sixteen she came back for me and put my name on the council books so they couldn't kick her and I out."

"Did you think about getting a job?"

"Me work? You are having a laugh. I can barely write my name and I was always on some drugs or another. Look at the state of me."

"Yes I can smell you from where I am sitting."

"I will shower later."

"If you are going to be my mate I think you should shower each day. Tell me more."

"From an early age I started begging in the City Centre where there were lots of overseas visitors. It was good money. I can make £200 to 300 when I score as well."

"What do you mean score?"

"Drug users know that beggars can get gear for them. Some will ask me to get some drugs. I tell them to wait where I beg. I will go to the guy who got the drugs. Or I will phone him and they will meet up but I don't get a good cut that way. Mostly I will pay the money for the drugs. Before I get back to the punter I will take a bit for myself and charge a bit of extra cash for it. He will be happy he has some gear to use. I would have made some drugs for my use and drinking money for myself."

"Do you drink and beg at the same time?"

"No I hide it with my bag of things when no one is looking. I have a sip, when that's finished I will buy another special brew. That the strongest one I like the best."

"What do you do with your money?"

"By the end of the day I will get some more and buy four cans and go in the park."

"Aren't the parks locked and there is a keeper?"

"Yes, I know all his times when he walks and the parks are massive. I made a little shelter in the deep bushes in the park but no one knows about it. That's where I sleep at night. I go there when the rest of the homeless go to their home or the places they live."

"What about your mum, do you see her?"

"She comes to the City Centre and begs as well."

"Does she get benefits and do you get any?"

"She and I are supposed to go and look for work and because we don't go and look for work we do not get any benefits. Mum goes to the Salvation Army and sleeps sometimes or with her men friends. You know I have not thought about her until now."

"What do you mean?"

"I never gave her a thought on the out. I suppose I was just surviving as well, not much of a life."

"I suppose that's what drugs do to you. Why did you start doing drugs?"

"She ran away from home to have me because her parents wanted her to have an abortion she was fifteen when she had me. She was a kid herself."

"I can help you to become someone here."

"In prison?"

"You can learn a trade here - read and write and better yourself. I will be your mentor if you like."

"What is a mentor?"

"I can guide you to do the right things such as no more drugs."

"I will be honest with you Danny I brought some in with me."

"You are joking me, how did you manage that?"

"It was not nice but I done it for two days at the nick."

"Where is it now? The same place? Have you used it?"

"Yes."

"Look at your cell. It's still dirty from the first day you came in. If you want to be my neighbour you have to change, starting from today."

"I want to change Danny but I will need help."

"I know boys like you in here end up giving blow jobs and other things for burn. Do you want to end up like that? Those men are watching you already Vincent."

"Cons are watching me now?"

"Yes mate, new meat. What will happen is your five year sentence will get longer and longer until you will never get out."

"At the end of five years I will not get out?"

"You will be reviewed and then they will decide. That's why it is very important that you do all the right things. The review board want to see prison change you for the better. If they don't see that you will not be released. Go and speak to a few cons who got that type of sentence. It means Extended Sentence for Public Protection."

"I thought after five years I will be out."

"You are right, but you have to prove that you are a changed person and be a benefit to the public. If not, you know what. Look if you want to change your life this is the place to do it. I am talking from experience. Trust me mate. I couldn't read and write before I came here."

"I don't want to be here after five years. I will try."

"How much is your gear worth?"

"About a hundred pounds?"

"Get it and give it to me and go to my shop and see Liam then get what cleaning stuff you need and any food you want."

"But…."

"But what? It's not going to last you forever. I am telling you now if you use drugs I do not want you as my neighbour, so you'd better move. I will see you later."

"Danny I have been doing one kind of a drug or another since I was seven years old or as long as I can remember. That's all I know."

"Look kid, you are a good looking boy when you clean yourself up. Men like kids like you. This is how things will go in here. People will ask you to look after drugs, booze, phones and other things that you are not allowed in here and they will pay in pills or drugs. When you are caught that goes on your record. Then men will want your body and they will use and bully you. I want you to think about what you are doing. Go to Liam at my shop and you can get £150 worth of stuff. You will find he has got some nice clothes there and any food stuff you want. Just give me the drugs you got."

"Can I go and see?"

"Yes you can. I will wait in your cell until you come back."

"Ok Danny."

After Vincent left Danny went by the window and moved the seal around until it opened and then he took all the phones and money out. He could not carry it all so he put the money in his pockets and then when in his cell got a black bin bag and went back and got the phones. He put the money in the toilet and put his laundry bag over it. Then he put the phones under the bed, then he went on the landing to look to see if he could see Liam or Larry. Vincent was now coming out of their cell.

Danny thought to himself about the kid. He was not going to give him the drugs. He was going to use it. He wouldn't bother with him anymore. Danny went back in his cell and lay on his bed, hoping that the kid would come.

Chapter Twenty Two

The next morning Danny went to class. Clare was taking the class and after the class was finished all the cons rushed out of the classroom. It was just Clare and him.

"How are things with you Danny? In the last letter you sent me you were not happy?"

"I have news from Banks. The judge will not let me change lawyers for my case but, as you know, I wanted Raj's company."

"What reason did they give?"

"They are saying I will be wasting tax payers' money, but I could pay private."

"How would you get the money?"

"I have a friend that will help me in here."

"But if you borrow from someone in here they will own you and how will you pay them back?"

"Yes, I know. I see my wife and kids are happy without me. I was not a caring husband or father so they will be better off without me. My life in prison is totally different from when I was outside. I had no ambition, was lazy and selfish and never thought of anyone else apart from myself."

"I can't believe that."

"It is true. My wife did everything in the house for me. Do you know I never looked at or kissed another woman until I met you? I am not sure I would please you with sex."

"Danny it's not about sex. I like and admire you for the way you turned your life around from being not able to read or write and you were on the verge of dying of obesity. You'd better get back to your wing now as it's getting late."

"Bye."

He got back to his block late but they were still serving dinner. He ran and got his plate and got his dinner. After that, as he went into his cell where Liam followed him.

"How is it going mate?"

"Bad news. One of our guys got caught while giving the drugs to this guy."

"Where was this?"

"It happened in the causeway between the education block and our block. Our man was giving the gear to the punter while other cons were going in both directions. Then two officers coming from opposite directions saw them and held them. Both were marched back to their cell and their cell was searched. They had to go up to the governor this afternoon."

"That was very stupid of our man. Did you put the word out that all our people need to be careful?"

"Yes I did. I went to the keeper last night and got the gear then I met our man in the gym first thing this morning and gave him the gear in the showers. There were no cameras in there when I gave him."

"Has he got your phone number?"

"Yes."

"Tell you what. Take the pin out of your phone and get a new one from a keeper. They might not check but we can't be too careful. They are so short staffed they've got no time to look at CCTV and some of them can't be bothered."

"Tomorrow is the big day boss. With all that's happened today the officers might be a bit more watchful because the four that caught our boys are the blue eyed boys now. The others might try and get a pat on the back as well by being extra vigilant."

"What does vigilant mean?

"I am not sure? I think it means look out a lot more or be on top of things."

"Looks like you are feeling uneasy about tomorrow?"

"A little."

"I don't blame you, but everything is set up. We are not going to get all our drugs through. If we get half through that's good. We have to go ahead as we've got little or no stock now. We're not going to make real money selling tobacco £25 to £55 per pack on the outside and getting double in here. We have a lot of cons working for us and we've got to look after them."

"Boss I know Clare is sweet on you, ever thought of asking her?"

"No not really, but when we can't get gear in, I might. Unless someone wants to pay for a big order up front."

"Boss I am not happy, not set up diversions."

"I think if we set one up with the officers how they are at the present time, everyone will get searched top to bottom and that will be no good. The governor knows what diversions are. Leave everything as it is. It is this climate with Cyril's murder. The officers are not in the good books of the prison governor. If we do a diversion he will lock down the prison and search everyone on the visit. I mean body search."

"Ok boss, wish me luck because my girlfriend is coming that day."

"I don't think you should have booked the same day, but it's done now so best of luck and you can give me a full report."

Liam was all dressed up to see his girlfriend. Smartly he walked up to the visit hall where quite a few of the cons were running to get in the queue first. Liam took his time when he got to the hall where the queue was about twenty deep. He waited like the rest. The first in the queue were not called first. The others behind the queue were called first depending on what names came up first to the officer that was calling the names. After their names were called, they were searched and allocated a number of their table. Liam was called and searched.

"Table number 13, next."

Liam went to table 13, sat and waited until he saw his girlfriend. She ran and kissed him on the cheek.

"How are you babe?"

"It's hard in here, did you bring it?"

"Yes. I will go and get some food. What do you want?"

"A coke and one burger and a bit of cake thanks love."

The visit hall was packed and two of the officers were patrolling up and down between the tables. Two were at the entrance Liam came in and about six to eight officers at the visit entrance under CCTV cameras.

"Thanks love."

"I really miss you Liam."

"I miss you as well but don't be mushy with me. I am going to eat then kiss me and pass the drugs into my mouth when we kiss. Do not look around, just kiss and when you finished say how much you love me so as to not to draw attention to us."

Visitors were laughing and joking. The place was very loud and the officers stopped walking between the tables.

"When you are ready love."

They kissed for a long time.

"Table 13 stop that now."

An officer came to table 13. "If you two behave like that that will be the end of your visit, stop that."

"Liam are you OK?"

"Let me drink some coke please. Have a look around over my shoulder. Can you see anything out of the normal?"

"Like what?"

"Nothing."

"Do you want anything else?"

"No, have you seen how big the queue is, just stay next to me so I could look at you."

"Don't be silly."

"Look behind you."

"What?"

"Six officers surrounded that table and they held the woman and now they are taking the man away."

"Why are you doing this to me, and my wife? I have done nothing nor has my wife."

"Munro, I saw you drop something on the table and you picked it up and swallowed it."

"Officer it was crumbs from my cake I picked up and put into my mouth."

"I made a mental note of your table. You had no cake on the table. Come on straight to segregation. The CCTV will tell the truth."

"Did that Munro get caught?"

"Think so, you best get going to miss the rush or they might keep visitors longer."

"Ok love take care. I love you."

"Love you, bye."

"Bye."

Later that day Liam went to Danny's cell. "How was your visit?"

"It's always nice to see my missus and I will be sad for the next few days."

"I know what it feels like mate, how did the other thing go?"

"As far as I know everyone got through apart from Munro."

"What happened?"

"I think he dropped the gear on the table and that McCarthy caught him picking it up and put it in his mouth. They have taken him to the segregation unit."

"Well we will know by tomorrow how many got through with the drugs. You better get that thing out of your system mate."

"Yea I will see you later.'

"Make sure the keeper gets it by tomorrow."

"Sure boss."

Chapter Twenty Three

There were many ways contraband drugs, phones and money got into prison. It could happen in the yard where prisoners have outside social activities.

Another way drugs, phones etc. might come in is using the team who would get their men on the outside to find out the name of companies that supply the prison with things such as toilet rolls, towels or anything the prison needs and find a way to make deals with these company employees to bring drugs with their supplies.

The prison also manufacture things and do small assembly work such as bike repairs, army camouflage and netting. There are so many ways the team can get things into prison.

Prisoners on visits are given a coloured band to put on over their clothes. It fits across the shoulder to the waist. There are several different colour bands. The officers make a note of what they are and they are allocated a seat number. They have cameras in the visit hall and some forty to fifty prisoners on visits and about fifteen officers, plus CCTV cameras.

Prisoners went on visits with friends and prearranged what shoes or trainers to wear. Then they exchanged shoes or trainers or kissed to pass the drugs over.

When the team brought drugs, phones etc. on the visits they created diversions by getting two of the team to start a fight on different tables. On the visit they do not care if there are children, the two or six people who are involved are taken to the separate cells and are strip searched. Then they will go back to their wing and sometime later they will get a nicking. The rest of the prisoners on visits will be searched and the usual suspects will be strip searched. Some of them will be caught with drugs. Lots of them will somehow get through with drugs or phones etc.

If you are in a local team you would have grown up together or know some of the officers from the area you live in. You could have gone to school or played football, gone to football matches or the pub with them. They could have married your cousin or sister so there are a lot of ways you will know the officer from outside. The wage officers get paid is chicken feed. They need to do a lot of overtime to get a decent wage. What they could earn if the bring in contraband for the team could be thousands a week so some take a chance. One of the screws even bought a yacht. He was so stupid with the bribes he took. The others who are not in the team normally get the officers they know to help them to get the best jobs like delivering tea, librarian, receptionist, gymnast, etc. when you get these jobs you are not banged up all day, but you can be out of your cell all day.

The best job to have is making tea for the officers because you have access to their kitchen and the officers always leave something in the fridge such as bacon, sausages and cheese. Food would be better than you might get to eat on the server and you're out till nine at night. There was a big queue for that job. They put their name down but they never get the job as it goes to officer's mates. There are other jobs such as wing representative, diversity, listener, separation rep, Shannon trust mentor.

When you come into prison, you process through reception where you are given toothpaste, a toothbrush, blankets, a sheet, plastic cup, plate, knife, fork, spoon, prison tracksuit, a top and bottoms, slippers and jeans, whether they fit or not. You then go with your plastic bag full of your items to the waiting room. They ask if you are Christian or not then may go to see the minister where you can chat for a very short time. Cons sometimes use religion as a way to get out of their cell by going to church or to Bible studies and other church activities.

So there were a lot cons that knew the system that wanted to see the minister. Danny went to church with his mum and brother every Sunday and Sunday school in the afternoon. He told the minster this and he said he would give Danny a bible when he came to church on Sunday. He was very quickly dealt with and told to go sit by a door. Danny waited for a good while then someone outside called him inside and told him to sit down on the chair by the desk and he sat opposite Danny and gave him a form, asking him to read it. He looked at him and did not say anything. For the first time in his life he was ashamed to say he could not read. When Danny did not say anything the man immediately knew. He read to Danny, read his name and the name of the prison.

"Danny would you like to do full time education instead of working? Here is a chance for you to learn to read and write."

"Would I have to be in a class with other people?"

"Yes but all of them will be the same level as you. Also there's a lot of people from other countries that don't know any English and if you need extra help I can organise that as well with a Shannon Trust Rep."

"Who is that trust?"

"The trust was set up by Shannon to help prisoners like yourself to learn to read and write. Other prisons volunteer to help prisoners one-to-one. They will come to your cell or in the classroom, anywhere which is private, to teach you."

"That's good, could you get someone for me?"

"Leave it with me. I will get back to you. Just give me all your details."

At Danny's wife's house, a letter arrived.

"Mum the post has come and you've got a letter."

"Leave it on the kitchen table. I will read it later."

"But mum it's from dad."

"How do you know?"

"It's got the prison stamp, shall I open then mum?"

"Yes, but your sister and you can read it to us in the kitchen."

Chapter Twenty Four

Danny had been in prison for coming up to eight years and he had been found guilty of murder. He was sentenced to twenty two years and he had been moved to a category B prison where he had learned the way of the prison. He had people working for him inside and outside. He still saw Clare and she was working at a high school, so there is was no conflict of interest. His wife had left him and took Amanda and Kim to live with Bill. Kim was at university just minutes away from her home. She came and visited him went she could. She had started her own investigation into her uncle's killer by going through all the people who ever met or knew her uncle and all the local newspapers.

Kim had visited her father as many times as possible. Danny now had a very big network in the prison and cons working for him. His right hand man was Frank and Bill was still working for him in the gardening business. Frank, his new partner's son, was also working for Danny and there were another seven staff working in the gardening business. Kim did office work and banking the money part time. When Danny first came to the B Category prison he met at induction an old officer, Jean Hughes.

On the way to class Danny was stopped by an officer.

"Are you the same Mundy I met eight years ago at Emely Prison?

"Yes miss I am."

"Where has all your weight gone?"

"Miss this is prison and I eat prison food."

"Ha ha."

"I got classes miss. Got to run."

Most of the prisoners were sitting around the dinner table but they were in their own groups.

"Excuse me, is your name Dave?"

"No its Danny."

"I heard something about you."

"You are kidding me, come to my cell now."

"Aren't you finishing your meal?"

"No this more important, come follow me."

They made their way to Danny's cell and Frank was in there eating.

"What is your name mate? "Daly."

"My name's Danny Mundy and that is Frank, my partner. Now tell me all that you know from the start to the finish. Do not miss anything out even if you think that it's not important."

"I was at Emely prison. You know some people can get sentenced for days or weeks or months. It is a short sentence prison and it's mainly a three man bang up. It was I and another inmate in the cell and they bought a newbie in with us. We had a bit of gear and some spice."

"What was the new person's name?

"Greg Page."

"Ok go on."

"I asked him what he was in for."

"Something stupid."

"Tell us."

"No no it's OK."

"So I got talking to him then he became a customer. I sold him some spice but he was not used to prison spice and he started talking more about himself and what he'd done. He said he got done for doing it in public with his partner."

"Police normally give a warning for that."

"Yes they do but his partner was a man and he had been warned before."

"He was not used to prison spice and he was saying the police don't know what they are doing half the time. They'd got an innocent man doing 25 years for killing his brother and he heard it was actually a jealous lover that killed John Mundy."

"Tell me who said that."

"I can't remember his name but he drinks in a pub in Canterbury."

"Which pub? What's the name of the pub or road it's on?"

"He moaned - What is this stuff you gave me - my head is going round and round. I want to take it out of my body. He started to bang his head on the wall then he lay on the floor and banged his head on the floor. We had to hold him and had to press the buzzer to let the nurse see him. He was going crazy because he was not used to prison spice. He started fighting us and punching and kicking. So we held him the best we could, then the door opened and the officer saw what was happening and said to wait for them to come back before they locked the door. What's that noise?"

"That's bang up time, quickly finish the story."

"Greg was still fighting and kicking even though we held him on the bed so he could not move. He was screaming and foaming at the mouth and spitting, it must have been hours or so it seemed, before officers and nurses came and got him. That was the last I saw of him."

"Thanks for that. I see you are alright. I might give you some work."

"Thanks Danny."

"You mean Mr. Mundy"

"No need for that Frank."

"I will see you soon."

"What you doing Daly? Just get back to your cell."

"Yes officer."

The door locked.

"Do you think he is telling the truth, this is a fourth hand story?

"Could you make up a story like that? Let's assume it's the truth. Now we need to get the name of everyone in Emely prison during that period.

"How are we going to get all those names Danny?"

"Lunch will be over soon. Got to see as many people as you can that might be able to help and I will do the same."

That night after bang up Frank came in.

"Danny I found someone that's good on the computers."

"That's good - get him to meet here."

"He is from a different wing. The only way to meet him is at the church on Sunday. I sent word to him to meet in the back row of the church."

"But is he on the list to go to Church of England or the Catholic Church? If he is not on the list the screw won't let him out to go to church. I am on the list."

"I know you are on the list. I sent word for him to put his name on the list for Church of England."

"What's his name?"

"Phillip Initt."

"What do you mean Initt?"

"That's his name, Phil Initt."

"What job are we going to give Daly?

"I was thinking of letting him start small and see if we can trust him. Let him sell burn. Let's start him off with two packets and let him sell them. Sixteenth, no bigger. We don't want our other people to lose out to him because he is going to be dealing tiny amounts and he answers to you at the end of the week."

"But Boss that is a very small amount."

"You want him to start? That how I started selling roll up for milk."

"All right Mr. Mundy."

The cell door opened.

"Why are you pressing the buzzer Mundy?

"Sorry officer, its church today. I need a shower and to get ready for church."

"Can't let you out yet. I need another officer here. It's only me alone."

"But Guv we are all church goers, we will not cause any trouble."

"Just as soon as the other officer comes I will let out."

"But Guv we will not have time to shower."

"Sorry mate."

"Just our luck Frank."

Then the door opened.

"Go and get your showers and come straight back to your cell."

"Thank you Sir."

Danny and Frank went to the showers where they thought they'd have the showers to themselves.

"Lot of people going to church this morning Frank."

"Must be pay day for some of us."

"Lots of naughtiness going on in church this morning Frank. Move over you. That's the best shower in the whole unit."

"Here you are Danny. It's all yours."

"I am only kidding mate."

"You have it Danny, I am finished. I will have it if you don't want it Danny."

"Get lost Frank."

"Come out of the showers and wait by your cells."

Everyone started shouting to the officer.

"Get out you pervert."

Everyone who was going to church was ready by their cell waiting for the call to go and the two officers were together on the ground floor on the radio, waiting for the message from Oscar to tell them when it was Danny's turn to leave the wing.

"What time is it Frank?"

"9.53 But they are taking their time."

"We will probably be the last in church today."

"Come on you Christians."

The main gate to the block was opened and everyone made their way down and out of the block which was about 2 to 3 minutes away from the church. When they got there it was a long queue to the entrance. There were two officers sitting on a chair and desk with all the names of who would be allowed to enter the church. If your name was not on the list, you would not be allowed in.

Danny was next in line.

"What's your name?"

"Danny Mundy, Sir."

"Have you got anything on your person that you shouldn't?"

"No Sir."

"Open your legs."

The officer patted down Mundy.

"What's this in your pocket?"

"Sorry sir, I forget I had my pencil and paper."

"You are a good Christian Mundy, making note of what the good preacher has to say."

"Sorry Sir."

"Shall we still let him in?"

"Wait on the side and don't block the way."

"Yes Sir."

The officer continued to check names and search cons until there were none left. The officer on the chairs spoke to Danny.

"In future check your pockets before you come to church."

The church on Sunday was where cons from all the different wings met and did their deals, swapping drugs, names, and phone numbers. In fact, you name it, they did it. The Father was in control of the church and he did the evicting or telling people to be quiet. The officers wouldn't interfere unless necessary. In the church they sat in each isle, with four at the back and two by the door. On the way out there were hardly any fights at church. (There were two gypsy families that hated each other and one family planned to kill the head man of the other family in church the next Sunday. That was the only way they would have access to each other as they were kept separate usually)

As Danny got into the main church all the back rows were filled but Frank saved a space in the front row. One of the officers pointed to the space by Frank so he went and sat next to him.

The head of the Church was father Peter. He loved table tennis. Often he got his very small bat and came to the wing to play table tennis with the cons and he won all his games. The cons lined up to play father Peter. The other person doing this service was Father John who is new and from Nigeria. He took bible studies and was very short - about five feet tall. Once he was coming to the wing and taking names of people who wanted to have extra bible studies. He had his big book of bibles and at the same time was trying to unlock the main gate to go out of the block and he was struggling to unlock the gate so one of the cons saw him struggling and came up to him.

"Give me the keys father and I will unlock the gate for you."

"Take it Eugene."

The con opened the gate and went out with him. Two officers came running.

"Eugene get back in here."

"I was just helping Father John as he was struggling."

The two officers came and got hold of Eugene.

"You are going to the segregation unit."

"But Sir all I was doing was helping the Father."

"Yes, he was helping me. He did nothing wrong."

"Sorry Father John this will have to be reported to the wing manager."

It went higher than the manager. It went to the governor of the prison and poor Father John got a warning and Eugene went to the segregation for a week.

On the way out of church Danny walked to the front and lit a candle and prayed for his wife and children. Trying to see Greg Page he was looking everywhere but neither he nor Frank could see him. Frank was next to Danny.

"Frank quickly go and see if you can see him."

Everyone was hustling to meet and make their deal but the officers were on top of them.

"Get a move on, do not stop to talk to anybody. Just go straight to your wing. Anyone caught passing anything will be reported."

Another officer shouted.

"I'm watching you, now get moving."

One of the cons covered his mouth and said, "Take it easy Hitler."

"Who said that?"

Danny and Frank were walking slowly to their wing when a tiny guy came up to them. He spoke with a stammer and was about five foot two inches, with thick rimmed glasses.

"Are you Frank?"

"Yes, what do you want?"

"You wanted to meet me. I am Initt."

"Yes but keep walking. Good to meet you. My name is Danny Mundy and I want you to do me a very big favour."

"I don't do favours, but for you Mr. Mundy I will."

"I will pay and you will come under my protection."

"I don't need protection. I've got someone doing that already, what do you want?"

"I need you to find Greg Page's address. He was in Emely Prison from 2011 to 2013. Maybe find any family that he may have and their address as well."

"That will be a lot of work as it will take me a lot of time, but I am not sure I can do it. I am near my wing so I have to go."

"I will come next week and see you, where do you work?"

"I work at the library."

"I will see you there."

Frank and Danny got back to the A wing and into their cell.

"Danny, that guy has use of all the library computers."

"Yes I know?"

"Find out who is protecting him and find out all you can about him. I want to try and get him in our wing?"

"That's a good idea."

"Kim is coming this afternoon. How old is she now?"

"She will be twenty one next month."

"What about Amanda?"

"Since she found out that Bill is her father she has gone a bit cold on me but I love her the same. I am not forcing her to come and see me. When she is ready, she will."

He got to the visit as normal, was searched and waited and waited then took seat number 12 which was the furthest from the barriers. Danny sat and waited for the main outside entrance door to be opened and then the visitors would wait by the barriers. They could see all their loved ones sitting on the chairs and tables. Lots of visitors were waiting at the barriers but he was looking for Kim and couldn't see her. When she comes she is normally first in the queue.

The officer at the barriers waved the visitors to come in but there was no sign of Kim. He had to look twice as it was Linda. He waved to her then she waved back. She had on a cream suit, miniskirt, a red shirt and red high heels. She was stunning. She came up to the table and hugged him then they both started to cry. She had little make up on so when she cried there was nothing on her face but tears. Then they sat down.

"Kim told me, when I come I must get the food straight away or it all goes."

"I am so happy you've finally come to see me. Don't worry about the food for the moment."

"Let me get you some food, maybe two burgers and two cans of coke?"

"No, just a coffee and cheese sandwich for me please."

"You have lost all of your weight. I would not have recognised you if you had not waved to me. You look sixteen again."

"I wish."

"Look the queue is getting big. I will go and get your coffee."

Danny looked at her walking to the queue and all eyes were on her. In the queue he noticed male and female officers were looking at her. She was so beautiful and he'd lost her. That was totally his fault yet he hoped she was happy now. A few moments later she returned.

"Here you are Dan, you look so different now."

"My life is changed. That's what prison does. How come you came instead of Kim?"

"No Kim is coming next week. I booked this visit myself."

"I read the notice board so quickly and assumed it was Kim. I only looked at the surname."

"Kim told me you are reading lots and now you are writing a book?"

"No I am thinking of writing a book."

"I hope you do it. You can say what a bad person I am."

He hugged her.

"No you are not, you were the best thing that happened to me, but I threw you away."

"Eat your sandwich. When you were at home I would have never told you to eat, lol. Did Kim tell you I gave her a box and all the lawyer's paperwork that Johnny had given to me to look after for him?"

"When did he give you that box?"

"Years ago. I thought she should have it as she is looking into your case."

"Ok I will speak to her when she comes to visit me. I am so glad to see you. Are you happy Linda?"

"Dan I am very happy. Billy has looked after me and the children. As you know both of them are doing very well with Bill's help."

"I know I was not a good father and husband, so I am happy for you. I wished I was the person I am now with you then."

"You have become a very clever man now, buying our council house in Kim's and my name. I don't want it so when you come out you can have my share."

"Linda you think I have become a clever man now but that is not true. I was too lazy. You did everything for me so I did not have to think."

"Dan I will always love you. You were my first love but I love someone else now and it's a different kind of love."

"I know Linda. Why did you come?"

"I wanted to see you."

"Time ladies and gentlemen. Visiting time is over."

"Linda it so nice to see you. How did you get here?"

"I drove."

"Drive?"

"All the children drive and have their own cars."

"What car do you have?"

"I've got a black Mini Copper."

"Time please, visiting time over."

They both said goodbye and he looked at her as she left and others cons were looking at her too. He wondered if she would wave back. Would she turn around?

Yes she did and waved goodbye. He noticed she still had his engagement and married ring on. What did that mean?

Danny was so happy walking back to the wing. Then someone came to him and asked, "Is your missus a model?"

He wanted to say she was not but said yes instead.

He ran back to A wing and went to his cell. Frank was in there.

"How was the visit?"

"Good. Very good. Linda was there. I got one or two things to do, mate. I see you later."

Frank could read him like a book. It was both their cell but he knew he wanted time to think.

Down in the outside visitor's car park in a Black Mini Cooper, Bill was in the passenger side reading as the door opened and Linda had a tissue in her hand. She had been crying again.

"Are you aright love?"

"I have not seen him for eight years and he is so different and understanding now. I do not know what to say. I am all confused now. I did not have the heart to ask him for a divorce Bill, sorry love, but I will ask next time I go and see him."

"You are going to see him again?"

That night nothing much happened. He was just thinking how sexy she was and realised he really fancied her all over again. It was never like this when he first came to prison. What had he lost? What was this box she was talking about that Johnny left? Frank did not say much to him.

"Frank tomorrow I want you to see all the boys that are working for us and check everything is up to date?"

"Boss I did that yesterday. A few bits need to be sorted out and my son said that Billy wants to quit, but I told you all this yesterday."

"Phone Billy and ask him to visit me."

"He has booked for Monday afternoon. Boss that visit has messed you up."

"You can say that again."

Danny went to the visiting room and again was waiting then seat number 12 came up and he was waiting again. Last time Billy came late and he had told him not to come late. This time he was on time though.

"How are you mate and how is business?"

"As you know, I want to quit."

"I can't understand why you want to quit as you helped me build up the gardening business. It's legitimate now that we have got a warehouse, shop front and ten people working for us."

"Kim can run the business by herself. I just want half the cash we've got in the bank and nothing else Danny. The pressure is getting to me, checking everyone's work and doing my jobs. I don't finish till nine or ten at night."

"Look I tell what we will do, you don't work anymore, just go and price the jobs, check that they are done properly and work in the office."

"Danny, Kim is in the office all day. She does not go to university any more. She does an evening course twice a week."

"Does she? Wait until I see her. Tell me the reason why you want to leave."

"I have been pressured by Wade and his boys and he has got bigger now. He does a lot of drug dealing now. I don't want him to find out how big the business is. That's why I want to leave. All he knows it that I work for Kim."

"Where does he live?"

"I am not sure. I think about twenty miles away and he does not drive but one of his boys does."

"Thanks for telling me the truth. I want you take a holiday for two weeks. Go to Spain. You can ask Kim for the money and tell her the reason why. But before that you find out where he lives or any of his boys."

"Thanks Danny. I've never been abroad. I will go to Spain then."

"Is there anything that Kim or the boys don't know how to do?"

"I will go over everything with Kim before I go."

"What does Wade know about you and the business?"

"He only saw me with the company van and stopped me for a chat, asking if I want to work for him. I told him I'd got a good job and don't want go back to prison and that was it."

"Ok buddy - you sort out your holiday and ring me when you come back."

"Let me get you something to eat. All this talking and I forgot to get food."

"See when we talk about things we can work it out. So remember that."

"Yes, let me get some food."

Danny went back to his wing quite pleased with himself for sorting things out. Or had he?

The wing was quiet, like something had happened. He walked up to his cell and Frank was inside going over the books.

"Everything OK?"

"No. Just a small handbag fight but they did not bother to lock down. Someone owed a packet and did not pay."

"Was it one of our customers?"

"Yes, he owed us two packets and he only paid one. He did not think he should pay double when he only took the packet in the morning. I think both of them will be taken to the segregation unit."

"Get word to our man at the segregation unit to tell him he still owes or his family with have to pay. Surely he knows we've got people on the outside working for us."

"He will by the end of tonight. He will know. How did it go with Billy?"

"He told me about Wade seeing him and I asked him to take two weeks off. Does your son know Wade?"

"I am not sure. I will ring him tonight and see what more I can find out."

"Danny I spoke to Jr Frank and he said he doesn't know Wade. He said that he thinks Billy is doing drugs and short changed Kim with the payment, saying customers are not paying the full amount but they do and he is keeping the rest."

"Why did he not tell you before?"

"He was not sure."

"Thanks Frank. I will deal with it. By the way, what is happening with Initt?"

"He said he is still looking."

"It's been a month now, what is happening?"

"I am not sure though a lot's been going on. I have been spending a lot of time on the big drop."

"I understand. I will go and see him myself at the library, thanks mate."

For the next few weeks everything was going good and Kim was meant to come later that afternoon.

Waiting at the table for her, she popped up and he waved to her then she waved back and all the other visitors were waving.

She walked up to the table and another girl followed her. It was his little Amanda and both of them came running towards him. He got up and lifted the both of them up and swung them around together. They were beautiful girls, just like their mother.

"Amanda I am so happy you came to see me and you Kim."

The three of them talked and talked and ate and drank. Looking at his girls, he thought they could be models if they wanted to, as both of them were tall and slim.

"Kim we've got a problem with Bill."

"I did not want to worry you but he didn't go on holiday. He came back and opened the safe but I leave nothing in the safe apart from the petty cash and he took it all. I think we should hire someone new to do the pricing of the jobs."

"Yes do that and offer a 5% bonus for all the jobs he gets, that's net, not gross."

"Look who is talking net Kim. Our dad's an accountant now."

"Our dad has been reading all those books on Maths, book keeping and all the books for Dummies."

"Yes I heard of them. Well done dad."

"Thanks love. By the way Kim if you find more than one, take both of them and you can cover a bigger area in the business."

"What shall I do with Bill?"

"Tell him he can leave when he comes back. I want you to check how much he has robbed or short changed us."

"How far shall I go back?" "Up to you love. You will have a lot on your plate now."

"Kim can handle it dad, don't worry."

"Time please ladies and gentlemen. Time's up."

"Dad I will come and see you again." "Amanda I love you. Please come again. Kim I love too, so take care and don't work too hard."

Danny stood up and hugged both of his girls, feeling so happy. They went to the barriers and waved goodbye. He did the same until they were out of sight. When he got back to the wing, Frank was in the cell.

Chapter Twenty Five

Kim and Amanda went outside and they got into Kim's car and sat down.

"Amanda how do you fell about seeing Danny?"

"Kim I consider him my dad as well. I've got two dads so double the presents."

"Good girl."

"Why did you not tell dad what was in the box?"

"It will hurt him to know what uncle Johnny has been doing. I don't know what to do."

"We have to do something now that the detective found out that the door of the landlady's house was broken into and the back yard fence was broken. He has photos of it and the date the photos were taken. We can tell him about that."

"But who supplies that evidence?"

"Little sis let me work on it. We will tell dad everything and that will implicate a lot of people."

"The landlady's house, the back door and the fence. Surely that's enough for a new trial?"

"No I don't think so."

"Have you read everything on the trial?"

"No."

"Have you read all of Uncle Johnny's paper work?"

"No I will be honest with you and there are some tapes as well. I looked at the tape for a few seconds and I could not watch it anymore."

"Why?"

"It was things that Uncle Johnny did with other people."

"You mean he was having sex with people and blackmailing them."

"Don't be so cruel."

"Kim I think it's too much for you. Why don't you hire someone? I will you give some of the money towards it?"

"I think you might be right. They can go through all the papers and tapes and then report to me, sorry us, and we will then decide what to do with the information we get."

"Drop me by the station. I've got to get something from the shops."

After dropping Amanda off, Kim went to her friend Mary's at the estate agents office where she worked.

"Hello Mary can I see you later?"

"I'm free now. Let's go and get a coffee."

In the coffee shop Kim found a quiet place in the corner while Mary got the coffee.

"This is cozy Kim, now tell me what this is this all about? You are not…?"

"Don't be silly. You know my Uncle Johnny?"

"Of course I do. I know all your family. Come on, we have been living in each other's pockets all our lives. Did you know when I used to come to the cottage I was jealous and envious of you?"

"What are you talking about? You were there every weekend when we did horse riding, swimming, tennis, we did everything together."

"I was jealous. I don't care what you say."

"What I am going to tell you is dangerous and I don't want you to tell anyone else. Johnny left a box with my mother. In the box was £10500 in the building society. And £800 in cash. There were pictures and photos, tapes etc. There are many suspects who could have killed him because he was blackmailing them. These are the notes in each file that he had on them."

'1. The Landlady. She did not want the friends and the neighbours to know she was having an affair with me. She was very posh and played the lady.'

"The landlady's husband died ten years before Johnny moved in and she had a six bedroom house where Johnny lived. She was in her late forties and very plain looking. From the day Johnny came to live in the room, she was very happy. She gave him evening meals for free and eventually she had an affair with him but she kept it quiet from everyone. I think Johnny was blackmailing her with a photo he had of them in bed doing things. You know what I mean."

"Yes I do, go on."

'2. Eden is the accountant at dad's work place. He wrote one night they went out drinking and he told her he was robbing the company with fake invoices. He bumped the prices up on certain items and put in the ledger it was less. He was in charge of all accounts in the firm."

Eden was the accountant at his work and he was married with a wife and two children. The accountant at Danny's work place could have lied about the clocking machine. The last thing he wanted was to lose his job as he would never get one again accounting.

'3. Big Ron's Grandson. He was in charge of all the roofing and tarmacking work. He also bought stolen cars and sent them to Ireland and vice versa.'

"Big Ron's grandson Ron did the same thing to the gypsies. He hated gays and he did the same thing to them. He would be cast out of their communities."

"Mary you will never guess the next one on his list. It is the M.P. for Canterbury."

"Mark Harris, I'm sure he was not an M.P then?"

'4. Mark Harris - chief executive at Canterbury city council. He was the top man in the council and his ambition was becoming a Conservative M.P. for Canterbury.'

"Mark Harris - he did the same with him. He got mum and dad's council house which I now have bought. He also must have taken money from him, but my uncle never got promotions in the council. He had the same job for ages."

"5. Kim, my auntie. He has some uncompromising photos of her."

"This one will shock you about Amanda's Father, Bill."

'6. Bill was involved.'

"No that cannot be true about Bill."

"I did not say Bill alone dummy."

"I am shocked at this. I never thought your Uncle was like that. If you were not showing proof of these things about your uncle I would never believe you."

"What about Bill?"

"Bill has always loved my mum and it was not until the water tank burst in the house that mum had to move to his cottage. She had nowhere to live so she had no choice but to live at his cottage and that I suppose made her fall in love with Bill. After dad went to prison, my Auntie Kim came and took us to the cottage to live."

"Sorry Kim. I know you don't like to talk about it."

"I know Bill loves your mum and he gives her anything she wants."

"That's not true. My mum never asks for anything from Bill. He just kept buying jewelry all the time and giving her things."

"Sorry you are right, now what do you want me to do?"

"Come with me. We are driving to the landlady's house. Come on. Mary, the landlady's back door and outside fence was broken. That was in the detective report that Bill hired. That report never came out even though it proves there could be someone else involved in the murder of Johnny."

A few minutes later the car parked outside the landlady's house. Knock, knock and the door opened.

"Hello I am Kim and this is Mary."

"Kim you have grown into a beautiful woman, come in."

They walked in and they were outside Johnny's room.

"Can I go into my uncle's old room and have look?"

"I have not rented that room since he has passed but yes you can go and have a look. I'll make us some tea."

"That will be good, is the kitchen in the same place?"

"Yes."

"OK we will come there. Come in quickly Mary."

"What are you taking out of your bag?"

"I've got a flat pack shoe box. I will put it together and make a box."

"For God's sake what are you doing woman?"

"You will see. Let's go in the kitchen now and drink our tea."

"What have you got there Kim?"

"It's my uncle's shoe box."

"Give it to me."

"No, don't try and grab it. Mary let's go."

"Give it to me. It's mine. I will call the police."

"Call them, they would love to see what's in this box, bye bye."

"Where are we driving to now?"

"Dads work place. We are going to see Eden as he was the one that told them about the clocking in times."

A few minutes later they were at Danny's old work place. Mary and Kim walked into the yard and asked where Eden's office happened to be. Someone pointed to the side door.

"There is the side door to the office."

"Knock on the door then Mary."

"Hello Eden, where are all the staff?"

"It that you Kim? They've gone."

"Yes it is and this is Mary - my friend. You have seen her before."

"What can I do for you?"

"I came to tell you we've got some new evidence. I have found Uncle Johnny's old shoe box which had a lot of papers in it. I think I've got some new evidence."

"That is great news for your father. Can I have look to see if I can help?"

"It's ok, I just wanted to tell you the good news. Bye."

"Wait. I am sure I can help. You can call me any time."

"Bye Eden."

The two of them got back in the car.

"Where are we going now?"

"To see Big Ron's grandson at the gypsy camp."

When they reached the gypsy site, they parked the car and started to walk into the site. Then four dogs came barking and running towards them and they were about to run back to the car when a voice shouted 'Stop!' and the dogs started to wine.

"What can I do for you lasses?"

"You look like Big Ron's Grandson."

"No I am not. I'm his cousin. Do you want him?"

"Yes."

"He is not here, he's at work."

"Tell him I am Kim, Johnny Mundy's niece."

"I remember you as a kid in the pub with your mum. She was a great singer."

"Tell Ron that I got some new evidence about Johnny Mundy. He left a shoe box full of paper and pictures."

"Ok love I will tell him."

"Bye."

They got into the car very quickly.

"I was so scared of those dogs, Kim."

"So was I."

"Where now? To see Mark Harris?"

"He will not see us or we will have to wait a long time to see him."

"If he is there he will see us. I am going to his offices now."

Kim drove to Mark Harris' offices and as they reached the car park she shouted.

"Kim, look his car is there."

Kim parked the car and they went and saw the receptionist and told them they wanted to see Mark. They were told he was very busy so he couldn't see anyone and they would have to make an appointment. Kim was insisting and mentioned Johnny.

"Go and tell him this is about Johnny Mundy. Now if you don't he will not like that."

The receptionist wrote the name down and went into the office. Minutes later, a man came out of the office.

"Would you like to come into the office please?"

They followed him into the office and took a seat which was offered.

"How can I help? You mentioned Johnny Mundy. What about him?"

"This is Mary and I am Kim - Johnny Mundy's niece. We have new evidence that can free my father from prison. My uncle left papers which were found about possible other suspects that could have killed him. He was blacking mailing them."

"Why come to see me? You need a lawyer to appeal to the judge for a retrial. I can't do nothing."

"Well I am sorry I wasted your time sir, thanks for the advice."

"By the way if you need a solicitor let me know."

"Thanks once again, we will be leaving now."

Later in the car.

"Why are we seeing all these people?"

"Remember I said this could be dangerous. I am setting myself up. The people we saw or their accomplices could kill us to get Johnny for the box."

"You have set yourself up as a target. I am not leaving your sight."

"Mary I made a mistake being a detective."

"What now?"

"Now I've got four people after me. I should have told one and waited a couple of weeks. If nothing happened then told the next one on the list and so on. Now I got four people after me. Any one of them could attack me or try and steal the box and I would not know who did it."

"What are you going to do now?"

"I will get CCTV fitted at the house and at the office now and put the box in a safety deposit box. It's at my office safe at the moment. I'll get double locks on all my doors."

"I will drive you back so you can use your phone and do that now. Here is the name of the CCTV we use at the estate."

"Let's change over now Mary."

"Ok."

"I've done all the calls. You want to go for a meal?"

"I am dead tired. Just take me home. Will you be ok?"

"Don't worry. I will drop you home then I will have an early night."

Kim got home when it was just getting dark. She parked her car outside her house and locked the car and walked to her front door. Just as she opened the door, someone pulled one of his arms around her neck and one over her mouth. She dropped to the floor to get out of his grip and ran upstairs and into the toilet. She thought 'Why did I come up here? Why did I not go to the kitchen and get a weapon?' The person started to kick the door but the bolt held up. He was kicking harder and harder and the bolt started to get loose. Kim got hold of the bathroom shower and turned on the hot water and sprayed it into the bath getting the water as hot as she could. The extension lead of the shower was long and she kept running the shower. The water was boiling hot and she was now ready for the person. The door burst open and Kim sprayed the water on him and then ran out but the person tripped her up and she fell to the floor by the bathroom door. She was in a daze. A large knife was pointed straight at her neck so she could not move. Then someone else came and knocked the person's hand. He held onto the knife and ran down the stairs."

"Who are you?"

"My name is Raymond. Your dad sent me to keep an eye on you."

"Go and see where that person went, I am ok."

Ring ring. "Hello."

"It's me, Kim. I have been attacked. I am OK, don't worry. Could you come and get me from my house straight away please? No questions, just park in the next block from my house and walk the rest of the way to my house."

"Ok Kim."

Kim put the kettle on then changed her mind and went to the drinks cabinet to pour herself a shot of rum. She drank it then poured herself another one. The door knocked and she went into the kitchen and got a knife, then opened the front room curtains a little. She saw it was Raymond so she opened the door.

"Come in Raymond. Did you see anything?"

"No - not a trace of him."

"What do you think I should do? Call the police?"

"I am not sure. I will have to hear what your dad says."

"Raymond I don't want you to tell my father. What about telling the police?"

"I think you should tell them, but you don't know what they are going to do and they will certainly go and question your father."

"Would you like a drink?"

"No thanks."

"My friend Mary should be here in a few minutes. I am thinking of staying with her tonight and if you like you can stay in the downstairs bedroom and you can help yourself to what's in the kitchen to eat."

"Yes I will stay here. When Mary comes I will go and get my things and come back. Have you got a spare key?"

"I am getting all my locks changed and CCTV tomorrow. Here is a spare key. Ah, the door. It must be Mary."

"I will open the door."

Raymond went to open the door and as he opened it, Mary ginger sprayed him.

"Stop, stop Mary. He is a friend."

Kim went in between the two of them so Mary stopped spraying Raymond.

"What are you trying to do? Kill me woman?"

"I am so sorry."

"Kim I am going before she sprays me to death, bye."

"Who is he?"

"My dad sent him to look after me."

"How did he know about the box?"

"He does not but he must have thought Bill would have given trouble."

"How? I'm all mixed up."

"No. Not my mum's boyfriend Bill, but Bill who works with me at the office."

"Yes you did tell me he was fixing the books and nicking money."

"That's it."

"Well tell me what happened then."

"As I came in the front door this person grabbed me. I got out of his grip and ran upstairs to the bathroom. He broke the door down and was about to knife me when Raymond came and rescued me."

"He is kind of cute, how old is he?"

"Tonight was the first time I met him, but thinking about him he is cute. I saw him first and I don't think he likes you after spraying him. He does look a bit like my uncle."

"Yes he does, I always liked your uncle growing up."

"Tell me which one of you girls did not have the hots for my uncle. Raymond is coming and sleeping here tonight, can I stay at yours for a bit?"

"Of course you can, are you ready?"

"I will just wait a bit. You go and look out the windows at the back to see if you can see anything and I will look out the front."

About an hour later Raymond came back and no one else came to the house.

"Kim shall we let Ray in?"

"No he's got a key. Come on, let's go now."

They passed each other in the hallway and said goodbye.

"Don't forget the cameras and locksmith are coming in the morning."

"I won't, be safe. Goodbye."

"Bye."

Mary's flat was above her estate agents office and there was parking at the back of the row of offices and flats. She was very proud of her place. She had it rent free. That night the girls talked about old times for a while and went to bed. In the morning Mary had to go to work and Kim had to go to the office and warehouse to let the engineers in to do the works.

Later that day Kim let her self-back into Mary's flat as she had the spare key. She was going through her dad's paperwork and she found Raj's paperwork and realised that was the lawyer her father wanted to defend him so she knew she could trust him. Mary was working downstairs in the office.

A few hours later.

"How was your day, did you make any money?"

"I think I got one with a nice commission."

"I think I found a lawyer I can trust. My father wanted him but the judge said it was a waste of tax payer's money to change lawyer's mid-stream. His name is Raj. I will email him and hopefully I can meet him on Monday."

"Why have you brought the box and all your dads' paperwork here?"

"I wanted to see if I can find out anything. Nobody knows your address. I checked last night if anyone followed us."

"So did I, but you never know."

"You are right, what shall I do?"

"Shall we go to your house and see what Raymond thinks?"

"You just want to see Raymond."

"You can't stay here the rest of your life, you've got to go home."

"Yes I am ready when you are, but wait a minute. Let's take a photo of all the paperwork we've got of uncle's. Here, you take that bundle of notes my uncle wrote and I will look through his case. I will ring Frank to go to the office and warehouse to let the CCTV men in."

A few hours later the girls had taken the photos and read through most of the papers Johnny had left.

"Let's stop at the office first then we are going to see lover boy Raymond."

"Ok."

Mary drove to Kim's office and the men were already doing the work. Frank was at the front desk.

"Good morning Kim."

"You are taking the mickey, its afternoon now Frank and this is Mary."

"Hello Mary but we have met already."

"How can I forget that you proposed to me at the Christmas party?"

"Sorry Mary I was drunk. By the way Bill phoned and he should be here now."

"That's good. I want to see him."

"Do you need me anymore?"

"Stay here till after Bill's gone. When he comes send him in the back office. Come on Mary - let's get a cuppa. Do you want one Frank?"

"No thanks. Look who's here."

"Come into the back office Bill."

"Sit down Bill."

"Do you want me in here with you and Bill?"

"Yes Mary you can be a witness to what's been said. Hope you don't mind Bill?"

"I don't care."

"Bill, you said you were going on holiday and did not. This bit about Wade is not true, so what is going on with you?"

"I just want to leave the job and get my share."

"What's your share?"

"I told your father that I wanted half the cash we got in the business account and he agreed."

"I know my father. If he does not answer you, that does not mean he agrees with you."

"I worked hard for this business before you came. I made your father a lot of money."

"Listen Bill if it was not you, my father would have found someone else to set up a business from prison with. You do not have the brains to build the business to what it is today. My dad phoned you every single night to tell you what to do in the business."

"Are you going to give me half the cash or not? I make it £6,350 is my share."

"You ring my father. If he says to give it to you I will."

"I don't want any money from the building society accounts."

"As I said when dad phones me and tells me to give it to you I will."

"Kim can you give me a couple of hundred, until your dad's phoned you? I will ring him tonight."

"I am sorry Bill. If you were still working you would have money. You've still got your job here pricing if you want it. By the way have you told dad about the customer that paid you the balance of money? That money was never paid into the office? It works out over the last two years over £22,000 were not accounted for. When you ring tonight tell him about that."

"I never."

"Don't deny. I know. I have checked. I think you'd better leave now."

"This is not fair Kim."

"That's right, it's not fair to cheat the hand that feeds you, now go."

After Bill left, Frank Jr came in the office.

"What a wanker. Excuse the language Kim. I was listening in case he gave you any trouble."

"I've got my minder Mary here. Frank do you mind staying until the workmen finish? You are on overtime by the way."

"Don't worry, I have booked overtime already. I have been answering the phone and booking some jobs to be priced."

"I think you'd better price the jobs yourself after you set your men up on Monday and make sure all the teams have got work as well."

"You've done it all on the time sheets."

"Just double check on all the jobs for me. I've got quite a bit going on this week.'

Over the next few days everything was OK, with no more attacks on Kim. Kim was meeting with Raj at his office.

"It is very nice to meet you Miss Mundy. I met your father over eight years ago and I am sorry I was unable the help him then. What is this new evidence you have?"

"I have my dad's case papers and my uncle left a box of paperwork with my mum. She did not remember it till after the trial. My uncle Johnny has been blackmailing people, at least five people, that he has written down and collected money from. Also the landlady lied. The back door and the fence in the back yard were broken."

"That is new evidence. Can you leave all your dad's case papers with me? I will read them and let you know if we've got a case for appeal."

"What about the list of people that my uncle was blackmailing, like Eden the accountant? He was that one that lied about the time my father left work and clocked him at the wrong time."

"I've got enough for the time being. Just give me the list of the people and the amount he was paid."

"I don't want legal aid on this. Here is £2,500 for a deposit. I can see my father trusted you. I want you to keep it very quiet for the moment."

"If I am happy to carry on I will give you a breakdown of my fees and the barristers. Once I have read all the papers and I am happy I will book a visit to your father, if that's OK with you?"

"That will be fine, I will take my leave now."

"Just a minute. I will give you a receipt for the money."

"Thanks Raj. Look forward to hearing from you, bye."

"Bye."

After Kim left Raj looked for the landlady's evidence and read the report where the back door and fence were broken. He spent the next few hours on the people that Johnny was blackmailing. The next day Raj went to the landlady's house and knocked on the door."

"Hello are you Miss Hilda Hunt?"

Raj looked official. The landlady was looking around to see if the neighbours were watching and quickly said, "Yes I am, come in."

Once inside the house they spoke.

"How can I help you officer?"

"Twelve years ago someone was murdered here and we think the wrong person is in prison, because of withheld evidence."

"I told the officers at the time all that I knew."

"I don't think you did. Do you know what the charge for perjury is? We know that the back door and the back yard fence were broken. Are you going tell me the truth or are we going?"

She interrupted Raj.

"No, no I will tell you the truth. I can hardly remember as it was so long ago. I was cleaning the kitchen and I heard noses but I took no notice of it."

"Why did you not tell us about it?"

"I got an envelope of money not to tell anyone about the back door."

"It that all it said?"

"Yes."

"Have you still got the envelope?"

"That was years ago so I threw it away."

"Are you willing to tell the truth now?"

"Yes, are you going to charge me for not tell the truth before?"

"I don't know. You will have to ask the police."

"I thought you said you were the police."

"I never said I was the police. I have our conversation on tape if you want to listen to it."

"Get out of my house now."

"Bye and thank you for the information."

A few days later Raj had read all about the case and was meeting Kim at her office.

"Hi Kim how are you?"

"I am fine."

"I've got some news. I went to the landlady who said she was paid a thousand pounds to keep quiet about the door and the back fence. She does not know who sent her the money. The good thing was I got her on tape saying all those things. I will go and see your father in a few days' time. I need to see the other paper work you've got of Johnny's."

"I'm not very happy to give it to you but my dad trusts you. Just wait here and I will go and get them."

A few minutes later.

"Here you are - the papers and the tapes."

"Can I quickly look through it?"

"Yes, do you still want me in the office?"

"You can stay. I just want to check something."

Raj flicked through the paperwork then asked a question.

"Has Johnny got another building society book or another bank book?"

"No I don't understand."

"He worked for the Canterbury City council and they pay their salary through a bank and you've got no other account for John. That means he has another bank book for his salary and I see there's no credit card. What has happened to all of that?"

"That is all my mum gave me. There is nothing else."

"Who killed him took his wallet and credit cards and money, if he had any."

"I was too young to remember what happened after Johnny was buried. I think mum paid for the funeral."

"Thanks for meeting, inspector Pat Robinson."

"Raj, is it OK to talk at the front desk here?"

"Yes."

"Have a seat."

"I am here about the Danny Mundy case."

"Mundy, I can't remember?"

"It was about eight years ago when he got convicted of murdering his brother."

"Yes he was in a state. He was cold all the time."

"Yes that's him. Danny Mundy. Do you remember what happened to his brother's wallet and his credits cards? Did you search his room? If those things were not there someone must have killed him for it."

"I see what you mean but I can't remember. That was years ago. I don't know."

"How can I see his clothes and shoes etc.?"

"I can't see that we will still have them. I don't think I can help you."

"When Johnny Mundy was killed, what happened to all his clothes and belongings?"

"I am really sorry Raj, it's so long ago. I wish I can help."

"You can Pat. Johnny Mundy's workplace was Canterbury City Council which will have his bank details. Please will you phone them up and find out his account details such as which bank or building society etc. See if there was money in his account and if his credits cards were used after Johnny Mundy's death."

"I brought the charge of murder to Mundy's brother and now you are saying it was a wrongful conviction?"

"Yes Pat. I have lots of new evidence that the landlady lied. I got her on tape that she lied in court and she was given £1,000 to keep quiet about the back fence and basement door being broken into. Johnny was blackmailing at least five I know of."

"I find it hard to believe I missed all of that."

"Come on Pat. You only just got promoted to inspector and you were not the only one on the case. It would be a feather in your cap if you were to show you got the wrong man and put it right. It would right a great wrong."

"Let's go into my private office."

Once in the office, "Do you want a drink?"

"Coffee, black will do."

Raj opened his briefcase and took some papers out and put them on the desk.

"Here you are - black coffee."

"That's the Canterbury phone number for the wages department."

"Raj give me a copy of the tape of the landlady and I will go to the council myself. I will get everything you need. Any chance of the five names being blackmailed?"

"When are you going?"

"After you leave the office."

"When will I get everything?"

"Once I have made copies I will drop them in the next 24 hours."

"Thanks for your help. Sorry, when you help me I will thank you."

"I will see you out."

Chapter Twenty Six

Danny was very happy going back to the wing. He got to see Frank and went in the cell where he was there doing some paperwork and looking at the calendar.

"Good visit?"

"Very good, what are you up to?"

"Danny, everything is set for tomorrow."

"OK but first get one of our drugs crew to go and keep an eye on Kim at the gardening business. I think we might get trouble with Bill as he did not go on holiday."

"Ok boss. Sorry to hear boss. I will sort that out straight away."

"Now you can explain how everything's going to work."

"Tomorrow B wing will have social activities in the yard by the outer wall. The yard has three gates and the one at the end leads back to A, B and C wings. The next at the other end leads to D and F wings and the last one is the middle gate in the passageway leading to the all the wings. That passageway is the only way the wings are connected and E wing is opposite the yard by the outer wall. The gated fences are over twelve feet tall and the outer wall is twenty feet high. We will have six men inside the yard and six men outside of the fence. These men will wear disguises such as hooded caps, bright colours such as red and green etc. The time the men from outside will throw the drugs over the outer wall and into the fence area will be at 2.30. Our men will pick up the drugs and then throw these to our people outside fence area. The drugs sometimes get thrown over in tennis balls or Germany made hand grenades with the drugs taped at the end of a thick stick. Then our men will run to the wings but before they reach the wings they will take off all their outer clothes and give them to our people to hide and sometime during the next 48 hours they give the drugs to our keepers. Then casually walk back to the yard and back to their wings."

"Sometimes others cons will try and get the packages but the officers will know them. They can't leave the yard without being searched. Imagine you are throwing meat to wild animals in a cage. Well that's what it is like when the packages are thrown over."

"Sometimes others prisoners in the yard will try and nick the drugs from cons then fights will take place and the guards will then stop the fights but not until they have more of them."

"It seems like a good plan. Last year when we did it nothing went to plan. Who are you using on the outside of the yard?"

"I have no choice. I have to use two keepers."

"I do not want the keepers to be involved in this. Get another two cons, I don't want the officers to have any idea who looks after our gear. Make sure everyone knows exactly what to do."

"I have gone over it with them for the last month. That only thing they don't know is when the gear is coming in."

"We lost a lot of money last time."

"But boss we made over £10,000."

"How much would we have made if everything went to plan?"

"Ok I understand boss."

The next day Frank went to the gym where he worked and Danny went to his computers class where he was doing code. This was so hard for him to understand. He had done so many computer courses yet this was the hardest one yet. He asked his teacher so many questions. He must be fed up with him. Danny was the only one asking him questions.

"Sir can I go to the library this afternoon to see if there are any other books on code?"

"Here is a pass. You can go now."

"Thanks Sir."

On his way to the library, he thought to himself he must have been glad to get rid of him. He showed his the pass and went in the library and to the desk. He asked the person at the desk.

"Where is Initt mate?"

"He was shipped out yesterday Danny."

"What happened?"

"He got caught on the computers with internet connections. He was on the stock exchange, he was making a mint."

"Just my luck. Anyway have you got any books on computer code?"

"Let me have a look for you Danny." Moments later, "Sorry Danny we have not. If you know the name of a book I can get it."

"No I don't. Never mind, I will see you later."

It was lunch time now. He went back to the wing and had his dinner in the halls. Frank joined him.

"What's up boss?"

"They have shipped Initt out, I am going to see Daly."

"How did it go with Daly?"

"He said that he thought the guy was lying but he was not sure. He admitted he wanted to get in our good books so that's why he said it. He did not know if the guy was lying or not."

"Shall we sack him for lying to us or misleading us?"

"How is he in the shop?"

"He is on point with everything. He is one of the best ones working for us and he makes a lot of money for us. It will be a shame to let him go."

"Go and tell him we will give him another chance but he will be on half wages."

"Ok Danny and everything's set for this afternoon."

"Good. I am going for a kip as it's going to be a long day and night"

The door unlocked and he looked around. There was no Frank and he looked at the time. It was 4.10 pm so he must have been sleeping all afternoon. He wondered how everything went. Frank would be there soon. The door opened.

"Frank, you let me sleep all day."

"I thought that will be good for you."

"Thanks buddy. That was needed, how did it go?"

"Eight packs of gear were thrown over and we got six. One of the team got caught by the officers but was not too bad, far better than last time. I will know more tonight and tomorrow."

"I'm so glad you let me sleep mate. Now for the next one. Let me get this right, the main stores get delivery from outside of toilet paper, tooth paste and basically everything that we cons use? Then all the stores are unloaded by hand held fork lift trucks and then taken into the main stores warehouse. When the wing orders stores, everything is packed to be delivered. The officers have got the keys. Three or four cons deliver, pulling a cart or large cages on wheels with all the stock in it. Then the guard opens the wing doors. Then the stores officer meets them and he had a con working with them and they unload their supply of the stores they order. So packets are loaded into the wing stores and our man over the next few days gets the gear and gives it to our keeper."

"I have put the word out that who got the other packets best return to me."

"Good. One thing in prison - not many cons grass has the packages given to the keepers yet so we're waiting for the rest by tomorrow and all will be sorted out."

"When is the main stores getting its delivery?"

"It's a morning delivery, not sure what time but we've got three men working in the main stores now."

"I thought we had more?"

"Yes we did but he got caught nicking a stereo that was meant for a con. He came with his slip to collect it, the stores manager saw it was delivered and then called the officers and they searched his cell and found it."

"That was stupid. All he had to do was put not received, don't we pay them enough?"

"We do. It's just he was going to sell it but got caught. We can't really stop them from making their own fiddles."

"So everything is set up for the morning?"

"I will speak to the guys in the stores already and I will ring the driver tonight. If it works out alright tomorrow, we will have a lot of stock."

"Frank I am supposed to be the forgetful one. All what we got today is going out apart from the drugs."

"Yes, yes. I have given all the account details to the buyers. Some of them have put the money in the account already."

"Good, I am going to give up coding 'cos it's killing me. I am not thinking straight and the teacher will be happy. Let's hope everything goes well tomorrow."

In the morning he went to his computers lesson and Frank went to the gym. He was not worried as they had things come through the main stores all the time and there'd been no problem. The only times the officers on the gate thoroughly search the driver is when there is a new one or a new van. The company that delivers knows that.

"Sir I am thinking about not doing code anymore as it is draining me. Is there another computer course I can do but not as hard?"

"I am sorry to hear that, you say the library has no books that can help you?"

"No sir."

"Leave it with me and I will see what I can do."

Danny was hoping he would send him back to the wing but he made him continue with the class. Danny just could not get into this code. He had this problem before when he was in a new class and there were things he'd never heard of. That was putting him off but his mind was not on it and day dreaming in class was no good. That's why he was thinking about Initt. Who was this Daly person? Were his wife and Amanda coming to see him? He was glad he slept the previous day.

"That's it lads. Class is over."

By then he was glad it was over. Everything should have been done and dusted. He hoped nothing went wrong. He was in his cell and had his lunch. There was no Frank so he must have stayed at the gym to clean up. Nobody talked to him, apart from Frank, about the business. He would see him tonight. He went into the cell and started to read.

The cell door opened.

"Danny how are you doing?"

"I am well, Miss Jean."

"I thought you appealed your case. I did not think you were guilty of killing your brother. I like the way you used the prison system to improve yourself and you are still improving yourself."

"Thank you Miss."

"Here is a couple of bars of chocolate for you to keep quiet about."

After she left he thought she fancied him. That was all he needed.

That night he got his lunch and went into his cell, getting worried and there was no Frank. It was all so quiet and he didn't like when it was like this. It was just his imagination thinking the worse. The cell door opened.

"Fucking hell Frank where have you been?"

"They kept me back at the gym to clean up the place, today of all days."

"You had me worried all day. The next time we have deliveries make sure the gym is tidy so they will not keep you in."

"Sorry Danny I thought about that on the way back to the wing. I must have had a lot of calls. I did hear something on the way. Someone got caught with drugs in their mouth when they searched him. The stupid idiot did not swallow the drugs and when they searched him he coughed and it came out of his mouth."

"Was he one of ours?"

"Yes."

"Make sure he does not work for us again doing that job. Tell him to get a job transfer to the bike shop. How many men have we got in there at the moment?"

"We've got two, another two or three would be good."

"How many cons in the bike class?"

"I think ten in the class."

"Get the word to one of the other eight that don't work for us to ask for a different job so our man can get in there quickly. My contacts tell me they are getting at least 15 bikes delivered to be refurbished very soon."

"Did you see what they've done to the social yard where we get the drugs thrown in?"

"I have been in a bit of a daze today. I would not notice anything."

"They have installed a net over the yard. So if anything is thrown over it will fall on the nets."

"We are lucky we've got so many other inlets into the prison."

"Danny, you explained how it works in the bike shop. You had that before I joined with you."

"It was the delivery driver for the main store who told me that the prison started to refurbish bikes and he knew the guy who does the charity for the bikes. He knew the manager who gives outside work to the prison and he said he will speak to the governor of the prison and see if they've got a spare workshop and that's how it started."

"Does the manager know about the bikes being filled with drugs?"

"What do you think? There are lots of other jobs the prison do for companies on the out."

"How do our people know what bikes have got what?"

"It will be special marks on the bikes so only the person and I know what the mark is. I suppose we will have to wait until tonight to see what came through."

"Yes Danny I will phone tonight."

That night in Frank and Danny's cell.

"Good news buddy, everything is good."

"They all know what to do with the gear?"

"They were all told they must give the gear to the keepers as soon as possible and when you've got time tomorrow go to all the keepers and check that they gave all they receive to them."

"They know I will check them and keep an eye on them for the future."

"Frank have you noticed anything happening on the block lately?"

"You mean these Muslims. They are a bit heavy but not to our people."

"I notice that they are trying to recruit the weak cons. They are not like the other ones I met in Emely prison. Those were very nice people."

"What are you going to do about it?"

"None of our cons complain about them."

"But the ones they can't recruit, they are bullying the weak ones and robbing them."

"How many men have we got on the block that work for us?"

 "I would say fourteen?"

"How many can handle themselves?"

"I say ten are heavy."

"How many do the Muslims have?"

"About twelve and more are getting transferred to this Wing."

"I met some very nice guys at Emely and they were very helpful to me when I needed it."

"We will not bother with them until we have to."

"Sounds about right mate. The last thing we need is trouble. I remember when my old mate Cyril got killed. The place was never the same with the screws. They were on top of everything we did so we were extra careful."

"But boss that's how it should be."

"By the way nobody is sending money to Bill's bank account are they?"

"No boss. I reorganised that the same day you told me to get someone to look after Kim. Boss since you were visited by your wife you have not been the same."

"I know mate and there is something else. Miss Jean Hughes fancies me and she gave me two bars of chocolate. Did you see them on the table?"

"I did."

The cell door knocked.

"Come in, Daly, what's up?"

"Four Muslims came to the shop and wanted ten tins of Tuna, two tins of peas and two packets of rice. I told them that is too much to give on our tick and we've got to know them first before we give that much out in one go."

"So what happened?"

"They walked away."

"Go and bring their order to me now."

"What are you doing Frank?"

A few minutes later Daly came back with the Muslim order.

"Here you are Danny."

"Thanks."

"What are you doing?"

"I will give them it."

"You want me to come with you?"

"No that's fine."

Knock, knock.

"How can I help you mate?"

"You came to my shop. Here are the things you wanted. Sorry my man did not give it to you."

"We no longer need it. We are not beggars."

"I am not giving it to you. I am lending it to you and if you want it you will have to pay the normal interest."

"In that case I will take it. Thank you and good bye."

"Over the last few weeks there were more Muslims coming to the wing and bullying the weak prisoners and some of them are our friends and customers."

"Like how?"

"Pushing in front of queues for lunch, dinner and going straight to the front of the queue on canteen days. It's not one or two that pushed in, it's five or more. They have been taking over the outside sink that everyone used to wash their dishes in and they wash their feet in it."

"Their excuse is that the prison should provide two on all the floors and landing."

"Why don't one of the boys complain to the wing manager?"

"They don't want to grass."

"Frank I will be honest with you. I have noticed all what has been going on with them. I am not sure how to handle this. I don't want it to explode and we all get shipped out to different prisons. We've got a good thing going on here. We are making a lot of money for our families."

"Why don't we handle it like we did in the past?"

"That was white cons against white cons."

"This is different?"

"Yes buddy, did I tell you I sort of had this come up before but these Muslims did not fight but they were very kind but only a few of them. Tell you what, let's get a few of our lads to see what jobs they have got and where."

"Have not noticed, though they are working on the wing most of them."

"I have noticed six working on the wing."

"You can add another two as they are cleaning the showers now."

"Did you speak to Daly?"

"Yes I did. I was wondering when you were going to bring that up. They've taken another 12 tins of tuna, rice, peas, 2 packs of toothpaste and five milks."

"I know that was one week ago and they still have not paid for the stuff I gave them before."

"I think we or you should go and see them."

"What is the name of the ones I gave the stuff to?"

"They are on the threes?"

"Yes I remember their names. It was Hamza and Amid. I am going to see them."

"Do you want me to come with you?"

"Just come up to the landing on the threes and stay out of sight. Sit down if you can or watch the boys play chess or something."

"Ok Danny."

A few moments later Danny knocked on the Muslim's cell door. The door opened.

"Danny come in. Would you like some tea?"

"Thanks."

"Here is a seat for you. My name is Hamza and that's Amid."

"Thanks for the tea."

The situation was tense and Danny did not want to ask about the stuff. He was hoping they would say something as he was sipping the tea.

"So how can we help you Danny?"

"You know Daly runs that shop for me."

"Yes we know that."

Danny was getting impatient so he drank all his tea and stood up, then sat down again.

"You owe me for all the food you took and it's been nearly a month. It adds up to a lot of stuff owed to the shop, what are you going to do about it?"

"I thought you gave us the first lot."

"You said you will pay for it Hamza and you did not want charity. What about the other stuff you took from the shop?"

"Amid and I did not take anything from your shop."

"Daly told me you sent two Muslim boys and they gave your name. It was for you. I'll tell you what, you keep the first amount of food I gave you. The second load of food I want back at the price Daly told the boys. I will find them myself and make them pay it back to the shop."

"What are you saying?"

"You know what I am talking about, thanks for the tea."

Danny left and pulled the cell door after himself and walked past Frank and back to his cell. He sat on the bed.

"Looks like we've got trouble boss?"

"Yes tell Daly not to give anything to the Muslims from the shop and put the word to the crew not to give any drugs to any white cons who are Muslim and nothing to all Muslims."

Over the next few days Danny was not sleeping but thinking of what he was going to do with the Muslims. Kim has not told him that she was attacked and Frank's man was keeping an eye on her. That day Kim told him about the attack so there were two men now looking after Kim?

"Frank. I got it."

"What have you got?"

"Don't take the piss. This is what we are going to do. We will get some weak cons to attack the Muslims in the showers and the ones that are doing the cleaning. Not really the weak ones, the ones that think that they are tough but are not if you understand what I mean."

"But Danny they will get mashed up by the Muslims."

"That's the idea. Then the managers and governors will think the Muslims started it and hopefully they will get shipped out to different prisons."

"Most of these Muslims are fit as they all come to the gym all the time and you see them doing press up and pull ups on the landing stairs all the time."

"So there is a good chance my plan will work. The governor should not have let so many Muslims on one wing. He should have spread them out in all the wings?"

Later that night in Danny and Frank's cell when everyone was banged up.

"I have sorted some of the cons I want to do the job on the Muslims. A couple of more days. I am jumping into bed and I will be on the phone."

Frank went into the toilet with the box and took the phone out then he put the box back on the table and went back into the toilet and closed the door. He had text messages from some of his contacts but the one he rang was Raymond.

"What's up Raymond?"

"Kim has been attacked. I managed to save her. I am now staying at the house and she is changing the locks and having cameras in all her places tomorrow. I am staying at the house and Matt is keeping an eye on her and Mary her friend. She does not know about Matt."

"Who was it that attacked her?"

"I did not manage to catch him or see his face because he wore a balaclava. Are you going to tell Danny?"

"No mate not at the moment. Get another person from the crew to keep an eye on Kim. I want her watched around the clock."

"I spoke to her about getting the police involved, but she has not given me an answer. What do you think?"

"No old Bill, tell her that as well. Make sure you catch him."

"Ok Frank."

"I will see."

"That was a long call."

"Yes things needs to be done."

"I don't know what I would do without you Frank."

"Who are you kidding? You had done all this before I met you."

"I just want to make you feel good Frank."

"Thanks boss, what's this about Jean Hughes?

"I first met her at Emely prison. She is 49 years old and she took a shine to me. She is like my Johnny. She wants to buy her own house. Her life is not a happy one and she finds solace in her job. She does all the overtime that she is allowed to do. That's why you see her all the time, she told me. When she has enough deposit for a house she will leave him. She says she will not give him her new address. He used to beat her until one day she threw him on the floor and then put an arm lock on him, until he begged for mercy. He has not tried that again. They don't have sex anymore. Her husband is a lazy sod."

"He sometimes don't go to work. He drinks, gambles on the horses and on the internet and does not contribute towards the household. She has twins that go to university and she is very worried about her twins not having enough money for university and has become a very lonely woman as the twins go out nearly every night when they are not studying."

"Why is she telling you all this?"

"She wants my body?"

"What are we going to about Clare and your wife?"

"You are jealous Frank, lol."

"Danny I am a bit like you on the out. I love my wife and I would never look at someone else."

"Fair play to you Frank, as I admire you. I was not a nice husband or father on the out."

"I still find it hard to believe you were like this on the out."

"Frank my week was like this. I went to work Monday to Friday 7.30am to 5pm. Once I got home I would eat by myself in the sitting room with the T.V. on, leave my plate on the table and fall asleep and wake up about 9pm and have a coffee and two burgers, which Linda would make. I spent no time with the children with homework or playing. Linda did it all without question. Wednesday night I would go and play pool with Johnny. Friday night was the only time we went out to the pub. Linda sang on the karaoke machine. She loved that and all the people in there, love her singing and sometimes the kids would sing with her. Saturday most of the time was overtime till 2pm and after that I would go to the pub for a few pints and sometimes I would stay all night. Linda would send Johnny to get me. I was a selfish man."

"Fucking hell Danny, I thought I was bad but I was never as bad as you."

"I have not finished yet. Sunday I would get up at 12noon and come back at 3pm and eat and sleep till 7 or 8pm and come downstairs and have a couple of burgers."

"Did Linda ever moan?"

"She did, but not a lot. If there was work to be done in the garden, I would start it and Johnny would finish it. I was not a family man Frank. If I was to live my life again it would be different."

"Tell you what Danny, you are a different man now. One day you will get released and all that you build up outside you and your kids will benefit from it."

"Thanks for that. Everyone that is working for us will be better off."

"Have you looked on the visit notice? You've got a legal visit."

"When is it?"

"This afternoon."

He had his shower and wore some nice clothes and Gucci trainers. Then made his way to the visit hall. He saw Miss Jean.

"I see you are all dressed up Danny."

"Yes it's nice to wear some nice clothes now and again."

"I must say you look very smart. Is it a legal visit or your girlfriend Clare?

"Legal Miss."

He started to walk quicker and she did the same. He wanted to lose her but she kept up with him. What did she know about Clare? He wondered if she was jealous as nothing had happened between her and him. He'd just got be careful with her.

"Where are you going Miss?"

"Same place as you."

"Oh I will walk with you then. It's my lawyer that's coming and I hope its good news."

"Let's hope together, I don't know if I told you but I don't think you killed your brother."

"I know I did not kill him. He was my best friend and he looked after me. We have reached the visit area so I better get in the queue to be searched."

After being searched he was told to go into a small room with chairs and a table.

"It can't be Mr. Danny Mundy?"

"It that you Raj?"

They hugged each.

"Have a seat Danny and how are you?"

"Thanks Raj it is really nice to see you and now you are going to handle my case."

"I must say prison has done you the world of good. When I met you last you were not a well man."

"Thank you Raj. I am a different person now."

"I can see that. I have met Kim. She is a very nice person and she gave me all your case paperwork. I met with the landlady and she assumed I was from the police. I went along with her and she spilled her guts out. She lied in court and did not tell about the back door and the fence in the back yard being broken. Someone gave her £1,000 not to tell about it. I have some very sad news for about your brother Johnny."

"Do you have to tell me?"

Danny was holding back the tears thinking about Johnny.

"I have to tell you, ok now?"

"Yes go ahead."

"Johnny knew a lot of people. He left a box with Linda which contains at least five people he was blackmailing."

"Stop for a minute, you are telling me Johnny was blackmailing people for money?"

"Yes and Kim's got all the proof and the money."

"Stop a moment. Let me take this in."

"Danny I know it's hard for you to take in but it's true and we've got to try and get a new trial and get you out of this prison."

"Yes, yes you are right. Thinking aloud, someone must have threatened him. That's why he wanted me at his house. As I walked there they must have killed him and went back through the back door and fence."

"I think we've got a strong case for a retrial."

"How much is this going to cost? I think about £25,000 without legal aid. Kim said that she did not want legal aid. She gave £2500 already."

"Could we get legal aid?"

"Yes I think we can. We have to apply for it. It would take some time."

"I am happy about you keeping that £2,500 for yourself and still applying for legal aid. You can still carry out all the works you need to do in the mean time before we get legal aid."

"I've got the legal paperwork with me. I will get them for you to sign."

Danny took the legal papers out to flick through them and sign without Raj telling him where to sign. Raj was impressed and smiled to himself.

"Danny I want you to know I have had case that was a lot stronger that yours. The judges still refused for a retrial. Do not build your hopes up too much, I will do my best for the retrial. I will try as of now and get the best barrister I can. Hope you don't mind. I will give him £2,000 up front to make sure he takes the case plus what legal aid will pay him if that is ok?"

"That's fine Raj. I trust you. Could you please take all the paperwork that Kim got pertaining to the people that Johnny was blackmailing and investigate them so we can find out who killed Johnny and who paid the landlady?"

"I had that in mind to do. You are a different man Danny."

"Could you book to see me in two weeks' time?"

"I might not have anything."

"I want to see."

"Ok Danny."

"Time please gentlemen. Mundy wait in there when you are done."

"Ok officer. Bye Danny."

"Bye. I have to wait in here. I will see you in two weeks' time, bye."

He was in a daze walking back to the wing, thinking about Johnny. That's how he always had money to buy the drinks and help Linda with the shopping. When Linda asked where he got all the money he told her he maxed out on his credit cards. He always did the right thing by Danny and he was not going to allow this news about him to stop him loving him. There was a chance he might be free in a years' time. What was he going to do on the out? At least he had the girls and the garden business. He would go into the building game and buy houses that need renovation and do them up and sell them. He would ask for a transfer into the painting class then the plumbing. He would go to all the building classes that the prison had to offer. As he got to the wing Frank was there in the queue waiting for evening meal.

"Here is your plate Danny and how did your visit go?"

"Not bad. There's nothing new. They're just trying to get more money from legal aid."

"Tell me more?"

"Let's get lunch and we will talk in our cell."

They got their lunch and he followed Frank up the stairs. He did not want to tell Frank about the new evidence as it might change how he thought and that could be very dangerous. He wouldn't tell him anything until he knew one way or another.

That night in Danny's cell.

"When are you planning the attack on the Muslims?"

"Tomorrow dinner time."

"Why not do it in the evening? If they do it before it's going to be lockdown and we will lose a lot of business."

"The reason is that not many Muslims will be in the wing. It will be a bit of a fairer fight."

"It's up to you Frank. I've got a feeling you are not happy with this plan."

"I don't like our boys getting beaten up by the Muslims."

"Well if you feel that way why don't we call it off and let it take its natural course with the Muslims? Frank I want you to be honest with me."

"Let's call it off Danny."

"Ok call it off but still pay the boys what you agreed to pay them."

"Thanks Danny."

"Is there anything outstanding?"

"It's only those two Muslims that owe us, what are we going to do about it?"

"Nothing! But none of them are getting nothing from our shops and our crews that deal with drugs is that right?"

"Yes."

He had already started thinking about being released. If he did not think about it, he would have given the go ahead to sort out the Muslims. It was the same reason why he was not telling Frank he might start to think differently. If the Muslims started taking the piss more he would have to do something about it.

"It's been a week now and the Muslims are still pushing their weight about. Some of our people are complaining. Not sure I can hold them back, what do you want me to do Danny?"

"As I have said they get nothing from us and we have to stay out of trouble for a while. We are making money Frank so why mess it up?"

"Danny honour."

"I've got a visit this afternoon. When I come back we will talk about it."

"Thanks Danny."

The visit.

"Hello Dad, you are looking well."

"Nice to see you. When were you going to tell me you left uni?"

"Dan you knew weeks ago, I don't want to talk about it."

"I am Dan now. OK young lady, tell me what's being happening?"

"I got new locks changed at all our places and cameras. I see what goes on from anywhere I am."

"What do you mean anywhere?"

"Yes Dad I can be at our house and look at my cameras and see the office or the warehouse. I gave Raj some money. Let me get you something to eat."

"Let's have a can of coke and a pasty."

"Is that all?"

"I want to keep my figure."

Kim came back from the café.

"Bill has gone. I don't suppose he rang you?"

"No he did not."

"I thought so. He wanted half the money in the business account. I told him to ring and if you said yes I would give it him."

"He's one stupid boy."

"You mean man. Do you remember my best friend Mary? She fancies Raymond. He looks like Uncle Johnny. He has blond hair, tall and handsome."

"Don't tell me you fancy him as well. I can still tell."

"Mary has first shout, so I will leave well alone. I took on two estimators and we are just getting new types of work such as extensions."

"Extensions?"

"Building extensions. One of the new guys I have taken on used to do that and he has the workmen as well. We start the first one next week."

"Well done Kim. If you are happy doing this job, I am happy as well."

"Dan I love doing this job and expanding the business. When you come out you will have something good in your life."

"That's a long way off."

"Did you see Raj?"

"Yes but I am not building my hopes up. I have seen so many prisoners get let down and it totally destroyed them for months after. They are not the same after that turmoil."

"But Dad."

"Don't talk about it. How is Amanda and your mum?"

"She was so happy to see you. She's back at university now. Mum was happy to see you but it's always sad to see you in a place like this. Did she ask you?"

"Ask what?"

"Oh nothing."

"It can't be nothing, tell me?"

"I should not have said anything. Dad leave it."

"Ok love when is Amanda coming again?"

"Not sure Dad. I think when she has holidays."

"It's very nice to see her after all these years and your Mum. There goes the bell. Visiting time over so you'd best get going so you will not get held up in the rush."

"You are so right Dan. We had to wait so long before we got out last time and they did not give us a reason why they kept us back. Love you lots Dad - bye."

"I am still your father but if you want you can call me Dan like your Mum always did. Bye love."

On his way back to the wing he came across Jean.

"Mundy make your way straight back to your wing."

"Yes Miss Jean, what's wrong?"

"Just get back to the wing."

Jean ran past Danny and a few more officers passed him, then Danny started to walk back to the wing quicker, once he was in the wing.

"Get to your cell straight away Mundy."

"Yes Sir."

"Frank what's going on?"

"Some Muslims were fighting in the showers and a few of our boys got hurt and they are at health care."

"What else, like who started it? Who came out worse?"

"I don't know too much. I came back from the Gym and I was told to go straight to my cell. The guy next door told me by the pipes, that's all I know."

"It will be lunch soon, we will know then."

"How was your visit?"

"Good my daughter Kim wanted to call me Dan. It slipped out a few times."

"She is growing up. I will check my phone in a few minutes time if anyone has texted or tried to ring."

"It not lunch for a half an hour so check the phone now. Go in the toilet."

"Ok."

"Fucking hell you are not going to like this. Hamza, Amid and a few Muslims robbed the shop. Daly and a few of the crew went after the Muslims in the showers and they got beaten to the punch. The Muslims knew they were going to do that and had men in the showers waiting for them when only Hamza and Amid went to shower. Daly thought it was only two of them but in fact it was twelve of them."

"I told them we did not want trouble. We have to do something now."

"You are saying they should not have done something."

"No, not really. Someone steals from us and we've got to do something. The only place we can do them is in the showers in the wing or in their cell, without getting caught."

"Danny do you remember the Godfather film?"

"Yes, yes I do. Good thinking Frank. We can do that, but a bit different. They all don't go to the Gym at the same time. We plan the attack at the Gym at exactly 2.15 pm then some officers from another wing will rush to the gym. At 2.20 we attack all the Muslims on this Wing and make sure they are in their cell or in the showers."

"That's a very good idea only one thing is we might be locked up or have education or some other activities those days."

"We will chose a day when we are open and go to the Gym."

"That sounds good, I suppose I have to organise it all?"

"Yes that's why you are getting the big bucks."

"Thanks a lot."

"When you've done that, go over the plan with me."

"I was waiting for that, are you getting involved?"

"I will personally deal with Hamza and Amid."

"Are you sure. You are getting on a bit."

"As I remember they are cleaners on the wing so we have to leave it for a bit."

"What about the shop?"

"We are still running the shop so restock Daly and put a watch on the shop all the time. Now tell the boys not to go in the shop but to play games on the landing, so they can see everything that goes on."

"Ok boss, I will start organising it now and I will put a watch on the Muslims now, so when we are ready to move I will know exactly what to do."

"Get me two thousand pounds for tomorrow afternoon. I've got a legal visit."

"Legal visit. Why?"

"She wants a divorce."

"How do you know?"

"Kim slipped up."

"Why do you want that much money?"

"They want me to admit adultery and I am going to fight it, that's why."

"Ok boss."

"Going back to the Muslims. When we do them it must not look like it's planned. No one grass. It was a plan and if the Muslims grass we must say they started it, if they're questioned by the officers.

The next afternoon Danny went to his legal visit with Raj in the same room he had before.

"Nice to see you Raj."

"Same. How are you?"

"I will be honest with you. It has affected me a bit thinking about being released."

"I am not going to bother with the things I've done but it's looking a lot better than the last time I saw you."

"Good, will you tell more anything positive?"

"I've got the landlady on tape lying and I saw Pat Robinson, he has been helpful so we will see."

Danny was looking through the glass door to see an officer outside. He stood up and knocked Raj briefly on the ground. When Raj was picking the brief case up and the paper, Danny took the money out of the back bottom and dropped it on floor.

"Put the money in your brief case, Raj."

Raj could not think. He did what he was told and picked up everything else and sat on his chair again.

"That's the money for the barrister. You keep the money Kim gave you. I know I should not have done that but sorry mate. I wanted to look after you."

"Danny don't do that again. I could lose my license."

"Have you heard from the judge?"

"I need some evidence, not a lot more. We are nearly there. I've just got to wait on that Pat Robinson to come back to me about some information I need."

"Tell me?"

"Why don't you wait and I will tell you when I've got something more positive for you?"

"You are right. I will wait, but it is so hard in here."

"Look at the time. My time is up, I shall leave you."

"Bye Raj. I have to wait in here."

After Raj left, an officer came in.

"Mundy you can go back to the wing now."

"Ok Sir."

On the way out, Mundy was searched. Then he made his way back to the wing, instead of going straight to his cell. Danny walked around the wing. He does not normally do that, taking stock of the Muslims. In the old days cons would look at him and wanted to fight him - saying things to him. The main one was, 'who are you looking at?' Then a fight would ensue and he knew he was in charge of the wing. He was the boss. What would happen to him on the out? He was used to 12 years of prison. Would he get back to a normal life without Linda? Would he be able to adjust to the life on the out? He wished Linda was back in his life as he still loved her with all his heart. He thought he would apply for a divorce. He thought that was what Kim was talking about. He had started the plumbing class now and he was going to do the painting but he couldn't get by without it. He would do the plumbing on the out.

Frank looked down from the landing.

"Danny what are you doing?"

"I will be up in a minute. Actually, I am coming up now, wait there."

"That was quick Danny."

"I am fit for an old bloke."

"What? You are younger than me."

"You live at the gym so that keeps you young."

"Everything is set."

"Good. Do me a favour. When you see Daly call him for me, I was looking for him."

"Did you look in the shop?

"Never mind. I will go to the shop."

"Every time you go to visits your head goes."

"Lots going on with the Muslims, I don't want to make a mistake."

"You know yourself there will be mistakes, no matter what we do."

"I am going to see Daly now."

"Hello Danny,- what's up?"

"You know what's go to happen?"

"Yes."

"Have you been allocated a job yet?"

"No and my boys at the shop neither."

"That's good 'cos on the day I want you to be on 3s landing and one of your boys to go to the shower at 2.20. I will be coming up at the time to do the Muslims. I want boys to go the 3s and try and stay out of sight."

"That will be very hard to do."

"Do the best you can. The main thing is we do not want the Muslims to know. Use the guys we got on the threes ok, they know what to do."

"Ok boss."

"I will see you later."

The next few days were quiet.

"Today is the day Danny."

"Everything checked."

"Everything is checked and double checked. You feel fit, you haven't done any fighting for a while so have you still got it?"

Danny held Frank in a neck hold.

"Yes you have still got it, now let me go."

"When this iron grip holds you that's it mate."

"You will be taking on two of them mate. You'd better be careful."

"I should be ok as I will be taking them by surprise hopefully. You make sure you are ok my old mate as well."

Frank had gone, the time was 2pm. Danny was getting ready. He put on his vest, then underpants then one pair of tracksuits and then another pair. He had a cap on and he looked at the time saying 2.15pm. He made his way up the landing where he saw his boys. Then he went in the shower room, took off one of his track suit tops and bottoms and asked his man to hold it. Then he put his cap on and made his way to the Muslim cell where he pushed the door wide open. He hit the one closest to him as hard as he could on the side of his face. He fell to the floor then the other came at him with the kettle. Danny kicked the kettle and punched Amid in the face and he fell to the floor. Both of them were on the floor. Hamza was still out and Amid was about to get up. Danny kicked him on his head and he was out. Danny got their little cupboard and tried to open it but could not. So he turned it to the back and kicked the back in and pulled out the broken back cover. He looked inside but it had nothing inside apart from a couple of roll ups and an address book which he took. He sat on the bed waiting for one of them to wake up. Hamza did. Danny was about to hit him again.

"Please don't hit me again, sorry we stole your stuff. I will pay you back."

"I am telling you if any one of you fucks with my shop or any of my people, I will come back and fuck you up, so you can never kneel to Muhammed again. Do you understand? I've got your address book so make sure you go and pay everything you owe my shop with interest. Do you understand?"

"Yes."

"I want you to stay in your cell for the next hour."

"Yes."

Danny went into the shower and took off the track suit he had on and pulled the other one on.

"Go take these to laundry. Tell him wash them straight away."

"Yes Danny."

"Not now. Wait till I have gone. Give me the black bag I gave you. Let me have it again, I need this."

Danny made his way back to his cell and just then the alarm went off and officers were coming out of their offices.

"Everyone in their cell now."

Lying on his bed, Danny thought to himself that was good timing. He always thought the Muslims were wealthy but those guys didn't have anything their cell. Nothing of value. Those two probably were not connected to the other ones that went to the gym. They wore all the expensive gear like Gucci, Praga, etc.

Danny would speak to Frank when he came back.

The cell door opened and Frank walks in then the door locked again.

"Hi Frank. Cup of tea? I will put the kettle."

"Sure I see no mark on you Danny, did you do them?"

"No they done me, don't ask a stupid question. How was it with you?"

"We did ok, but one of my boys went over the top with a 12.5 kilo weight. He broke one of the Muslim's jaws and he was taken to health care and Munro was taken to the segregation unit."

"Munro again. He is a fucking idiot. What can we do about him?"

"What can we do? Nothing."

"You're right Frank. While he is in the seg we are not earning and we still have to pay him. I don't mind but he is such an idiot."

"Those Muslims you did at the gym, are they rich? Or have they a lot of bread?"

"I think so. On Saturday their canteen bags are full so they can hardly carry all the stuff they buy on their canteen sheets. Plus they ask other people to buy for them. Their families on the out put money into the cons' canteen account and they buy what they want each week."

"I thought the two that I did on the threes were the same as them."

"Aren't they?"

"When I done them, they were lying on the floor. I broke their little cupboard and it had nothing inside apart from a couple of roll ups. They had nothing of worth in their cell. I don't think they are connected only by being Muslims. Hamza and Amid haven't a pot to piss in."

"What? Are you feeling sorry for them?"

"I don't know what I am thinking, I don't think they will report me, but we will see. Did you hear anything the officers said on the way here back from Gym?"

"No."

"We will know a lot more tomorrow."

"Something seems to be troubling you?"

"No nothing Frank."

"You are thinking about the two Muslims you sorted?"

"Yes mate. The Muslims were very good to me when I first came to prison. I can't forget that. I would not be the man I am today without them. It's a matter of honour."

"You think someone set them up?"

"I am not sure. No smell of smoke in their cell, no food stock and they were like beggars. Someone could have put them up to it, but who?"

"Did you take anything out of the cell?"

"Silly me. I got their address book, let me look through it. I can't see any names I know. You look in it and see if you know any names. Here you are."

"Thanks."

After Frank looked at the book.

"I have had a look at it. Nothing. We've just got to watch them to see who they talk to, or you can go and question them. Who paid them to steal from us?"

"Frank let's wait until tomorrow and see if we get any come backs."

"I will organise that tonight."

"When was the last time you spoke to our cell mates either side of us?"

"They know the drill when the pipes is just knocked hard once."

"Yes and I've got the broom stick ready."

"Sorry Frank just checking, one day we might get a surprise visit."

"Anyone who knows us will never try it."

"Yea you are right Frank.

The next morning in Danny's cell.

"Come on Frank it's 6.30. Time to wake up and do our exercises. Your tea is made. It's on the bedside cabinet."

"I am up. We start at 6.45 ok, as I was up late making phone calls."

"Yes I noticed, pull the other one."

"That was good, what time it is now?"

"The clock is just here Danny. Look at it, coming up to 7.55."

"They should be opening up soon. Do you want me to get your cereal ready?"

"Yes please."

The rest of the day went well without trouble from with any Muslim or anyone and Danny was still thinking about the two Muslims.

"Hi Daly let me have four tins of Tuna and two bags of rice please."

"Here you are Boss."

Danny went up to the threes and knocked on the Muslims. Hamza opened the door.

"I am sorry I got nothing to pay you back. We've got no one outside that can help us. We just get our wage for cleaning the wing. When we get our canteen sheets we will bring it to you and you can buy what you want."

"I want to know who set you up to steal from my shop."

"No one."

"I know you are lying as you have nothing of value in your cell. That means what you stole you have given to someone else. Now tell me the truth."

"Hamza tell him the truth. He might stop them from bullying us and taking all our stuff."

"No, no we can't tell or they will beat us up more."

"You tell me Amid and I will stop them from bulling you two."

"It's the Muslims on the ground floor next to the office."

"Thanks Amid you will not regret it."

"The numbers are 2, 4, and 6. They are all next to each other, thanks Hamza."

"What are you going to do?"

"I don't know at the moment, here I brought this for you."

"Thank you Mr. Mundy. We will pay you back."

"When you get your canteen sheet go and give it to Daly in the shop ok."

"We will and thank you once again."

Danny made his way back to the cell and Frank was waiting for him.

"You couldn't help yourself could you?"

"Frank you are always right, stick the kettle on."

"I made the tea mate. It's by the bed."

"This tea is horrible."

"I thought you were going to drink your tea without any sugar."

"You could have warned me. I will drink it just to show you I can."

"Nice isn't it."

"Yes it is, it was the Muslims on the ground floor that put them up for stealing from us apparently. They are bullies and you know what I think about bullies. The only trouble is they are next to the office."

"I think we have done two of them in the gym as well. I think there are six to eight of them on the ground floor mate."

"Those two I think are very weak, I feel bad what I've done to them. They will tell the Muslims they told me about them."

"I will tell all our crews to be careful and be on the lookout all the time."

The door knocked and they opened it as both of them were lying on their beds.

"Miss Jean how can I help you?"

"I hope you can Danny. Go outside Frank. I want to speak to Danny."

"Ok, Miss, we done nothing."

"How can I help you Jean?"

"I've got two chocolates and some cans."

"Thanks Miss."

"I see you got a visit tomorrow. Clare, who is she to you?"

"Just a friend."

"I can do a lot for you if you like me."

"I do like you, you are a very kind person Jean."

Danny stood up from his bed and walked towards her and held her hand and was about to kiss when the door opened.

"Officer with post coming up the stairs Danny."

"Make sure I don't see that again Mr. Mundy."

"Yes Miss."

After the post was delivered back in their cell.

"That was a close shave, I was about to kiss her. I will be honest to you she is alright. I remember her when I first came to prison. She had a soft side to her."

The next day Danny had his visits from Clare and they talked.

"Danny can I meet your daughter Kim for a coffee?"

"I'd rather you did not Clare."

"Why?"

"I don't think its right at this moment in time. She's got a lot on her plate with the business."

"When you come out you will be living with me, won't you?"

"That's a long way off, I don't want you to give up your life for me."

"Danny what do you think I have been doing for the last twelve years?"

"I am sorry you gave me the last twelve years but no one knows what's going to happen in the future."

"Do you want me to stop seeing you?

"It's up to you. I love to see you but I don't want you to give up your life for me. If you are going to do that then of course stop."

"I am going now. Bye Danny."

"I did not mean it like that, I was thinking about you. You are a young woman. Try and meet someone else. I've got another 13 years in here and that's if I get parole. I am thinking of you Clare."

"Time please. Visit time is up."

The both of them stood up and hugged each other for a long time. Clare started to cry then she left. Nothing more was said.

Over the next few days the whole prison was quiet. It must have been England playing in the world cup. One thing in prison the cons loved was football and all the soaps on T.V.

Danny had just got back from his plumbing class when Daly came to him and said, "The two Muslims gave me their canteen sheets. What shall I do?"

"Use half of the money they got on the sheets to buy things for the shop and let them keep the rest."

"Why? That means they will never pay back what they stole from us."

"Sometimes in life we give people a chance to put things right even if they can't afford it."

"You are the boss."

Danny went to his cell.

"I didn't think you were here yet Frank."

"I am here normal time."

"Those two Muslims are paying some money towards what they owe. Daly just told me."

The cell door swung open with a bang and six Muslims came running in slashing with toothbrush made knives. Only three could fit between the single beds and three were behind and trying to cut Danny. Danny was first in line so he put his hands to stop his face being cut. He fell back on the bed and started to kick. That gave him a little time to get himself room to grab his quilt that was folded at the end of the bed. He got it and opened it. While still being cut to bits on both of his hands he managed to somehow throw the quit over them. Then started to punch and high kick. Frank banged the Pipe with the heel of his shoes then took out the broom and lit it. The flame was big as he had glue on the badges around the broom handle. Then he started to push the flames in the Muslim faces. The quilt caught on fire. Then the cons from either side of Danny's cell came in the cell. They took aim and hit the Muslims on their back and on their heads with their socks stuffed with tins of tuna and pool balls. They were taken fully by surprise then fell to the ground one after another. When they fell to the ground they were kicked dozens of times by Danny and his crew. There was not enough room on the floor for everyone.

"Shut the door. Don't let the Muslims out. We are going to give them a good hiding."

"Yes Danny."

Door slammed shut

"We have had enough. Sorry, sorry."

"Frank grab the quilt."

"I will throw water on it. Look it's nearly out."

"Take it and the broom. Dip it in the toilet and run the sink water on the quilt."

"The cell's filled with smoke. Munro open the windows the best you can."

"Sure boss."

All the Muslims were on the floor on top of each other. Some were bleeding while some in a daze, their knives were on the floor so they were helpless. Frank picked up all the knives that were on the floor.

"Listen you load of wankers, you will be paying protection money to me and my crew inside. It is £200 per month and outside £400. I don't care how you split it. That is the price.

"Search them. Frank and Munro you help him."

"What are we looking for?"

"When you see it you will know. Munro go to their cell downstairs and search it for addresses and tobacco and anything that we may need like addresses of their family on the out."

"No need to do all that. We will pay the money inside. The family can afford it."

"I don't trust them. Frank are you done here?"

"Can't find anything."

"Go downstairs and help Munro have a clear out of everything."

"Ok boss."

"You rich Muslims will know how it feels to have nothing."

"We will pay the money Mr. Mundy."

"I know you will. I will have my people on the out visit your family and your shops and make sure you pay."

Danny's two hands were bleeding badly now.

"You Muslim lot can go. Do not try and stop Frank for taking what he wants in your cells".

"We will not. He can take what he wants, no trouble."

As the Muslims were leaving, Frank and Munro were coming up the stairs.

"Look they are coming up now."

"Danny what shall we do with all the stuff?"

"Let Munro sort it out and make a list. You keep all the paperwork. I am bleeding badly so get some clean sheets out and strip them to make into bandages. Have we got any disinfection?"

"We've only got mouthwash."

"Put some on a clean towel and wipe my arms, then wrap them."

The crew were still standing in Danny's cell, waiting to see what Danny was going to do next. Danny was now sitting on Frank's bed. Frank was wiping Danny's arms with the mouthwash.

"Ouch that burns."

"Danny's blood is still coming out of one of the big cuts. It's very deep."

"Bandage that whole arm now and tightly. You boys that are standing, if you don't mind mop all the blood off the floor and tidy my bed and take all the bedding to be washed."

One of them said, "The laundry man can never get rid of all the blood. Throw it all. I've got more clean sheets, quilts and pillow cases. I will go and bring them."

"Ok mate, the rest of you tidy this place up."

Danny passed out on the bed for a second and Frank finished bandaging him.

"Danny, Danny, wake up mate. I think you need to go to healthcare as you have lost lots of blood."

"Yea let's go to the office. Just get my jacket."

"Here you are Danny, what are you going to tell the officers?"

"I will think of something by the time I get there."

They reached the office and knocked on the door and waited.

"They can see us. Why don't they open?"

"You know that, Frank, they always make us wait. When they come out tell them I am self-harming myself."

"What do you want?"

"Sir, Danny Mundy has been self-harming himself. I think he has over done it as he has fainted a few times."

"Is that true, Mundy?"

"Yes Sir."

He unlocked the gate and said, "Go to healthcare now and I will phone them that you are coming."

Frank and Danny were making their way outside the wing's gate.

"Where are you going? Only Mundy."

"But sir he might fall on the way there. He needs someone to take him."

"Ok make sure you go straight back to the wing."

Danny and Frank walked along the underground causeway until they reached the steps up to healthcare. Then they walked to the healthcare gate and it was locked. Frank shouted, "Health care, hello."

Then he pushed the metal gates so it made a loud noise, banging together. A nurse came out.

"What's the problem?"

They were still talking through the metal gate.

"Didn't my wing ring you?"

"No, what's the matter?"

"The officer at my wing said he was going to call. My mate Mundy is self-harming himself, take your jacket off Danny."

As Danny did that with the help of Frank, blood was dripping on the floor. When the nurse saw this, she opened the gate and said, "Come inside, before you collapse."

She held Danny, took him inside and locked the gate after she went inside.

"Get back to the wing. I will take care of him."

She took him into the medical room and put him on a bed.

"Lay down on the bed and put your arms in the air and keep them there. I will be back in a minute."

Then the nurse and a doctor came in.

"What have you done to yourself? Let the nurse take these things off, so we can see what damage you have done to yourself."

The nurse cut the sheet off very slowly around the right hand.

"The blood has congealed and the sheets are sticking to his arms, doctor."

"Slowly does it nurse, what did you use to disinfect it sir?

"Mouthwash doctor."

"At least you used something. This does not look like normal self-harm. Carry on nurse, and this arm does not need any stitches. Keep your arms up please. We will clean this arm and dress it. Your left arm seems to be the worse one with the amount of blood that's come through the sheet."

"You are right. I did that arm last after I felt dizzy and I fainted. My friend brought me to the office and they sent me here."

"Stay still please, while the nurse finishes your right arm. She is nearly done."

"That arm is done, doctor."

"Before you do the next arm, let me give an injection. Turn to your side please."

The doctor pulled down his pants and injected Danny's bum.

"Try to keep your arm in the air please, it looks like the bleeding has stopped nurse.

Please can you get him a hot drink?"

"What is your name sir?"

"My name is Danny Mundy miss."

"What would you like to drink?"

"Coffee please."

The doctor got out a form.

"Danny Mundy what wing are you from?"

"A wing sir."

"Who sent you here?"

"I am not sure, it was a new officer and I don't know his name."

"Ok Danny when the nurse comes back with a drink we will look at the next arm. Here she is now, how does your hand feel now with the new bandage?"

"It feels ok but is still throbbing a bit. I can hold the cup with it."

After they all had their drinks, the doctor decided to cut the sheet bandages off Danny. He started to cut.

"Blood is a strong glue. You really wrapped the bandages tightly around your arm. Slowly does it. I have done yet a little blood is starting to come out. I am going to take it all out now. It might hurt a bit."

"I am good doctor. Go ahead."

"Nurse get the stitches ready. I'm going to do some sewing now. You are very lucky Mundy. There is only one very deep. It should be ok once we stitch and clean it up."

"Shall I finish and bandage him Doctor?"

"That's a good idea nurse thanks. There's quite a bit of paperwork to do, thank you."

It was very late when Danny got back to the wing. He banged at the iron gates then a bit later an office came to open it.

"Where you been Mundy?"

"I was sent to Healthcare early on today."

Another came and said, "Where you been?"

"Healthcare Sir."

"Get to your cell now."

He went to his cell door but it was locked. He waited at the door hoping for an officer to come and open it. He opened the flap and Frank saw him. He put his thumb up. Then he went back to the office and knocked on the door.

A few moments later.

"You again Mundy, what do you want?

"Sir my cell is locked, can you open it please?"

The officer came out with a huff and quickly went and opened up open. Danny went in and he locked it straight after him. He was not happy.

"Are you OK mate?"

"The nurse did a good job. They were going to keep me in but I told them I was OK. Did they get the count wrong today?"

"Yes, how did you know? The officers seem to not know where I was today. They seemed surprised when they saw me at the gate."

"They kept coming and opening my flap and saw you were missing but never thought to ask me where you were."

"Any more problems with the Muslims after I left?"

"Good as gold. They had a lot of stuff. I have organised for the keepers to get some gear tomorrow. And the shops as well in the other blocks."

"I am very tired. I am going to bed. The injection is also putting me to sleep."

"Ok buddy, I am falling asleep myself."

Over the next few days it was quiet and this afternoon Frank had a visitor. Danny went to the plumbing class. Then later that evening, after dinner, they were in their cell.

"By the way, how was your visit?"

"Very good. My son and missus came and it was very nice to see them. I really miss her."

"How long have you got left to serve?"

"About the same as you. 12 to 15 left. My son said your Kim is doing a great job with the business and he is like her second in command. He has learned how to price jobs now and he is looking over a big workforce of men and one girl."

"So my Kim is looking after him wage wise?"

"Think so. He and his girlfriend are saving to buy a house."

"You bought your council house?"

"My missus is happy with money in the bank, I know what you are thinking. Silly woman."

"Look mate in here we have no choice. What woman do it's up to them how to run everything."

"Junior was telling me there is a new thing coming out called, I forgot its name. You fly in remote in the roofs of very high buildings, scaffold holders use it when pricing jobs."

"I think someone told me about it, drum it's called."

"No Danny it's called drones. They can fly for miles in the sky and by remote control. You fly it anywhere and it's got a camera so you can see where it is."

"Are you thinking what I am thinking?"

"Yes I am. Junior has bought one."

"How much gear can it carry?"

"Not sure."

"If you don't mind asking JR to test the one he has got and learn to use it properly or hire a bigger one that can carry the type of weight we need to carry drugs and phones. I am sure he can hire one which tells the weight it can carry. Tell him when he finds the correct one to buy it with cash out of the area, like London and pay cash for it and give a false name so he will not be traced. Just in case we get caught, then the police can't trace him."

A couple of weeks later.

"Danny JR is testing the drone which is stopping by our cell tonight."

"What time?"

"Midnight. Did you tell him we've got to be able to hold it still for at least ten seconds or more to get the gear from it?"

"I told him 20 seconds."

"Does it make a lot of noise Frank?"

"Not sure Danny though we will know tonight."

Minutes to midnight.

"Can you see it Frank?"

"No. What time is it now?"

"11.59. It should be here now. Would it have a light fitted?"

"It should have Danny, it must see where it's going. Let's check our phone for any messages."

"It says midnight is the test run, if any problems will call."

"I cannot see the drone Danny but I can hear noises."

"Frank, push your hand out of the window. The cameras on the drone might see it. I will phone Frank Jr."

"Don't do that. He is handling the remote control. We just have to wait and see what he does. I have put my hand outside."

"The phone is vibrating let me get it. It says, "Got to go because guards are patrolling the outside of the prison gates, so it must be two of them. We've just got to try again. They have seen what time the guards come to inspect the outside wall before they try and do it again."

Danny and Frank lay on their beds.

"I am a bit disappointed Danny."

"Listen mate. No need for that in life. Nothing goes smooth the first time. That's how business is. I am happy no one got caught and we have learned from this. The next time we put a white T shirt and some underwear outside and if the screws see it they will think our washing is out to dry. You said you heard noises?"

"Yes I did."

"Was it very loud to draw attention from the screws?"

"Not sure. I will wait a while then I will ring and hear what he has to say."

"Ring him now. He will be OK. I will go by the door to listen for any screw."

Afterwards Frank spoke to his son.

"Danny he says he handled the drone fine. He saw my hand so everything was pinpointed and it was ready to bring the drone to our window. Then one of the lookouts told him guards were coming. He had two lookouts by the way. He did not see the guards and they did not see him or his lookouts. I told him the next time there will be a white T shirt and some underwear out of my window."

"It's been a long day and I am going to bed now mate. See you in the morning.

"OK."

The next morning, after the officer unlocked the doors, the door knocked.

"Come in."

"Good morning boss, did you hear the noise last night?"

"No, what did it sound like?"

"Like a whistle, I think it was a drone."

"OK Munro we will keep an eye out for it, thanks for telling us."

"Danny if he heard it, so must the officers on duty patrolling the grounds. I don't think we should do this."

"Why? It could be very lucrative for our business."

"I don't mean not to do it. In the past we always got our crew to do our work. Why not on this? I mean get one of the crew to do it and he must be on the 3rd floor so it will not be seen or heard too much. It can hover on top of the roof then come down direct by the window. My son has the drawing of the building in the prison, no problem."

"Very good thinking Frank because of your son. I thought that's why you wanted us to do it. Our crew will not know it's your son ok."

"The only thing I am worried about is the noise the drone makes. I think we should do it when it's raining."

"Good shout Frank, what would I do without you?"

"You have built this business before you met me and gave me a chance to make good money. I will never forget that."

"Thanks Frank. You'd better organise with the right crew member for that job and he has to be quiet about it. Tell him on the day to phone them after bang up. Tell them you will be phoning them. You know what they are like on the phone as they spend the whole night checking on their missus. Most of the men in prison like to show off even if they have nothing. Did I tell about the con I met when I first came to prison? He used prison toothpaste and found an empty Colgate tube and squeezed the prison toothpaste into the empty Colgate tube. He did the same with the shampoo. It was crazy."

"Ok Danny."

Chapter Twenty Seven

Kim and Amanda met their mum for coffee in the city Canterbury City Centre.

"I shall get the coffees. Mum, you and Amanda find a nice seat by the window."

"OK love."

"Do you want a hand Kim?"

"No I am fine sis."

A few minutes later...

"Here we are, Latté for you Amanda and black coffee for you mum. I am dying to know what this meeting is for Mum."

"I must say you girls. I am very proud of you and you both are so beautiful."

"Mum get to the point."

"Here read this."

"Mum I don't blame dad."

"Nor do I mum."

"My last visit with dad I wanted to ask him for a divorce. I did not have the heart to ask him though he must have known. That's why he sent me the divorce papers. He still can read me like a book."

"What are you going to do Mum?"

"Amanda it makes sense to divorce dad. Bill wants to marry me, what do you say Kim?"

"I think you should, but I have spoken to Raj the solicitors. He thinks there is a very good chance dad will be released soon. He has applied to have a retrial because the landlady lied. But she has passed away. Someone payed her £1000 to keep quiet about the back gate and fence being broken."

"Kim this is the first I heard of this. Are you sure there could be a retrial?"

"Yes mum, but I think you should get a divorce as dad is not the same man he used to be. He wants a lot more out of life and is a better man for it."

"Amanda what have you to say?"

"I've got Bills name already. I think you should divorce dad and marry dad, sorry mum lol."

"Mum I am buying one these city flats as an investments. Here are some pictures."

After showing the pictures on her phone, Amanda said, "Mum I am thinking of leaving university and join Kim in dad's business."

"No way my little girl. Both of your fathers would not like that and I certainly don't want that."

"But mum."

"No Amanda and that's the last I want to hear of it and Kim would agree with me."

"Mum is right. I only left university to help dad in the business and that gives him something to live for in prison. If I had my choice, I would not have done it."

"You see Amanda."

"Aright, I might take a year out."

"That will be fine dear."

Later they all said their goodbyes. That night Linda phoned Kim.

Linda wanted to know more about Danny's appeal. Kim told her that there was a very good chance that he would be released soon. The shoe box contained lots of bad things that Johnny had done to people. Any one of them could have killed him. Kim told her mother that Kim and her brother Bill was in the blackmail book and they had paid thousands of pounds to Johnny. Linda was shocked and was speechless for a long period of time and told Kim she would ring back another day.

But she rang back the same evening saying that she would not believe that of Johnny. Linda was told again it was all in black and white what was paid. Linda said if she had given that shoe box to the police dad would not have gone to prison. Kim told her she did not know that for sure.

"Do not think about that mum, dad is a better person for being in prison. I will change the subject mum. Do you fancy coming and working for us? I am a person short. I'd rather you work for us than me getting someone new."

Kim was told she would speak to Bill and let her know the next day.

Over the next few days there was no come back from the Muslims they fought with. The Wing was quiet and nothing much of note happened, only some of the Muslims left the jail. Frank told the ones that were left that they were still responsible to pay the money.

In Danny's cell.

"I got the guys on the threes to do the drone job. Eddie and Leon. They live directly above us and they will do the job. I told them to put out white T shirts every day. Everything is set for tomorrow."

"So you are not going to wait for rain?"

"The drone does not work properly in the rain."

"Ok you are in charge."

The next day Frank spoke to his son and everything was set for midnight. At 8pm Frank phoned Leon and told him at midnight the drone would be at their window. He asked him not to use his phone at all and not to fuck this up. After all it had cost a lot of money to organise this.

Jr set the drone off and it was a clear night sky. The drone flew very high and stayed on top of the roof of the wing a couple of minutes before the drop. The drone was making a buzzing noise. Leon and Eddie heard it and were ready. Then at midnight they dropped the package by Leon's window. Leon unhooked the parcel, then the drone flew off into the sky. Eddie put the parcel into a washing bag and dropped it to the ground floor to Spencer's cell window. Spence took it into his cell. Later that morning, they all texted Frank that everything went according to plan.

"We did it Danny but I could hear the noise - it was like a lawn mower."

"Well done. We will know tomorrow if we have any come backs. I don't think the noise was that bad, does Spence know what to do with the parcel?"

"Yes boss."

"Long day. I am going to bed."

"Danny not sure I can sleep. Too excited."

In the morning Danny went to his class and Frank went to the gym. Both of them were eager to hear if there was any come back about last night. They did their morning sessions and when they got back to the Wing they both said they heard nothing. Over the next few weeks they used the drone a few more time but now cons were talking about drones and the noises. There were more guards outside the prison and more torch lights being flashed at night by the guards and more patrols inside the prison.

All the Muslims had left the block. Frank and Danny talked about seeking their family but both of them decided not to bother with them anymore.

A couple of days later in Danny's cell.

"Have you seen what they are doing on Wing one?"

"Someone said something about windows."

"They are building metal frames around all the windows."

"You are joking."

"And nets are going up as well."

"What do you mean by nets Frank?"

"Metal nets or plastic nets are going over the building as well, you know what that means?"

"Yes, we had a good run anyway."

"Danny do you think we should do a last drop before they put nets over our block?"

"We are seeing what they are doing in prison. What about the things the screws don't see? Like improve cameras, under cover guards outside. Forget it, we had a good run. We got the bike shop, the store, we got cons bringing gear all the time. We got those two bent officers. I think we are good not to take a chance with the drones again."

"Once again you are right Danny. You would make a great businessman outside."

"If you speak to my soon to be ex-wife she will not agree with you. Even with my business outside and that doing very well since Kim started working there full time."

"Did you say ex-wife?"

"Yes I did, I was sure when she last visited me that was the reason she came and she did not have the heart to ask or tell me she wanted a divorce. I still love her and because I love her I can let her go, she is happy where she is."

"Fair play to you mate."

"I spoke to Kim last night and she told me money coming from C wing is short. Normally she receives £850 to £1150 per week though over the last two weeks it's drop to £600. It's never been that low. Do you know if anything is going on there?"

"No but I will speak to Ben Murphy as he runs things there."

"Who is the keeper there?

"Robert Scott. He says his stock is running low as well."

"Did your son tell you he was leaving the business?"

"Yes he did. I told him to tell himself personal, I assume he did not."

"No he did not, why is he leaving?"

"He is going to get married. His girlfriend is from Wales and he is moving there."

"I am not happy. He didn't tell himself anyway. I will tell Kim to give him a nice present and thank him for all his help in the business."

"Thanks boss for understanding".

"I am going for a walk."

As Danny went outside of his door he looked into Munro's door and he was watching T.V. Danny called him to walk with him. They went on the ground floor where the table tennis table and pool tables were.

"Do you know the guys on C wing that work for us?"

"Yes Robert and Ben."

"I want you to go and check that wing out with your contact to see if there is any fiddle going and if anyone has been threatening my people, because the take is down?"

"I know one of your old enemies is there Burns?"

"I did not know that, how long has he been in there?"

"I am not sure about two months."

"By the way, do not tell Frank what I have asked you to do."

"I will not say anything when I have anything to report I will call you to play pool or something."

"That fine, I will see you later."

Over the last few days Danny has been checking all the stocks of gear and money going out to Kim. He spoke to all his crew, making sure everything was Ok and updating himself. Over the last few months he had left everything to Frank. Only one wing was not on point - C wing/

1st of December 2013

"Danny are you ok?"

"What do you mean?"

"Danny are you checking up on me?"

"No I am not. I just want to update myself on my business. I leave everything to you and it's not fair to you. I have become lazy and left you to do everything."

"I don't mind doing it boss - cup of tea?"

"Good idea. I prefer to have coffee if you don't mind?"

"Sit down boss. I will bring it over to you."

Danny took out the book of contacts and looked through the pages, stopping at C wing and studied it.

"Here you are Danny."

"Thanks Frank."

Danny put the book down and taste the coffee.

"That tasted good Frank. You did not tell me one of my old enemies is at C Wing."

"I did not want to worry you."

"That is something for me to think about and we are down nearly £500 a week for the last two weeks and is the stock being used or with the keeper?"

"I don't know Danny?"

"What have you done to find out?"

"I will be honest with you. I did not realise it was that much down."

"But Frank even if it was down £100 you should be on it and find out why it's down? Just enjoy your tea and I will finish this lovely cup of coffee you made."

"I will try and figure it out."

"Frank we are not supplying any more drugs for C Wing. Only the shop is running from now on. Go and get all the remainder of the drugs that did not sell and bring it back to our wing. You've still got your Red Band?"

"Yes Frank but what happens if customers from C Wing want gear?"

"Tell them to come to our wing and Daly or Munro will sort it out for them."

"You are the boss, but that's going to be a lot more work and we will be taking a lot more chances. Good chance we might get caught doing that."

"Well what do you suggest then Frank?"

"I suppose that's the way it has to be, the crew will take extra care".

"But only until we sort out C wing. Go there tomorrow morning and see Robert and Scott. See what they have to say. It should be no problem because you got the Red Band. You can go anywhere in the prison with that. Its bang up soon, I need to see someone quick."

Munro's cell door was open and Danny called him. They went down on the ground floor.

"I came to see you earlier but Frank was in there so I did not bother. One of your old enemies is at C Wing."

"Who?"

"Burns though he has only one eye!"

"You are joking? Only one eye, shit so the rumour is true. I did that to him, that was years ago. Tell me more."

"He is taking things from the shop and from the keeper and not paying back."

"How the fuck does he know Robert is the keeper? Why is Robert giving it to him? He is not supposed to give anything out apart from to give to Ben at the shop."

"I don't know?"

"Frank is going to C Wing tomorrow and we will know more then. There goes the buzzer at bang up."

They both walked up to their cells then as Danny got into the cell, Frank put the phone away.

"Everything ok Frank?"

"Yes boss. You'll never guess what happened to the nets the screws put all around the top of all the building?"

"Go on - tell me."

"You know it's been snowing for the last few days?"

"Yes."

"The heavy snow has pulled all the nets down so we are in business again with our drones."

"That's one bit of good news, so tomorrow you're going to sort everything out."

"Yes everything will be sorted out tomorrow."

The next morning at Bill's mansion in the kitchen.

"Kim has asked me to work with her for a little while until she gets a replacement. What do you think Bill?"

"I have never told you what to do, its fine with me. I see Danny has sent you the divorce paper you just left there?"

"Yes it's there. I've got to fill it in. Can I ask you a question Bill?"

"This sounds serious. Of course you can love."

"Was Johnny blackmailing you and Kim?"

"No. I lent him money as he was in the middle of buying a house he found in Canterbury."

"That is not what he wrote in the book he left."

"Linda I was not being blackmailed by Johnny. I am late for work. I have got to see the accountant today. Can we talk about it tonight?"

"I will take the temporary job with Kim."

"That's fine, Bye love."

After Bill left, Linda sat in her chair thinking. If she had given the shoe box to the police, Danny might not be in prison. She started to feel guilty and thinking what she could do to help free Danny from prison. About half an hour later she phoned Bill's sister. The phone rang for a while.

"Hi Kim. Can you come round as I would like to speak to you?"

"What's wrong love?"

"Come round and I we will speak then or do you want me to come to you?"

"That's fine. I will come around."

After the phone call Linda phoned her daughter. The phone rang.

"Garden World. Kim speaking."

"Hi love. I will take that job you offered me. When can I start?"

"Mum you can start tomorrow."

"That's good. 9am?"

"No mum 8am, is that ok?"

"Yes love, I want to help to get dad a retrial. What can I do?"

"That's great news mum. I will speak to Raj and Peter. I think dad will be out soon as there are too many other suspects and the landlady lied. I've got another call mum. I will see you tomorrow."

"Bye love."

"Kim come in. How are you?"

"Fine."

"I will come straight to the point, has Johnny been blackmailing you?"

"Yes he was. He had pictures of myself and him in uncompromising photos and a video of ourselves and he threatened me that if I didn't lend money to buy his house he'd sell them to the papers."

"Was he blackmailing Bill?"

"No he was not. Johnny wanted money from him also. He told him about the video of us and Bill paid money for them but he did not give the photo or the videos to me. Johnny was a nasty piece of work Linda and we all treated him so well."

"I am so sorry that he did that to you Kim."

"You mentioned something about a shoe box of papers and tapes, who has them?"

"I think Kim gave a copy to the lawyer and she's got a copy in the safety box."

"Do you think I can have all the copies myself of the photos and tapes?"

"Of course you can have them, but I think the lawyer will want to check with the police first but I don't know if you can have them when everyone is finished with them. I don't see why not."

"Can I get myself a drink? Do you want one?"

"A small one please."

"Kim you have been like a sister to me. You looked after me, I cannot thank you enough. Somehow I don't think you are telling me all of the truth. I don't want to go and see the tapes. So please tell me the truth?"

Kim burst out crying.

"The truth was very painful, Johnny, Bill a few friends and I we had orgies in the pool. Well you can imagine the rest and Johnny had a secret camera taking videos of us all."

"So any one of you could have killed Johnny for the tapes?"

"I love Johnny but all he wanted was to use me and take my money."

"What about Bill?"

"Linda you will have to speak to him, I am so sorry to tell all this."

"Have another drink Kim, I will have a double."

"Double for me as well."

Later that afternoon Linda met her daughter at her old house. Linda told her.

"Kim I am leaving Bill and moving back to our house. I am not sure but I think Kim and her brother Bill had something to do with Johnny's death."

"Mum I have been sleeping in your bedroom, do you want it back?"

"Yes love you say dad will be out soon?"

"That's what Raj told me - a matter of days."

"I brought some of my clothes and other things. If you don't mind love moving your things out today. I am going back tonight at Bill's and telling him in the morning."

"No problem mum, I will not go back to work today or I might ask the tenants to leave my flat in the city and live there."

"Up to you love."

"Dad will want to be part of the business when he comes out. Mum he is not the same man that went into prison."

"I know love. He has become the man I always wanted now. I am going back and packing the rest of my things."

Raj had dropped all the copies to Patrick at the police station.

Patrick was at his office with lots of paperwork on his desk and he read through them. Then he opened the parcel Raj had left. A few hours later he then went to see his boss.

"Come in Pat what can I do for you? Sir we've got a wrong man in prison."

"What do you mean wrong man?"

"Danny Mundy Sir."

"As I remember that was your case and who else?"

"Sir there were quite a few things I did not check it was one of my first cases. I believed what I saw and what an eye witness said. I was a novice I know Sir."

"Pat tell me everything now."

"Danny Mundy was saw holding the dead body of his brother Johnny and the landlady said she saw the knife in his hand. I now found out she lied. Her back gate and door of the house was broken in."

"Did you not search the house and the grounds?"

"No sir, I thought it was an open and shut case. She was paid £1,000 not to say who came in from the back."

"Bring her in for questioning."

"I can't sir. She took her life, which I am investigating at present. She took all of Johnny Mundy's money, credit cards and all his paperwork. She left a note to say that Mark Harris gave the thousand pounds."

"Mark Harris our M.P.?"

"Yes Sir. As I was saying, not to tell he came in from the back door. She also says that Mark and Johnny were arguing in the passage of the house and she thought Johnny was still alive went he left. Johnny Mundy was blackmailing at least five people that we know of."

"But who killed Johnny Mundy?"

"I have no idea Sir but now we have people with motives whereas Danny Mundy did not have a motive."

"I want you to interview all the suspects."

"I have that to do Sir."

"Tread very carefully with Mark Harris."

"Yes Sir."

2nd of December 2013 12noon.

The door of Danny's cell opened at 8.45am.

"They are late this morning. I wanted a shower before I go to class. I've got plumbing today. You are going to C wing before gym or later?"

"I will go before and later on as well."

Everyone was rushing around to get to class and work etc. Frank spoke to some cons at C Wing after the morning session. Everyone was going back to their Wing.

Danny was in a hurry to get back to the Wing as he wanted to shower. He rushed to his cell. Frank was there.

"I'll just get my towel bag. I will speak to you later about C Wing."

"Will you?"

Danny was in a rush which meant he did not notice a couple of new men on the Wing landing. He went straight in the shower. As he went into the shower four men followed him.

"Frank."

"What do you want Munro?"

"Four new men have gone in the showers after Danny."

"Never mind it's my son Burns and a few of his friends, Mundy is finished."

"What do you mean Frank?"

"That cunt causes my son to lose an eye he is a dead man now."

2nd of December 2013

Linda and Bill were in the kitchen of their mansion.

"I spoke to Kim yesterday and she told me everything. I am leaving you Bill. I just can't bear thinking of you doing all those things in the video that Johnny had."

"Please stay. Don't go. I love you with all my heart Linda?"

"I stayed with you last night because I loved you and you cared for me and my girls but no more, I am leaving you."

"You can't go. I killed for you."

"What did you say? You killed Johnny?"

"Yes I killed Johnny. He was going to tell you everything. I begged him not to but he wanted more and more money and I played him. But when he said he will still tell you we started to fight and he went under the bed to get a knife. We both struggled and the knife somehow got into his side and it must have hit his heart and he died. I left in a hurry and Kim my sister was my alibi in case the police came and asked questions."

"Bill I think you should go to the police and tell them the truth."

"I can't do that. I will get life."

"Bill you have to tell the truth or I will."

"You will not tell them love, will you?"

Both of them were crying and hugging each other.

"Bill you have to tell the police. They will give you a light sentence if you come forward because if you don't tell I will go to the police station myself and tell them."

"Ok I will go, but you drive there. I will go and change and I will make a list of what Kim has to do with all my business."

They reached the police station and Bill hugged Linda and kissed around 2pm.

"You will come and see me Linda."

"Of course I will love."

2nd of December 2013

Bill walked from Linda's car to the police station and waited at the desk and pressed the bell at the counter. A few minutes later a policewoman came to the desk.

"How can I help Sir?"

"I would like to confess to the murder of John Mundy?"

"What did you say Sir?"

"I murdered John Mundy."

The police lifted up the flap and opened the half door.

"Come this way Sir. Stay in this room and I will get an inspector to take your statement. I won't be long."

About ten minutes later the door opened.

"Hello Sir would you like to follow me to the statement room?"

They got to the room, with a table in the middle of it and two chairs either side of it. He was told to have a seat.

Later that day.

Linda was getting the house ready for Danny's coming home party when the phone rang it was on a small table by the steps.

"Hello Kim."

After a while on the phone. She hangs up the phone and sat on the steps and did not move.

The end

The book is pure fiction and any names use its pure coincidental to anyone.

www.ingramcontent.com/pod-product-compliance
Lightning Source LLC
Chambersburg PA
CBHW040517170726
48295CB00012B/240